MEGHAN MONARCH

Meghan Monarch LLC

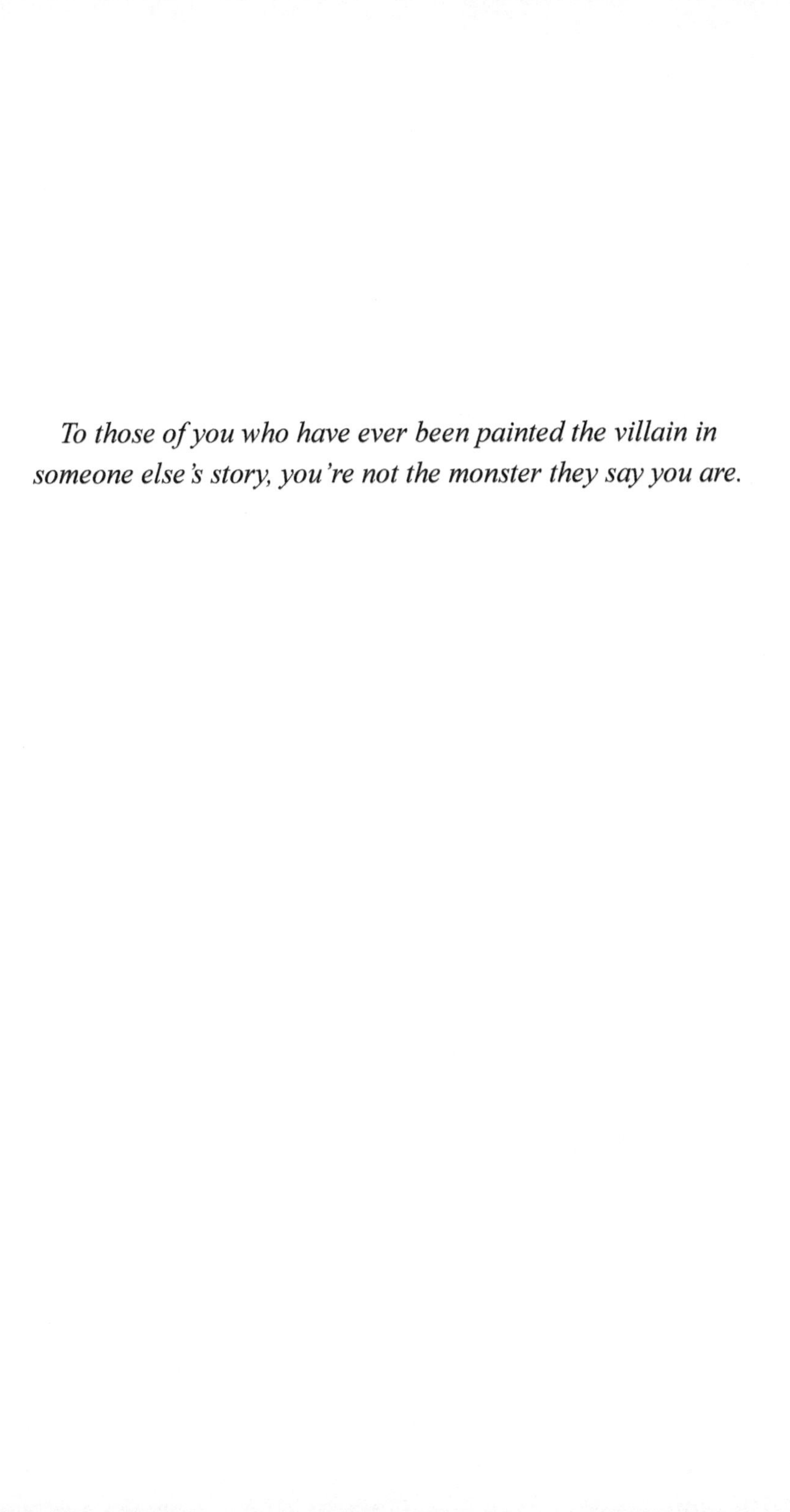

To those of you who have ever been painted the villain in someone else's story, you're not the monster they say you are.

A NOTE TO THE READER

Thank you for deciding to read Saving Tatum! AH! This is happening!

If you are as obsessed with superheroes as I am, I really hope you'll love this book. I wrote it for the fans in all of us who've always wondered what it'd be like to date a superhero like Captain America or Superman (not to be specific). HA.

As a fellow reader, I thought it'd be helpful to list some content warnings before you decide to jump in. Not everyone likes surprises, and I can understand that. So, if you'd like some warning as to what possible triggers can be found in this book, please read the paragraph below. If you'd rather not know, feel free to skip that part.

Saving Tatum contains references to alcohol consumption, violence using superpowers, anxiety and panic attacks, various forms of domestic abuse, a toxic parent-child dynamic, and death/murder.

Please read with care and enjoy your journey.

XOXO—Meghan

"You are nothing but an eyesore in this damn house," my father seethes through his clenched teeth.

Back pressed to the hallway wall, the cold seeping into my skin doing nothing to help the shivers racking my body, I move my feet centimeter-by-centimeter, closing the distance between me and the stairs as subtly as possible.

"Wh-what—" I grit my teeth against the chattering, hating how his eyes light up at my obvious fear. "What did I do this time?" I swing my long ponytail back behind my shoulders, suddenly afraid he'll try to grab onto it and pull.

His low chuckle quietly slithers through the small bit of air separating us. "What did you do?" He scoffs. "What *haven't* you done?"

My chest tightens, panic coursing through every vessel and capillary, adrenaline traveling at lightning speed straight toward my heart. The fact that this man contributed to the creation of me is the greatest burden I carry by far.

As my breath starts to come out in smaller puffs by the second, he takes a long, languid step closer, head cocked back, his cognac-brown eyes darkening to pitch. As he takes another step, running a hand roughly over his disheveled dusting of facial hair, the hall light gleams off the police badge pinned to his black polo.

He's so entirely average-looking: average height, average build, average features, average everything—he's the epitome of a middle-class father. He just happens to have the temper of a wild hippo.

"Have anything to say for yourself?" He looms closer, dizziness clouding my head as his petrifying whisper travels through the still morning air. If he just raises his voice a little more, Mom will hear—Mom will help. She—

"Everything okay up here?" My eyes dart to my mother's

silhouette in the dark hallway, granting me the tiniest bit of reprieve. "Tatum?" I spot a dot of worry in the etchings of her eyebrows.

My dad's hand abruptly brushes down my arm, and I flinch. "She's having some trouble with her breathing again. I think I helped calm her down."

The floor creaks as my mother moves closer, and I force a deep breath, conscious of my father's too-tight grip—a warning grip—on my arm. "Another panic attack? Tatum, are you sure you're all right?"

My head nods a sliver. I force myself to speak slowly, to control the shivers. "I'm okay."

"If you're sure... Are you ready to go get Jay?"

Born ready. A rush of relief threatens to dizzy me again, but I nod anyway. "Lead the way."

She does, rubbing my arm comfortingly and kissing my father on the cheek before descending the stairs. As I move to follow her, his grip tightens painfully on my wrist, one last whisper hissing in my ear: "Not a word."

Ears burning, eyes welling, I blink back the tears and hurry down the stairs after my mom.

"Honey? You sure you're okay?" Mom's hand softly squeezes my knee, helping me release a shaky breath that was stuck in my chest for far too long.

I prop my hand on top of hers, her warmth seeping through my chilled skin. "Fine, Mom. Just nervous to see Jay. It's been a long time."

"Well, I am very excited to have him back around. I think it'll be good for you." Her voice softens, almost sadly. "He's always been able to understand you in ways I never have, and with what you've been going through lately, I think you're in need of your own superhero."

"Superhero? Mom, Jay is my best friend. It's not his job to figure out what's going on with me. I don't want him to know about all this."

"But—"

"Mom, no. Please don't—"

"Tatum, is it really all that bad to have a hero in your life?"

Of course it's not. But the idea of Jay knowing about my panic attacks, about my father's threats and intimidation…

He would try and do something about it. I know he would. And the image of him standing between me and my father…

I didn't even want to think about it.

CHAPTER ONE

Six months doesn't seem like a long time, but damn...it really is. Especially without my best friend here to start our freshman year of college together. College is already hard enough, but knowing we were supposed to begin this journey together has made it a lot more daunting.

"Jay and I didn't get to talk much while he was in Beijing because of the time difference. I'm going to try to text him and see if he remembers what it's like to be in the same time zone," I tell my mom, typing furiously on my phone.

Jay was offered a chance to help with opening a new hub for his father's company in China; a once-in-a-lifetime opportunity that will help him take over the family business someday, or so he says. What Jay really wants to do is comic art, but he claims he can do both at the same time. I'm not sure CEO screams having tons of free time for side comic gigs, but who am I to argue?

> Me: I cannot wait to see you. Hurry up and get off that plane!

I hit send, grinning from ear to ear.

"He's going to be here any minute now! The Delta app says his plane has landed," I squeal at my mom, who's waiting ever so patiently with me. She chuckles, and for the first time in months, I actually feel like myself. Like a weight I didn't know I was carrying is finally growing lighter.

It's hard to tell if my mom realizes just how much I've changed since my father came back into our lives, or if I'm really that good at hiding it.

That's the other reason Jay's absence has been difficult to handle.

Ever since my dad showed up on our doorstep—oddly enough, the same day Jay left for his internship—after leaving us twelve years ago, my world has been turned upside down, plaguing me with debilitating anxiety and panic attacks. Therapy has helped—at least enough to help me hide all my problems from Jay—but I always feel like I'm walking on eggshells, worried about when the next burst of terror will come.

I don't want to tell Jay anything just yet. I don't want to burden him with my drama after he's been away for so long, but honestly…I don't want to talk about it in general. Sometimes when you have stellar parents like Jay's, it's hard to actually fathom the fact that others don't have the same luxury.

I've already had a hell of a time dealing with the fact that my dad seems to only treat me like shit. Everything is hunky-dory in front of my mom, or whoever else we're around. That's actually what has me in absolute fits. Sometimes, I'm not even sure what I'm experiencing is real.

"Should we take bets on what superhero shirt he chose to wear today?" Mom asks, pulling me from my stupor.

"Five bucks says it's Captain America. Gosh, I've missed that nerd."

"Me too. It'll be nice to have him back. What's going on with school for him?"

"He isn't starting until the second semester." Which will mark the end of the only stretch of my life I've ever braved school without Jay.

We've actually been best friends since we were kids; the minute we reached high school, Jay really grew into his looks, but no one ever noticed because he was a total geek. I didn't care. We got to be geeks together, and that's always meant so much to me.

"You know Jay," I added with a shrug and a smile. "He's going to rock this college thing, no matter when he starts."

"So are you," she replies kindly, stroking my cheek with the back of her hand.

Before I can reply, my phone buzzes in my hand. I rip my eyes away from my mother and stare intensely at the notification, swiping the lock screen away as fast as I can.

> Jay: Do you know how many texts I just had to read through? You are still way too much. Watch the door; I'm second behind Harry Potter's Aunt Marge :p

Shoving the phone into my pocket and pushing my purse into my mom's hands, I adjust my pants and prepare to run toward the exit next to customs. I almost put in all the work to get checked in so I could wait by the gates, but I figured that was probably a bit overboard.

I have to cover my mouth when people begin exiting, though, because Jay was not kidding when he said there was a lady who looks identical to Harry's Aunt Marge. My eyes take in the hideous brown blazer covering her arms and shoulders, a heinous suede skirt falling just below her knees, and if you can believe it, she even dons the exact short haircut to boot.

It's about time that woman deflated and landed somewhere else.

"Those clothes are horrendous, aren't they?" Mom asks, which sends me into another fit of laughter.

Before I continue our conversation, my heart nearly stops at the sight of the most beautiful man I think I've ever laid eyes on.

My eyes peruse his well-built body. *Is this dude real?*

His toned arms barely remain contained beneath the aqua blue, cotton-like fabric of his long-sleeved shirt. His light-washed jeans tightly hug his muscular thighs, while the rest of his straight-legged pants just barely bunch up around the ends of his extremely long legs.

When my eyes reach his face, his olive-toned skin accentuates his baby-blue eyes that stare straight into my soul as I continue to assess him, finally reaching the wonderfully messy brown hair sitting atop his head.

Familiar baby-blues. Familiar messy brown hair.

"Jay?" I whisper, knowing full well that there is no way this man could possibly be him; not my nerdy, comic book-loving, glasses-wearing, one-and-only friend in the whole world.

But those eyes… I'd know them anywhere.

Looking at my mom, I ask, "Is that…?" Then, thinking better of it—because come on, that cannot be him—I start looking behind the godlike man walking confidently toward us. "Do you see Jay anywhere?"

She frowns at me, looking a bit confused. "That is Jay, sweetheart. Something wrong?"

If I thought Jay was good-looking before, those looks were nothing compared to the man I'm looking at right now. *What happened to his glasses?*

I shake off the confusion and beg my legs to start moving. They start off with a brisk walk, and I am so oblivious to everything around me, I hope I don't end up being the asshole who gets in everyone's way.

Just as I am about to close in on him, a kid happens to run right in front of me. I twist and turn my body to try and maneuver around him, but I end up losing my footing anyway, and I'm suddenly plunged into one of those slow-motion trips, watching everyone's faces swirl around me as I fight to keep my balance.

Unfortunately, I lose my footing completely, and start my descent to what I'm sure is an extremely germy floor of the Detroit Metro Airport.

Luckily enough for me, before I actually make contact with the hideously blue, swirly airport carpeting, a muscular, broad-chested pillow catches my face.

Strong arms wrap around my back, but the fall never stops. I land on top of the Greek god formerly known as Jay with a loud *oomph*.

He feels as different as he looks. His arms feel stronger, his chest firmer. Even the way his arms are fastened around me feels different…a gentle pressure like what I imagine a straight jacket must feel like.

I definitely think I need one, because my first reaction to being caught by him is not "Thanks, bud" or "Good catch!" but instead, upon catching a whiff of his delicious cologne, a very obvious "Mmm."

"Is that really how you're going to greet me after six months?" Jay's extra-manly voice prods, sending my eyelids flinging wide open.

Clearing my throat, I try to find a place to put my hands

besides the manly chest of this gorgeous stud—I mean, my beautiful frie—no, I mean my *best friend*, and push myself up.

Pull it together, T. What the hell? I ask myself, brushing off the weird feelings whirring inside my body. How come it seems like Jay and I are just now meeting for the first time? And why do I want to reach out and touch every line of muscle on his newly extra-chiseled body?

"Sorry! Got more awkward while you were gone. Clumsier, too. I missed you so much!" I laugh, pushing myself up off of Jay and reaching my hand out to help pull him up. He barely puts any pressure on my arm as he stands, practically floating to his feet.

The second he is standing, I throw my arms around his waist, immediately realizing just how much I've missed this. He has no idea what these past few months have been like without him, and I plan on keeping it that way.

The remorse begins to eat away at me—not only for the secret I already planned to keep, but now a new secret—I'm totally attracted to the new man Jay has become.

This year is going to be interesting.

CHAPTER TWO

"Are you sure you're okay?" Jay's deep voice vibrates my eardrums once more, and my cheeks flush automatically…such a stupid response. *No more blushing, Tatum!*

"Would you shut up? I'm fine," I answer, smacking his surprisingly rigid pectoral at the same time.

Rubbing the back of my hand, my angel of a mother swoops in to save the day. "Tatum, honey, let me through. I want to hug Jay too!" She bumps me to the side and rushes in full-throttle to wrap him in her arms. I smile as I watch him bend down to rest his head on top of hers while shooting me a megawatt grin.

Feeling dizzy, I roll my eyes; now I need to add the brightest white, charming smile to the list of newly hot traits my once-dorky best friend has suddenly acquired.

"Is this really happening?"

"What?" Jay and my mom ask at the same time, making me go rigid.

"Shit, did I say that out loud?"

Jay raspberries air through his lips. "Uh, yeah? You sure you didn't smack your head when you fell?"

I titter, trying my best to hide the nerves as he pulls away from my mom and they both prepare to leave.

"You ready?" Jay questions, throwing his heavy arm over my shoulders.

I nod as I grab onto his hand—the hand that is dangling dangerously close to my chest—and walk out with him, speedily brushing all these tricky, hot-and-bothered feelings away.

My best friend is back, and I'm not letting my weirdness —or unexpected attraction—get in the way. We can continue everything as it was six months ago.

Normalcy. That's all I want.

Sliding into the backseat with him, I blow out a big breath as I pull on the seatbelt, only to have it come out about five inches before stopping.

Lovely. As if I haven't been awkward enough as it is.

"Come the hell on. Are you kidding me right now?" I plop my head back against the headrest in defeat.

I smell him before I feel him, and I freeze as I watch one buff arm reach across my body and gently grab the belt. Of course, it easily slides out for him, and I have to squeeze my eyes closed as I feel it snake across my body.

He continues to pull it, heat rushing over the areas he touches. Not even seatbelts can resist him, and I can't say I blame them.

When it clicks, it sends a chill through my body. "Thanks, Jay."

"No problem, T," he answers, bumping me with his shoulder. I smirk over at him playfully.

"Are you still staying the night, Jay, honey?"

My eyes go wide when they meet my mother's in the rearview mirror. "Staying?"

Turning to Jay, I find him shrugging in the most adorable

way. "Surprise?" he replies meekly. "Your mom and I planned this at the last minute."

Damn it! I just can't win today, can I?

Stuck in my thoughts, I vaguely hear Jay save me with a quick, "Yes, I am. Thank you, Ms. B."

"Would you just call me Mom, already? I've known you since you were five, Jay. Really."

I look out the window and listen to his amazing laugh until the buzzing of my phone brings me back to reality.

> Jay: Do you not want me to stay?

T, you haven't seen your best friend in six months. CUT. IT. OUT! I yell at myself before trying yet again to shake out all the uneasiness and force myself to go back to the Tatum that Jay remembers and needs.

> Me: No, I do. I'm sorry. It's just been a long few months without you. I feel like I don't know how to be JT anymore.

> Jay: It's fine. We'll stay up all night snacking on chips and binge-watching superhero movies. Once we catch up, we'll be back to normal before you know it.

> Me: JT forever.

> Jay: And always.

> Me: ☺

> Jay: I missed you, Tatum. So much.

His words send my stomach fluttering. I'm not sure if I'm

looking too much into it, but those six words seem to hold so much more in them than the letters that make them up on the screen.

Fighting the butterflies fluttering around my insides, I formulate a reply.

> Me: Yeah, yeah. What else is new?

Slipping my phone under my legs, I bump into his shoulder and catch sight of his Adam's apple shaking with silent laughter. Glancing down and away from his neck, I find myself having trouble containing my smile, and finally feel back to normal when I notice the Captain America symbol on his shirt. I must've missed it before, what with all the hubbub.

"You owe me five bucks, Ma," I tease.

"Well, crap. I was hoping you wouldn't notice."

Both of us laugh at the look of confusion on Jay's face. I lean into him and close my eyes, thankful he's finally back.

At some point during the hour-long drive home from the airport, I fell asleep. I don't fully begin to wake until I feel stone-like arms slide out from beneath me.

Jay somehow managed to wrangle me from the back seat, carry me through the house, *and* up the stairs.

Fully alert, I wait and listen to his breathing as he sits at the foot of my bed. When he sighs loudly, worry starts to prickle at my insides.

I'm just about to tell him I'm awake when his silky voice fills the void. "Please don't let us change, T. I saw the look on your face when you noticed my transformation, but please don't let it push you away. I need you."

Hearing those whispered pleas, I try to quietly take one of those slow, cleansing breaths my therapist is always talking about to reset.

Quietly yawning, I stretch out and place my freezing cold feet onto Jay's back. He stiffens, and I rip them off him, waiting a moment before saying his name.

"Jay? Is everything all right?"

Though I can only make out his silhouette, I can still see his hand run through his hair. He pauses a beat, clearing his throat before answering. "Yeah, everything is fine. How was your nap?"

"Freaking phenomenal. Although, it was rude of me to fall asleep the minute you got home."

What he doesn't know is that actual rest has been hard to come by lately.

"Did the store run out of Ben and Jerry's while I was away?"

"And what the hell is that supposed to mean?" I ask sarcastically, crossing my arms over my chest once I am sitting up.

"You lost weight while I was gone. Last I checked, string bean wasn't a flavor of theirs." His laughter is contagious, but I don't miss his attempt at a cover-up, hoping I didn't hear what he whispered mere moments ago. He's slick like that.

I decide to play along. "I guess you should be thankful your internship had a gym nearby. Maybe it just finally gave you enough muscle to fling me around with those new and improved Hulk arms you now have."

Before he can even formulate a reply, I leap onto his back and wrap my arms around his neck. He quickly stands up and catches my dangling feet. It only takes seconds for his hands to find the bottom of them. The tickling sends me writhing on his back.

"No! Stop! Stop it! You know how much I hate it!"

He is relentless. And if I wasn't dangling from the back of his skyscraper-like height, I'd find a way to fall off and escape.

"Jay, STOPPPPPP!"

The attack continues for a few more seconds until the fakest friendly voice from downstairs causes Jay to go still.

"I'm really trying to pretend everything happening up there is appropriate!"

Yup. There we go… Adam trying to play "Dad."

Reaching both of his arms around, he assists me in sliding back down to the ground. I race over to the door, sighing in relief when I hear the lock click into place.

"Who is that?" Jay questions, sounding confused. My mom should've never asked him to stay. This is already going south, and it's his first night home. "And why are you locking the door?"

"No one," I answer, ignoring the second question, and leaning my head against the wood. I'm going to have such a hard time keeping this secret. I tell Jay everything. But for some reason, I have a hard time telling him and my mom about Adam. To everyone else, he seems wonderful, but when it's just me? I see a different side of him. And that's the part I fear will make me look crazy.

I know Jay would believe me, but he is also a fixer. And in this situation, there's not much to fix. I mean, my dad is a cop. What can anyone do to him, really?

It's not like he's all bad—only to me, which is where the

anxiety and panic attacks have really come into play. Jay doesn't need to see the mess I've become.

Besides, it's hard to make others believe that someone treats you differently when they're the master of acting a certain way in front of others. It's easier to just hide everything away. I can take it.

Jay turns me around and lifts my chin, gently coaxing my gaze to his. "Who the hell is that, T? And don't you dare lie to me." His eyes flicker back and forth between mine beseechingly.

"My dad." The truth comes out far too easily.

He freezes. "What? Adam?"

"Yeah." I gulp. "He showed up a bit after you left, actually." I glance down, my hands finding each other before they begin to writhe around each other of their own accord.

"I don't understand. Why didn't you tell me?" I can see the inquisition looming in his eyes. He's on to me.

I shrug, keeping my eyes downcast, finding it hard to muster any words to explain why I've kept this to myself for so long.

"Tatum."

My eyes move up to his, "Hm?"

I study him as he processes my reply for a few short moments before he repeats, "Why didn't you tell me?"

My head twitches, "No idea." And I don't. Well, I sort of do. How do you tell your best friend over the phone that the man who left you as a child decided to show back up the same day he left? And how do you then tell him that he seems perfect, but is actually a complete ass to only you?

Jay obviously knows who my dad is. With how long we've been friends, he knows everything about me. My dad left when I was six, a year after I met Jay, but we were so young, he wouldn't remember much about him. I know I don't. Well, besides the fighting between him and my mom…

Holding my chin still, I finally force his hand down and walk to my closet. I cannot look into Jay's eyes much longer before I finally cave into his demands for the truth.

Looking back, I find him watching me. "We're not going to talk about this?"

I close the door to my walk-in closet behind me and use the brief reprieve to change into some leggings and one of Jay's old t-shirts before going back out and sidling up next to him.

"What do you want to do first?" I ask, trying my best to move past my admission.

"I'm hungry." Good—he's letting it slide, at least for now.

But I know him—he's going to use this trip to the kitchen as an excuse to check things out and assess the situation with Adam. So I scan the room, looking for something to have him do.

"Okay, dig through my movies and surprise me while I go get us some snacks."

"How about I go grab the snacks, and you pick a movie? I know my way around," he counters, reaching for the doorknob.

I snatch his hand just in time and squeeze it briefly. "I've got it. Plus, I don't want things to be awkward with my dad tonight. I just got you back, and I really don't feel like introductions. He already thinks it's weird that a girl and a guy are best friends and have sleepovers at our age. Just pick a damn movie and chill out."

Rushing out the door, I pull it closed and lean against it, begging my breathing to slow down. I hear Jay flick my light on and quietly sigh when his shadow finally moves away from the door.

I wipe the sweat from my forehead and reach for the phone in my pocket to text my mom.

Me: Is everything okay down there?

Mom: Fine. How are you feeling?

Me: Okay. I told him about Dad.

Mom: That's good. And the anxiety?

Me: No…I don't need him looking at me like I'm injured. Please don't say anything.

Mom: As your best friend, he deserves to know. But yes, I promise, for you. It just doesn't make much sense.

If only it did make sense to her. If only it made sense to me. I don't even know how to describe it.

It almost feels like this dark, ominous cloud is looming over me, messing with my emotions, pleading with me to keep this a secret. Something just tells me it's easier this way.

Me: You know him, Mom. He'll just try to save the day, like usual.

Mom: And that's a bad thing?

Rather than keep arguing, I swiftly push the phone back into my pocket and quietly tiptoe down the stairs to the kitchen.

The house is dark and quiet when I finally make it down.

Bringing my phone out a second time, I turn on the flashlight and lay it on the counter, light pointing up, to be as invisible as possible.

Glancing toward my mom's room, I find the door closed, but know that I need to hurry. The last thing I need is Jay coming down here and making some kind of ruckus to draw my parents back out of their room.

I scan the freezer and finally lock eyes on the two pints of Ben and Jerry's that I picked up for us this week: fudge brownie and cookie dough. Carefully setting them onto the counter, I reach into the fridge for two water bottles and set them next to the ice cream. So far, so good.

Pondering about how I'm going to manage to carry all of this up without making any noise, I softly pull open the silverware drawer and grab out two spoons. Like all the nights before this, I hurry to push the spoons into a pocket of my leggings and slip my phone into the other, light on and all.

As my hands slither through the darkness, I'm able to swoop up the ice cream in one arm, but the minute I reach for the bottles of water, one slips from my grasp. The dull crinkling sound rings ten times louder in my ears than it probably actually sounds, but suddenly stops. My muscles tighten in fear, unsure who—or what—is here in the dark with me.

When the hairs on the back of my neck stand up, I find myself backing up toward the fridge until my body collides with something that feels awfully human.

Terror filling every bone in my body, I gulp and ready myself to run, but find myself unable to move. My feet are cemented to the floor.

"I got the runaway water. Are you scared of the dark now, too?" Jay whispers, bringing tears of relief to my eyes once I know it's just him in here with me. How did he get down here without me noticing?

"A little bit. Let's go," I whisper back, ushering him toward the stairs before any other sounds erupt.

Finally arriving at my room, I flick my light back on and quickly close and lock the door, taking a quick breath to right myself.

Jay needs normal. I can do normal. I need it just as badly as he does; I just wish my body would calm down and enjoy the familiarity.

Turning around, I come face-to-face with Jay—yet again, his forehead is creased and scrunched.

"Can I help you?" I ask, arching my eyebrows in question.

Squinting at me, he replies, "Why are you being so weird? And why did you lock the door again?"

I peek at the door once more, unlocking it after he points it out. "You don't feel like all of this is weird? We haven't seen each other in six months! And we've barely talked. That's half of a year, Jay! I've been by myself the entire time, so yeah, it's a bit odd. I just have to get used to this all over again." My hands gesture between us.

"What do you mean you've been by yourself?"

Throwing my hands up in frustration, I march over to my bed and throw myself down onto it, face first, groaning in frustration. "Of course that's the only part you decide to focus on. Jiminy Cricket, Jay."

My cheek rubs against the comforter as he plops himself onto the bed right next to me. I flip myself over and stare at the ceiling.

A minute passes by as I wait for Jay to ask again. "Why have you been alone?"

"After graduation, I spent the summer working at the

campground full time. I filled up the rest of my time with reading and going for walks. Jana, Toree, and Lex were gone all summer on a road trip. I couldn't go because of work. You know Mom needs me to help her sometimes. Once college started, the girls just…didn't talk to me as much. None of us share any classes, so seeing each other has been hard to come by. I mean, we still talk, but it hasn't been the same. It's not like high school. So, I spent the last few months doing my own thing and trying to talk to you whenever I was able to."

When he doesn't answer, I tilt my head to the side to look at him and find him sitting with his head in his hands, quiet as a mouse. I reach out to him, but pause for a second, not sure of exactly what to do.

"I'm sorry," he whispers.

"For?"

"For leaving you. I should've stayed." Looking down at me, I notice his eyes have grown glossy, and it brings forth the tears I've been holding in for what feels like a millennium. They fall down my face like leaves in autumn, chasing the freeing relief of letting go.

I drag myself off the bed and walk around to face him. When I bend down to give him a hug, he pulls me onto his lap and engulfs me in his arms. The gesture has us squeezing each other harder, my tears turning into quiet sobs. Jay's hugs have always been cathartic.

I don't know how long we hold each other, but my cries eventually quiet, my tears drying up. I finally buck up the nerve to look into his eyes and am crushed to find sadness still lingering within them. "You shouldn't be sorry, Jay. You went to do something that's going to help shape your future. Your dad needed you to do this." I stroke his forehead softly.

"Don't feel bad. You can't be there to save me from everything. I had to learn to fly on my own eventually."

The flash in his eyes has me wondering what he's thinking about, but his words distract me. "I'll always try to save you, T. I'm sorry; I just missed you."

Jay has always been protective over me. In fact, he's always treated me a bit like a glass sculpture. Ever since my dad left, it's as if I became fragile in his eyes.

From nightmares and monsters under the bed, leaving my lunch at home, sleeping through my alarm, and forgetting to finish my homework to feeling abandoned by my dad to judging my looks, and getting picked on by bullies in school, Jay has always been my hero—always there to save the day or cheer me up however he can.

"I missed you too, ya goon. Now, let's just relax. Everything is fine. What movie did you pick?" I try my best to change the subject and lighten the mood.

"*Captain America: Civil War*."

Mentally first bumping the air, I say, "Thank God. I was hoping I'd get to watch America's ass!"

The minute the words leave my mouth, I feel Jay's arms pull taut. Confusion sweeping through me, I finally peel his claw-like arms off of me and get up to put the movie in.

Hearing his movement behind me, I spin around to make my way to the bed, but freeze in my tracks when my eyes fall upon Jay's eight pack of rigid abs staring right back at me. Every section of pure muscle is like a slice of what I can only relate to as heaven itself. My eyes peruse the deliciousness in front of me, not ready to let up any time soon. *Is this dude for real?*

Jay always sleeps with his shirt off because he's had night sweats since he was little. However, he might just have to sweat it out tonight, because I'm not too sure how to handle this sort of predicament.

The temperature in my room starts to climb to dangerous heights. I clear my throat and briskly make my way to the closet, where I whip on a pair of shorts to accommodate for the change in condition. This is going to be a long and sleepless night.

Once I close the closet door behind me, I pull my hair up into a ponytail, smiling at the all-too-familiar scene I return to. The bedroom light is off, minus my Marvel-themed twinkle lights, the movie has started, and Jay is under my blankets, snacking on some cookie dough ice cream. It suddenly feels as if no time has passed at all. I grin at the floor as I walk around the bed.

Excited to have some normalcy, I grab my fudge brownie ice cream and snuggle under the blankets on the opposite side, trying to keep a little bit of distance between us, but not missing the gravitational pull that begs to bring us closer.

"Feeling warm?" His voice vibrates right through me, my skin tingling with energy.

"Not at all, why?" I ask, keeping my eyes trained on the screen. My mind tries to conjure up as many pictures of snowmen living in igloos on the polar ice cap as it can.

Pushing the blankets down a bit, he licks his spoon before answering, "Just wondering why you put shorts on."

"I figure shorts go better with a t-shirt. Any more questions?" I stare into his eyes, trying with all my might to figure out what he's playing at.

Gracing me with a sexy half-grin, he answers, "Nope. I'll shut up now."

"About damn time."

Per usual, I don't make it through the movie, and I'm only aware of it because I wake up feeling way too hot, even in my damn shorts Jay gave me the fifth degree about.

Suddenly panicking about possibly falling asleep with my ice cream, I swing to sit up, expecting it to be melted all over my bed, but a weight keeps me pinned down. Looking over at Jay, I find his arm draping right over me, holding me down close to his toasty body. My eyes widen in shock.

Oh no, no, no, no, no. Nope. This can't happen. No way, José. I have got to find a way to get him off of me.

Trying to lift his thousand-pound arm to no avail, I pause for a break. We have always slept like this, so why am I suddenly finding it so different?

Because Jay got hot as hell, T. That's why! my subconscious screams at me. I roll my eyes at her. She really is too much sometimes.

Finally freeing myself, I walk across my room to grab a drink and find both of the ice cream containers in the trash and the television turned off. Jay must have finished off the rest of my pint. Typical. I'm happy to know that his time away hasn't changed everything about him. Well…besides his new godlike physique.

Just as I'm about to get back to bed, a blinking light on my phone catches my eye. I pick it up and notice the extra-bright 3:05 AM timestamp before swiping to unlock it. I sneak a peek back at Jay before opening the message.

Mom: Dad bought bagels for the both of you to enjoy in the morning. He's taking me out to breakfast early before he goes to work.

I squeeze my eyes closed. Maybe I am going crazy. How can he play the part of the perfect dad to everyone else, but completely transform in front of me?

Suddenly concerned, I turn back around and begin to formulate a reply, but freeze at the rustling of my sheets. I stand as still as a statue, hoping Jay will quickly fall back asleep.

"T? What are you doing?" The croaky tiredness in his voice sends a chill down my spine.

"You were giving me a fever, so I got up to get some water and thought I'd check my phone. I'll be there in a sec."

"Texting your boyfriend?" I smile when I hear the aggravation in his voice. Could that be a hint of possible jealousy?

"Now, why would I have a boyfriend when I have such a fine piece of ass laying just a few feet away from me?" *Shit. Did I really just say that?*

"Quit being a dick, T. I can't sleep with you over there. Hurry the hell up."

I think about what it would be like to snuggle up to him as more than just his best friend, but push the thought out of my mind as swiftly as it came.

I read back over my reply before hitting send, finding myself able to reply with only one word.

Me: Thanks.

I place my phone upside down on the dresser and make my way back to the bed.

The minute my legs make it under the covers, Jay pulls me close again. I snuggle into my pillow and close my eyes.

"Night, T."

"Night, Jay. Thanks for staying with me."

A snore is his only reply. I quickly drift off right after him. His embrace is the first feeling of safety I've had in months. He has no idea how badly I've needed him. I just hope he never finds out about what's really going on in my life, as selfish as that is. And if he ever does find out, I just hope he believes me, because I already find it hard enough to believe myself.

CHAPTER THREE

I open my eyes to sunlight and the soft, rustling sound of bags. When I turn over to search for Jay, the rustling stops. Confusion flows through me like a river as my very well-rested mind tries to catch up and recall all of last night's events.

"Shit, sorry, T. I was trying to be quiet."

Wiping the sleep out of both of my eyes, the dread starts to set in as I catch sight of him mid-packing, reminding me that Jay cannot be here all the time. He eventually has to go home and see his own parents. I'm already lucky that they didn't mind missing him for another day on my behalf.

"It's okay. I'd rather be up so I can see you for a little before you go. Want to go grab some breakfast at The Crow before you leave?" I'd put off visiting our favorite downtown Portside café since Jay left.

Setting his bags down, he casually wanders over to me without saying a word. The look on his face says it all. I shoot up, my heart falling. "You have to leave right now, don't you? What? Were you going to leave without saying goodbye?" The hurt I feel is far worse than I thought it would be.

"Of course not. You know me better than that, T. Our separation hasn't made me an asshole, jeez." He sits next to me on the bed and places his hand on my leg. "I was going to wake you the minute I was done. You didn't sleep very well last night, and I didn't want to disturb you until I absolutely needed to."

That's funny… I feel like I slept better last night than I have in months.

I know I'm being ridiculous, but I grab his hand and give it a squeeze of reassurance anyway. "Sorry, I'm being stupid. It's just hard to think about you leaving when I haven't seen you in so long."

After spinning the bill of his hat to the back of his head, he leans in closer. I go still, suddenly aware of his body closing in on mine. I feel the heat of his kiss on the skin of my temple. The surprisingly sweet touch makes my hands go clammy. Suddenly, I feel embarrassed.

I snake my arms around his neck and it takes everything in me not to jump up and wrap my legs around his waist. Anything to be closer to him.

Before I know it, we're wrapped in a tight embrace, and I find myself drifting through all of the memories we have shared over the years, using them to reassure myself that we are fine.

I tilt my head into his neck and breathe in his woodsy, familiar scent. "Do you need help carrying anything out?"

With a snort, he answers, "Are you kidding? With these big, beefy arms? I can carry my bags and yours without breaking a sweat; you said it yourself."

I dramatically roll my eyes, "Oh, puh-lease. I never should've said that."

His chuckles turn into full on laughter as he pulls away, pushing a strand of hair back from my face. I turn away as soon as I feel the blush creep along my cheekbones, feeling like I'm on display.

The moment he moves to attend to his things, I notice the sudden drop in temperature. I feel the panic start to set in, but I try my best to push it aside. I haven't felt anxious since the moment Jay returned, and I'll be damned if I let him see the mess I've become while he's been away. He wouldn't even be able to recognize me.

"Not my problem you finally noticed how hot I've gotten."

Well, shit. Forget the drop in temperature. Now my hands have gone clammy. I wring them until I feel the tension start to dissipate.

"T?"

"Yeah?"

"You okay?" he asks with a grunt as he lifts his duffle bag onto his shoulder. I don't miss the thick veins of his forearms, twitching in ways that make my mouth go drier than the Sahara desert. *Where is some water when you need it?*

I stand up and brush my clothes down. Lifting my hands, I assess the bedhead situation, suddenly thankful I put my hair up last night. Only a few hairs have snuck out from behind the elastic, all of them seeming to be sticking up in different directions. "I'm fine. Do you need me to order an Uber?"

"Nope, my mom will be here in five minutes. I texted her right before you woke up."

With anxiety brewing in my belly, I want nothing more than to get this over with so that he doesn't witness a breakdown. "Okay, let's head on down. Do you have everything?"

"For the hundredth time, yes. Stop worrying, T. Everything is fine."

"I know, I know. I just hate the idea of you leaving again."

Putting his free arm around me, he ushers me to my bedroom door. The panic starts to level up...not only at the thought of him leaving, but now because I'm not sure if Adam has left the house yet.

That reminds me. I guess I should mention the bagels…

Squeezing me closer, he says, "I'm just going home. It's not like I'm heading to a different country. How about we hang out tomorrow, and on Thanksgiving? Shall we do our annual flip-flop "Fill Your Gut" Thanksgiving dinner tradition?"

"Let me talk with Mom and let you know," I shrug, unsure how things will go now that my dad is here. "By the way, I guess my dad got us breakfast. It's downstairs."

His eyebrows raise while his lips push together. "Wow. That was nice of him."

I nod, opening the door to let him through.

Leaving the safety and isolation of my bedroom, I feel the anxiety shooting off throughout my body like fireworks. My skin burns like gasoline set to flame. The quicker I get him to the door, the quicker I can usher him out and escape back to my room.

The minute our feet hit the landing, my mom bursts through the kitchen doorway to find us, "Jay, sweetie, we are so glad to have you home. Your mom is so excited to see you too. Please apologize again for us hogging you all night."

"You talked to her?" I ask.

"Yes, she just pulled up outside, so we chatted for a few minutes." She turns back to Jay, handing him something wrapped in a paper towel. "I'm sure Tatum told you that her dad is back in the picture. Well, he grabbed some fresh bagels for the both of you, and I thought you might want to take it with you."

I nod along with her and rub my arms to try and warm up. Jay sets his bag down and walks over to my mother. My worry is briefly forgotten as I latch onto the sway of his wide, muscular back. I'll take anything to get me out of my head, except this sight has my spit slipping down the wrong tube. I choke, making my eyes water.

Jay quickly turns around, "Are you okay?" he asks yet again, pounding on my back.

How embarrassing. "Yeah, I'm fine."

Problem is, I'm all but fine. My first problem was the anxiety and impending panic attack, but add on Jay's back, and I'm the farthest from fine. My thoughts are running in way too many different directions.

After grabbing the bagel and hugging my mom, Jay walks back over to me and opens his arms. Without hesitation, I dive into them and am encased in his safety and warmth.

I feel the knob of his chin on top of my head and try to breathe through the panic that's begging me to cling on and never let him go. I'm fully aware that he's here to stay, but ever since my diagnosis, I tend to worry about the most random things. I blame it on the daddy issues.

"Thanks for everything, T. And you too, Ms. B. I'll see you guys tomorrow, okay?" He unzips his duffle before pushing his breakfast inside. "Oh, and tell Mr. B I said thank you."

Finding it suddenly hard to breathe, I remain quiet as I feel my mom place an arm around me and pat my shoulder, trying her best to ground me. Why is it that my mind can never stay right where it is when these things happen? Instead, it slips through cracked doors and hidden crevices to hide from the boogeyman who plagues my life.

"Bye, Jay," I whisper through the tears beginning to gather in the corners of my eyes.

With a quick sweep of my cheek, he grins and turns toward the open door.

That's when things go south. Jay's image goes fuzzy, because I am unexpectedly staring down a dark tunnel. Not wanting him to see what's going on, I try my best to turn and find the stairs, but fall to my knees in a jumbled mess of what appears to be a mix of sobs and heavy breathing.

Everything around me disappears as my heart beats out of my chest. All I can think about is how there's no air and that my life is ending and and and—

I'm going to die.

I'm lost in my own panic when a voice tears through the darkness: "T! What the hell is wrong? Tatum!"

It's Jay—*my Jay*. He's still here. I try to follow his voice, but it's too far. Before I make it to him, I'm sucked in again. Clawing at my throat, I beg my body to take in the air it needs.

"Ms. B, what's happening? What the hell is wrong with her?" Jay keeps talking, but it's muffled and hard to hear. *Damn it!*

The moment I feel my mom's arms around me, the darkness lightens by a fraction, but not nearly enough. I'm just able to make out her reply, "It's okay, honey. She's having a panic attack. You can go; I can take it from here."

I'm finally able to take in a little bit of air, but my vision is still nowhere to be found. I strain to hear what Jay says next, and I hate hearing the way his voice cracks and wavers. "Since when does Tatum have panic attacks? What the fuck is happening right now?"

He must really be scared if he's swearing in front of my mom.

"It's just something she has. Really, Jay, it's okay. Your

mother is going to get worried. Tatum just has to settle down, and then I'll have her call you." Thank God for Mom's calmness.

"I'm not going anywhere. My mom can wait. Ms. B, please answer me. Since when does Tatum have panic attacks? What happened?"

Mentally screaming at my mother not to say anything, I feel my soul leave my body the moment the words leave her mouth. "Her first one happened the day you left."

Damn it, Mom. He wasn't supposed to know! Can you hear my thoughts, woman? He's going to think it's his fault!

It's not until I feel Jay's hands cupping my cheeks that the sun decides to shine again. It's like taking your first breath of crisp, fall air the moment you wake up. Slowly, but surely, the clouds start to drift away, revealing the light hidden beneath.

Finally able to see clearly again, I take in the biggest gulp of air I can possibly absorb and look into his eyes. The blue in them is paler than usual, but it's the hurt I find in them that takes the newly acquired air right back out of my lungs.

Trying my best to diffuse the tension, I offer him the finest smile I can possibly muster, but I can instantaneously tell that it does nothing to soothe him.

"T, why didn't you tell me?"

"I didn't want you to feel bad. I knew you'd want to come home and be there for me, but you needed to stay right where you were, Jay. I couldn't have you missing out on this opportunity."

Dropping his forehead to mine, he stares far too intensely into my eyes. "You really are thick, you know. I'd do anything for you. I just wish you would've said something."

Finally feeling a little more alert, I reach up and pull his hands from my face and cradle them in my lap. The action takes maximum effort on my part.

Looking toward my mother, I slowly nod to her and watch her get up to head outside. Even that much movement is draining.

"Jay, I'm sorry I didn't tell you, but I was just trying to save you for once."

"From wha—"

I place a finger over his lips to silence him, my eyes pleading with him to let me continue, fearing my exhaustion might stop me.

"Please let me finish." Once he nods, I carry on, "I know you don't need saving, but I was just trying to spare you from giving up a trip of a lifetime; and that truly is what that was. One day, you are going to be in charge of TI Industries. I couldn't stand in the way of that. I know how important this opportunity was for you. Our lives are changing. Things won't always be this way."

The ache that fills my chest at that last thought nearly kills me. I wish we could just stay JT forever and always like we always say, but eventually we will graduate college and get married and move on. Life will steal him away from me more than it already has, and I'm not sure I'll be able to survive it.

He's been there ever since we were five, saving me from my bully, Evan Durthrop; sharing his lunch whenever I forgot mine; reading my last-minute papers fifteen minutes before their cutoff time. Jay has stood by me time and time again, no matter what.

Now that I think about it, I'm sure he suffers from some sort of hero complex. Sometimes I wonder if it's due to the fact that he has always kind of "had it all" growing up, so he felt like he needed to make up for all the things I was missing.

With a newfound determination in his eyes, he argues, "If you even think our lives are going to change enough to the point where I won't be there for you, you have another thing coming, T." Before I can even form a reply, he pulls me back up and into his arms for one last, chaste hug.

"Text me when you get home, and tell your parents I say hi." Folding my arms across my chest, I ready myself for a redo goodbye. *He is just going home, Tatum. He's here now. Everything is fine,* I chant repeatedly in my head.

Sensing my unease, he cups my elbow and softly squeezes, "I love you, T. Never forget that."

"Love you too, ya sap. Now, get out of here before your mom busts down my door," I laugh, waving him toward the front of the house, albeit with trembling arms.

Throwing his hands up in defeat, he steadily backs toward the door and is almost knocked over when my mom opens it behind him. "Ope. Sorry, honey! I didn't know you were going to be right there."

A small smack of a kiss on her cheek sends her blushing as Jay passes by. "Love you, Ms.—" She pins him with *the* look, and he quickly adjusts, "—I mean, Mom!"

One hand over her heart, she uses the other to wave at him. "Love you too, sweetheart."

Grinning through my sadness, I wave right along with her, grateful for the last smile Jay gives me before pulling away.

The moment the door closes, the loneliness that plagued me the entire time Jay was gone starts to settle in like an old friend. I make for the stairs before my mom can watch the breakdown, but her low voice stops me in my tracks. "Tatum, dear."

Peering down at the carpeted stairs, I count the tears that

fall down and disappear into the dark fibers as if they never existed. "Yeah?"

"It's okay to be sad."

"I know, Mom. I just hate it. I feel…defective."

"You're not defective, Tatum. Maybe the panic attacks will get better now that Jay is back."

All I can do is silently nod at her small gleam of hope, but I have a bad feeling that things are only going to get more complicated.

When she doesn't reply, I hold myself together the best I can until reaching my cracked-open bedroom door.

Walking in, the silence seems all too loud, and I hate it. I miss the way things used to be.

Totally unsure of how much time has passed, I finally peel my eyes away from the old star sticker I placed on the wall next to my bed from homecoming our freshman year of high school. Jay brought a single star to place on the corner of my eye. He had no idea how silly I'd look, but the thoughtful notion didn't go unnoticed.

After the night was over, I stuck it to my wall to remind me that Jay will always be there—a shining star in the darkest night.

A couple hours later, I've changed into a clean set of pajamas and am snuggling into bed when I hear my cell phone buzz from across the room. Groaning, I force myself to get up and cross the threshold to get it. I wait to check the message until I make it back to my bed.

Hurrying to get back under the warm covers, I finally swipe open the screen, and smile when I see who the text is from.

> Jay: My stomach hasn't been right since I left your house. How's it going, Tater Tot?

A tear slips out of my eye when I laugh. It's been a long time since Jay has called me that.

> Me: Nausea, heartburn, indigestion, upset stomach, or diarrhea? :p

> Jay: On second thought, my worry has suddenly subsided, you jerk.

> Me: You really do need to quit fussing. I'm fine. How's Ma and Pa?

> Jay: They're more than fine. Ma said you came over here once a week while I was gone?

Running a hand down my face, I realize that I forgot to ask Jay's parents not to mention my weekly visits. Ughhh. I'm shocked it's taken this long for her to mention it to him.

> Me: Yes, andddd?

> Jay: T, what is going on?

Looking all around my room, I plead with the reply gods to give me an answer that will satisfy him.

> Me: Nothing. It's not a big deal. I just missed seeing your parents, and I knew they were missing you, so I went over for dinner every week to keep them company.

I refresh our text thread for what seems like five minutes before he finally replies. The puff of air I release blows my unbrushed ash-brown hair dangling in my face up for a short second, only to have it land right back in my eyes.

> Jay: I just worry about you. I guess I didn't realize how much I missed taking care of you while I was gone. Thanks for keeping the 'rents company. Apparently, they love you more than me now. LOL!

> Me: I mean, I am quite lovable. ;)

> Jay: You have no idea.

Unsure of his meaning, I don't respond again. As I set my phone down, those last few words echo in my head, long after it hits the pillow, and Jay's remaining scent wafts into my nose.

Although things are complicated, life feels like it's getting better.

CHAPTER FOUR

I wake with a gasp that pulls me upright. Clutching my chest, I hurriedly blink the blur out of my eyes, wondering what could've woken me like that. *Did I have a nightmare?*

Throwing my blankets off, I run to the door and just about rip it off its hinges. Facing my ear toward the main level of the house, I'm met with silence.

Thankful, I close the door and slide down to the cold floor, my heart almost beating out of my chest. I don't know why I continuously worry about something happening to my mom. Adam doesn't seem to have a problem with her. Still, the concern creeps in from time to time.

Cradling my head in my hands, a few tears slip down my face. My emotions have been all over the place since my panic attack.

After a few minutes, I eventually calm down. I push myself up off the floor and walk to my bed, noticing the temperature has dropped quite a bit in my room. I shiver in response, casting a glimpse toward my bedroom window. It's cracked open, the long black-and-white chevron curtains just barely moving with the light breeze.

"When did I open that?" I ask no one.

Reaching the window, I pause, the hairs on the back of my neck standing on end, bringing a wave of anxiety with them. I look back toward my room and smooth them down, trying my best to soothe my nerves. It's not like anyone could ever even get to my room on the second floor. I'm being ridiculous.

"Everything is fine. No one is here. It's just you. You are okay." Those are the sort of phrases my therapist tells me to chant whenever I feel like I'm spiraling about something.

Wringing my hands, I somehow am able to ground myself by the time I turn back to face the window again.

Sweeping the area once more, I manage to catch a glimpse of a shadow that almost seems to be floating in the trees. I squint, trying to see better. If I didn't know better, I'd swear it was a man. But that can't be possible, can it?

Before I can even blink to check if what I'm seeing is real, the shadow takes off up toward the sky, faster than lightning.

I'm not dreaming. There's no way. My eyes sweep left and right, scanning the clouds for any sight of the shadow again.

When I come up with nothing, full-on hysteria starts to set in. I slam the window shut and lock it, hoping like hell I was hallucinating. Then again, I'm not sure I want that for myself either.

I search my room, desperate for something to secure the window. Thankfully, Jay must've forgotten his belt yesterday, because I find it on the floor next to my bedside table. I hurry and loop it through the two handles, pulling it tight. Hopefully, this will keep out whoever that was.

If that was even a *who*. Oh my gosh…am I losing my mind?

Jay, I just need Jay, my subconscious tells me. I decide to listen and run to my bed to slink down under the covers, the same way I used to try hiding from imaginary monsters as a kid. The comforter settles softly atop every inch of my body, my breath like a warm breeze on a humid summer night.

Finally finding my phone, I dial Jay at superspeed and listen to the ringing. "Please answer, please answer, please a—"

"Hello?" he answers in a groggy voice.

"Jay? Thank God you answered. Holy shit, you won't b-"

"Whoa, slow down, T. Is everything okay?"

"There was a man outside my window."

Silence, then, "A man? Are you sure?"

The anger inside me grows rapidly. Suddenly feeling defensive, I reply, "Yes! He was floating up high in the trees!"

Totally unfazed, Jay yawns loudly in my ear. The insensitive gesture starts to make me come unglued.

"You know what, Jay? Forget it!"

"Tatum, whoa, hold—"

I hang up before he gets the chance to finish, slamming my phone down on the bed.

The vibration of him returning my call only makes me more angry. I know I'm being a bit irrational, but my emotions are still in a bit of disarray. I hold down the power button and watch the screen go dark. If he doesn't want to believe me, then there's nothing to talk about.

I roll my eyes at myself. It's obvious he now thinks I've cracked after watching me in the midst of my panic attack.

Jay has always trusted every word I've said. Has my secret already planted a seed of doubt in his mind about my sanity?

He's also very easygoing, so maybe this is his way of trying to comfort me, but it definitely didn't work.

Overwhelmed with sadness, a little bit of fear, and a lot of frustration, I squeeze my eyes shut and beg for even a sliver of reprieve…

The creak of my bedroom floor sends my eyes flying open, carried-over nerves being awoken from hours prior.

When the familiar jangle of keys and a phone being set on my desk reaches my ear, I have already solved the puzzle. No one has set their things on my desk in months—it's Jay. Great, I'm already annoyed, and by the looks of my alarm clock, it's only 9:00 AM.

"I'm too tired to deal with your shit," I announce, anger seeping through every syllable like maple sap—sticky and undeterred.

"T, don't be like that." His reply has me getting out of bed in a flash and stomping to my closet to change.

"Don't 'T' me. I'm really angry with you. Just get out."

Finally reaching my destination of solitude, I'm stopped by a pillar of muscle. I'm too angry to even acknowledge the recurring attraction bubbling just beneath the surface whenever he's near.

Moving to his side, I push him as hard as I can, but he doesn't budge, not even an inch. Instead, he grabs my hands and brings them to his cheeks, drawing my attention to his face.

"Tatum, look at me." My eyes meet his, the blue color of his irises almost crystal-clear, the brilliant shade steadying me, making me think of the somewhat-calm lake of our Michigan hometown.

"What?" seems to be the only word my brain can produce right about now.

"I always forget how green your eyes are," he whispers.

My anger starts to dwindle, along with my worries from a few moments ago. "What?"

"Listen, I'm sorry about last night. I believe you. I really do…but how could someone be floating outside of your window? It doesn't make sense."

And with that, my anger returns. I push him out of the way before he realizes what's happening, throw myself into my closet, slam the door, and lock him out. I have no idea why the closets in this house have locks on the inside of them, but they've come in handy as of late.

The doorknob jiggles for a few before I hear Jay's forehead smack into the wood. "Tatum, why are you being like this?"

"Like what? *Crazy*?"

"*Crazy*? No, of course not. Just open this damn door."

"Now that you've seen my panic attacks, is that what you think of me? That I'm crazy? Delusional? Hate to break it to you, Jay, but ever since the day you left, my life has been thrown upside down. I'm different, life is different, we are different." The word vomit sends me into yet another crying fit, and before I can even change out of my pajamas, I'm crawling my way under the hanging clothes to hide.

I cry so hard that I don't even notice the sound of the door opening, or the arms that pull me out. The minute I smell him, I am brought back to the present, his touch instantly calming me and bringing me out from the fog.

"How did you get in here?" I ask between shaky breaths.

He holds up the emergency key pin I keep hidden on the top of the closet door frame, his mouth in a gentle closed-lip smile.

Tilting my gaze back down, I notice that his lap is covered in DC pajama pants.

"Are you in your Superman PJs, JJ?" I whisper.

"That's all it took to make you talk to me? Really?" He laughs loudly, shaking both of us.

Listening to his beautiful laughter is the one thing that brings some sort of peace to me at this very moment. I guess my mom was right. Jay really might be the key to my anxiety. I guess life can be pretty impossible to manage without your best friend.

I'm not sure how long we sit like this. I pick at the seam near the bottom of his shirt and continue to bask in the wonderful warmth of his presence, trying like hell to forget all about the highs and lows that have shown up since he got back home.

"Tatum," his deep voice says.

"Hm?"

"Talk to me?"

I sigh, "About what?"

"What is going on with you? This is not the girl I know and love."

"I was diagnosed with anxiety and panic attacks six months ago," I vaguely reply. "That's all."

"But why?"

"No idea," I shrug, "I had my first one the day you left." It's amazing how easy it is for me to slip into this lie.

"And you've had them ever since?" He tilts my chin up and searches my eyes for more information than I'm giving him.

"Yes."

"I'm sorry. I never should've left."

"We talked about this, Jay. That was never the answer. You leaving, and then everything else that happened after you left, just catapulted me into a sort of chaos, I guess."

Squinting one eye, he goes on, "What else happened after I left?"

My eyes widen, suddenly realizing I've said too much. I reach for something I've already mentioned. "You know."

"No, I don't."

"With the girls being weird, and my summer revolving around a summer camp work schedule, it left me to just be alone, probably too much." I know for a damn fact that he will not be happy with that answer, but I can't tell him the truth. Not right now.

Thankfully, he lets it go for now. "So what had you flying out of bed last night?"

I blink. Frown. "How do you know I flew out of bed?"

Without hesitation, he answers, "You were breathing like you'd just run a marathon on the phone."

I stare into his eyes a moment longer, letting go of the uncertainty that twitches in my mind.

"I already told you what happened. There was a shadow in the tree, and then I watched it float away. It looked just like a man. You don't have to believe me—I'm very well aware of how insane it sounds."

"Do you want me to stay the night tonight and keep a lookout?"

Smiling up at him, I nod my head in agreement. Another sleepover, just like the good old days, will work just fine, especially since Adam will be on patrol all night.

"So, seeing as I'm here at what feels like the asscrack of dawn, what should we do today?"

I glance at the ceiling, thinking about what our day could

be filled with. Shopping? Movie theater? Arcade? PJ day? It all sounds wonderful.

"Arcade and lunch?"

Jay chuckles before standing up. "Do you still have some of my clothes here?"

Part of me blushes just thinking about how often I wore his clothes while he was gone…and how many times I sniffed the sample bottle of his cologne hidden on a shelf in my closet.

"Yeah, one second." I rifle through the hangers closest to the door, grabbing a black v-neck and a pair of jeans. Here's hoping they'll still fit his new physique.

"Thank you." His voice echoes right in my ear, making me jump just a little, his warm breath tickling my skin.

"What the hell, Jay?" I spin around, smacking him playfully on the chest.

His laughter starts to disappear as I leave the closet and shut the door, trying my best to catch my breath.

"Don't even think about it."

"About what?" I answer sarcastically.

"Locking me in here," he replies, already walking out fully dressed.

My eyebrows furrow. "How did you do that so fast?"

"Wouldn't you like to know? Come on, slowpoke." He bumps me jokingly.

I wait a moment before following him. "You know that door can only be locked from the inside, right?"

Seeing the arcade sign in the distance puts a wide smile on my face. It's been almost a year since we were last here. I look over at Jay and find him donning a similar look.

Jay gets out and rounds the back of his car, yanking on the handle and extending his hand to help me out. He turns his back to me and stands still.

I almost slam into him. "What the hell are you doing?" I question.

He points a thumb down over his back. "Do you not want a free ride or not?"

I puff out a laugh and hop on, loosely wrapping my arms around his neck.

Jay moves without a single sign of difficulty. I smile against his shoulder and anxiously wait to pass through the doors.

After clearing the entrance, Jay gingerly lowers me to the ground. Once I right myself, he dashes out a hand to tickle my side, sending me scrambling backward.

"Would you stop it? You are such a jerk!" I call out, batting at his hand.

"Bet you can't beat this jerk at any of the games today."

I scoff. "Yeah, right."

He runs off into the forest of games. "Loser buys lunch!"

***

Hours later, it's my debit card buying our food. I can't help but roll my eyes at the thought of Jay being so good at literally every single thing he does. He willingly extended the competition longer to keep giving me chances, but we had to call it before we were skipping lunch and buying dinner instead. I mean, it's just not fair. How can someone be so naturally talented?

"What are you thinking about?" Jay prods, finally pulling up to my house.

Now that we're here, it's more than just Jay's wins that I'm thinking about. My eyes run over my dad's truck parked next to us, reminding me that the fun is over for the day. Only a couple more hours before he'll be leaving for work.

"Hey," Jay continues, his fingers moving my gaze to meet his. "What's going on?" His eyes dance between mine.

"Nothing." I grab his hand and gently pull it from my face.

"T."

I force a smile, "Do you have to be good at everything? You never answered me. I mean, really…it gets old." His gentle laughter calms me. "Movie night?"

Jay nods, following me out of the car and up the sidewalk. His silence is deafening as he stares into the window of the truck. "Jay?"

"What?"

"Is everything okay?" I reach for his wrist and try to pull him back away from the door.

He pins me with his gaze, his body stiff and his eyes lifeless. "Yep. Peachy keen. Ready?" He points his head toward the door.

Following him inside, my body freezes when Adam appears in the doorway of the kitchen. His stern eyes burn a hole into my soul briefly before softening—in preparation for a good show, I'm sure.

"Hello, Mr. …" Jay pauses, waiting for Adam to give him a preferred name to call him by.

My dad extends a friendly arm, the lines of muscle twitching ever so slightly. "Call me Adam, son."

"Mr. Adam?"

"No," he chuckles. "Just Adam."

Jay rubs his palms together, his steps breaching the doorway as Adam makes room for us to enter. My muscles tighten.

"Jay? Tatum? Is that you?" My mom's angelic voice drifts in from the kitchen.

"It's us, Mom," I respond shakily.

She appears in the doorway, shooting a glance at me before placing her hand tenderly on Adam's shoulder. "Movie night?"

"Yes. We're just going to head up now. Goodnight." I grab Jay's hand and whisk him up the stairway.

"Before you go," Adam starts. I shiver as a chill runs through me. "Would you like to join us for some ice cream?"

What?

"Actually, that sounds great," Jay answers.

Unable to find words, I nod along, unsure of what will come of this.

My mom turns around, heading for the kitchen as Adam leads us to the dining room table.

We all pick one of the chairs, settling in while we wait for the ice cream.

"So, Jay, I've heard a lot about you. You're going to college with Tatum?" Adam asks.

Jay nods. "Yes. I'm taking my general ed classes right now while I intern for my dad."

"Where at?"

"TI Industries, actually. The plan is for me to take over someday."

Adam's head bobs up and down as he listens before focusing his attention on me. "You didn't tell me what a successful young man Jay already is, Tatum."

I smile awkwardly. "Yeah. He's really great."

Mom makes her way into the dining room, balancing bowls along her forearms and in her hands.

Adam flies out of his chair, making me jump, which in turn draws Jay's attention to me. His eyebrows pull down in confusion.

"Anne, honey, let me help you." My dad reaches out to grab some of the bowls and helps her pass them out.

"Thank you," Jay and I say at the same time.

"You're welcome, my dears," Mom replies as she takes a bite of her dessert.

The rest of our time passes by with idle chit-chat and the clinking of our spoons inside our bowls.

As we finish up, I grab our dishes and make my way to the kitchen, rinsing them out in the sink before placing them in the dishwasher.

"He's nice." Adam's voice almost catapults through the air, and even though my body doesn't show it, I flinch in shock.

I glance over my shoulder, noticing him leaning against the kitchen counter with a bottle of water in his hand. "He sure is."

"What's wrong?" he asks. As he moves closer, an almost sinister look crosses his eyes.

Rapidly closing the dishwasher, I dry off my hands with a towel and back up a few steps.

I'm about to answer when Jay's voice floats through the doorway. "Thank you so much for the dessert, guys. You know I can't resist ice cream."

I deflate with relief as Adam's attention shifts to Jay and my mom, giving me time to put the towel back on the rack and walk over to them.

"That I do know," Mom laughs. "Thanks for spending time with us."

Setting the bottle down, Adam moves closer to Jay, extending his hand. "It was wonderful to chat with you, even if only for a short time. We won't keep you any longer. Enjoy your movie night." Jay shakes his hand, and I notice his head tilt briefly just before Adam turns toward my mom. "Anne? Ready for bed?"

Mom kisses my head. "Yes. Goodnight, sweetie. See you both in the morning."

Taking Jay's hand, I lead him through the house and up the stairs, pulling him into my room as I shut the door behind us.

I scramble around the room, changing in my closet and placing an *Avengers* movie in the DVD player.

"Whoa, whoa, whoa. Tatum."

I freeze, finger hovering over the play button. "What?"

"Slow down. You are moving a million miles a minute. It's stressing me the hell out."

I plop down on my bed. "Sorry. You meeting my dad really freaked me out. I just want to lay down and relax."

His narrowed eyes are teeming with questions, but for whatever reason, he doesn't ask. Instead, he runs into my closet and comes out in sweats. "Then let's do this."

I grin and snuggle under the covers with him. Even though it's not very late, I only make it through one movie before my eyes start to grow heavy. Jay pulls me closer and places his chin on the top of my head, his steady heartbeat lulling me to sleep.

I wake in the morning to my hair tickling my face. I find myself lying on my back, eyes darting so quickly, it's hard to take anything in. I nearly jump out of my skin, and when I feel someone grab my arm, I let loose an animalistic scream that I'm sure will wake the whole house.

"Tatum, calm down! It's me."

Clutching my chest, I look into the calming blue eyes that I forgot were there. "Shit. I'm sorry, Jay. I totally forgot you were here."

"You slept so well last night. I'm sad to see you jumpy in the morning," he coos, rubbing his hands up and down my arms. The constant affection is starting to make me feel funny around him.

"Jay."

"Yeah?"

"Why do you keep touching me so much?"

He drops his arms to his sides awkwardly. The loss of contact has me feeling surprisingly empty.

"I mean…we've always been touchy and cuddly and shit. Sorry. I didn't know everything had changed since I left."

"Well, not in the way you think."

He smirks at me and his eyes start to glimmer mischievously in the early morning light.

"Why are you looking at me like that?"

"I didn't know you felt that way."

"What way?" Heat flushes over my cheeks. If I could see them, they would probably be fire-hydrant red.

"You like me."

Shit. Shit shit shit. Play it off, T. "Of course I like you, you idiot," I tease, smacking him in the shoulder.

He shakes his head and laughs. "Oh no, you don't, Tatum. I know you better than you think. I know you like me, but I can see that your feelings are changing. About damn time, too."

As we both move to sit up against the headboard, my jaw drops after his declaration.

"What?"

"You can't tell me you really had no idea."

Well, now I'm actually confused. "No idea about *what*?"

"That I've had a crush on you for years now."

The floor practically falls out from under my feet.

I don't know how long I sat there staring, mouth gaping, unable to remember a single word one might say to answer such a declaration…but it must've been too long, because Jay finally breaks my shock by snapping in my face. "Hello? Earth to Tatum?"

"Obviously I didn't know," I squeak out. "Why didn't you say something?"

"I didn't think I had to! I wasn't exactly subtle, T. I just figured you didn't want to complicate our friendship."

I search his eyes, looking for any slight hint that all of this could be a lie. Finding nothing, I continue, "So, why tell me now?"

"Not only did my time away from you nearly suck the life right out of me, but the moment I laid eyes on you when I got off that plane, I felt it." He grabs my chin and forces my eyes to his once again.

"Felt what?" I rewind to what I remember when he arrived at the airport two short days ago, but all I can recall is how different he suddenly looked to me—sexy, muscular, dreamy… I shake my head; this is my best friend. I can't possibly look at him that way.

"That I'm in love with you."

Jumping back, I leap off the bed, "Come again?"

He spins his legs to the side and stands up in slow motion, trying not to scare me after his confession, "I'm in love with you, Tatum. It has taken me years to realize it, and even longer to admit, but I do in fact *love you*. I knew it the moment I got off that plane and your big green eyes were looking at me like you were seeing me in a whole new way."

I slowly back away, ready to run out the door at any moment. "I didn't look at you in any certain way."

"Yes, you did," his deep voice murmurs, pulling me deeper under his spell; his voice is like a siren's song to me, one I would follow to the very ends of the earth. "In fact, you're looking at me that way right now."

I'm vaguely aware that Jay has somehow ended up standing directly in front of me. As his hands wrap around both sides of my face and pull me closer, I see nothing but blue.

When his lips brush softly against mine, my knees go weak. He keeps one hand against my cheek and uses the other to hold me up; when his hand braces my waist, it's as if fireworks have been set off inside my body.

His mouth moves gracefully against mine, supplying me with the burst of life I didn't know I was missing.

I pull away, but have yet to open my eyes when Jay's voice breaks through the silence: "Well?"

Meeting his gaze once more, I gasp and place my hand over my lips as I flee once again to my closet. Jay doesn't chase me this time, and he doesn't fight with the doorknob when I lock it on him for the second time in forty-eight hours.

Slinking against the door and down to the floor, I touch the parts of my face where Jay held me seconds ago. I imagine Jay on the other side of the door, watching the minutes pass by on his watch as he waits for me to reappear. It's not until I hear him gather his things off of my desk that I make the effort to leave this tiny space and find out what the hell just happened between us.

"Jay?" I call out, unhooking the lock and preparing for him to ambush me.

When there's no answer, I swing the door wide open and scan the room, "Jay?" Once again, the alarming feelings set in. Have I really scared him off?

Crossing the room in record time, I stomp my way down the stairs to find the house empty. And when I pull open the small curtain that looks out into the driveway, I see that his car is gone. "What the hell have I done now?" I ask myself aloud. Jay hasn't even been home for an entire week, and I've already made his life a living hell.

Running back up the stairs, I sift through the covers for my phone, and dial Jay's number. It rings once before going straight to voicemail.

Just as I feel the tears form in my eyes, my phone vibrates against my ear. My eyes whip to the screen. "Jay," I breathe out in relief.

Jay: I'm sorry. I just couldn't help myself. I know you might not want to accept what I've said to you, or what happened in your room, but I'll say it only once more: I've had feelings for you for a while, and I've waited six long-ass months to kiss your perfect lips. I won't say another word while you figure out your feelings. Until then, JT forever and always.

That's when the tears really fall. Not only is Jay the most

wonderful best friend I could've ever asked for, but even after admitting his feelings for me, he isn't pushing me, and he's trying his best to keep our relationship what it always has been.

He obviously knows the feelings I have for him now, but I can't chance it. With the way my life has turned out to be over these past few months, I can't add on one more thing—not when I feel like I'm barely surviving as is.

Not to mention, I'll never put our friendship at risk. Ever.

My fingers shake as they prepare a response that I'm praying won't rip Jay apart.

Me: I obviously can't hide my feelings from you, and I appreciate you telling me the truth about how you feel about me, but I can't do that with you right now, Jay. I'm not sure I'll ever be ready. I care about you too much to lose you over a risk like this. I hope you understand. I love you.

Jay: Love you too.

I hang my head in defeat, knowing that was not the answer he was looking for. Maybe I'll change my mind in the future, but with the ocean of darkness that I'm drowning in, I need him to be the hero he's always been for me, without changing anything else.

CHAPTER FIVE

Jay wasn't kidding when he said our friendship would continue as normal after his big admission. Thanksgiving and all the days of the month after have gone just as smoothly as they did before he ever left. I still notice the heated way he stares at me when he thinks I'm not watching, and the way he gets a little too close when we share my bed during sleepovers, but he doesn't push me.

I can't say I don't like it. No. The complete opposite, in fact. But I won't tell him that.

My anxiety and panic attacks have almost disappeared. Mom claims it's because Jay is home, but I think it's because Adam has been better. He's hardly home, and when he actually is, he doesn't try to bother me in the slightest. I don't know why work has him so busy, but I'll take it.

As I stand here looking in the mirror at my red and green Christmas dress draping softly on my body, I wrap the battery operated Christmas lights around me.

Jay had this silly idea a few days ago to "wear our Christmas spirit," so here I am. I wonder how ridiculous he's going to look. Although, I can't imagine someone like Jay looking ridiculous in anything.

My phone buzzes the moment I finish attaching the end of the lights to the top of my dress. I snort at the text.

Jay: These lights are poking me in places that no one should. Get your ass out here, pronto.

Me: Don't forget, this was your idea :p

Grabbing my purse off the hook on the back of my door, I close the door behind me and head down the stairs, hesitating at the sound of a man's voice.

"Any idea why that boy is out there?" Adam asks almost sternly.

"Tatum is going to Jay's to celebrate Christmas over there. His mother always put together a nice dinner."

"She spends a lot of time with him." It's not a question, and doesn't seem like a threat. It's simply a thought. To me, it seems like he's searching for something.

Uncertainty stops me from continuing down the stairs, my anxiety roaring back. It's Adam's voice that breathes life back into it. The fact that I picked up on the slightest hint of sternness in his voice makes me nervous.

I start to tiptoe down the last few steps and stand as still as a statue on the carpeted landing, pausing to gauge whether I can sneak by without being seen. My eyes flick between my feet and the front door, trying to guess how many more steps I'll need to take before reaching my destination.

I make a break for it, but jump out of my skin as a shadow slides into the doorway to the kitchen. I grip my chest. "You scared me."

Adam's evil sneer makes me shiver in fear. "Where the hell do you think you're going?" His voice is a harsh whisper.

"I'm going to Jay's for Christmas dinner."

"So, you just don't care about this family anymore?" He

leans in, gripping the doorway until his knuckles go white. I back up a step toward the door, unsure of where to go.

"Everything okay?"

Adam casts a glance over his shoulder before dropping his hands and plastering a fake smile onto his face. My mom's grin falls a bit when she sees me. I can't even imagine what my face looks like right now, because it feels numb to me.

"Just fine. Tatum is just feeling a little down about all of us not being together for the holiday," Adam answers, kissing her cheek. She closes her eyes, her concern slipping away like dust in the wind.

She places her hand on his shoulder, looking over at me. "Don't worry about us, sweetie. We will have our Christmas tomorrow." With that, she walks between us and squeezes into the bathroom beneath the stairs.

Backing me up against the front door, Adam pins me with wide, animalistic eyes that have a panic attack brewing in the pit of my stomach, its tentacles crawling their way through my organs.

My throat constricts, and just as I start to think I'm going to pass out, a knock on the door stops me in my tracks. My skin jumps as the vibrations shudder through the wood. I swallow hard, watching as Adam's face blazes red, as if smoke could start billowing out of his ears at any moment.

There's no telling how he'll react with my mom so close, but I desperately need Jay to get me out of here. I reach for the doorknob, pining for any bit of relief I can possibly find.

With a tight face, Adam mouths, "Don't even dare." But I refuse to listen. I crack the door open and give Jay the best smile I can muster. His gorgeous smile slips as he stares into my eyes, his face going slack.

"Are you okay?" he prods, slipping in to shut the door behind him, his eyes never wavering from mine.

The toilet flushes as I nod and glance toward the doorway. Adam's face has now begun to fade to a pink color covering both his cheeks and the space between his eyebrows, but I can see the danger in his eyes. My mom comes out from the bathroom and smiles at Jay, but her gaze remains confused. Can she really not sense Adam's anger? Is she just choosing to ignore it? I can't be sure.

Jay stares between both of them, and I watch as he stands taller than he was when he entered, his chest puffing out as he gives a curt nod in their direction.

"Hi, sweetie," my mom says quietly, "Thank you for inviting Tatum over for dinner."

"It's no problem, Ms. B. My mom would love to see you too, if you'd like to join us." *I don't think that's a good idea. Shut up, Jay.*

If you didn't know him, you'd never notice, but the twitch in Adam's eyebrow is just the beginning of the blow building inside of him. "We actually have plans, don't we?" he says almost too kindly, hugging my mom against him. She beams up at him, making my stomach twist and turn.

We need to get the hell out of here before he thinks about showing Jay his true colors. Adam might be downright evil, but he loves to put on a good show for everyone. He wouldn't dare to make a bad move in front of Jay for such a trivial reason. At least, I hope not...

I catch the threatening hint, but Jay doesn't, or maybe he just flat-out refuses to acknowledge it. He just continues to stand there, staring at both of them, undeterred. You would think someone turned on Fight Night with the amount of testosterone filtering through the air around us.

"Well, you two should get going, but thank you for the invite. Tatum, you have your phone?" Thank goodness my mother is able to at least sense the awkwardness in the air. Her response seems to shake everyone from their daze.

Patting my purse, I just barely bob my head up and down. As I pull on Jay's sweater, I usher him out of the house, fear still swimming through my veins.

Once I get the door closed, he stomps his way to the car, leaving me in a cloud of snowy dust. *This won't be good.*

It takes everything in me to lift my cement-like feet from the doorstep. I quickly look over my shoulder, hoping and praying my mom continues to be spared from the monster taking up residence in our home.

Keeping my head down, I sigh and head in the direction of the car, slipping into the passenger seat. I reach for the buckle, but drop it when the slamming of Jay's door sends me leaping out of my skin. Jay is breathing heavily, fist tight against the wheel he just punched. The lights covering his body tremble under his quaking fury as a wild expression crosses his gaze.

"Do you want to tell me what the hell is going on? What is up with your dad? Why are we leaving your mom here with this psycho? And what is he doing to her? Talk to me, T, before I lose it."

The gears in my mind creak with the exhaustion of constantly needing to produce an excuse that appeases him. I hate lying to him more than anything else in this world. Even more, I want to know how he figured this out, and why he thinks my dad has done something to my mom…

Nothing's happened to my mom; not yet. Just me.

My hands ache from the way my nails are biting into the skin of my palms, "Jay," I whisper, trying to think of something to keep up my charade. Anything to get us past this.

Gripping the steering wheel, his eyes stay trained forward. "Please don't 'Jay' me. Just tell me what the hell is going on! I've kept my mouth shut long enough." His loud voice fills the space around us. I've actually never heard him get this loud in all the years I've known him. And for some reason, that calms me. The fact that his tone doesn't even alarm me only proves one thing—Jay truly is nothing like Adam, for which I'm forever grateful.

"My dad is just…different."

The stillness is paralyzing—uncomfortably so.

"Are we really going to sit here and pretend we didn't notice a whole lot of crazy in those eyes? Something is wrong, and you're hiding it from me. Now, spill."

Completely clueless as to how he was able to pick up on that much about my dad has me reeling with confusion. Hanging my head low, locking eyes with a few chunks of ice salt on the gray carpeting of Jay's car, I realize Jay—and my mom—are right in their own ways. I have to be honest. He's my best friend. I can't lie to him anymore…and maybe instead of Jay saving the day, maybe he can actually help me save myself this time. Especially when my mom seems to be so oblivious to everything going on right under her nose.

I sigh. "Not here."

My eyes scour the outside of the car, desperately searching for something to latch onto; anything to distract me from my world crumbling in on itself. I don't know what I expected to come of all this. I guess I was just trying to survive, hoping that if no one else truly knew what had happened within the confines of our walls, that maybe it would all feel like some strange nightmare, dissipating as soon as the sun came up.

I feel the heat of his gaze as he turns his attention to me. "Why?"

"You won't like it, and I don't want to be here when I tell you. Please, just drive to your house—or a random parking lot for all I care—and ask your parents if I can talk to you before we celebrate."

Putting the car in drive, he backs out, reaching for his phone at the same time.

Once we're on the road, he pushes some buttons on the screen, and holds it to his ear. "Hey, Ma. Yes, sorry we're late. Can we push back dinner a bit?"

He pauses a moment, and I take the time to finally look at him. I suppress a chuckle at his bizarre red-and-green plaid dress pants, but the giggling comes to a stop when my eyes move up to his extremely tight red button-up. The silky material hugs every crease of muscle on his chest and arms.

Finding it hard to breathe, I clear my throat, almost choking on my spit. Jay glances over to check on me, and it's his mischievous grin that has me whipping my head straight ahead to stare at the road once more.

"Thanks, Ma. See you in a few. Love you." I hear the flirtatious grin in his voice. I shift in my seat at the sound.

My eyes follow his veiny hand as it pushes the phone back into its pocket, an action that shouldn't look as sexy as it does, especially with all that I'm about to admit to him. I remain quiet, waiting for my heart rate to return to normal…if that's even possible.

It doesn't take long for us to reach Jay's house, but when we do, Jay turns the car off and sits thoughtfully for a few minutes. "Everything okay?" I ask.

When he looks at me, it's with the most sincere love in his eyes. I can't help but smile. "I'm sorry," he says.

"What the hell for?"

"With everything going on, I never got to tell you how beautiful you looked when I walked in that door. I've never seen Christmas lights look so perfect."

His declaration is enough to make me melt. Without a second thought, I lean over the console and peck him on the cheek. Choosing not to wait for his reaction, I slip out the door, anxiously wanting to avoid that conversation for as long as possible. It takes him a minute, but he quickly follows suit, his smile finding me when his eyes meet mine over the hood of his car. I can't help but smirk in return.

"Wait right there," he starts, "Don't move a muscle."

I obey as he comes around to grasp my hand, and we walk up the sidewalk together. The warmth helps to chase away the storm brewing just under the thin layer of my skin.

The moment Jay and I reach the fork in the sidewalk, Mrs. Tenlin swings the front door of their house wide open, her gaze sweeping side to side until her eyes land on us.

She smacks her hand to her chest, her curly, brown hair falling in waves around her shoulders. I smile at her. "It's good to see you, Ma."

She races down the steps and sweeps me into a tight embrace. "Sweetie, where have you been? We haven't seen you since Jay's been home," she answers, brushing the hair off my face. "Is everything all right? Jay says we need to push back dinner for a bit." My head spins as she assesses me, her gaze drifting back and forth between Jay and me.

With a tight-lipped grin, I reply, "Everything is fine. We'll be down shortly. I just have to adjust my lights."

She kisses me on the cheek and gives me one more tight squeeze before letting us go. I feel bad lying to her, but not as much as I do about lying to Jay. I have a feeling that she knows anyway. I visited every week while Jay was gone, and as the weeks drifted by, the somber looks had increased in frequency, eating away at my conscience.

With lightning speed, Jay pulls me toward the back of the house. "Where are we going?" I ask.

"I moved to the guest house. This college boy wanted his own space." He shoots me a megawatt smile.

Once we trudge through the snow-covered backyard and enter the guest house, he takes me by surprise as he thrusts me against the door and encases me between his arms, palms flat against the wooden barricade.

I wait for what he might do next with bated breath, but by the heaving of his chest, I'm not sure I'm prepared for what he might want to do. The closeness has my mind conjuring up things that are only found in steamy romance novels, things that have my cheeks blushing once more.

We stand there for what feels like a lifetime, staring into each other's eyes before he finally speaks, "You have no idea what you do to me."

Gulping loudly, I stammer, "I-I didn't d-do anything."

The wicked smirk that crosses his face tells me the complete opposite. "You think you can be as sexy as you are in that dress, hug my mom like you're family, and cuddle up to me at night like I'm the last bit of warmth in this world, and call it nothing?"

I shrug as my mind goes blank. All I can focus on is the size of his deep, muscular chest, and how close it is to mine.

"Why won't you just admit your feelings for me, T? I want you for myself." His words have my mouth watering and my knees feeling weak and wobbly.

"I thought you wanted to talk about what happened back there."

"Maybe I want an answer to this question first."

Pushing his arms down before I am left with no energy to resist, I manage to calm him a smidge. "Jay, this is important. Your mom is going to be expecting us. Can I please just tell you what's been going on?"

I don't miss the way his pupils deflate a little. Guilt weighs down my gut, but I'm not sacrificing the survival of this friendship over some attraction.

Pivoting away from me, he moves to sit down on the couch and pats the area next to him. "Go on," he urges. My body freezes in hesitation as my gaze sweeps about the small house, noticing all the changes since Jay has moved in.

Blue neon lights border the top of every wall, definitely giving it a bachelor-pad vibe. The dark wood floors and white walls give a stark contrast to each other, the navy-blue couch looking a little out of place.

I happen upon a hidden bottle of courage somewhere deep inside myself that snaps me out of the brief daze and propels me forward to sit beside him.

I cannot do this. There's no way I can do this. My head starts to shake before Jay catches my chin between his pointer finger and thumb and draws my face to his. My eyes find him like magnetic poles fighting to pull the other closer.

The warmth in his eyes is enough to urge me on.

"This is going to hurt you, Jay."

"That's okay. It's hurting you more. Let me take some of the burden off of you."

I'm not sure what I ever did to score this man as my best friend, but I could live a thousand lifetimes and never deserve him.

"As you know, the day you left was the same day that I had my first panic attack." I take a deep breath, pushing it out hard. "But the truth of it is…that's also the day my dad showed up."

"Wait…the same day? He's been there that long?"

"Yes." I pause. "He came knocking on our door and basically said he wanted to get to know me. He felt bad for missing out on so many years."

He scoffs. "I mean, not even sending a damn birthday card for a decade-plus will do that to you." Not exactly the response I was anticipating, but I get it.

"Yeah…but it's been hell ever since."

The couch bounces a little when Jay shoots up to pace the floor in front of me. His wood floor creaks beneath his weight. "I knew it. What's his deal?" He whips around to face me, his wide eyes almost bulging. "And why did you lie?" He runs his hands through his hair, ruining the gelled-down combover he obviously worked so hard on.

"You're not going to like the reason."

Getting down on his knees, he takes both of my hands in his and silently begs me to continue.

"He makes me feel like I'm crazy, Jay…everyone thinks he's so perfect, even my mom! I mean, he's been rocking his job in law enforcement, so the community thinks he walks on water." I throw my hands up, slamming them back down onto my knees before continuing, "But he hates me."

Before my eyes finally float up to meet his, searching for anything to gauge his reaction, he pulls me up off the couch, plops back down, and cradles me in his lap. That's when I feel the tears running down my cheeks.

After giving me a few minutes to collect myself, Jay tucks a piece of my hair behind my ear and lifts my chin to force our eyes to meet once more. His droopy blue eyes sadden me.

"Has he touched you? If he's hurt you—"

"Shh." I silence him with my finger. "He hasn't hurt me. He tries to scare me, that's all."

"If he is so terrible, why does your mom let him stay?"

I look down at my hands that are wringing themselves into oblivion in my lap. "Well, she hasn't seen it…or at least, I don't think so. I would hope my mom wouldn't be ignoring what's going on. But she's glad to have him back… and…I mean, there's nothing I could say anyway. He's a cop."

"What the hell does that have to do with anything?"

I force his gaze to mine, hoping this conversation is almost over. "He has a lot of pull in this town. Not only would no one believe me, but what proof could I possibly use against him?"

"Damn," he answers, dropping his head in defeat. I can't help but lift my hand to stroke the hair on the back of his head. He leans his head into my chest and breathes me in. My eyes scan his movie case, noticing the slew of superhero movies housed on each shelf. If only superheroes were real. I'd give just about anything for one of them to swoop in and save the day.

"Let me protect you, T." I smile as I picture Jay dressed up as a knight, slaying dangerous dragons to rescue me from my dark tower. If only it was that easy.

"Don't be silly. I'm fine. I may be stuck at home because our community college still has no dorms to escape to, but I'll be out before you know it. And who knows, maybe he'll leave again before I even get the chance. I can do this."

When he looks at me again, I notice a glassy sheen move across his eyes. "Please."

Scrunching my brows, I ask, "Please what?"

"Let me protect you. I should've been here for you. If I

could've come home, you know I would have. All you had to do was ask."

"You would've ruined your internship." He shakes his head at me, his lips twitching as if fighting to keep his mouth closed. "What, Jay?"

"I wasn't just there for the internship."

My head jerks back a smidgen. "What are you talking about?"

"Nothing." He shakes his head. "Just forget about it. Thank you for being honest with me."

With all the emotions swirling around in my head, I decide not to press him about it because I want nothing more than for this whole conversation to be over. I just want to eat some dinner and enjoy a holiday with my best friend and his family.

"Can we go in now? I'm starving."

He squeezes me closer, giving me a moment to feel the muscles restrained under his shirt. I sigh, but his quiet laughter interrupts my moment of silence and muscle appreciation. "What are you laughing about?" I ask.

"You have your appetite back. Move your ass and let's go!"

"Whatever. Most guys want us women to starve ourselves," I chastise him, finally standing up straight and smoothing my dress down.

Shaking his head, he grabs my face in his large hands while towering over me. "I'm not most guys. I like my women fed." He drops his hands to grab one of mine, pulling me toward the door before he turns to face me once more. "That goes for all of you, too." He winks, his pointer finger moving up and down in front of me. My temperature begins to skyrocket.

I shut the door softly behind us with the one free hand I

have and whisper, "Do you have to be so swoon-worthy all the damn time?"

For a moment, I worry he heard me, because he stills for a millisecond.

Before we even move off of the porch, he faces me and locks eyes with mine, but something is different. His eyes have a glow to them, like blue streaks of lightning are running through them. My eyebrows twitch.

With just the right amount of force, Jay walks me backward to gently push me against the door and silences me with his mouth. It's the type of kiss that literally sucks the soul right out of you.

I find it hard to open my eyes until I hear Jay clear his throat. "You okay?"

"What the hell was that?" I ask in a gravelly voice, forcing one eye open at a time.

Raising his eyebrows humorously, he titters. "A kiss?"

"What was up with your eyes?"

His eyes widen a small fraction, just barely, making me wonder if they really did light up. I tilt my head to the side, anxiously awaiting his response.

"What do you mean?"

"They were glowing blue."

He runs his hand through his hair and I watch as some pieces fall back onto his forehead, "They are blue."

I shake my head, wondering if everything is just getting to me. I decide to momentarily forget about it. "Let's just go."

"Gotta feed my girl."

I try to nudge him down the walkway, but his great size overpowers me. "Would you quit that?"

This time, he yanks my arm and literally glues my body to his, his lips touching my ear. I shiver in suspense, wondering if we'll ever make it to the house with the amount of times we've stopped. I chance a glimpse at the sliding glass door to be sure Jay's parents aren't watching us.

"What is it exactly that you'd like me to *quit* doing?"

I am rendered speechless, wanting to close my eyes and feel his hot breath touch my ear over and over again. All I am able to do is shake my head and whisper, "Nothing."

"That's what I thought, " he says with a grin, turning a final time and grasping my hand to finally pull me toward the house.

Of one thing, I am certain: I don't remember Jay being this seductively tempting before he left.

Dinner with Jay and his family is going as smoothly as I hoped it would. Although, I can't help but feel a twinge of sadness as I think about my own family at home; one I sometimes wish could be more like Jay's. I picture what something like that might be like.

I let my mind wander for a few more minutes once we all move to the living room couch to watch Christmas movies. I lean my head against Jay's shoulder until I feel his hand cradle my cheek and gently push my stare to his. "What's wrong?" he asks, concern filling his eyes.

"I was just thinking about how everything is going back at home," I reply, hating that I have to admit this type of bullshit to him.

His thumb strokes my cheek, and for a brief moment, I forget my troubles. What would it take to be this calm all the time?

"Come with me," he asks, standing and offering his hand

to me. I smile and take it, getting up from my chair to follow him to wherever he plans on taking me. Anything to get out of my own head. "Close your eyes."

I snicker and close my eyes, holding my opposite hand out to feel for anything Jay might accidentally run me into. I shiver when I feel the cold air brush my skin, leaving a slew of goosebumps in its wake.

Before I get the chance to voice my discomfort, I breathe in Jay's cologne as he covers me in his jacket. His mouth touches my ear once more: "Are you ready?"

I tremble a bit, but nod, a big smile taking over my face. He lifts his hand from my eyes, and I blink the blurriness away as I gasp at the sight in front of me. All of the trees in his backyard—that I somehow missed on our way to the guest house—are covered in hundreds of Christmas lights, suddenly making me feel right at home in my ridiculous Christmas light-up dress.

"Jay, this is beautiful. But you never decorate your backyard. What gives?"

When he doesn't answer, I whip around to find him. My hand flies to my mouth when I find him standing behind me, a rose clutched in his fist, "What are you doing?"

"Would you just be quiet for two seconds?"

I cross my arms over my chest and raise an eyebrow at his choice of words.

"Sorry. Will you hear me out? Please?"

I pretend to think about it for a second, but when Jay gets that adorably impatient look about him, I offer him a nod.

"About damn time. Anyway…" He clears his throat. I smile at the nervousness in his gaze as he continues, "Tatum, we have been best friends for the longest time, and our friendship has been the biggest blessing in my entire life. However,

I cannot let go of these feelings I have for you. You can keep fighting me, but I see the desire in your eyes every time you look at me. Friends make the best lovers. Let me be your best friend, your lover, your confidant, *and* your hero. Please. I promise I'll never let you down."

His proposition has me dreaming about all the possibilities—dreams that could never possibly work in my favor.

The love shining in his eyes is enough to make me wonder if it's worth it to keep fighting back with every reason why I should refuse.

Stepping carefully over the blanket of snow on the ground, I move directly in front of him and take his face in my hands. "Jay, that was incredibly sweet, but we can't do this. Not only do I not want to ruin our friendship, but I just have so much going on. I..." I pause to heave a dreadful sigh. "I can't."

His eyes grow dark and slack for a short second, taking me aback. "Yes, you can. Stop pushing me away. We're not going to ruin anything, and as for everything you have going on, let me help you. I can carry the weight of the world that's been sitting on your shoulders since I left."

"Jay..." I look down. "Stop."

"No. Please don't be like this. I just know we can make it work. Please."

It would be easier to keep saying no if everything in me wasn't screaming to say yes.

Is this really the worst thing that could happen to me? I mean, Jay is perfect in every way. Not only is he my best friend in the whole wide world, but he loves me—really loves me. So, for once, for Jay, for me, I take the leap.

"Ugh, *fine*," I tease. "If you insist."

I watch his eyes light up as the corners of his mouth rise,

and I leap into his arms. He holds me for a bit before slowly letting me slip down his body and plopping me in front of him.

"I'll never let you down, " he softly assures me, sliding a simple silver ring down from the stem of the rose.

I gasp, suddenly feeling overwhelmed. And as I look closer, I see that it has two letters engraved on it: JT.

"JT forever," he says, answering my questioning look.

"Forever and always," I reply, pulling his face to mine as we melt into a soft, tender kiss. Nothing has felt right until this very moment. If Jay can really save me, I'll give him anything he wants, for as long as he'll have me.

CHAPTER SIX

After a surprisingly relaxing end to our Christmas break, the beginning of my second semester—and the new year—of community college has been pretty uneventful. A full time schedule of general education classes has both Jay and me pretty busy, but not busy enough that we don't see much of each other.

Being in a relationship with Jay is just as I expected it to be—amazing, yet simple. He has made sure to still keep our friendship alive as we stick to our sleepover movie nights and random trips to the mall. My mom has no problem with him still staying; she trusts me, after all. The only person I haven't told is my dad. I don't think I really plan to, either.

As of late, my dad has actually been doing okay. There haven't been any run-ins between us, but the anxiety still sits just below my skin, waiting to erupt at any sign of hostility.

Jay must feel something is off, because even though he doesn't think so, I've noticed him coming around more often since my admission. I'm grateful he loves looking out for me so much.

The sun is shining through my bedroom windows, lighting up my walls to appear a shade lighter than my normal orange. I'm laying my head in Jay's lap as he quizzes me for our biology test, staring up at the glow-in-the-dark stars speckling the white ceiling, when he drops the bomb.

"I'm going to be out of town all of next week," he says nonchalantly, his eyes locked on the card he was just about to quiz me on.

I sit up and spin to look at his face, wondering if he's being serious. "You're what?"

His eyes soften as he stares down at me. "I won't be in town next week," he says, his thumb tracing my cheek, "but it'll be a quick trip."

"Where are you going?"

He pauses for a moment, and I don't miss the wheels turning in his head. *Is he lying to me about something? No, Jay would never. Right?*

"Remember that comic book internship I applied for?"

"Yessss," I drawl.

He grins. "I've been offered a spot to attend a weeklong conference for comic book writers in Beijing."

"Beijing? *Again?*" I close my eyes as the palm of his hand cups my cheek. I rest my head there, helplessness setting in.

He clears his throat. "Listen, I have to go. I'll be back as soon as I can, but this is a great opportunity." He pushes my hair behind my ears. "I need you to promise me something, though."

As much as I hate to see him go, I don't want to hold him back from his dream, but I can't deny that I'm scared about what I might go through the moment he leaves. "What's that?" I ask.

"A couple things: first, stay out of your dad's way while I'm gone. Second, if something goes wrong, go stay with my parents. The guest house is always open to you." He continues to tick away the list on his fingers. "Third, with my schedule and the time difference, I won't have much time with my phone, so if you absolutely need me, you need to call the number on this card." He pauses, handing me a white card with three, red diagonal lines that stretch from the top right corner to the bottom left. I notice the oddity of this card only having a phone number on it, but I don't question it. "Lastly, please don't ever take your ring off."

I scrunch up my eyebrows, "Why?" I glance down at the silver band and run my finger over the J and T engraved into it, curious what hidden wonders lie within the metals it's made of.

Taking my hand in his and kissing the band, he answers, "Just don't, okay? Promise."

"I promise." And I do, but I have no doubt there's something he's not telling me. I'll be patient—for now—but eventually, I'll have to know what's really going on.

In the meantime, the imminent goodbye has me filled with dread. *Who's going to protect me while he's away?*

I've gotten so used to seeing Jay on a daily basis that sitting on his bed, looking at the suitcase he's holding, is enough to bring tears to my eyes. I'm trying my best to fight them back while he's not looking, but the minute he turns around to lock eyes with me, they immediately break down the gates.

"Baby," he coos, rushing over to me and landing on his knees to get a good look at my face, "don't do this. It's going to be okay. I'll be back before you know it."

If only he could feel what I'm feeling right now. He cannot guarantee me that everything will be okay while he's gone, and that thought frightens the shit out of me.

I hang my head low and watch as the tears fall onto my jeans, leaving small wet spots in their wake. All I can do is shake my head, but he quickly stops me and holds it still as he presses his lips hard to mine, his mouth warm and possessive. His warm connection is like the first cozy, spring day thawing out the icy pinch of winter's frost.

When he pulls back, the scorching look in his eyes sends liquid lava flowing through my veins. I leap into his arms, his grip pulling me in close.

Jay stands up, keeping me tightly locked to his body. I quickly wrap my legs around his waist. He lays me down on the bed and gently hovers over me, his left hand brushing through my hair as he stares deep into my eyes.

"Are you okay?" Jay whispers, his eyes jerking back and forth between mine. "I can—"

I don't give him the chance to finish. Instead, I grab the back of his head with both of my hands, bringing his soft mouth down to meet mine.

My skin tingles as his hand wraps around the side of my face like they do in all those romance movies, and the gesture makes my heart melt. I don't think I'll ever get tired of the way he touches me.

When he pulls away, he gives me one more kiss and slides off of me. I suddenly feel cold. "Jay? Is something wrong?"

"I could lay with you in that bed all day long, but unfortunately, I can't be late for my flight…" His eyes soften as he tries to deliver the news as lightly as possible.

The realization that Jay is about to leave for seven days slams its way back to the forefront of my mind. I swallow loudly. "I don't want you to go." My voice is barely a whisper.

"T, I know, but I have to. Please don't make me feel worse

than I already do." The heartbreak that flashes across his eyes is enough to tear me in two.

"I'm sorry, I know. I'm just really going to miss you." I get up and pull him to stand in front of me before wrapping my arms around his middle and laying my head against his broad chest, listening to the comforting thumps of his heart. I try my best to commit them to memory.

After only a moment, he wraps his arms around me in return and squeezes me as tight as he can without hurting me.

"Jay, honey! Are you ready?" Mrs. Tenlin yells through the intercom connecting Jay's guest house to the main house. I stare in the direction of the intercom, dread filling my stomach.

I throw a mask over my face, already knowing how hard it's going to be for Jay to leave not only me, but his family too. This won't be easy for him, and I need to keep some composure. It's only one week... Seven days. One hundred sixty-eight hours. Ten thousand, eighty minutes. (Shoutout to Google for giving me those exact numbers when I couldn't sleep at four in the morning, tucked into Jay's side). I try to recall the tranquility of his features as I stared at him. He sleeps with the windows open—something I'm still not brave enough to do on my own—so the moonlight made it easy for me to see his face.

I can do this. It's going to be fine.

A small kiss on the cheek pulls my gaze back to Jay's face as he searches my eyes for any reason to stay. "Ready, baby?" he asks sweetly.

I offer him a smile of reassurance. "Yeah. Let's go."

I admire Jay's back the entire trip to the house—giving myself something else to focus my mind on—and try to talk myself into believing that all of this isn't a big deal.

That is, until we clear the threshold and I stumble upon Jay and his mom embracing in a near death grip with tears rolling down her face.

Isn't he just going to a comic book art convention of some sort? The hug they are exchanging appears to say much more.

"Everything okay?" I question.

Jay looks at me over his mom's shoulder, and confusion swarms in my belly at the vacant look in his eyes. "What's going on?" I try to hide my panicked tone, but it feels like I'm sucking at it. Remind me to not consider acting as a future career.

Mrs. Tenlin gives him a peck on the cheek and whispers something in his ear before shuffling off to the kitchen. Jay's dad comes up next and nearly smothers Jay in a tight embrace. If there's one thing I know about Jay's dad, it's that he's not really a hugger. I have no clue what to make of this.

Once they disappear, Jay avoids my gaze at all costs. The uneasy feelings from earlier are now back with a vengeance, and I don't see them disappearing anytime soon. This silence is deafening.

"Jay?" I'm met with those beautiful blue eyes again, but they're darker than usual, resembling the deepest parts of the ocean. I see chaos swimming in those waters, turbulent waves blanketing the unknown that lies just under the surface. What would it take to harpoon those troubles and drag them to shore?

"Hm?"

"What aren't you telling me? Why did your mom just act like you're going off to war?"

Jay reaches for both my hands and pulls me in. He waits a beat too long before answering. "She's just being a mom, ya know?" His eyes continue to dart to the doorway behind me as he looks anywhere but in my eyes.

"You're lying." My tone is not kind. "We're together now, Jay. Quit acting like I'm an outsider. I deserve to know."

For a moment, I can almost guarantee he's going to confess as he stares into my soul, but I watch the thought evaporate into a cloud of smoke just as speedily as it appeared. "There's nothing to tell." His tone is stale, lacking the very life he seems to breathe into everything he does.

I close my eyes for a brief moment, shaking my head in quiet frustration. "Forget it."

Once I find his gaze again, his eyes droop a bit, and guilt builds in my gut. Touching his arm in passing, I make my way out the door. I just need a moment to breathe…away from him.

I sit down on the cold cement, hoping and praying that everything about this whole ordeal is a total dream, or maybe it's just turning out to be an utter nightmare. It's hard for me to tell.

My back straightens the minute I hear the door open behind me, the hair on the back of my neck standing at attention. I stand and beeline for the car.

"T," Jay calls from behind me, "Why are you doing this?"

"Why do you think?" I seethe, holding my hand on the door handle, ready to leap in at any moment. The anger I spew is surprising.

The minute I hear the doors unlock, I whip the door open and drop myself into the passenger side, shivering once my ass hits the cold leather seats.

"Well?" Jay prods, taking his seat next to me and buckling himself in. I cannot believe he's being so dense right now.

What does he expect me to say? And why can't he just leave it alone so I don't have to feel like an utter bitch?

"You're lying to me."

He grips onto the wheel and lays his forehead against it. "About what?" His tone is dull and deflated.

"Can you please just drive? You're going to be late." He heaves a heavy sigh at my remark, and I find myself instantly wishing I could take it all back.

What the hell, T? The love of your life is going to Beijing for an entire week. Why are you being like this? I roll my eyes at myself for being such an asshole, but I've already lit the fire; there's too much gasoline left for it to simmer just yet.

Our ride to the airport is quiet, but with every passing minute, my remorse piles higher. Jay hasn't looked my way, nor has he uttered a single word, which only makes me feel like an even bigger bitch. I can't even remember a time when Jay has ever ignored me; in fact, I can't really recall a time we've ever fought like this.

Suddenly, he feels lightyears away.

The moment we pass the Detroit Metro Airport sign, the regret and anxiety mix together in my stomach to create a truly terrible acid that is casually working its way up to becoming projectile vomit. I swallow repeatedly, trying to keep it buried deep down.

Jay parks his black Chrysler 300 in the short term parking lot, and hands me his keys before quietly getting out to grab his bag. Meanwhile, I wait in the car and watch him in the reflection of the passenger side mirror. His downcast eyes remain unmoving, and my chest expands with a sigh. I get out and gently close the door behind me, waiting for Jay to meet me, but as he gets nearer, his eyes stay locked on the building.

"Jay?"

"I don't want to fight with you, Tatum. I need to go." He says it like he has no choice.

I grab his hand, begging him to look my way. The moment I have his attention, I answer hurriedly, "I don't either. I'm sorry."

"For what?"

"Getting angry. I just know when you're lying to me, and it makes me feel like you don't trust me."

He nods slightly, no reply to what I've just said. Looks like I'm not getting anywhere with this.

Once we're inside at the drop-off area, he turns to me with glossy eyes. "Do you remember what you promised me?"

"Avoid my dad, go to your house if I need to, call the number on the creepy card in case of an emergency, and don't take off my ring." He leans in and kisses me on the cheek, but it's a cold, strange kiss that has me conjuring up all sorts of possibilities. Something really doesn't feel right. "Jay…"

"Yes?" he replies sadly.

"What are you not telling me?" My eyes search his desperately.

Dropping his bag on the floor, he wraps both hands around my face and leans down to seal his mouth over mine in what feels like a goodbye kiss. *No, that can't be.* I've never had a goodbye kiss. I wouldn't even know what that feels like, would I?

"I love you," he whispers. I melt at the realization that this is the first time he's said that to me as his girlfriend, not just his best friend.

"I love you too, but Jay…" I grab both of his hands and squeeze them. "You know you can tell me anything. I can take it."

While I should be utterly speechless over the fact that this man has admitted he loves me, the atmosphere around us weighs so heavily that I can't bear to change the subject.

"I'm just going to miss you. That's all." I let go of his hands and slam into his chest for one last hug, taking a huge sniff of my favorite smell. If I could bottle his scent, there's no doubt it'd sell for top dollar.

"I'll miss you too. Be safe."

"Always," he answers.

With one last kiss, he picks up his bag and starts to turn around. Everything around me becomes blurry as the tears swim into my vision. I close my eyes and feel his calloused hand grip mine and softly pull just enough that only my hand follows.

Once his touch is gone and my hand falls back down to my side, I know he's gone. I turn and waste no time in getting out of this place, the thought of watching him leave too unbearable.

The walk back to Jay's car that I'm borrowing for the week is both quick and irrelevant. I'm not sure how I found my way back to it, let alone got inside, but it's nothing compared to the crushing sadness taking over me. My chest heaves with the small, silent cries rushing their way out of my body.

I would do anything to be with Jay every minute of every day because this hollowness is enough to convince me that there's no hope I'll make it through this in one piece. How did I make it through those six months without him? And why does one short week feel even more daunting to survive?

For the first time in a while, I feel a panic attack brewing in my stomach.

"No! No, you will not do this!" I scream at myself,

begging my anxiety to go away, but it's back with a vengeance. It feeds on fear and the unknown.

Unfortunately, I'm consumed by both: fear because Jay is gone, and the unknown…

Jay has lied to me for the first time ever.

Who knew things could change so easily?

And with that last thought, the darkness pulls me under and swallows me whole.

CHAPTER SEVEN

Days 1 and 2:

Very uneventful. I dropped Jay off on Friday and spent the rest of the weekend in bed, crying. Mom came to check on me a few times, but other than that, I laid there with my phone in my hand the entire time. Who knew looking back at old pictures of us would make it feel like we've always been together? I guess in a way, we have.

My phone never goes off. It's been two days since I've talked to him. Two horrifically, long, dreadful, lonely, sad days…

Day 3:

I'm admiring the extra dark color of the bags under my eyes when a pounding on my bedroom door makes me jump higher than a jack rabbit. "Shit," I say under my breath, my heart thumping wildly.

"Tatum Louise Bellini, you open this door right now!" Adam's voice booms, sending shockwaves of terror through my blood vessels. I am frozen in fear, but my feet move of their own accord when the door shakes against my dad's fist a second time.

"Coming," I squeak out, my voice unbearably small compared to his. My hand pauses on the doorknob, but I finally click it unlocked. I duck out of the way just in time as the door goes whooshing past my face.

"Sit your ass down!" His screams slam into my face, saliva plopping on my skin like rain. I'd give anything to wipe it off, but the truth is, I'm too scared to even move. "You heard me!"

I hold my hands up like I'm being rushed by a gunman and back up until the edge of my bed buckles my knees. I sink down with an *umph*.

"Do you want to tell me why that dickbag's car is in our driveway and you've been holed up in here sobbing for two days?" The vein in his neck throbs with seething rage, waiting just under the surface like a lion stalking its prey.

"I-I just m-miss Jay…" I whisper, careful to keep my voice as quiet as possible.

"And *why do you have his car*?" he screams, his face so close that his powerful voice blows my hair back a little. My core vibrates as my anxiety builds.

Keeping my head down, I answer, "He let me borrow it while he's gone for the week."

I jump back when his finger almost grazes my naked eye and squint at him as if the sight of him might blind me. I can see the tunnel vision starting in the recesses of my vision, but beg it to stay hidden for now. Being that vulnerable will only fuel his fire.

"Why the hell would he do that? Huh? What are you not telling me, Tatum?"

I hold up my hands in defense and scan both of his cold, dark eyes, searching for the right answer to appease him. "He needed a ride to the airport, so he drove us in his car and just told me to use it this week—"

"Why wouldn't his parents just drive him? Are you two dating? You have NO business having a boyfriend."

The manic look in his eyes tells me the worst thing I could do is confirm that thought, so I plead the fifth, remaining silent.

"Answer me this instant, you little shit," he seethes. I close my eyes and try my best to block him out, just as my head is yanked back by my ponytail and held tight, my hair follicles gripping my skull like their lives depend on it. I scream silently, my neck being stretched at an angle that makes it hard to get out a noise. "If you want to ignore me, you have another thing coming. I will get the truth out of you."

His hot breath covers my face, bringing tears to my eyes.

Just as I'm about to beg him to leave, my head swings forward with release. I jump back as he storms out, slamming the door behind him; I quickly run over to lock it. Slamming my fist against the door, I'm instantly paralyzed in pain. My lungs burn. I try my best to crawl over to my bed, but I can't move. Instead, I fall back against the door, gripping my throat as I slide down to the cold, hard floor.

My breaths come out in small gasps, and I watch as everything around me falls prey to the invading dark tunnel stealing my vision, sucking me deep into the darkness closing in.

I'm going to die here. This time I know it. I'm going to die here...

The door rattling against my back with knocks shakes me awake, catapulting me back into my nightmare. I never thought I'd have to live through this sort of reality.

I grab at my chest again, my quick breaths instantly slowing as I place the quiet, gentle knocks. *Mom.*

I huff out a relieved sigh, grateful my lungs still function properly. That was the absolute worst panic attack I've ever had. *How am I even alive right now?*

"Tatum, sweetie? Can I come in?" Hearing my mom's sweet voice has tears collecting along the rims of my eyes. It takes me forever to get up and gather myself, but I try my best to calm down before letting her in.

I turn the knob to pop the lock and slowly swing open the door. "Hey, Mom," I whisper.

Concern floods her eyes as she assesses me from head to toe. I can only imagine what I look like right now.

"What's wrong?" she asks quickly, slipping in to quietly close the door behind her and relock it. "What happened?"

She wraps her arms around me and helps walk me to my bed as I tremble in her arms, wondering if we need to turn up the heat. When we're seated, I snuggle farther into her, hoping her warm, comforting scent will pull me in and erase my memory.

She squeezes me tighter. "Baby, talk to me. What happened?"

"It was nothing, Mom. I just miss Jay."

She sighs, her breath tickling my hair a little…the hair I'm so thankful is actually still there. "Do not think you can lie to me and I won't know. Something happened. Tell me."

I give her a piece of the truth. "Adam was upset with me. I think he's figured out Jay and I are dating. He raised his voice. It scared me. That's all." The staccato pace I'm speaking at feels rehearsed.

"Did he lay his hands on you?" My heart sinks as I try to find some reassuring words for her, but I wait a beat too long.

"Tatum?" Her voice sounds more urgent, worrying me into almost telling the truth, but for her sake, I resist.

"No, Mom. Of course not. I'm fine, just shook up. I think I'm going to try to call Jay."

She softly pats my head and kisses me on the temple. "I'm sorry, baby. It might've been a bad day at work. You have class tomorrow, right? Maybe getting out of the house will help."

I nod my head. "Don't be sorry, Mom. It's not your fault." And it's not; she just can't see what's really happening.

I wish Adam had never come back.

Days 4 and 5:

Still nothing from Jay. I've texted him numerous times, but have received nothing in return. I even tried to call his phone after what happened with my dad, but it went straight to voicemail, and I chose not to leave a message.

My mom was right. Being out of the house away from Adam has helped somewhat, but I feel like I'm not really here. After my two classes yesterday, and science today, I chose to stay on campus and enjoy some lunch in the student center to extend my time. It's too bad college classes don't seem to last as long as a school day does in high school.

I've barely touched my food when someone manages to pull me out of my daydream.

"Tatum? Are you okay?"

I immediately recognize Toree's voice and shift my attention to distract me from the sinking feeling inside. I smile, hoping it appears happy enough—she looks so pretty today. She's always had gorgeous red hair with those typical brown eyes that accompany it, but she's now added in some light blonde highlights. They suit her.

"Hey." I push some hair behind my ear, adjusting in my seat. "Yes, I'm okay. Your hair looks great."

"Thank you," she replies sweetly, swinging her backpack to the floor and sitting across from me. "I feel like I haven't talked to you in forever."

Because you haven't, Tor. I don't say that. It's not entirely her fault. I could've reached out just as easily as her.

"I know. I'm sorry. I had a lot going on this summer, and by the time classes started, I just felt so overwhelmed with all of...this." I wave my hands around me. "Ever since Jay got back, I've kind of been MIA." I shrug, unsure of what else to say.

She reaches across the table and grabs my hand. "I'm sorry too. I could've called at any time, same for Jana and Lex, but we thought you were mad at us for a little bit there. I...we should've done better. I'm so sorry."

I squeeze her hand and stare straight into her eyes which suddenly look so big. "I forgive you, Tor. I've missed you too. I'm sorry for the misunderstanding."

She smiles sweetly at me, her eyes going a bit glossy before shaking herself out of her stupor with a sigh, her hands smacking the tabletop. "That's it, I'm texting the girls. Let's fix this."

I laugh for the first time since Jay left. I can't wait to have my girls back.

Within minutes, Jana and Lex join us at the table, and I'm quickly surrounded by the girls I've known for what feels like forever. Toree and Lex have been in my life since kinder-garten, and Jana joined our posse in sixth grade. We've been inseparable ever since—that is, until Jay left and I became a hermit all summer, on top of starting our first year of college, which resulted in never seeing each other and radio silence between all of us. I didn't even end up in any of the same college classes as them.

My eyes scan the three of them, wondering if they have any classes together. It's odd that they're finished for the day and happen to be in the student center the same time as me. That must mean they have at least one together today. I suddenly feel even more regretful about not reaching out.

Besides Toree's bright-colored hair, which was done by her sister who recently enrolled in cosmetology school, Lex's hair is darker—a result of wanting to go for a more "serious" look for college—and Jana has a nose piercing from the end of a somewhat-rebellious summer fling with a tattoo artist. Apparently, I wasn't the only one who had a mental break this summer.

"So, T, give us the deets." The sneaky look in Lex's eyes makes me blush. I know exactly what she wants to know.

I shrug. "About what?"

"We are not oblivious to Jay's newly enhanced, newly buff bod. Tell us!" Jana spouts.

A blush flows across my cheeks in embarrassment, followed by a small pang of jealousy—if my friends have noticed how attractive Jay has gotten, it means other students have, too.

"Well, we're sort of dating now."

All three of their eyes grow wide.

"*Sort of?*" they all screech at the same time.

"Okay, we're dating…officially. He asked me out on Christmas and was pretty adamant, but if I'm being honest, we've been into each other since he got home. I was just too scared to admit it."

They squeal, fawning all over me like I just showed them

an engagement ring, but their volume only rises when Jana feels the band around my finger.

She pulls on my hand to bring it closer to her brown eyes, "And he got you a *ring*? Chica!"

I nod in response, biting my lip when I think back to that special Christmas day. "It's just like a friendship-promise ring. Nothing crazy."

"Friendship-promise ring? Okay, T," Lex mocks, bumping into Toree.

I smirk. "He's amazing, guys," I say with a dreamy sigh.

They all roll their eyes at me, scoffing at my success in finding a solid man. All of them have had their fair share of jerk boyfriends. It's about time one of us found a keeper.

"I'm sure he is," Jana says sarcastically, wiggling her eyebrows at me.

"What does that mean?" I cross my arms, silently begging her to get her mind out of the gutter—because now that she's mentioned it, all I can imagine is Jay with his shirt off, sweat coating his skin as he's leaning inside the hood of his car. Maybe I should ask Jay to look at his car just to make that dream a reality. *No, no. Get that fantasy out of your head.*

Smacking me in the shoulder, Lex takes over, "Oh, come on, T. Don't hold out on us."

"I know exactly what you guys mean, and I hate to break it to you, but *that* has not happened."

"Why?" Lex asks, her blue eyes stretching wide with wonder. She sets her chin on her hand to prop her head up, apparently ready for a story.

I look at all three of them, waiting anxiously and quietly for me to explain. I huff out a breath. "Jay will want to make it special. He is that type of guy."

They immediately melt further into their hands, their eyes

growing doughy with admiration. I nod and grin in agreement, not sure what else to say.

"You lucky dog," Jana sing-songs, leaning against my shoulder to softly bop her head against mine.

While I finish eating, we spend time catching up, talking about all the things we've missed since the last time we talked. Everything from the flat tire the girls got on their road trip to Florida, the pottery class Jana enrolled in at the local art center because she heard the teacher was hot, Lex almost quitting college before it even started because she was offered a pretty sweet nannying gig before the family up and moved out of the country, and Toree trying out for the dance group of the Detroit Pistons basketball team.

After three hours have passed, we go our separate ways, and I can't help but think about how this is the first time I've been this happy since Jay left. I've missed my girls, and when I glance back at our circle, my heart is so warm it feels like it might be cooking inside my body. Just wait until Jay hears about this.

Day 6:

Friday Eve has finally arrived. I don't know what I was thinking when I chose a 9:00 AM speech class on Thursday mornings to end my course week. Talk about the longest two hours of my life.

Jay comes home tomorrow, and I cannot wait to see him. I hope everything has gone okay for him, because I haven't heard from him once the entire time.

Even though I thought about calling that number on the card, I never had an absolute emergency to use for an excuse. I guess I was more curious than anything else about who would pick up the phone connected to such an odd-looking card.

Pulling into the driveway, I'm ready to skip inside, knowing this is the last day I have to be without Jay. That is, until I notice a gray pickup truck in the driveway. Great…my dad's home. He's the last person I want to see.

Glancing up at the clock, I dig in my purse for my phone and check it for anything from Jay before opening up to type a new message to my mom.

> Me: Where are you?

I almost type more, but stop myself. Instead, I look out the window and try to patiently wait for her reply before having to face Adam alone. If my mom's here, he'll be less likely to get physical with me again. I obviously need a buffer now.

A message pings in. I swipe the screen and read my mom's name, my stomach dropping.

> Mom: Sorry, sweetie. I got stuck at work.
> I'm running to the grocery store quickly
> before I head home. Is something wrong?

Well, this is just great. Now what do I say?

> Me: No. Just wondering. See you soon.
> *hugs*

I lean my head back and breathe out a long, exhausted sigh, absolutely dreading going inside that house.

There are a few options: wait out here and risk Adam seeing the car and wondering what I'm doing, run in and hope he doesn't notice me, go to the Tenlin house, or drive somewhere else. Either way, there's no guarantee he won't get mad. He seems to always be mad at me these days.

My anxiety starts to creep in, trying its best to stop me

from opening this door and going into the possible hell standing before me. *Just lock the door and wait for your mom,* it tells me. *Start this car and go hide out somewhere until she leaves the store,* it begs.

Swallowing down the fear, I whip the door open and scramble out before I can change my mind. If Jay isn't here to protect me, I need to be as brave as I can be alone. I refuse to let Adam bully me out of my own home.

Besides, heroes can't always be there to save the day when they have a world of problems to look after. I grab my things and try to puff out my chest like Jay does, ready to take on anything, reminding myself that *my* hero will be back tomorrow.

I take a deep breath before quietly unlocking the door and slipping inside. My eyes close as I silently shut it behind me before opening them again and looking around, taking stock of my surroundings. I don't notice anything, other than the ticking of the nearby clock. *Thank God.*

Tiptoeing over to the stairs, I use just the balls of my feet to silently creep up them, but let out a scream when a gripping pain shoots up my arm as Adam yanks me back down the way I came.

"Ow, ow! You're hurting me!" I yell, trying to squirm out of the near death grip around my upper arm. Tears form in my eyes when his hot breath runs over my ear.

"Where the hell do you think you're sneaking off to?" he whispers in the most sinister voice, fear bubbling in my stomach like lava that's about to burst.

My tears threaten to escape, but I try my best to contain them. Instead, my emotions come out in a whiny voice: "I-I'm not sn-sneaking anywhere. Please stop."

The evil cackle that erupts out of his mouth is mad enough

to rattle my bones. His breath reeks of alcohol, turning my stomach more than once. This was the wrong day to be brave.

"I want to know why you were sneaking up the stairs. Are you scared of me?" His evil sneer produces acid in my gut, nausea swarming its way through my body. *Be strong, T.*

When he squeezes tighter, my vision goes red. I've had enough of my jackass of a dad, and I won't stand for it any longer. "Get the hell off of me!" I fight to yank my arm away.

When he crushes my arm tight enough that my muscles start to cry out in agony, I scream at the top of my lungs, knowing he'll surely leave a bruise this time. When he finally lets go, he throws me onto the stairs like the trash on garbage day. My hands fly out, just barely catching me, but I have no fight left. I just want to get away from this lunatic and never see him again.

"Look at me," he orders.

A panic attack begins brewing again. This will be the second one in his presence in under a week. I refuse to give him the satisfaction he craves. Instead, I beg the panic to stay away for a few more moments and look at him.

What I see in his eyes is enough to fuel a nightmare. Darkness clouds the color, evil lurking beneath.

When he came back into my life, I honestly thought he'd be the dad I had always hoped for. I hoped I would finally see love in his eyes, but I see nothing there but hatred and evil.

He ended up being my worst nightmare.

"What did I do?" I choke out.

"You thought you could defy me. You run around this house thinking I don't matter." He violently jabs his pointer finger into his chest. "I am the man of this house, and what I say goes. You and your mother are nothing without me. You will *never* escape me—"

Before he can go on, I hear my mother's car beep when it locks. In the split second he takes to look out the window, I get up as quick as I can and make a break for my room, embracing what I can of my arm.

He doesn't stop me, or utter a single word, for which I'm thankful. I slam the door shut behind me, locking it hard with shaking hands. Once I know I'm safe from Adam's psychotic ass, I walk over to my mirror and delicately lift the sleeve of my shirt to inspect my arm.

There are already fingerprint bruises that dot along the injury, a stretching cloud of purple imprinted into my skin.

My fingers softly drift over the tinged skin, agonizing pain following in their wake. I tightly close my eyes. Adam has grabbed me by my ponytail in an effort to get me to comply before, but this is his first time leaving bruises.

I can't believe this. I really can't. How could a father do this to his child? *How*?

The cry that crawls out of my throat is one I've never heard myself make ever before. I cry for the sad girl whose dad left all those years ago, for the hopeful girl who invited him back into her life for a second chance, and for the disappointed girl who should never have to fear what her dad will do next.

I was better off without him, and that's a sobering tale of heartbreak; one I never thought I'd have to live.

I cannot tell my mom; she will never forgive herself. But one thought keeps replaying in my head: Adam needs to go.

Most importantly, Jay cannot know. That's why I've avoided the number on the card *and* his parent's house. He would lose his mind, and I don't need anything happening to him on my account. But he comes home tomorrow.

How on earth am I going to hide this from him?

CHAPTER EIGHT

I wake up the next morning feeling more refreshed than I have in the past week. Jay is coming home today. I haven't heard from him once while he's been gone, but I try not to think about it. He *has* to be okay.

He has to.

My phone dings next to me, and I rush to grab it, ready to see Jay's name…

My smile falls as his mom's name flashes on the screen.

> **Mrs. T:** Hi, honey. We missed you this week. I just wanted you to know that Jay's flight got delayed and we're not sure when he will get in. I'll keep you updated.

> **Me:** Miss you guys, too! Thanks, Ma. Just let me know and I will go get him. :)

Knowing I probably have more time than I thought this morning, I decide to forego changing out of my cozy pajamas just yet. The bonus to not scheduling classes on Fridays is that my weekend always starts early. Sometimes, I even get the house to myself, depending on if my parents have to work or not.

Snuggling down into my warm blankets, I turn on the television across the room and start to scour the channels. I finally settle on *Harry Potter and the Half-Blood Prince.* Nothing quite compares to a *Harry Potter* movie. Plus, this gives me more distraction time than anything else.

By the time the movie ends, it's lunch time and I haven't moved from my bed, but I quickly jump at the sound of car doors slamming shut outside, and realize that I should probably get ready for the day in case my parents need me to come out of my room at some point. Is it wrong of me to refuse to leave the confines of my personal space until Jay's back, though?

I whip the blankets off and shiver at the cold air surrounding me. *Curse these hardwood floors,* I think as I shove my feet into a fuzzy pair of black slippers I leave next to my bed.

I wonder what eyeshadow colors I should go for today. I want to look my best for Jay, even though I know he won't care either way. The best part about dating your best friend is that they've already seen you at your absolute worst, so it doesn't matter how you look at any other time; they're still going to think you look great.

I gather up my makeup materials from the top of my dresser and sneak out of my bedroom and into the hall. Some quiet chatter downstairs catches my attention, but I can't quite make out who's talking, or what's being said.

I shrug, deciding to ignore it—if it's my dad, there's no way in hell I'm going down there. After our run-ins this week, I'm avoiding him like the plague.

Around ten minutes and a quick sweep of powder foundation, a golden-brown eyeshadow dusting, eyelash curling, and hairbrushing later, I'm back in my room. Dancing to the closet, I ponder what I should wear. I think I'll go for something simple since Jay and I probably won't be doing much.

"Hmm, hmm, hmm," I hum, fingering through my hangers of clothes. "No, no, I guess," I say aloud, stopping at a brown, crocheted sweater that will hide my bruise wonderfully.

I dread it, but I slip out of my nightshirt and clip my bra on when suddenly, everything grows a little colder than it was moments ago. I freeze, trying my best to keep my eyes from bulging out of their sockets, terrified that Adam might've found his way into my room. I just can't bear to look over and lock eyes with that monster—not again.

Please say I'm being ridiculous, please say I'm being ridiculous, I chant over and over in my head.

The gears in my brain turn repeatedly, sifting through all the things I could do, when they finally beg me to turn my head and check for myself. How can I make a decision when I don't even know what the hell is going on?

Maybe if I turn slowly enough, he won't see me. I'll move quietly, hoping I'll develop a last-minute superpower and become invisible. That could happen, right?

I silently curse, wishing I would've had the forethought to shut my closet door. This is the one with the lock on the inside. It could keep me safe.

Finally finding the doorway, I lock onto a familiar pair of neon-like blue eyes. *Jay?*

I slowly turn to face him, but dare not to move out of fear of driving him away. The emotion roiling in his eyes right now is enough to chill anyone to the bone; I shiver. He is the most perfect mixture of seething anger, smoldering sexiness, and impenetrable mystery I've ever laid eyes on.

But why does he look so furious? *Is he not happy to see me? Did something happen while he was gone?*

My feet move of their own accord, but stop when Jay

holds his hand up to keep me back. His eyes close as he shakes his head, and I fear what I'll see when he opens them —but when he does, there's only sadness left.

He's fixated on my arm.

My heart sinks. He's seen the bruise. *Shit, shit, shit.*

I am stuck in place as he stalks over to me, but quickly breathe in his musky cologne scent the moment he's near. His smell is enough to calm any storm, but I'm not sure this storm will stay away for long.

The second his fingers brush my skin, they send a bolt of electricity through every pore he touches and erase the pain that was resting there seconds before.

"Baby," he whispers, his voice quavering pitifully, sending my heart slamming against my ribcage. Tears gather in my eyes at the pain in his voice. "Why didn't you call me?" His low voice rises a few octaves in growing anger.

"I'm fine, baby. Really—"

"You're not! I swear, I will fucking kill him." His eyes begin scanning me for any other injuries, his body trembling with rage.

I take his head in my hands, my eyes searching his face, begging his gaze to ultimately find mine. When they do, a sob nearly escapes my throat for a multitude of reasons…not only has it been way too long since I've seen him, but the shattered look in his eyes is enough to bring me to my knees.

"Just leave it be, okay? I am fine, and now that you're here, I've got nothing to worry about." I whisper, softly cradling his cheeks.

While this seems to briefly calm him, I can tell that the darkness never leaves his mind. He will never forget this.

Neither will I.

The droop of his shoulders has my insides tumbling,

almost urging me to rush to the bathroom. I think I might be sick.

"Why didn't you call me? I would've been here so fast."

"Jay, you were in Beijing, on a whole other time schedule. Are you kidding? And besides, I *did* call you,"

"You did?" When I nod, his eyebrows scrunch, his eyes swarming with confusion as he looks off at something I'm not entirely sure I could even see. "I guess something must've gone wrong on my phone."

"It's okay. I'm okay."

He shakes his head, moving my hands with it. "You don't understand."

"Don't understand what?" What the hell is he talking about?

"Nothing. Just…I would've been here."

Unwilling to listen to much more, I move in slowly and press my mouth to his. It's like all the lightning that was stored in his eyes is now striking my lips. "What are you doing here, anyway?"

His eyes snap open, "What do you mean?"

I shrug. "Your parents were going to text me. I was supposed to pick you up."

"I planned to surprise you all along. They were in on it."

Before I can continue, Jay breaks away from me and leans down to throw me over his shoulder, bra and all. I close my eyes and smile. It feels so good to be in his arms again.

With only the back of Jay's jeans in my view, I try to count the steps he takes to guess where he's taking me. A plethora of colors fly around me as I'm softly thrown onto the bed in a fit of laughter, but all that stops when I see the serious look in Jay's eyes as he stands over me. It feels like he's memorizing every single one of my features in case I disappear.

My mouth goes dry when Jay slowly descends to hover above me on the bed. He is the most beautiful man I've ever laid eyes on, and my hands want to run over every inch of his body.

Would he pull away if I did that?

As Jay gets closer to my head, he pauses to carefully run his mouth over the bruises on my arm. It's as if he's sucked all of the pain out of the marks and taken it upon himself to dispose of it. I'm relieved to forget about the ache, even if only for a short amount of time.

His mouth continues to crawl closer to my face; over my shoulder, into the crook of my neck where he pauses to take in my scent, and up to my earlobe. He sucks the lobe into his mouth, sending me writhing beneath his weight.

"Jay," I whimper, pleading for something I'm not entirely sure of. He smiles against my cheek, then leans back to look into my eyes. Those neon-blue streaks are back again, the ones I'm tired of asking about because I get no answer. It must be all in my head. That's the only thing that makes sense.

I finally grow tired of waiting and place my hand on the back of his neck to pull him down to me. Our lips connect in that electrifying way again, and I'm lost.

I know Jay would never push me to do anything before I'm ready, and I'm so lucky to have that. Everyone deserves to feel this kind of safety; the assurance of testing boundaries and not fearing the other's pressure.

When Jay breaks our kiss, I keep my eyes closed and listen to his labored breathing, ensuring he's really here with me.

Jay swiftly gathers me to him and rolls us to the edge of the bed before sitting up and hugging me to his chest. How he does it, I'll never know.

Pulling back, I study the lines of his hard muscle. They clench tightly as he continues to hold me on his lap. He is so strong and safe. I'm not sure I've ever seen something quite like him before.

Jay smoothly moves me off his thighs, setting me on the bed before he rises from it. "Let's go," he requests, holding his hand out to me. I grab it and allow him to help me up. "Go get dressed. We're going somewhere."

"Where?" I chuckle. He knows I'm awful with surprises. He laughs back and shakes his head, leaving me no choice but to go get dressed.

I squeal as Jay's fingers wiggle into my sides. My body involuntarily jumps as he continues to tickle me.

I twist out of his grasp and run into my closet. Once inside, I dress quickly and take a look in the mirror on the back of my closet door. I have a little more color than usual, thank God.

When I emerge, I find Jay packing my duffle bag. Drawing my eyebrows up in confusion, "What are you doing?" I ask.

"Packing you a bag." He shoves my deodorant, phone charger, and hairbrush inside. "You're staying at my house for the week."

"What? Jay, come on. You can't force me to stay."

He pauses before turning to face me, some of my belongings still being held in his strong grip. His fingers squeeze around them, threatening to crush them easily. "Listen, I haven't seen or talked to you in a week. Then, I come back to find the most suffocating look in your eyes and your arm covered with horrific bruises. I would never force you to do anything you didn't want to do, but I'm not letting you out of my sight. Can you really fault me for that?"

My feet slowly carry me over to Jay. I take the bag from his hands and set it on the floor, never breaking eye contact. Once the items are on the ground, I throw my arms around his neck and squeeze him with everything I've got.

Jay releases a heavy breath, his chest growing smaller with the loss of air. "I'm sorry," he whispers, "I know I can't make you. I just…I got caught up. Too angry…please forgive me."

When his loving embrace molds me to him, the tears break through the dam. This is what a man's touch should feel like: soft, yet strong; loving, yet tough and protective. It shouldn't hurt, and with Jay, it never does.

"You're my hero," I whisper in his ear. "Heroes never need forgiveness."

Kissing me on the cheek, he replies, "You'll always be safe with me. Every single part of you."

It's in that moment that I realize Jay is slowly healing me —saving me from not only the pain within, but the pain I live with. I will never know fear when he is around. No matter what happens, I can consistently count on him. He will always be there to save the day.

Jay's arms ease up and let me go. "Would you like to spend some time at my house?" His eyes squint briefly, his fingers twitching in anticipation.

"Of course." Why wouldn't I want to go there and escape? We finish packing my things and I grab my phone off of the bed before slipping it into my pocket.

"Is Adam home?" I ask, hesitating before we step out into the hallway.

Jay stills when he hears the name of the monster that hurt me. His response instantly makes me wish I could take the question back. He shouldn't feel bad about what happened. None of this is his fault.

Jay shakes his head, but says nothing.

We quietly make our way downstairs, and I can hear Mom moving around in the kitchen.

"I'll be right back," I tell Jay. I need a few minutes alone with my mom to let her know what's going on.

"Mom?" I quietly call to her. She sets down the pans she was putting away and looks over at me. The darkness around her eyes slams into my chest. "What's wrong?"

"Nothing," she whispers, but I hear the wavered tone near the end. She's about to break.

Her head drops forward and I hear a sniff. I run over and wrap her in my arms, trying my best to transfer some love and warmth over to her. She doesn't deserve this. No one does.

"It's okay, Mom. It's all going to be okay." When she shakes her head, it slightly nuzzles against mine.

"It's not okay. None of this is okay. We should've never let him back into our lives. I don't know how I didn't notice it before. Every time he's around, I feel so happy; everything always seems perfect." She grabs my arms and gently pulls them off of her, but keeps my hands in hers to turn my attention on her face. I hate seeing her cry. "I've seen the change in you this week without Jay, and as much as you don't want to admit it, I know something happened between you and Adam. I know you feel like talking to me about it will be a bother, but honey, I'm your mom. I will always protect you. I feel like you don't trust me to keep you safe."

She'll never be able to get him out...there is no making him leave. Why doesn't she get that?

"You don't need to carry my burdens."

Her eyes widen. "Burdens?" She carefully places her hands upon my cheeks. "You don't ever need to worry about weighing me down with anything. I'm your mother and I will fight every battle I possibly can for you. It's my life's mission. Now, tell me, did he hurt you?"

I think of the bruise on my arm. I think about what Jay saw.

Would he tell her? No, he wouldn't. Would he?

I smile at her, but I can feel the way my smile doesn't quite reach my eyes, "No, Mom. Everything is fine. I prom- ise." It's easier this way. Getting involved with law enforce- ment could get messy. "I have to get going. I'm staying at Jay's—"

She stares at me for a bit too long, speculation clouding her eyes as she assesses me. "For the week. I know." Her cold lips kiss my forehead. "He loves you far more than you know, sweetheart."

"I know. Please call me if you need me, okay? Promise."

"I will. Now get going before Jay comes in here to whip you over his shoulders. That man has been waiting a whole week to see you."

No sooner does she say that than Jay knocks on the door- frame leading to the kitchen, peeking in at us. "Am I inter- rupting?"

"No, sweetie. Come on in here. I want to hug you before you go. Tatum isn't the only woman who was missing you."

The laugh that comes from his mouth is so beautiful that I can't help but smile. He walks into my mom's open arms and bends down to hug her. "I missed you too, Ms. B."

"Mom, honey. Call me Mom."

"Okay, Mom. Are you sure you're okay with Tatum staying with me for the week?"

"Of course." I study the looks they exchange. My mom peers in his gaze, almost as if she's searching for something. Is she hoping he'll tell her what happened?

Without another word, Jay breaks away, looking back toward me. I stare between them, thankful to have not only one, but two heroes. That's a debt I'll never be able to repay.

Jay holds out his hand to me, and I look into his endearing eyes—eyes that hold so much love for me I sometimes can't even believe he's looking at me that way.

"Get going, hon." My mom kisses me on the cheek and pats my back in the direction of Jay. I take his hand and let him lead me out. I hope he's leading me to safety. I hope he's leading me to freedom.

We slip out the door, only making it to the porch when Jay stills.

"And where the fuck do you think you're going?"

I jump at the alarming boom of Adam's voice as he stands between his car and Jay's. *Where the hell did he come from?*

Jay scoops me behind him, shielding me. "She's coming with me."

My dad slams a fist down on the hood of Jay's car, a seemingly devastating dent left behind before stalking toward us. I squint my eyes to check for clarity. "Like hell she is!"

I slip out from behind Jay, "Dad, it's fine! I'll be back later. Stay—"

"You little piece of shit!" he cuts me off, reaching his large hands out to grab me, but Jay is faster. Like lightning, he flashes farther in front of me, my hair flying back with a gust of wind.

"Jay, no!" I scream. I watch as Jay uses both of his hands

to shove my dad straight into the passenger side of his pickup. He whips through the air, and my hands shoot up to cover my ears, my eyes closing at the loud slam.

When I open them, my jaw drops as I assess the damage. The dent on Adam's truck looks like someone threw it against a glacier, which I'm sure can't be right. I mean, it would take another vehicle to cause that sort of damage. Right?

"Now, get up and get the fuck out of here. Do you hear me? Leave Tatum and her mother alone." Jay yanks Adam up by the collar of his shirt. "I don't want to see you back here until you can act like a decent human being, you scumbag."

All of a sudden, my body starts to twitch. Absolutely crippling fear seizes all of my muscles, and I start to feel like I'm falling as I look at Adam. He is leering at me in an almost too-focused way. I know it's impossible, but it almost feels like something invisible is holding me in place, forcing a paralyzing panic through me.

Adam tries to grab onto Jay's wrist, sneering at him with teeth that almost seem sharp and pointed.

Jay slams him into the side of the car a second time. Adam winces in pain. Instantly, I break free from the imaginary hold.

It takes another second before I wake from my stupor and find myself able to move. My feet walk slowly toward Jay, my mind unsure if it should urge me to run toward him, or away from him; a surprising battle I thought I'd never have to face.

"J-Jay, let him go. We can't make him leave—"

But to my surprise, a glossy sheen flows across Adam's eyes. He steps away from Jay and begins walking down the driveway toward the street, his limbs moving robotically.

"Where's he going?" I choke.

"He is leaving. Can you please get in the car while I go talk to your mom?"

I shift away from him. "No! I need to—"

He grabs my shoulders, but his touch suddenly feels scalding hot. "T, everything is going to be okay. Please, let me talk to her, and then I'll have you come in."

"I don't understand." My hands start to tremble at my sides, and I freeze when Jay picks me up to place me on the porch steps, finding it difficult to move even after he leaves.

Terror begins to clog up every artery in my body, but as soon as the blockages form, a cooling trickle of peace seems to sweep them away just as fast. Where it comes from, I have no idea. Somehow, the presence feels foreign, yet friendly.

Once the door clicks closed behind me, I find my mind reeling through everything that's happened in the last five minutes. Glancing back at the truck, the dent takes my breath away again.

I remember reading an article a few years ago about a thirteen-year-old boy experiencing a surge of adrenaline after watching his dad get crushed by a truck. Scientists say that he was able to lift the truck off of his dad because the adrenaline gave him almost-godlike power. It was weird, but I guess it made sense.

Is that what happened to Jay? Did his adrenaline kick in? Is that how he could possibly exude that much power? And how in the world was he able to make my dad leave?

No...he couldn't have. Maybe my dad just thought it was easier to leave. Maybe he knew he should before doing more damage, because hurting a twenty-year-old guy would most definitely lead to trouble with the police force. There's no way he could afford trouble like that.

Then again, none of this makes sense. I feel like I'm

grasping at straws to try and decipher what just happened. Does all of this connect with the way Jay's eyes seem to glow sometimes? I mean, he has been different since he came home: bigger muscles, larger stature, intimidating—

"T?" Jay just barely towers over me as I dangle my legs over the porch. Dazed, I look up into his beautiful blue eyes. "Are you okay?" He reaches down to push a bit of hair behind my ear.

"Okay? Yeah, I'm okay. Why wouldn't I be? I'm fine. Totally fine."

"Hey." He crouches down, softly grasping my chin. "Take a breath. You're safe. I'm here. Everything is okay." He quietly chants these things in my ear as I heave heavy breaths, begging my heartbeat to slow down.

"Is Mom okay?"

"Why don't you go in and find out?"

My head snaps back at him once I'm standing, "You're not coming?"

"I'm going to wait out here for you. I think it's best if you do this alone." He just barely touches my hand and heads toward the driveway.

"Tatum?" My mom whispers, her worried face poking out between the door and its frame. "What happened?"

I rush to her, the overwhelming need to protect her consuming me, and close the door behind us. "Jay took care of everything. I don't think Dad will be back for a while, but I'm not so sure I should leave now." My teeth start to worry my lip, a small bout of anxiety settling in my chest.

"No, honey. Please go. Everything is all right. Jay took care of everything. I just wanted to make sure you were okay."

"Wait. Jay told you what happened?" I pause. "Then why did you ask me? I'm confused."

She reaches up to caress my cheek, her touch suddenly feeling unknown, her gaze distant.

"Mom, are you okay?"

"Absolutely. Maybe this was a wake-up call for your dad. I'm sure he'll be back, but probably not for a while. There's no need to worry. I think I might even go stay with my friend, Tonya, while you're away. That way we can both make sure we're safe."

I sigh in relief. "That would definitely help." It's best if we both make ourselves scarce for a little bit.

All my thoughts start to twist in my head, confusion warping everything. At this point, I'm not entirely sure how I should be feeling.

"Sweetie, I'm going to go pack. You head on out with Jay. I think we both need some time away from this place for a while. Don't fret, I'll check in."

I squeeze her once more. "I love you so much. Please call me if you need anything."

"Love you most," she coos, rubbing my back.

"Ready, T?" Jay calls from the other side of the front door.

I face away from her and toward his voice. "Coming!" Although, I'm not sure if I should be going so easily.

Jay's stunning smile greets me as he opens the door and reaches in to grip my hand and pull me out of the house. "Bye, Mom!" he calls behind us.

"Bye, loves! Take care!" She seems unusually chipper for what just happened. Am I missing something?

Jay carefully pulls me down the stairs, but I drop my hand when I spot Adam's truck. The dent is gone; completely gone. I walk over to it, running my fingers over the paint to inspect it closer. The one on the hood has disappeared too. Scratches are left behind, but there are also scratches on some parts of the truck that weren't touched.

"You good?" Jay asks.

I point at the truck, "What happened to the dents?"

"What dents?"

Looking between him and the vehicle, my heart rate picks up. "Adam…and then you… There was a…you *saw* it. I-"

"Tatum, there's no dent. I know a lot just happened, but it's okay. Let's head to my house and take it easy. We can talk more about it later."

Jay puts his arm around me. I can feel him ushering me along, even though it feels like I'm still staying in place. Maybe I'm in shock…

We both slip into his car at the same time. I spare one last look out the window, catching my mom staring out at us with a small grin on her friendly face. I lift my hand and blow her a kiss that she quickly catches and holds close to her heart.

CHAPTER NINE

Jay is quiet the entire ride to his house, but his need to constantly touch me is enough conversation for the both of us. I close my eyes as his thumb rubs back and forth on my hand in a repetitive pattern, quickly putting me to sleep. My mind yearns for rest.

My eyes don't open again until I feel Jay nuzzling my neck. A quick ten-minute nap has me feeling revitalized. "Baby, wake up. We're here." The deep timbre of his voice is like melted caramel—sweet and sticky. I almost consider keeping my eyes closed just so he'll continue, but my giggling gives me away.

"I'm up, I'm up," I repeat, slinking away toward the door with some tricks up my sleeve; I have to know if the things I've been seeing are really there, or if I am indeed losing my mind. I lean forward just enough, but as soon as he closes his eyes to move closer, I slip out the door and around him— quick as lightning—and dash for the backyard at a breakneck pace.

I pass the front porch and round the corner when Jay jumps out from behind the house and lands in front of me. I squint my eyes and look behind me, trying to think of every possible way he could've possibly made it out of the car and around the side and back of the house by the time I just passed the porch. "How did you—?"

"You can't outrun me, T."

Clearly, but how the hell did he get from the car to there so fast? It doesn't make sense. There's no way. I've just attempted to think of how in the span of a few seconds, and have yet to come up with something feasible.

I guess at the number of steps between us and know for a fact that I can at least round this corner before he will catch me. There's no way he's that fast when I'm already standing at the corner of the house.

"Don't make me chase you again, T."

I can't help it. I have to know what will happen. My mind won't rest until I test my theory.

I see the edge of the wall in my peripheral and whip around to run again. The silence assures me he is still stationary.

I lift my foot and take off, but am immediately engulfed in muscular arms before I even get the chance to move. Jay picks me up and swings me in a circle. I squeal loudly out of surprise. "Put me down!"

He laughs, "You thought you could outrun me, but I'll always catch you." He kisses my cheek, but I can't help but feel uneasy about all of this. *Why is he acting so normal? How did he get to me so fast?*

"How did you catch me, Jay?" I ask seriously when he finally sets me down.

"You're obviously as slow as a sloth."

My hands find his forearms and slide up to his biceps. It's enough to get his attention. "Jay, I'm being serious. There's no way you could've gotten to me that fast two different times. What the hell is going on with you?" His eyes widen a small fraction, but quickly reset back to normal. I don't miss it. "Jay."

"Babe, you're being silly. I'm just fast. I work out, remember?" Something about his answer makes me uneasy, like there's so much more to say.

I cross my arms, utterly fed up with whatever is going on with him. "You may think you are the only one who can tell when the other is lying, but you're sadly mistaken. You're keeping something from me. I know it."

The silence between us stretches on for what feels like a lifetime as I wait for an answer.

"You know what, Jay? Forget it. I'm so over this." I stomp past him to the car and grab my bag.

I'm surprised Jay has not followed me this time. He would normally fight me to grab my things. I don't fuss over it for too long. Instead, I make my way up the stairs and let myself in.

"Jay, sweetie? Is that you?" I squeeze my eyes closed to rid myself of the anger I'm feeling long enough to talk with Jay's mom; I forgot about the guest house. *Ugh.*

"No, Ma. It's me, Tatum," I call out, hoping she won't try to seek me out.

Footsteps sound down the hall, and before I know it, Jay's mother is walking toward me with outstretched arms. *Where the hell is Jay?*

"My sweet Tatum. We thought for sure that you'd be over this week. We've missed you, dear. I'm so glad you're staying for a few days." She kisses both of my cheeks as she draws me in for a hug. "Where is that son of mine?"

The mention of Jay has my temper soaring again.

Without blinking an eye, Ma sighs and asks, "What did he do?"

I roll my eyes and try my best to grin innocently enough so that she'll forget about it. "What don't boys do?"

Her left eye squints at me. She doesn't buy it, but I remain silent on the subject. "I'm going to head out back to unpack," I add. "I'm exhausted."

"Go ahead, love. Dinner won't be ready for a couple of hours anyway."

"Thanks, Ma." I stretch up on my tiptoes and softly kiss her cheek. Her shoulders relax a bit, but it doesn't even touch the fire in her eyes. Mrs. T is not one you want to mess with—momma bear extraordinaire.

I pick my bag back up off the floor and start toward the back door to head to Jay's house. The jittery feeling of Jay potentially lying to me starts to weigh heavily on me; far heavier than this damn bag. There's absolutely no way all of this could be a coincidence.

The minute I make it to the door, I plop the bag down to give my shoulder a break before switching it to the other side. The front door finally closes, alerting me that Jay has finally made his way indoors.

Mumbled voices push me to a standstill. I shouldn't eavesdrop, but I can't help it. I have to know what Jay is keeping from me.

"Why don't you just tell her? It's Tatum, Jay."

I leave the duffle and start to slink closer. *Did I hear her right?*

"You know I can't, Ma. I can't."

"One day, you'll have to."

The conversation doesn't make me feel any better, but it does at least assure me that I was right. Jay is hiding something, and I'm determined to find out what.

After making it inside the guest house, I set my things down in his room and decide to lay down until Jay comes in. I don't stir as he sits atop the bed, lacking zest to show him that I'm awake, because I'm not in the mood to talk when it won't lead to the answer I want. Why waste energy?

Jay's body curls around mine as his fingers run through my hair. "Please don't make me tell you. It will change everything."

He says those words barely above a whisper, but I hear them loud and clear.

Does he not trust me? What could he possibly be hiding that scares him so much?

I sit up when the door clicks, surprised that Jay really left me in here. Well, I take that back. I guess I can understand. Who in the world would want to be in the same room with someone who is on to the secret you refuse to tell?

My skin starts to itch with concern. We tell each other everything. What's so different about this?

Then again, I didn't want to tell him about Adam…maybe he's hiding this for the same reason I hid that. To protect me.

After a few minutes, it's obvious that Jay isn't planning on coming back anytime soon, so I give myself the opportunity to be nosy by pulling open the bottom drawer of his bedside table. Nothing unusual…some of his favorite comic books and a reading light are stashed inside.

The top drawer isn't much different. There are some cough drops, nose spray, and his remotes.

As I slide it closed, my eyes latch onto a tiny white corner of paper peeking out from under the drawer's contents. I glance at his bedroom door before my fingers carefully grip the piece of paper and pull it out like it might rip.

The paper sounds like a heavy cabinet being pushed across a hardwood floor to my nervous ears. Everything always seems ten times louder when you're sneaking around.

When it finally pops out from beneath the rubbish, I'm shocked at what I find. It's a photograph of a younger me, sleeping in Jay's bed. I run my finger along my problem-free face, reminiscing on my life before my dad came back into it. Was life really that easy before? Has Jay always watched over me while I slept? How did I not notice his feelings before now?

Jay must take a phone call, because his voice travels down the hall from somewhere near the front of the house. I swiftly shove the picture back underneath the items in the drawer and lay back down.

"T?" Jay whispers when he opens the door.

"Hm?"

"Are you feeling okay?" His footsteps sound against the floor as he travels over to the bed to sit down.

"I'm fine." The anger has somewhat dissipated, but I'm still not happy he's consciously choosing to keep something from me…something that's obviously important.

At this point, my mind is so jumbled, I have no idea whether I should be making a bigger deal about this or not. All I know is that I'm sitting with my best friend, in his bedroom that feels oh so safe, in his family's guest house; I feel like I'm home. So, if I'm somewhere *safe*, why do I still feel so uneasy? And if I'm feeling uneasy, why do I feel the need to stay and figure things out?

When he doesn't answer, I turn to make sure he's still there, finding him resting his head in his hands.

The guilt starts to eat away at me. There are so many things I need to know, but maybe they *can* wait until later. Jay did take care of my dad, after all. And my mom seemed fine with everything. Maybe my anxiety is just getting the best of me. If I'm patient, I'm sure there's a perfectly logical explanation Jay will give me very soon.

The covers are easy to push off as I slide from beneath them and crawl over to him. I place one of my legs on each side of him and lean against his strong back, wrapping my arms tightly around his waist. He winces when I squeeze him in a hug. "What's wrong?" I question.

"Nothing. I—uh—I'm just sore."

"From?" I probe.

Jay's back straightens, but he lets me stay close, placing his hands over mine. "I took a boxing class in Beijing while I was gone."

"Oh. I see." *Right...of course you did.*

"T…" he pleads. I don't have to see his face to know he is desperate for me to leave this alone. Whatever he is keeping from me is serious enough that he can't take much more fishing.

"It's fine, Jay," I start. My lips kiss his back softly. "Whatever it is you're keeping from me, I hope you trust me enough to tell me someday. Until then, I'll try not to bug you about it." Doesn't mean it won't bother me, though. The curiosity is piling high enough to build a totem pole at this rate.

He pulls my arms from around him, and for a second, I fear I've upset him. Standing up, he slips his shirt off and tosses it on his desk. I gulp loudly, admiring the muscle covering his torso. I can see the bruises from his "boxing classes" now, and they not only prove his point, but also make him that much sexier.

I remain rooted to the spot, bewitched by his electric blue gaze.

Making it to the edge of the bed, he leans down to encase me between both of his very large, veiny arms, trapping me in a muscular prison. We stare into each other's eyes, trying to read the other's emotions—searching for any indication as to where this might go next. Jay answers for me by giving me a very heated, yet calming kiss; his urgency forceful, yet his mouth soft and warm.

Something inside of me snaps. My hand finds its way to the back of his head and I pull him over me, falling back onto the comforter. His strong arms hold him up as his tongue slides between my lips and into my mouth—something I've never experienced before. The action pulls a groan out of me, which only excites both of us more.

My tongue meets his, and then he's on top of me. We are a mess of mouths and limbs. I keep my eyes closed, enjoying everything happening between us. The energy surrounding us is magnetizing enough to fuel a compass.

Without realizing what I'm doing, I move my hands to the bottom of my shirt and tug it over my head in between kisses. Jay stills, his eyes running over every inch of me in what I hope is appreciation. For the first time since he came home, his gaze never wanders toward where my new bruise is housed. I'm thankful.

Jay's head descends to my neck where he licks and nibbles the skin. The effects he is having on my body right now are enough to paralyze me. My muscles twitch and jump every time he changes up his actions.

Finding it hard to control myself, I wrap my leg around his waist, and with some effort, roll him onto his back. Sitting up, I run my hands up and down his very well defined abs, licking my lips as I go.

"Keep licking those lips, and I won't be able to stop whatever comes next." His admission has me biting down on the skin of my mouth, slowly dipping toward his ear.

"I think we both know we don't want to sto—"

The knock on the front door shuts me up. Thank God Jay thought to lock it. I sit up, covering my mouth to hide my humor at the sight of Jay's wide eyes. His hands hold my hips still.

"Jay? Tatum? Dinner is ready," Jay's mother says through the speaker, her voice wafting through the room.

"Coming, Mom," Jay croaks, his finger on a button above his bed I never noticed before, clearing his throat right after. I chortle at his disheveled state. I guess I didn't realize how much of an effect I have on him.

"All right. Don't be long. Your father's hungry."

"How long do you think we really have?" I tease, wiggling my hips. Jay's Adam's apple twitches as he swallows loudly. His grip on my hips loosens.

I'm too far in to stop whatever this is now, but his hands on my shoulders halt me in my tracks anyway.

"We can't…"

"And why not?" I groan. He laughs as he sits up beneath me, holding me close to his chest.

"Because. I never should've even let it get this far just now. I want to make it special. I just find it hard to keep my hands off of you sometimes." He places a kiss on my nose. "I promise it will be worth it."

My lip pouts out, trying to convince him otherwise. The hormones coursing through my veins right now are too much for me to merely head over for dinner like nothing happened.

"Please don't do that. I'm too frazzled to resist your cute ass." His rough hands lightly push me off of him. My eyes are glued to his back as he walks over to put his shirt back on. *Damn it.* Can't this be a shirtless dinner party?

When Jay turns around to look at me, I swear I see sparks of light in his blue eyes.

"Jay." My voice sounds much more sensual than I mean it to, but I can't help it. He does things to me.

"T, stop. Let's go to dinner, and I promise to give you a teaser later." The wink he shoots me has enough power to knock my panties off as it passes through my body.

Moving onto my knees, I crawl across the bed toward him. His eyes go wide. "Who knew the little girl I used to make fun of for wearing leggings and sweatshirts all the time would grow up to someday be crawling across my bed in nothing but a bra and pants. I gotta say, I don't hate it." He leans against the door frame, his beefy arms crossed over his torso. Each vein pops like daisies growing out of the ground.

I plop down on the edge of the bed, disappointed that Jay is not going to give in at the moment. That's okay, I have a plan: make sure dinner is very interesting so he'll be anxiously waiting to give me that teaser later.

Tatum, you're a genius, my subconscious applauds. Sometimes, I wonder if I should give her a name.

Let the coercion begin.

"Who knew the little boy I made fun of for constantly being in a superhero shirt would grow up to still be wearing them, but would also be hiding a Greek god of a body underneath?" I wink and get right to getting dressed, fully ignoring his looks I can literally feel peppering off my skin.

"Okay, Aphrodite," he jokes. "You ready?"

I nod and quickly glimpse at his bedside table, ensuring I

closed it back up. I don't need anything else getting in the way of my "promising" night.

"Let's go," I urge, grabbing his hand to pull him out of the house and through the yard.

Jay's mom gives us a once-over when we make it into the dining room, and for a moment, I worry about the state of my hair, but just smile and hope for the best. Too late to turn back now.

"Hey, Ma. Hey, Pa." I say, taking my seat close to Jay. His eyebrows twitch up in curiosity as I squeakily scooch my chair even closer to his.

"Hi, honey," they reply in unison. "We're so glad you could come for the week."

"There's nowhere else I'd rather be." I smile from ear to ear. This house has always been a home away from home for me. I'll never be able to thank them enough for including me in their family in their own way.

I don't miss the sad smile from Jay's mom, though. I'm positive Jay has told her what happened with my dad, but I can't be sure. Here's to hoping it won't become a hot topic of our dinner conversation, especially when I'm trying to seduce her son.

Oh my word, should I even be thinking these things at their dinner table—in their *house*? Who am I? What has gotten into me?

I squint an eye in Jay's direction, suddenly very curious about the chances of him being a warlock of some sort, putting me under a spell. His cheeky grin convinces me otherwise.

The dinner on the table smells divine: spaghetti and meatballs, with a side of garlic bread. I breathe it in and close my eyes. Jay's mom is one hell of a cook, being a chef and all.

Once we are all plated, the conversation starts to flow effortlessly.

"Tatum, do you have any universities picked out to apply to once you finish up at the community college?" Jay's dad asks.

"No, not really. I mean, I've thought of a few, but I have absolutely no idea what I want to do."

"You might want to talk to Jay. He has a few schools he's already applied to."

That declaration sends my eyes flying open wide. Why wouldn't Jay tell me he's been applying to universities? He's not even finished with community college.

Maybe he doesn't want me going to the same school. I turn my gaze toward him, waiting for any inclination of trouble, but all I see is my heartwarming Jay.

"There's just been so much going on that I didn't mention it, but I've had a running list for you sitting on my desk since I started filling out the apps."

A sigh escapes my mouth, thankful that it wasn't what I thought it was. Curse my anxiety-ridden, worrywart self…

"I'd love to look at them." My hand slides off of my lap and steadily finds Jay's. He coughs and quickly leans forward.

"You okay, sweetie?" Ma prods.

"I'm fine. Spit went down the wrong tube."

Ha. Gotcha!

"I hate when that happens," I chime in, squeezing his knee before sliding my hand up his thigh.

No sooner does my attack begin than Jay's hand smoothly takes mine and flips it over. I'm about to pull it back and try again in a few minutes, but stop when his finger begins drawing circles in the middle of my palm. The action is both incredibly sweet and surprisingly arousing.

The rest of dinner passes by with idle chit-chat, and I find myself mindlessly giggling more than I have in all the months since my dad has returned to our house. It feels so good to just be a regular person again.

I've been trapped inside a coffin of myself for so long that I've forgotten what the outside world was truly like.

"Coming?" Jay calls. I look around at the cleared out chairs. When did he get up and put his things in the kitchen?

I get up, cringing when my chair squeaks across the floor, "I'm going to help your mom clean up first. I'll be over there in a second."

He grins at me and leaves without another word.

Jay's mom starts to wash the dishes. "You don't have to do that, sweetie. I've got it. You're our guest."

"I don't think I've been a guest in over a decade, Ma."

She laughs with me. "You know what? I think you're right." She picks up the next dish as I move over to start drying the ones she's finished. "Tatum?"

"Yes?"

"Can I ask you a question?" Her worried tone sends tingles along the back of my neck.

"Of course," I answer, a small twinge of anxiety settling in the pit of my stomach. It's crazy how foreign it feels there, almost like this house is too harsh of an environment for it to thrive inside of. I can only appreciate how much of a difference being with Jay in a safe place has had on my body.

"Are you okay?"

The question almost sends me stumbling backwards. When was the last time someone asked me that? Let me correct myself—when was the last time someone outside of my immediate family asked me that in such a caring way? Like they might actually have enough power to change something about everything going on?

"I am, especially now that Jay is back."

A heartwarming smile spreads across her face. She pats my hand, a few droplets of water running over my skin. "He loves you in more ways than you can imagine, honey. I know you've been worried, but just trust that when he's ready, he'll tell you everything."

I stare at her in shock. How does she know I've been wondering about what he's hiding from me? "What do you mean?"

"You know exactly what I mean. Now, let's leave that alone. Get on outside before Jay comes chasing after you."

I fold the towel and lay it down before embracing her, breathing in her homey scent, and make my way through the kitchen and out the back door toward Jay's house. I smile up at the door as my hand wraps around the knob. I'm so very lucky to have him in my life.

Stepping into the house, I am greeted with darkness and wonder if he's already asleep.

Something in the shadows grabs me after I shut the door behind me, making me shriek, but I'm quickly silenced when a hand covers my mouth a second later. I try to tell myself that it has to be Jay, but part of me isn't so sure.

"It's just me, baby," Jay breathes in my ear. His hot breath prickles across my skin. "Ready for that teaser?"

I press my cheek to his in relief and nod in agreement.

A moment later, his hand leaves my mouth, and I feel him move from behind me before he bends down to place both of his hands on the backs of my legs. He lifts me with ease, and I quickly wrap my legs around his waist.

He takes a few steps and presses me against the door where his mouth hovers over mine, acting like a magnet seeking out the deepest parts of me.

Just before I feel like I can't take it anymore, he leans in the rest of the way, and I swear I feel electric shocks radiating between his lips and mine. His breath is refreshingly minty, only urging me on more.

Our lips glide over one another in a heated attack of passion that I hope and pray never ends, so when he breaks away to take a breath, I kiss my way along his jaw and up to his ear.

"I've waited all night for this," I whisper.

"You? If my mother knew what you were trying to pull under the table, she'd have a panic attack of her own." He stills when he realizes what he just said…and I do too. "I'm sorry. I shouldn't have said that."

"It's fine, babe. I know you didn't mean it." The aura in the air shifts, taking on a shadowy form. I can feel the stress plaguing Jay's body and permeating the area around us.

Sure enough, I've lost him.

CHAPTER TEN

"I'LL KILL YOU, YOU PIECE OF SHIT," ADAM BELLOWS, charging right for me. He looks different: glowing dark purple eyes boring holes through my head, his skin an ashen gray. "You thought you could hide from me? All along, you have been figuring me out. You've ruined everything, and you'll pay for this!"

I feel around in the darkness, hoping like hell to find a doorknob or even a trapdoor to fall through. My chest tightens, a panic attack swimming just beneath the surface.

"I have no idea what you're talking about! Please." I hold up my hands to try to stop him. "Leave me alone!"

My hair whips around my face as a blast of wind surges around me.

"Get away from her!"

Could it be? There's no way...

"Jay?" I squint in the darkness, my pupils attempting to soak up every possible speck of light they can possibly find. My hand clutches my chest when the figure turns around because I'd know those electric blue eyes anywhere.

"Jay!" I call out...before realizing there is something different about those eyes.

They might be the very familiar color I've always known, but there's more to them. The lightning I have spotted on *more than one occasion seems to be alive; the streaks darting through the darkness toward Adam. They resemble whips and lassos, flying through the air to try and wrangle a wild bull.*

I don't know what to do, where to go, or who to trust. I run for Jay, hoping he is the right answer.

After running in place, the darkness shifts, sliding me closer to the scene. Red and blue lines of energy spark around me, my eyes flinching with each bright burst.

"Jay! Help!"

Adam collides into me. I scream and fall backwards. My arms and legs thrash in an attempt to get him away, but it's no use. I'm too weak.

Suddenly, his weight is pulled off of me, and I watch as Jay slams his head against Adam's before throwing him into the darkness, seemingly never to be seen again.

I look up, watching in anticipation, my throat constricting as Jay turns back to me. Those eyes are piercing and petrifying in their own way. I scramble back, fear clenching around my heart like a straight jacket.

"What are you?" I whisper. He darts for me, and I scream as loud as I can.

"Tatum! Tatum! Wake up!" Jay yells, shaking me awake. "You're having a nightmare."

I yelp, diving off the bed, using my hands and feet to push me against the wall beneath his window. My eyes catch a glimpse of the clock…2:30 AM. I barely remember what happened before we fell asleep. Yesterday almost seems like a haze.

Turning my gaze once more, my eyes latch onto Jay's. That glow is there, but it's quickly dimming as he stares down at me.

The bed moans as he shifts to get up. My hand shoots up faster, "No. Stay right there. Please."

"T, what is wrong?"

My eyes dart between his as he dangles off the side of his bed, "N-nothing. I just…I just…"

But within the millisecond it takes to blink, Jay is in front of me, softly holding my cheeks in his hands. I bat him away, scrambling across his wood floor. "No! Stop! Don't touch me!" I scream as he reaches for me again. I push myself up, bumping into the wall as I move.

Darting toward the bedroom door, I'm halted when Jay wraps his arms around me, pinning my arms to my body. "Tatum, everything is fine."

"No. No, it's most certainly not! I feel like I'm going crazy!" I try with all my might to lift my arms up and get his arms from around me, but it's no use. He's too strong. "Jayson, you need to get the fuck off of me! *Right now!*"

Like magic, his hold disappears. I spin around and watch as Jay huffs and puffs, standing rigid, vacancy taking over those beautiful blue orbs. "You never call me Jayson." He takes a step back, "What the hell is going on?"

"You tell me! Is Jayson even your real name?"

He scoffs, "Don't be ridiculous! Of course it is. What are you going on about?"

"Something is wrong with you! I know it! Your eyes glow, and I swear they have lightning in them sometimes. You move way too fast. Oh, and you apparently have incredible strength," my arms begin to flail through the air, "and you *did* something to my mom, okay, because there is no way she was fine with me leaving after you literally threw my dad against his own truck so hard that you created a glacier-sized dent, and—" I stop dead. "Wait a damn minute! Did you do something to me to get me to come here? Is that why yesterday feels like a daze? Did you *hypnotize me*?"

"What? No! Tatum—" Jay stalks toward me, but freezes when I move away from him again. "You don't understand. I just—this—you—I can't."

Jay slowly drifts down to the floor, his hands aggressively yanking at his hair as he rocks back and forth. His chest shakes as his breathing goes ragged. If I didn't know better, I'd say a complete stranger was kneeling before me, fighting a battle all his own.

Moving ever so slowly, I slink back toward his bedroom door and slide down against it to the floor. "Jay…" His body twitches, and my eyes widen when he looks up at me; his irises have now darkened to a deep pantone, the slick glassiness grasping at my heartstrings. "I need to know… Please. I'm scared…scared enough that now *you* are in my nightmares."

The pain that flashes across his face has my heart in a vise. He breathes out a heavy sigh that seems to carry so much more than just air. At this point, the fear bubbling in my gut is waiting for the perfect moment to take over.

I apprehensively take his hand in mine and stroke the rough skin of his calloused palms, completely unsure if I should even be this close to him, but all I want to do is comfort him.

"While I am utterly terrified of what you're about to tell me, I am not oblivious to the fact that I've known you my entire life. I am putting every ounce of trust I can find in me into that right now. You have to give me something, Jay. You have to."

His hand runs through his messy hair again, and I watch

as the muscles of his forearms twitch back and forth. The truth has been kept from me for way too long.

"I have been friends with you for a long time, Tatum," he begins. "I grew up like any regular kid did, but there was a day when I was told something very serious.

"My dad has owned his business for a long time. What I didn't know was that his business covered what he was actually doing…Tatum? What?"

I break my stare. "You're shaking." I run my hands through my hair. "Why are you so afraid to tell me, Jay?"

His eyebrows pull together and move lower, a shattering look sweeping over his face. "Because…my secrets are going to change everything."

I don't know what it is, or where it comes from, but something cracks deep inside of me; a carnal need to know what is haunting him, and how to fix it. If I'm not mistaken, I'd call this bravery. "I can take it."

"My dad owns a top-secret company called RED. It is a science research facility, specializing in human modification. They've created a serum injection to…enhance the human body. Everyone who receives it becomes better in certain aspects: faster, stronger…but it can also give you something else."

"Okay?"

"Every RED that has been given the injection develops a…um, a power."

I fly up and look straight into his eyes, "A power? Are you telling me you're a wizard?" He shakes his head at my question, so I try a different route. "A superhero?"

He freezes at that one.

"Wait, like the comics?" The life in his eyes deflates a little as he looks at me with worry. "Jay, are you playing with me right now?" But the look on his face says it all...he's completely serious.

My eyes sweep up and down his body, assessing his structure. "I suppose you aren't. I mean, look at you." I point at him. "This is some pretty big proof. You're really not joking, are you?"

"No, I'm not. I'm called a RED. When my dad approached me about helping with the family business, of course I agreed. And once he showed me everything, I agreed to receive my injection over the summer."

"So Beijing, the comic convention...they were all so you could go fight bad guys?"

The use of that last word makes him laugh sadly. "Something like that. I was actually going through a transition period here before harnessing my power, training, and going out on my first mission." He shifts on the floor, staring deep into my soul. "I'm sorry that I had to hide it from you." His voice cracks under the pressure of his apology.

My eyes blink rapidly as I wonder out loud, "How were you able to hide these secrets all this time, Jay? We've been friends for far too long. How did you do it? And why?"

"I mean, why do you think I was gone for all that time? It was easier to be away, going through a shitty transition, than to be right in front of you hiding so many things. It was already the hardest thing to not tell you anything.

"Do you know how hard it is to watch someone you love deflate a little each time they're made to feel like what they're seeing isn't real, yet yearning so hard for that same person to figure it all out; to really see you? To discover what you've become?"

I glance down at my hands. I need to know all of it before

cracking open that oyster. "So, let me get this straight…you are super strong, crazy fast, and—"

"I can also fly," he says nonchalantly, playing with his hands.

"Fly? Is that your unique power?"

"Actually…" I startle at the popping of his knuckles. "All of us REDs can fly, too. My unique power happens to be mind control."

"Mind control?" My thoughts drift to Scarlet Witch. Mind control is one of her powers. She ended up being a hero, right? She was able to sneak into people's heads and save others. "You get inside people's heads and tell them what to do?"

"Kinda. There's more to it than that. The most helpful thing is that I can literally wipe people's memories and replace them with new ones. Let's say I happen to come across a disaster, and there are things we don't want people to remember. I can look into their minds and calm them down. And once they're receptive to the intrusion, I can wipe the bad stuff and give them the good."

Realization dawns on me. My legs lift me up of their own accord. "Wait. Is that what happened at my house? Did you replace our memories?"

Jay rises, moving closer. "T, listen to me. All I did was calm you guys down. You have suffered enough at the hands of Adam. You didn't need any more stress. I just wanted you to—"

I lift my hand to his face, keeping his focus on me. "Is this the first time?"

"What?"

"Is this the first time?" I seethe through my teeth.

"Yes! I swear it! I didn't want to have to do it, Tatum, but

I couldn't bear it any longer. Watching you and your mom have to deal with your dad like that, it's unfair! I had to do it. I had to get rid of him, but you both needed a little bit of peace, too."

I start to pace, the wood floor creaking beneath my feet. My mind starts to work in overdrive. This is too much information. "So, is that it then? Is that everything?" I stop and stare at him, waiting for his response, but no words ever come. Instead, his face goes white. "Jay?"

"T, please come sit down."

"Okay." The panic in my voice makes me want to break down. And immediately, our future comes storming into the forefront of my mind. Could whatever is left be enough for me to call it quits between us? Is there a limit to what I can handle? Am I even handling this properly right now?

I slowly step my way to the bed and sit on the edge, wringing my hands in my lap. His answer could change everything. Will I be able to accept it?

He sighs and moves to sit next to me, taking my hand in his. I almost think about pulling it away, but the warmth in his touch settles something deep inside me.

The beat of silence seems to go on for eternity.

"Immortality."

A single word. One word that delivers a big punch to my gut.

He will live forever?

And before he says anything else, his mouth is on mine, sealing it in a kiss of fiery passion I'm sure is meant for distraction; one that lets every bit of emotion he's feeling seep into every fiber of my being, making it feel like he's somehow embedding parts of himself deep within my soul. I want nothing more than to surrender to him, but I can't. I pull away, silently begging him to answer me.

"Jay, enough. Finish. Let me know what I'm in for."

He holds up his hands and answers exasperatingly, "The side effect to this injection, besides all of the powers and abilities, is that I will never age. The way you see me right now? That's it." His hands move up and down along his torso. "Not only does the injection alter the strands of DNA to make some parts almost robotic, it freezes them completely. It stops the aging process altogether."

Wait...

No. No way.

"Hold up...what?" *This can't be.* "No. That's not possible." I stand up and back away toward the wall opposite us again, my eyes widening frantically. "I can believe the *superhero* part, strangely enough. Shit, I can even believe the developing powers part. But immortality? No. That's vampire-legend-type shit."

"Tatum."

"No. No, no, no. Stop." I hold my hand up to him, not sure I can possibly handle him being near me much longer. I think I've officially reached my capacity for psycho-babble bullshit.

"Wait just a minute. So, the part that freaks you out the most is the fact that I won't age? That I can stay this way forever?"

I look at him like he's crazy. Is he really that dense?

I mean, I can't say I'm that surprised at his ignorance. Jay was the one who thought girls stick pads directly to their lady parts when I started my period in middle school.

We both just stare at each other in silence. I give him time to process his own catastrophic news, hoping and praying he'll actually answer with something that surprisingly makes sense.

Ultimately, I'm forced to burst the reality bubble. "Jayson Joseph, of course that's the part that freaks me out the most. Where the hell does that leave me? An ancient-looking woman, sixty years from now, next to *you*, a buff young guy who looks like my grandson visiting me in the nursing home?"

When his shoulders slam down, he looks at me with sunken, tired eyes.

All at once, it hits me. He never thought about it. He never thought about how he will stay the way he is forever, while I will age into an old woman and eventually die, leaving him alone.

"Tatum, I swear I never thought about it that way. I really didn't." He rushes over to me and sweeps me into his arms, crushing me against him with his strength, bringing tears to my eyes. The sobs rack through me quicker than I realize I am actually crying.

"Jay, what about us?" I whimper.

"What *about* us?"

"You'll have to watch me fade away someday. We'll be together for my forever, but then you'll be alone. You'll have to watch your friends and family disappear, and then finally, me…that seems like a terrible way to live, knowing that everyone around you is constantly running out of time, and you have to observe it all."

"Let's not think about it," he says into my ear. "Let's not worry about the future. We're here together right now, right where we're meant to be."

"I can't help it. This is all too much," I breathe. I push

away from him a smidgen, my eyes and hands running over his chest. "But for some strange reason, it all makes sense…"

Clarity, safety, understanding, and acceptance seem to join forces and try to clean up the aftermath of everything in me. There's a part of me—somewhere deep inside—that is grieving what Jay once was; what *us* meant before he revealed his new truth. I'm not sure if I'll ever be okay with this, but for now, I have to at least *try* to be okay, because Jay needs me.

"Why?" he croaks.

"You've always had this strange hero complex, constantly coming to my rescue for the smallest of obstacles that I didn't need saving from. I've always known I'm safe with you; I just had no idea it was to this degree."

While there's a part of me who knows I really don't have anything to fear when it comes to Jay, there's another part of me that doesn't know what to think of his admission. I'm not sure if my mind is being warped, or if I'm just batshit crazy, but I guess knowing the truth changed something inside of me. Even after all the superhero movies we've watched, I'm skeptical.

Staring at him for a beat, I move back and head for the door, suddenly seeking space after what I've just been told. Talk about emotional whiplash.

"T? What's wrong?"

I hold up my hands, "I-I think I need a minute." He moves toward me. "No. Please, Jay. Just let me go."

"But…I love you, T," he says softly, pity blanketing his tone.

I close my eyes, relishing in those words. "I know, but this is…this is big." I almost think about telling him how I practically wish I could go home, but I'm not exactly sure it's safe for me there.

Slipping out of his room and down the hall, I walk through the front door and out into the crisp, cold night, desperately seeking a view of the stars.

I hold my arms, gazing up at the full moon, wondering what else could be real out there if superhumans are real here.

Without thinking, I make my way to the house, phone in hand that I grabbed as I walked past the kitchen. One of the only other things somewhat holding me together is that Ma and Pa obviously know Jay's secret. If they feel safe with him, there shouldn't be a reason that I can't.

I try the back door, knowing Jay's parents sometimes leave it unlocked in case we need something. When it opens, I sneak inside, breathing in the familiar scent I've spent so much of my life growing accustomed to.

"Tatum?" Ma whispers, making me jump. "What are you doing up? Are you okay?"

My face crumples at the sound of her voice, and I shake my head furiously.

She pushes up from the table, the length of her white robe billowing around her legs. Leaving her cup behind, she moves briskly toward me. "He told you?"

I nod, finding it hard to utter any words at all, when she wraps me in her arms, holding me as tight as she possibly can.

Sobs rack through me, my body trembling and bumping against her. "Shh," she coos, softly rubbing my back. "I know. I know. It's hard to believe."

Giving her one last squeeze, I lean back, desperation surging through me. "I don't know what to do, Ma."

Her eyes grow glossy, "Oh, honey. Come here. Why don't you sleep in Jay's old room tonight? I'll let him know you're here. Maybe the familiarity will help. We can talk more about this in the morning. Does that sound okay?"

My head bobs up and down of its own accord. "Yeah. That would be nice. I'm not sure what to say right now, anyway."

"I know." Her hands rest on my shoulders. "Darling, this is a lot to take in. It's going to be hard for you to fall asleep, but I want you to think of everything you could possibly want to know while you lay in that room. The minute you wake up, you come get me. I'll answer your questions, and we'll go from there."

"Okay."

I don't know what to think, but all I know is that Jay has been my best friend for basically my entire life. Focusing on that aspect, there has to be some unspoken acceptance that comes from knowing someone forever. Right?

"You're safe here," Ma whispers, kissing my cheek as I enter Jay's old room, pulling the door shut behind me.

Making my way to his bed, there are a few final thoughts swimming as I close my eyes: my boyfriend is a superhuman with supernatural powers and timelessness, but is bound by a deal he made. His admission changes everything, but will it change us? That is something I won't know. Not yet, anyway, but I'm willing to hear him out.

He'd do it for me.

I know it.

CHAPTER ELEVEN

my cheek. "Sweetie…"

"Mom?" I call out quietly.

Opening my eyes and blinking away the sleep, I startle at my surroundings. Instead of orange walls, I find a deep navy. *Jay's room.* I forgot.

I push myself up, backing against the headboard when Jay's mom catches my eye.

"Honey, it's okay. It's just me." She doesn't reach for me this time; just watches me sadly, her hands in her lap.

I clutch at my chest, my breaths attempting to regulate themselves. "Sorry, Ma. You scared me."

Her smile is small. "No apologies necessary, Tatum." She glances out the window. "Jay is worried about you, honey. I thought I'd come chat with you and see if you're up to going back to his place."

Pulling my knees up to my chest, I fold my arms over them, cradling my head against my forearms while I study his baby blue comforter. "I'm trying not to be scared, Ma."

"I'd understand if you were. This is a lot to take in. Even knowing all along, I still have a hard time wrapping my head around it."

"Is he...safe? You know, to be around?" I ask, dread filling my every pore.

She sighs, "Tatum, my dear. Jay is my son—my only son—and while something of this magnitude may seem scary, besides his father, there's no one else in the world I trust more. He is a good man; safe to the very core."

"I know. I'm sorry, I don't know why I asked that." I shake the thought out of my head. "How do we move on from here?"

"Well..." She moves up to sit beside me, lifting her arm around my shoulders, and pulling me to her. "When you love someone, there is always movement. Moving takes you on a journey, while staying behind keeps you in the past. And while all of this seems like a dream, isn't that what you and Jay have always been after? You read all those books and comics, and watch all those movies, deep down wishing and hoping for more out of this mundane life. Now you have it. It's time to move. Maybe you don't know in which way just yet, but it's still time to go in a new direction."

I tilt my head against her cheek. "My whole existence, I hoped superheroes were real, waiting to be a part of something bigger. I'm not sure if Jay told you, but things haven't been good with my dad. While Jay was gone, I hoped and prayed for a hero to save me. And now that I know I actually have one, it suddenly feels all too real."

"That he's a hero?"

"No, that I've been living with a monster...I was hoping those nightmares were just that, all in my head. Now I know for a fact that it's all true."

Her fingers wrap around my hand and bring it to her face. "That tells me the timing couldn't have been any better."

"So what do I do now, Ma?"

She smiles, suddenly looking tired. How long has she been carrying this on her own? "You talk to Jay, hon. You see for yourself if this is something you're up for."

The rest of the weekend at Jay's was far too quiet. We've been tiptoeing around the truth admitted to me, and I'm still stuck wondering if I'm reacting correctly. It's not like there's anyone else I can really ask about this, besides Jay and his family.

I wonder if his dad is a RED too.

I look down at my watch. My class is set to end in about ten minutes.

Once Jay and I had our second semester schedules made, we made a plan to meet every Monday after our morning classes to snag lunch in the student center.

I love the freedom aspect of college; I love getting to make a schedule that grants me more time to do things like this. But sometimes, I find myself wondering if the other students can see right through us. Do they know I'm dating a superhero? What's it like to be oblivious on the outside?

When I make it to the entrance of the lunch space, I find Jay leaning against the frame of the exit door, facing the parking lot. I take a moment to stand and stare without him knowing.

The jeans he is wearing nicely define his muscular thighs. My eyes start to scan all the way up his torso to his powerful jawline, but just as my skin starts to tingle, I know I've been caught.

My gaze locks with Jay's in a heated stare. He ups the ante

by flashing that million-dollar smile I've missed so badly these last couple days. My knees almost buckle.

I begin to make my way over to him, noticing how deserted the café is. January is like a transition period for students to get back in the groove of school again. So without many people to embarrass myself in front of, I make a last-minute decision, running as fast as my legs will carry me to Jay.

Just to be safe, I drop my backpack a few steps away and leap into his arms. His eyes fly open in surprise and I hear his phone clatter to the ground, but it's quickly forgotten when his strong, muscular arms envelop me, pulling me against him. *Damn, does he smell good.*

"What has gotten into you, T?" Jay asks, laughing deeply.

I breathe him in once more. "I've just missed you these last few days. You finally seem like yourself again." I would assume some normalcy is bound to return at some point. Is this it?

His laughter rattles against my chest, and by the feel of the vibrations, it's real.

"It's so good to hear you laugh." I slide down his body until my feet hit the floor.

"I laugh often, thank you very much." His attempt at looking intimidating is hilarious.

"But they haven't been real laughs, Jay. I'm not dumb. Now, wipe that smug look off your face. It's not working."

He tickles my side as revenge. Slipping away before he can continue his attack, I stop short at the crunchy sound beneath my foot.

We both cringe. "Shit," Jay mutters under his breath.

Lifting my foot carefully, I lean down and pick up the

phone like it's a dirty sock, scared it might be done for. "I'm so sorry."

His fingers brush mine as he reaches to take a look for himself. His eyes scan the screen, but his face shows no emotion. "Is it bad?" I ask.

"The screen is cracked, but it still works. Don't worry about it, T." I grab his phone and press the power button to check for myself.

My eyes lock onto my sleeping face. I smile warmly, touched at the sweet gesture. "Why do you have that picture as your lock screen?"

He kisses my cheek and pushes his phone into his pocket, "I love watching you sleep. You're most at peace when you're dreaming." *Except for when it's a nightmare.*

"You're cute. Let's get going." I hoist my backpack over my shoulder, grabbing his shirt and pulling him along behind me, to get in line for food. "I'm getting bosco sticks," I say over my shoulder, shooting him a wink.

Hours later, I glance at the superhero posters covering parts of Jay's bedroom walls. He might've moved up in the world, starting college, moving to the guest house, and becoming a sort of superbeing, but his nerdy tendencies haven't changed. I love that about him.

Jay and I decide to eat dinner in his room tonight, just wanting to enjoy our time together now that things seem somewhat mulled over.

I wish life could always be like this. Why did Adam have to come back and ruin everything? It would've been one thing if he came back and was the amazing father I always hoped would swoop in and be there for me every single day, but he's the complete opposite. He's the darkness of the night, the source of nightmares, the cause of terrible pain. I'd give anything for him to leave again…anything to have my life go back to the way it was.

I wonder if Jay could make him leave forever, but I have a feeling that's not how Jay sending him away will work out for me. Still, superheroes are supposed to defeat the bad guys…so why not?

I'm pulled from my thoughts when I feel something mushy on my cheek.

"Ahh! Are you kidding me?" I reach up to touch it. "Mashed potatoes, really?" I scoop most of it off and flick it onto my plate.

Jay's gorgeous laughter sounds next to me. "You were ignoring me. I had to get your attention somehow. I'm thinking you should use potatoes for foundation from now on." He howls, gripping his stomach as he falls backward. I grab some of the applesauce off of my plate and pounce on him. My palm smacks as it makes contact with the whole middle of his face. *Victory!*

"Maybe you should use applesauce for *your* foundation then!" I lick the rest of the applesauce from my hand and move to get off of him, but his arm captures my waist before I'm able to escape. I squeal.

"Should we compare?"

"You better not, Jay Tenlin! Don't you dare!"

"Sorry, I can't hear you through the applesauce." He rubs his face against mine, the chunks of applesauce getting into my lashes, eyebrows, and mixing with the leftover potatoes. I can't help but cackle.

I take the onslaught up a notch and run my tongue up the length of his cheek, collecting the remnants of food as I go.

Jay stills and grips my hip tighter. "What are you doing?" he prods, the huskiness of his voice making my insides quiver.

"Oh, nothing. I was just finishing up my dinner," I continue, now kissing my way down his neck.

Before I realize what's happening, Jay has me on my back, his adorable, food-covered face incredibly close to mine. His hot breath trickles over my skin as he stares into my eyes.

There's that electricity again. I swear it only appears when he looks at me with this heated gaze. The air crackles around us with tension.

When he leans back, he slips off his shirt—which he seems to do a lot when we're in these compromising positions —and wipes my face off with it, cleaning his right after, then whipping it to the ground without tearing his eyes from mine. My stare is glued to his, my chest heaving with rushed breaths. I want nothing more than for him to kiss me at this exact moment.

"I love you," he whispers, pushing my hair out of my eyes.

"I love you too," I answer. He slowly inches down toward me, but not nearly fast enough. *Get down here already!*

I feel the weight of him on top of me and close my eyes to soak it all in. He feels heavy, but not in a bad way. The pressure is tranquilizing.

The moment his lips find mine, I'm lost. I kiss him with everything I have, transferring every emotion and feeling I have for him through my kiss. I hope he can feel how much I love him, how I'm trying with everything I have to acclimate to the new us.

Our mouths collide for what feels like a lifetime.

I sink further down into the mattress when I feel his lips move along my jaw, over my ear, down my neck, and along my clavicle. The feeling of his mouth on me is utterly divine. I'm not sure I'll be able to keep it PG for much longer.

"Jay," I breathe.

"Hm?" He never stops running his mouth over different parts of my body, slowly driving me wild.

"Did you lock the front door?" And as if I'm an electric chair, Jay flies off of me, scaring me half to death. "What the hell? Are you okay?"

He walks over to his dresser and slips on a new shirt, a much tighter shirt that has my mouth watering. "We can't do this."

I smack my hands onto his comforter, frustration building. "Oh my word, Jay. Stop being so ridiculous. Yes, we can. Now, get back over here."

"Oh no, you don't. I'm not coming anywhere near you. You know how important it is for me to make this special, but you try to pull me in every chance you get." He starts to point at me, a sporadic twitch in his hand. "You're a siren, that's what you are."

I can't help but laugh. "You're being ridiculous."

"Tatum, do not push this. Please."

Why are we torturing each other?

I roll my eyes, getting up and placing my sticky hands on my hips. "You know what, Jay? Then quit seducing me every moment you get. I'm sick of it. You're making this damn near impossible for me, and I won't do it anymore. Quit taking your shirt off every moment you get. Oh, and keep your hands to yourself," I argue.

His eyes widen as his mouth goes slack. His hands raise in defense, "Sorry, babe. I'll stop."

I nod and stomp away to grab a book from my bag, heading out to the living room.

The next two days of my time at Jay's are still pretty quiet. In fact, I am starting to worry that I might have leprosy with the way he's been avoiding my touch.

The night before the last day, I decide I can't take it anymore.

Making my way to his room, I find Jay drawing some of his comics at his desk after cleaning up dinner. "I think I'm going to head home."

The pencil is his hand stills. He turns around and gives me a conflicted stare, "Please don't go, T."

As he moves to get up, I hold my hand up to stop him. If he so much as gets within a few inches of me with his bulky muscle and brilliant blue eyes, I'll cave. *No way, José.*

"Jay, we've had basically a full week together. I think it's about time I go home so we can regroup."

"Give me one more day."

"For what? To continue sleeping on opposite sides of the bed?" I snap.

"No." He shakes his head. "Listen, I have a surprise for you tomorrow, but you need to promise you'll stay."

He is literally going to drive me insane. What are men good for anyway? "And what about that surprise is going to make me *want* to stay?"

Heat grows in his eyes, and before I know it, my hand is slowly falling back to my side. I don't register the moment he stands, or when he walks toward me. But when his cologne fills my nostrils, I know I'm going to have a hard time refusing whatever he throws at me.

His mouth comes dangerously close to my ear, so close that I could probably guess the temperature of his breath. I shiver with excitement, "My parents will be gone tomorrow. I want us to have one last night alone. Will you please stay?"

A night *alone* with Jay? I mean, his guest house is already separate from the house, but if his parents are gone too? That's different. How can I resist that?

Are we going to do what I think we're going to do?

Tatum, keep it together, girl. You have to at least pretend to think it over. I shake myself out of my daydream and look up at his smiling face. It's not a smile that would necessarily say, *You know you're going to stay.* It's a hopeful smile; one that has me returning a smile of my own.

"Fine." I should've said more than that, but I don't want to sound desperate. His quick peck on my cheek spreads some warmth through my body; enough to satiate my desire…for now. He retreats back to his desk, leaving me standing in a bundled mess of hormones. "What are you drawing over there?"

"Oh, nothing."

"Can I see?"

His head whips around, stopping me dead in my tracks. "No! This is a surprise too. Please, don't look." I wish he could see how damn cute he is. How could anyone ever refuse anything he asks?

When it is finally dark enough to be considered bedtime, I almost catapult myself into the bed.

Jay's chuckling draws my eyes to him as he finishes taking off his shirt—in his normal way this time—and tying his basketball shorts in place. "Eager, are we?"

His wink almost makes me faint. He cannot do that. It's not fair!

"Nope. Just tired." I pat my pillow enthusiastically, fluffing its insides this way and that, and snuggle into Jay's familiar scent with a smile plastered on my face. This is the best mood I've been in all week. I cannot wait to see what tomorrow brings.

CHAPTER TWELVE

I wake up in an eerily silent room. The bed is cozy, and the sunlight is shining beautifully, despite a fresh layer of snow outside. This day is already off to a wonderful start. I flip onto my back, pull the comforter under my arms, and stare at the ceiling, thinking about how even though this week was crazy to say the least, it was still so much better than being at home.

Despite the complication of being away from home, my mom seems to be having a wonderful time with her friend, Tonya. They've been shopping and watching old television shows together. Meanwhile, I wonder how life is going to play out after all of this…do Jay's powers eventually wear off? Will Adam be back? What will happen if we see him again?

My worry temporarily vanishes at the sound of footsteps coming down the hall. My teeth latch onto my lip of their own accord, anxiously awaiting what's to come.

The door creaks open, and the first thing I see is a cake with candles on top squeezing through the door frame. The view makes me chuckle. "What the hell are you up to?"

But when Jay's face appears in the crack of the door, I'm thrown by his look of confusion.

"What do you mean?"

"Why do you have a cake?" I ask, pointing at the food in his hands.

"T, it's your birthday."

Wait, what? How the hell did I miss my own birthday? Why has my mom not texted me?

I snatch my phone off of the bedside table and look at the date. Sure enough, January 30th. "Holy shit."

As Jay sings his own rendition of a birthday song, his eyes grow ten times brighter than all of those candles combined. I can't help but bask in the fuzzy warmth of his love for me.

Once he finishes his singing, he makes it to the bed and nods for me to sit up before taking a seat next to me.

I close my eyes to make my wish and blow out the candles.

"What did you wish for?" Jay wiggles his eyebrows at me.

I grin, wondering if I could ever share my wish with him, but I decide not to. It's a dark wish…a selfish thing to think about, but it's true.

If I could have anything in the world, it would be for Adam to leave—forever. I never needed my dad, and I definitely don't need him now.

Shit, what a terrible thought. There are kids out there with no parents at all, and here I am wishing one of mine away. But we all have our demons. Some of us just so happen to have ones that come in nice-looking packages that are internally made of explosives.

"That's for me to know and you to never find out." I stick my tongue out at him.

"Whatever. Happy birthday, baby. Nineteen. How does it feel? One more year and you'll catch up to me."

I tap my forehead in thought. "Well. I don't know. After forgetting that today was even my birthday, I guess it's a refreshing surprise. How did you feel on your birthday?" I balk before saying anything else, suddenly realizing he would've literally stopped aging after turning twenty this year.

"Like it was just another day." Sadness briefly flashes in his eyes. Jay is a year older than me, even though we're in the same grade. He started school late because his parents wanted him to have an extra year of preschool, which worked out in my favor because he ended up being in class with me.

That being said, we didn't get to do something like this for his birthday. He was in Beijing, apparently morphing into a superhero. If I would've known it was the last actual birthday for him, I would've made it special. Now it's too late, and the topic is too fresh and sensitive. I decide not to push the subject.

Looking over at him, I still can't help but wonder what it's like to know you'll be twenty forever. "It sort of feels like that for me too."

He gives me a sorrowful smile. "Well, I'm determined to make this birthday better than any of your others." He seals my lips in a soft kiss. It may not be as heated as I would like, but I can feel the spark hidden deep down inside.

"What are you up to?" I ask. He shrugs, jutting out an extremely pouty lip before leaving the room. "Jay!" I call after him.

I briefly consider following him, but I'll be honest; there's no way I'm leaving this bed, especially with a cake laying right next to me.

Holy shit! Is that cream cheese frosting?

Please be funfetti. Please be funfetti.

Just as I'm about to stick my finger in for a quick taste,

Jay comes back into the room. "What do you think you're doing?"

My finger freezes in midair. "Nothing."

"Jeez. I cannot leave you alone with sweets for even one minute. I was just going to grab some plates and silverware." He sets everything on his desk and then comes to grab the cake. I contemplate fighting him for it, but don't want to risk spilling it on the ground. That'd truly be a tragedy.

"Where's Ma and Pa?" I ask, wondering why no one but Jay has wished me a happy birthday.

"They already left. I talked to them and your mom about letting me have you to myself for the day, but they all gave me something for you." He saunters over and picks up my phone from where it sits next to me on the bed. Um, what is going on?

When he turns it around, it's a picture of my mom's smiling face. "What is that? How did you know it was on there?" I grin, waiting anxiously.

Jay looks down at me with pure love in his eyes. "It's a video I just shared to you when I went back to the kitchen. Why don't you check it out?" He smiles and walks back to the cake, leaving me to enjoy this surprise on my own.

I touch the screen and watch as it comes to life. My mother waves at me, her smile warm and beautiful. "Hi, sweetie! Oh my gosh! I cannot believe you are nineteen years old. It feels like just yesterday that I held you in my arms for the first time. Your hair was such an icy blonde—I mean, who knew it would end up being a beautiful ashy brown? And don't even get me started on your gorgeous green eyes." She sighs. "You are everything I could've ever hoped for and more, and I'll never be able to tell you how proud I am of you. You are such a strong, unique, truly amazing being. I don't deserve you."

She kisses her fingertips and brings them to the camera, briefly blocking my view of her before continuing, "I love you more than all the stars in the sky, my girl. Happy birthday."

I wipe the tears from under my eyes after she disappears from the screen, Ma and Pa appearing a moment later. Pa looks a little lost, but Ma appears extremely excited. It makes me smile.

"Hey, sweet girl. I hope you know that you have been part of the Tenlin family from the first moment we met you. We couldn't ask for a better best friend and girlfriend for our boy. You bring out the most beautiful things in the darkest parts of this world, and while you may not always feel like you have it all together, I promise that you are a true warrior. We love you so much and we wish you the happiest of birthdays. Lord knows you deserve it." She blows me a two-handed kiss and shoots her husband a scrunched-up look.

Her mouth twists as her hand collides with his shoulder.

"Ouch! What was that for?" he barks.

"Wish Tatum a happy birthday, you baboon."

He crinkles his nose back at her, and their banter has me giggling through the lump in my throat. "I'm not a man of many words, as you know, but I will say this—Tatum, you're a very special girl with some of the brightest light shining in your eyes. Never let it fade. Happy birthday."

My phone drops to my lap as I cradle my face in my hands, tugging the neck of my shirt up to wipe away the tears.

When Jay spins around and spots my tears, he zooms over to me. "T, what's wrong?" His strong hand rubs my back.

How? How is this man real? I'll never deserve him, not even in a million lifetimes.

I try to swallow down the lump, but the tears don't stop. "Jay, that was the most beautiful gift I think I've ever received. Thank you."

He gives me a sad smile. "You deserve it, babe."

I grab his face and fling my mouth onto his, giving him everything I have.

This is it. This is that moment. I'll give him all of me and never think twice about it.

When we become a jumbled pile of arms and legs, Jay hugs me to him. I can't help but feel like he's trying to hold me still. "What is it?"

"While I'd love to continue this, we not only have cake to eat, but your next surprise is in an hour."

"Jay, there's no way there's more."

He laughs against me. "Oh, but there is. Let me get you some cake." His lips softly touch my forehead before he slips out from around me and walks back to the dessert. I don't even fight him this time.

"*Funfetti*?" I shriek, super excited that my hopes were correct. There is nothing better than cake for breakfast, which makes me think of my grandparents. Growing up, they used to let me eat ice cream in the morning because Papa would argue that it has dairy in it. Can't disagree with that!

He snickers. "Of course. Now, hurry up. I have to take you to your next surprise."

I shovel the cake in my face, barely able to contain my excitement.

After we clean up and get ready for what's next, Jay ushers me to the car. "If you don't hurry up, we are going to be late."

"Excuse me! I am the princess today. I work on my own time."

His eyes roll so far back into his head, I'm almost sure he took a look at his brain. I pinch him playfully and get into his car.

Jay keeps his hand on my thigh the entire ride as I lean my head back and watch the city pass us by.

Our short ride comes to an end when Jay pulls up to a spa. "What is all this about?" I ask.

"With everything going on, I thought you could use a relaxing day."

A smile grows on my face, "Are we getting a couple's massage?" I wiggle my brows at him. He shakes his head, making me curious.

Inclining his head in the direction of the front door, he goes on, "Nope. You are having some time to yourself while I prepare your last surprise." I mentally squeal, trying to keep my composure. "You are going in there for a manicure, pedicure, and a massage. The works." He winks at me.

"Superheroes must make some damn good money, because you are way too good to me." I lean over the console and peck his cheek.

Jay grasps my chin and pulls me in for a loving kiss. "Guess so. But for the record, it's you that's way too good for me."

My conscience swoons. *Back off, lady. He's mine,* I snark at her.

"What are you going to do?" I wonder, grabbing the door handle, ready to throw myself out of here due to all the excitement bubbling in my gut.

"I already told you. Now, get in there before I steal the show."

Starting with his backward hat, my eyes begin to wander down Jay's very handsome face. He's sporting an Iron Man shirt today that does a very good job at hugging those beefy arms I love so much. Are the REDs like a version of the Avengers? I'm determined to find out.

I want to reach out and touch him, but I resist. He really needs to get going. There's no way I'm letting the ladies in that spa get all googly-eyed over my man.

I give him a wink in return that I hope is much better than what I've seen when I practice in the mirror. "Get out of here. We don't need any prying eyes. I love you."

"And I super love you."

Well, that's new. Nice play on words. I will never tire of hearing that man tell me how much he loves me.

After I get out, I push the door closed behind me and wave at him as he fades from view.

Time to get this party started, I tell myself, rubbing my hands together. It's about time this girl got some relaxation.

The moment I spot Jay's car outside, I'm exiting the building and jumping into his arms before he even has time to turn around from opening up my door. "Damn, girl. Plow me over, why don't you?"

"I love you more than anything on this planet, Jay. Thank you." I pepper his face with kisses.

He hugs me tighter. "You deserve it, T. You deserve to be happy. I still love you more, though. JT forever, ya know?"

"And always," I tease, smacking his hard chest. I can't help but wonder what forever and always mean for us now.

"Get your ass in this car."

"Sheesh. I'm going, I'm going!" My butt stings as he plants a smack on it. I rub the cheek in small circles, hoping it'll ease the pain. "Ass!"

"Don't act like you didn't like it."

I blush at his words, turning my head away from him as he closes the door. Our laughter fills the car the entire ride home, and by the time we pull into the driveway, I realize how dark it's gotten.

This is the most special birthday I've had in my entire life. Jay is a dream, and I'm not sure what I did to deserve him or this amazing day, but I'll take it. Man, I'll take it.

"Couldn't even fly me home, huh? Now that'd be a great experience!" I wiggle my brows in his direction.

The uncomfortable silence sends my gaze over to Jay. He clicks the car into park and takes a deep breath, and when I really look at him, I can see the tension and worry almost wafting off of him in waves. I'm actually not sure I've ever seen Jay look quite so…well, nervous.

I brush his hair back and play with his ear, bringing his attention back to me. "Everything okay?"

Swallowing hard, he blinks a few times before he finally answers. "Yeah, just fine."

If I didn't know better, I'd say he was second-guessing something about my last gift. I'm not sure why, because I know I'm going to love anything he gives me.

Both of our doors bang shut at the same time as we get out. My breath comes out in a cloud of smoke and goosebumps travel up my arms. I rub them to try to warm up. *Was it this cold when we left the spa?*

My eyes follow the driveway to the sidewalk path where Jay is waiting ever so patiently for me with his outstretched hand. I give him the happiest smile I can and bound up the pavement, careful to avoid any ice that's formed along the way.

Placing my hand in his, I follow him along the path, my face slamming into his concrete-like back when he stops abruptly in front of the fork that separates the path to the front door of the main house from the one that leads around to the back where the guest house is.

"Before we head back there, I just want you to know that I have never loved someone the way I love you. I knew from the moment I laid eyes on you on that playground that I was going to wind up with you someday. What I have planned is something I pray you'll feel safe with, but you can say no. Okay?"

"Yeah, yeah. Let's go, you blubber head." But really, his words bring tears to my eyes. I bat them away. I'm excited for my surprise, but it is damn cold out here. The last thing I want is a tear turning into an icicle on my face!

"T." He has a seriousness in his voice that has my mind conjuring up numerous possibilities. It actually starts to make me worry. What kind of surprise is this anyway?

I kiss his back. "Okay, baby."

He waits another beat and then turns around. One arm hugs around my shoulders, the other linking behind my knees as he lifts me up. I yelp with surprise.

"Close your eyes," he mutters.

I scrunch my eyes closed and throw a hand over them for good measure. It has to be something really big for Jay to be so nervous, and there's no way I'm going to ruin that.

A cold breeze presses against the top of my head and

shoulders as I feel a sudden and forceful tension pushing down on me, almost like the one from going up in an elevator. I squeal, clutching Jay close.

"Okay. You can open your eyes now," he says.

I drop my hand first and open one eye at a time, instantly smacking my hand to my mouth, my jaw hanging loose in shock. The view of the neighborhood is great and all, but it's the close proximity to the night sky that really takes my breath away.

All my life, I've looked up, admiring the sparkle and shine of the stars, all while spilling my secrets to the moon. "It's—"

"Ethereal," Jay breathes. I glance at his face, and the look he's giving me is enough to stop my heart. I was looking at the stars. Meanwhile, he was looking at me.

"This is… I…thank you."

His mouth seals over mine, his hot breath caressing my face. I know we're still in the air, but frankly, I don't give a damn at the moment.

Jay breaks away, giving me a soft smile. "You're welcome." His eyes train forward as he angles slightly, flying us down toward the guest house.

"No wings, huh?" My eyebrows quiver up and down.

He laughs, "Nope. No wings." His feet hit the ground with a thud, gently setting me on mine beside him, and grasping my hand in his, leading me toward his place. "Are you willing to close your eyes again?"

"After all that? Absolutely!" My eyes snap shut, my skin crawling with excitement as I listen to the door creak.

When it feels okay enough to look again, I stare in astonishment at what must be hundreds of twinkling lights hanging from the ceiling. It feels like I'm back up in the sky.

"Baby, is this real?" My feet wander inside before I register what's going on.

Suddenly, I'm surrounded by lights and I can't help taking a little spin in the middle of them. "It feels like I'm up with the stars."

Jay doesn't answer, and I start to look around for a few seconds until I find his glowing blue eyes staring at me, drawing me in like a mirage of water in the hottest desert. I'm not quite sure how, but they shine brighter than all the lights in this room combined.

"There's more," he says, holding his hand out to me.

I roll my eyes in disbelief. If I hear the word 'more' one more time, I'm going to sock him. "Please leave the lights up," I request, staring once more in awe.

A small chuckle comes from him. "I wouldn't dare take them down."

I grab his hand again and let him lead me to his bedroom. For a moment, I wonder if this surprise is far more intimate than what has been happening in here lately, but I push the thought away. Jay has made it very clear that we are going to make that special, but I can't help feeling like this day is special enough to be meant for it.

Arriving at his room, he pushes the door back and signals for me to enter first. More twinkle lights cover the walls, while candles sit atop every available surface, and rose petals cover the bed. "This is so romantic, Jay."

When I'm met with silence once more, I turn around to give him some grief, but am blown away when I find him on one knee before me.

"Oh, hell no! You are not proposing to me, Jayson Joseph Tenlin." Calling him by his full name feels weird in my mouth. "We have not been together nearly long enough, and we are way too damn young—"

"Would you shut up?" he interrupts, sending my eyes open wide. Did he just interrupt the birthday girl? And did he really have to use the words *shut up*? "Listen to me. This is not a damn proposal, you crazy woman! Will you please come here? I've been planning this for what feels like a lifetime and would like to get it out before all my speech practice goes to waste."

A grin grows on my face and spreads from ear-to-ear, a blush crawling up my neck to my cheeks, putting my embarrassment on full display. I clear my throat and move closer to him, keeping a little bit of a distance, because I'm not exactly sure what he has planned. "I'm sorry," I whisper.

He holds up the most beautiful bouquet of tie-dyed roses and takes a deep breath before starting, "Tatum Rose Bellini, I've already told you that I've been in awe of you since we were kids, but if I knew that coming back home would have you looking at me in a whole different way, I would've left much sooner. I wish I could put into words just how much I actually love you, but there aren't any passionate enough words to tell you that. Trust me, I've looked. The closest I could find was 'redamancy'—the act of loving one who loves you; a love returned in full." He pauses, moving the roses a little lower. "You are everything and more to me."

My eyes start to blur from the tears covering them. I feel them slip down my face, completely speechless as the words pour from his mouth and straight into my soul. I know they're true, because I can literally feel what he's saying.

"I promise to always protect you, even from your darkest nightmares. I promise that you will always be safe with me, no matter what we are doing, or where we are. And I love you so much that I can feel how deeply your hooks are sunk into me. There's not a single thing you could do that would change my mind about you." I leap into his arms, my lips crashing to his in a fierce moment of fire and ice, but he stops me. "T, let me make love to you, okay?"

I nod at him, and after kissing my hand, he takes it in his once more and leads me to his bed.

I pause, suddenly nervous to move any further. "Jay, I have no idea what I'm doing."

Does he know what he's doing? How will I know when to do, you know, stuff? What does Jay like, and how do I know? Where do I put my hands? Do I look into his eyes? Is that too weird? Am I thinking too much? Shit, where were we?

"T," he calls, my eyes locking with his. "This is a first for both of us. Just relax, okay? You're safe here." I have no idea what I'm worrying about. Jay has got me, and knowing that this is also his first time makes me feel even more relaxed.

I push up on my tiptoes and kiss him sweetly on the cheek. "Are you saying we're going to just figure this out as we go?" I smirk at him.

He answers with a loud gulp, pulling me back in for a heated kiss.

Moments later, he lowers me to the bed, where we quickly become a jumbled heap of ripped-off clothes, tangled limbs, and heavy breaths.

Jay stills, leaning back to allow his eyes the chance to peruse every inch of me. "Absolutely stunning," he mumbles.

I grow nervous and try to cover myself, but he grabs hold of my hands, bringing them to his chest. "Please don't hide from me," he whispers, his eyes growing dark. "You never have to hide from me."

As my eyes devour his sculpted body, I reply, "But…look at you, compared to me."

"What does that mean?"

"You're…well, you. My body will never even come close to being as perfect as yours."

His eyebrows scrunch in almost anguish. "You don't see it, do you?"

I look around us before my eyes meet his again, "See what?"

He lowers his upper body to mine, his mouth moving over my ear. "You are a work of art, Tatum. And I plan to study and appreciate every piece of you."

My skin instantly heats, my core temperature climbing to scalding heights, but no words formulate in my mind.

Jay's hands maneuver over me, and every touch sends a surge of energy through each limb of my body, while each bundle of nerves tingles with euphoric passion as we explore each other, endlessly searching for more.

"Are you okay?" he questions, his gaze dancing across my face.

I nod. "More than okay."

He kisses the space between my eyebrows. "Be honest with me, baby. If you need me to stop, or you want to try something, use that angelic voice of yours."

"Now that you mention it," I start, and his brows quirk up in surprise. "May I have a seat so I can do a little exploring?"

Before I register what's happening, Jay takes a hold of my hips, flipping the both of us simultaneously, coming to a stop when I am seated atop his waist.

My eyes greedily eat up every bit of him, watching as his mouth slowly morphs into a full-blown grin, obviously loving every second of this.

I plan to take my time with this—with him—and enjoy a whole slew of firsts with the man I feel safest with. And all I know is that my soul has never felt more certain of anything before. This is where I'm meant to be.

Jay is it for me.

CHAPTER THIRTEEN

I wake up the next day, a little stiff and sore, engulfed in a scent I've never smelled before. It's a smell that is the perfect blend of both of us; the masculine cologne that always covers his skin and the candied flowers smell that is mixed into my hair. It's the most amazing concoction ever.

Carefully turning over, I find Jay with his eyes closed. Ever since his return, there has been a certain amount of stress sitting around his features, but after yesterday and last night, he seems much more relaxed.

Once my eyes travel down the rest of his face to his very attractive mouth, I find my thoughts traveling to last night's events. The fact that Jay and I finally slept together last night is enough to satisfy me for the rest of my life.

Not once did I feel rushed or awkward, which means he was obviously right. Every single part of me was safe with him. Then again, I don't think I ever doubted that.

My thoughts continue to drift through memories of last night. Jay moved incredibly slowly, making me feel cherished, like I'm the center of his universe.

I remember how amazing it felt to have his lips running over every part of my body, his hands following in their wake. A shiver runs through me as I reminisce.

Staring at his sleeping face a little longer, I can't help but reach out my hand and run my finger along his lip before quickly pulling back, trying not to wake him.

Too late. His blue eyes flash wide, staring deep into my soul.

He gives me a sleepy smile, "Can't resist touching me, huh? I knew I was smoking hot, but I guess I didn't know it was this bad."

"You are such a cocky piece of shit, you know that?"

"Hey, you have to be nice to me. I gave you the best day of your life yesterday."

He's right. It really was the best. He put in more effort than anyone's ever put in for my birthday before, but it's a new day, which means it's time for new strikes to his very large ego.

Jay's hand slowly rises to push some strands of my hair behind my ear. "I love waking up to the feeling of you touching me."

I gulp loudly as his eyes dart to my mouth and cloud with desire. "That was yesterday, this is to—"

But I never get to finish, because Jay silences me with his very seductive mouth, pulling me back in for round two.

After a second *lovely* morning—no pun intended—I finish packing my things so that Jay can finally take me home after class later. Thank God we thought to take an afternoon slot this semester.

My eyes bounce between him and my bag. "You okay?" I ask, noticing the tension in his shoulders as he sits at the edge of the bed.

"I'm..." He jumps a little and sits back. I watch the gears

in his head spin 'round and 'round, searching for the right words. "I'm just scared for you to go home."

I don't have the heart to tell him that he should be, but at the same time, he shouldn't be. My dad is a scary man, but after this weekend, I feel different. I almost feel like Jay has healed me in a way that the therapists and medication never could. I can feel myself getting stronger and stronger inside. I'm not entirely sure how he's done it, but I'm grateful.

I pull my hair over my shoulder and walk to stand directly in front of him. His eyes drift upward to look at me, and the sadness in them nearly rips my heart in two.

"I think you just want to keep me locked in your bedroom for days on end," I tease, a short laugh slipping out. I can't help but try to make light of very serious situations; I'm just not good with them.

His hands snake around my waist, pulling me close enough to lay his head against my stomach. "You know what I mean, T."

I touch the short, soft hair on the back of his head, rubbing up and down in hopes of calming him. "You don't have to be scared."

His hands slide down my back and land behind my knees, where he uses them to knock my legs out from under me. I almost yell out at the feeling of falling.

I drop, landing on his lap, and our arms find their way around each other. We sit like that for a few minutes, the apprehension hiding within his body pulsing against my skin.

Before saying another word, Jay reaches for my hand and touches the ring he got me. "Good, you still wear it."

"Why wouldn't I?"

"Just promise me that you'll always keep it on." If only he

knew that I never took it off, not even when I'm in the shower.

"Why does it matter if I keep it on?" He leans back and stares into my eyes with a stern look I feel shouldn't be questioned. Some things are just better left alone. "The ring is staying on," I assure him.

He nods his thanks to me as I move off of his lap.

The rest of my packing goes on in silence. I can't help but feel like I'm going to completely fall apart when I see my house at the end of my driveway. Not only was the Tenlin house my second home growing up, but this guest house has completely morphed from our childhood hideout to a sort of new beginning. His room will forever hold a piece of my heart within its walls. This is where I completely gave myself over to Jay, in the most intimate way possible, and I'll never forget it.

Pounding through the hall, I'm happy to find that the twinkle lights are still up and lit. The sight brings a smile to my face as I recall how the most beautiful day of my life already feels like a lifetime ago. Why do the best days always pass by like a dream?

Before Jay opens the door, he spins around and almost nails me to the nearest wall with his serious gaze. "What?" I barely breathe out.

"Do you have any regrets about this weekend? Any at all?" He drops my bag to the ground with a thud and takes both of my hands in his.

The look in his eyes confuses me. "Jay, no. Are you kidding? These were some of the best days of my life."

"I just thought…"

"You thought I'd regret one of the best things we could've

ever done together?" My eyes widen in disbelief. I thought we both enjoyed it, but maybe I was wrong.

"Partly, but I was actually concerned about how I set it all up…" His head hangs in shame.

I raise my hand to lift his chin back up, his scruff tickling my skin. "That was the most thoughtful part, Jay. You have no idea how much I love that so many of the memories of our friendship have taken place here, and with everything that's happened this year, it's become a symbol of safety in a way. This was the best place you could've ever chosen for me."

I smile, hoping it will cheer him up in a small way. When he smiles back, I know that I have finally broken down his walls.

***

"Do we really have to be here?" I ask as we pull into the school parking lot.

Jay puts the car in park, sighing as he takes off his seatbelt. "Only a few more months, T. We're almost there."

It's hard to believe that today is already the first day of February; an unfortunate downfall of having a birthday so late in the month. If I hadn't had so many other things on my mind, I would've spent the whole month prepping for the special day, but now it's already come and gone.

In a couple more months, we will officially wrap up our first year of college, and now that I'm nineteen, it's time to get rid of Adam forever. We shouldn't have to deal with him anymore.

"Ready?" Jay asks, already opening the car door for me and reaching out his hand.

I take it in mine, and am just about to ask how he made it over there so fast, but his admission comes skirting to the forefront of my mind. "I'm never going to get used to that, ya know?"

He winks, "I don't know what you're talking about."

I bump my hip into his, giggling. "You need to be careful. People could see."

He quickly whispers in my ear, "I haven't been caught yet," before kissing me on the cheek and shutting the door behind me.

"Tatum!" Lex yells from in front of the building. "How does it feel to be in the last of your teen years?"

I shoot her a thumbs-up as I blush, noticing all the heads turning to look at me.

"Hey," Jay starts, stopping me before we move much further. "You know you can't tell anyone, right?"

That seems fairly obvious. Isn't it code to not announce to the world that you're dating a superhero? It's not like I've ever heard of these REDs before. Unless they make the news like the Avengers do in all their movies, I'm keeping my mouth sealed.

"I don't know what you're talking about." I act out locking my mouth closed, and smile as I pretend to throw away the imaginary key, using his own words against him.

He kisses my cheek again, letting my hand go as I head in the direction of Lex. I look over my shoulder at him, "See you after class. Love you."

"Super love you," he whispers, purposefully lagging a few feet behind me.

The minute I notice Toree and Jana have joined Lex and see that they're now holding up a birthday banner in front of them, I take off at what feels like lightning speed toward them. I wonder what it's like to move as fast as Jay does, making a mental note to ask him to show me later.

"Happy Belated Birthday, T!" they scream in unison.

I collide into them, pulling them in for a group hug as the banner drifts against our legs on its descent down to the pavement.

"Ready to go get drunk in Canada?" Jana questions. I glance over as Jay walks by, his eyes growing wide. I shake my head at him.

Lex smacks his shoulder as he passes, "We do see you, Jay. And we saw that look. Is it the technical underage drinking you're worried about, or the possibility of Canadian strip clubs?" The girls all bend over, cackling loudly.

"Very funny, ladies. I don't think T will be needing that anymore, though."

My cheeks blaze as I pin him with a serious look.

The collective gasps pull my attention over to them. "I'm going to be late," I remind them.

Looking back over, I notice Jay has completely disappeared. How fitting.

"*Did you sleep with him?*" Toree whisper-yells, shaking my shoulders.

"Can we please talk about this later? I'm going to be late," I beg, noticing I have three minutes until my class starts. My professor cannot help but call out late students in front of the entire class, which is not something I feel like enduring today.

Jana groans, her hands aggressively pulling at her cheeks. "You're really going to hold out on us like that?"

"I promise it's worth the wait," I reply, walking backwards and shooting them all a kiss. I whip around, fishing my phone out of my pocket to send Jay a message.

"Better be!" Lex yells at my back as I almost jog to calculus.

Me: You're a real ass, you know that?

Jay: I mean, my ass is real. And from what your thoughts tell me, you think it's real nice. ;p

Me: Get out of my head!

Jay: Make me.

Once classes are over for the day, Jay drops me back at home, and I urge him to not come in. After being apart, Mom and I really need to get our bearings back and figure out where to go from here.

"Mom?" I whisper, listening for any sign of distress.

I gasp as I watch her dash out from the kitchen, looking utterly breathtaking. "Tatum, honey! Oh, I have missed you."

I snatch her up in a tight hug, "Are you okay?"

"Absolutely! Oh my gosh, I had the best time with Tonya, and I've so looked forward to you coming back home."

My eyes wander from doorway to doorway, "Adam hasn't come back?"

She reaches up to hold my cheek. "He left a note saying he's leaving. We're safe, honey. He's gone."

My eyebrows rise in surprise. "Why did he leave his truck?"

Something doesn't seem right. This all feels too easy. *Maybe it has something to do with what Jay did to him?*

"No idea. He left the keys on the counter, so I say we not worry about it right now. He's a goner, as far as I'm concerned." She smiles, leaning back to look me up and down. "I know you just turned nineteen, but you look different; glowy almost."

I look down as my cheeks flush. "I'm just happy."

"Well, it looks good on you, sweetie. Now, go get changed and get down here for dinner. The chicken will be done in about ten minutes."

Racing upstairs, I fling my things onto my bed, rushing to get my phone out and tell Jay everything.

Jay: Good. Looks like my plan worked.

Jay: I'm glad you're safe. XO

CHAPTER FOURTEEN

The end of February is approaching, I've been nineteen for a couple weeks now, and not once has my dad made a return visit. My anxiety and panic attacks have pretty much disappeared, and being a superhero's girlfriend really isn't all that exciting; at least for the present moment.

All of that is about to change, because I really feel like I deserve to see more of Jay's world.

"Can I meet the other heroes?" I ask Jay, who is sprawled out on my new black rug beside my bed, doodling on a blank-covered journal I just bought. I love his artwork, and I think it will be great to have something at school that no one else will have, because it will be the only one of its kind. "Oh, and can you draw a giraffe on there too, please?"

"A giraffe? But ostriches are your favorite."

I turn over on my side to watch him work. "Yeah, I feel like that's changed. Did you hear my first question?"

His pen hovers over the cover. "Did you know that giraffes have the same number of bones in their neck as humans? Theirs are just bigger."

"Jay..."

He lets the pen fall from his hand, his gaze sweeping over to me. "Why, T? Why do you want to meet them?"

"I just want to know more about your world. I want to meet other people like you and see what their lives are like."

"Can't this wait until we're out of school or something?"

I sit up on the bed, crossing my legs into a pretzel. "That's still three months away. Don't you think it'd be nice to be close with them in case I need anything the next time you go on a mission?"

"I mean…" His hands rub down his face. "You have a point. But I'll warn you, some of them are friendlier than others. Not all of them joined under the best circumstances."

"What do you mean?" Jay's dad wouldn't have kidnapped people to try out this injection on, right? There's no way.

Jay leans up off the ground before extending his legs perpendicular to the floor and moving over to the desk with my journal in hand. Watching him use his powers never ceases to amaze me.

"Story for another day," he adds.

He sets the journal down, and I watch him from across the room, searching his eyes for a little more information. Will I ever get to see him in full battle mode? Do the heroes of RED work like the Avengers do? Is there training? There are so many questions that I've waited to ask. "Field trip in exchange for my patience?"

He laughs a deep, throaty laugh that sends shivers all the way to the tips of my toes. We lock eyes, the blue of his irises sparking to life. "And if I say deal?" His gaze becomes utterly predatory as he begins stalking toward me like a lion.

I gulp, stretching out my legs as I lean back on my elbows and watch. Once he makes it to the edge of the bed, his eyes roll over me, his chest expanding with large breaths. "I'm starting to think the deal you're looking to make has nothing to do with the other heroes," I breathe.

He almost growls, "Oh no. Just me." His large hand splays against my chest, just under where both of my collarbones meet, and he pushes me back onto the bed.

Leaning over me, his lips find mine, his tongue slipping inside. I close my eyes, relishing in his touch.

"You okay?" he whispers a moment later.

Our gazes lock, and I latch onto his triceps with my hands…until a pinprick dances across each of my fingertips.

"Ouch!" I cry. "You shocked me!"

"Sorry!" he shouts, staggering back from me.

I cock my head when I notice the color of his eyes flickering like a flame in the wind. "You okay?"

"Yeah." He shakes his head, giving me a strange look. "I think the shock made me glitch. That's never happened before."

I chuckle. "Maybe you're malfunctioning. Now, wipe that worried look off your face and get back down here."

And he does, without uttering a word—so unlike him—which has my eyes peering at him during his entire descent.

That was weird.

***

The Michigan temperature can fluctuate a *lot* near the end of March. Some days, you need your winter jacket; others, you can probably get away with slipping on a pair of shorts.

All I know is that the past month has been the longest month of my life. I've been busy with classwork and begging Jay to introduce me to some of the other REDs, but he claims they've been on all sorts of missions and trainings.

However, we are finally meeting them now, because

spring break is around the corner, and several of them will be getting time off.

"I am *so* excited!" I squeal, nearly coming off Jay's passenger seat. "I feel like I'm meeting the Avengers or something!"

His hand wanders over to my knee, squeezing it gently. "Calm down. Remember, this is top secret. We don't get visitors much, so don't freak them out by going all number-one-fan on them."

I scoff, "Like I'd ever do that." I watch out the window as Tenlin Industries comes into view. "And you're sure your dad is okay with this?"

"Yes. He's fine with it. He just really needs you to make sure all of this is kept secret."

I pretend to grab a thought from my head and toss it out the window, giving him a hurried thumbs-up.

"You're fucking cute, you know that?" He takes my chin between his thumb and forefinger, giving it a small shake.

I shoot him a quick wink. "I know."

A leisurely grin spreads across his face, his eyes scanning me up-and-down as he puts the car in park.

"Don't look at me like that. We're here."

Before I can blink, he's out the door and around the car, opening my side and unbuckling me before I even have time to turn my head. His mouth brushes against my ear before he says, "How am I looking at you?"

My heart skips a beat, but I try my best to contain it, hoping like hell he doesn't try to get inside my head and see what's going on in there. I push him away playfully, "You're such a tease. Let's go." I hop out of the car, take his hand, and incline my head toward the building. "I'm so ready."

Once we enter TI—Tenlin Industries—we step into the familiar glass elevator. My mind races through all of our childhood memories here: playing in the playroom for staff members' kids, racing through the hallways, and going up and down on the elevator multiple times a day. This place holds a lot of nostalgia.

Jay places his pointer finger inside a hole next to a blank black panel above the floor buttons. My eyes widen when the panel slides open to reveal a new set of glowing red buttons. They're so bright, they draw me in.

"Going down," Jay states, pressing R1 along the top.

I stand on my tiptoes behind him, "How many R floors are there?"

He slides the panel closed, looking over his shoulder at me. "So many questions."

I smile as he kisses me on the nose. "You know, I've always wanted to do it in an elevator." My eyebrows wiggle up and down, sending Jay into a fit of laughter.

"And I'm sure that fantasy has always been about an elevator with clear glass doors?" He motions toward the glass as the lift settles into alignment with floor R1.

I smack his chest. "Shut up. I forgot."

The doors open with a symphonic *DING,* and I step through, feeling like I've just entered the future. "Never say never," Jay mutters beside me.

"About wha—" But then I blush, putting two-and-two together. "You're awful, Jayson Tenlin."

He nudges me with his elbow. "Awful good." He takes me by the hand, pulling me beside him. "Now, come along. There's someone I want you to meet first."

A sturdy man with broad shoulders, warm brown skin, and wavy black hair looks up from a desk donned with at least four computer monitors as we enter. His smile is blindingly bright, and when he stands up from the computer to make his way toward us, his towering height and thick torso remind me of a defensive tackle.

"Tatum, this is Maleko. Maleko," Jay pauses, pointing his hand in my direction, "This is my girlfriend, Tatum."

Maleko's three middle fingers curl into his palm, his pinky and thumb left up as he shakes his hand back and forth in the air. "*Aloha*, Tatum. It's nice to finally meet you."

I nod at him and smile. "You too."

"Sorry, Jay. I'm the only one here today. Some of the REDs got sent on a mission." He signals around him at the empty desk spaces throughout the room.

"Really? Is everything okay?" Jay asks, casting a glance down at his watch.

Maleko waves his hand through the air, dismissing the question. "Absolutely, *Hoaloha*. Your father sent them on a training mission."

My eyes scan the floor we are on. There is not a single window to look outside of. The walls are instead covered with tiny, pinhole-sized lights that seem to be much more natural than they should. They somehow offset the artificiality of the lights lining the ceiling.

About ten sleek white desks scatter the office space we are currently standing in, Maleko's desk being the only one with that many computer monitors. Everyone else's has only one.

The individual trinkets spread out among the desks are what catch my attention as Jay and Maleko continue a quiet conversation. Some desks are bare, but the ones that aren't have name tags sitting near the edge: Koral, Nate, Dola,

Maze, and obviously Maleko. At least, those are the ones I see just in this area.

A stuffed turtle is draped over the tower on Maleko's main computer, two leis dangling from his desk chair.

Koral's desk is empty except for a brown cup covered with tree sticks, a single black pencil resting inside.

Dola and Maze's seem quite similar. They're stocked with colorful pens and utensils, along with neon-colored mouse pads that pop out against the white color of the desk.

Nate's is the most interesting of all; almost every inch is covered with animal encyclopedias and art prints. I'm guessing he and Jay get along, just judging by the artwork.

Tearing my eyes away from their belongings, I gaze down at the slate-gray floors, then up to the inner wall's floor-to-ceiling windows that put each room on display. Doors line the back walls, a hallway running along them.

"How many of you guys are there?" I question, breaking the almost-silence.

"Only six," Jay starts. "Me, Maleko, the McCoy twins, Nate, and Koral."

My jaw drops. "How many women?" Yes, I just know they are the most badass of all.

They both laugh. "Two, babe. Dola—one of the twins—and Koral."

"And trust me, they are fierce," Maleko adds. "Koral can knock me on my back in two seconds flat. Get her and Dola together, and they can bring down the house with us dudes."

I glance between him and Jay, amazed by how highly they speak of these women. "I want to meet them. Can we come back?"

Jay smiles. "Yep. Maleko, when is the next in-house training? She can meet them then, and after, I can show her what I can do too." He shoots me a sideways wink, taking my breath away.

"Your dad just switched it to the summer so you'd be more available, so…three months from now?"

I inwardly groan, but jump at the sound of a wailing alarm sounding from Maleko's desk, gold lights flashing across the ceiling.

"Sorry. I gotta get that. You guys should get out of here." He starts to jog back to his desk. "*A hui hou*, Tatum. It was nice meeting you."

Jay grabs my hand and starts escorting me the way we came. "Bye, Mal."

I smile over my shoulder, loving Jay's use of nicknames. "See you soon!" I shout.

We whisk ourselves into the elevator, and I watch as Jay slides his finger into the slot once more, this time clicking numerous buttons. When we begin our ascent, he looks at me, his gaze piercing. I stumble back, glancing at the windowed walls.

"Jay?" Suddenly, the air is too hot in here.

He stalks over to me slowly, his eyes traveling up and down my body. "Do you know how perfect you are?" He stops, his fingers trailing down the side of my face.

"Thank you, but I have no idea what you're talking about."

"This. Here." His hands signal at our surroundings. "The fact that you are so invested and accepting of me and what we do here. It's a major turn-on."

I blush, peeking up at him from under my lashes. Feeling frazzled, I try to calm him down. "I'm glad to hear that, big guy. How about we head home?"

He flashes over to the panel, his hand flying out against

the emergency stop button, eyes never leaving mine. "I think it's time we fulfill that little fantasy of yours."

I gulp, "Jay, we can't." I back up against the wall. "Th-the windows."

Even though we are in between floors, there's no guarantee someone won't start the elevator back up and spot us.

His brows furrow, but that doesn't stop him from walking up to the glass. The tip of his pointer finger barely touches the clear enclosure, and I flinch as frost splinters out, freezing over every inch slowly.

I watch in awe, trying to remember what Jay said about the powers each of the REDs receive from their injection. I didn't realize he had more than one unique power. That's new… I thought each RED only received one?

I stash the question into the back of my mind before it dissipates, swept away with the rushing of a tide; a tide I am sucked into within Jay's neon-blue eyes.

He strides toward me again, this time with wide steps and a quick pace, placing one arm on the wall above my head as he leans so close to my face, our noses are touching.

"You smell like vanilla," he breathes against my skin, smelling me as he moves down to my neck where he kisses it softly. "Tell me to stop before your scent takes me too far out."

"Too far out?" I quip, my chest hauling between the wall and Jay's chest, I'm breathing so hard.

"From shore," he says around my earlobe, giving it a little nip. He drops it a second later, "If we make it too far out, I'll never make it back to shore. And I sure as hell wouldn't mind drifting away for days on end."

I shakily place my hand against his chest—almost sure I feel the elevator rumble back to life—and achingly push him back barely a smidgen. "We…" I lock eyes with him, the temperature of his skin through his shirt almost burning my palm. "We should go."

He smirks to the side, his right eyebrow lifting in question. "You sure about that?"

I close my eyes, taking a deep breath. When I open them again, I notice we made it back to R1 at some point.

My eyes go wide as they fasten onto Maleko's stare. His mouth is hanging wide open as he gapes at us through the disappearing frost.

"Oh shit." I move behind Jay, fisting his shirt.

His laughter bounces off every surface of the elevator, "Right on. Eh, Mal?"

"He can't hear you through these walls," I grit through my teeth.

"*Pololei ma.* Though, you might want to take this party home." His hearty, deep laugh sweeps through the elevator speaker on the ceiling.

I peer around Jay's wide shoulders to see Maleko pressing a button next to the glass. RED apparently has a thing with buttons. I roll my eyes.

Jay pulls away, heading off to play with the control panel again.

"Is he not going up? Why was he standing there?" I prod, leaning against the wall as the elevator surges upward.

"We're always alerted when the elevator arrives on the floor. He was probably checking to see if the others were back."

I smooth my hair down, suddenly feeling slightly disheveled. "I see."

"Shall we take this party home?" Jay asks, sporting the

most devilish smirk I've seen on him before, making my knees grow shaky.

We seem to make it back to Jay's place in record time, my body shivering with eagerness. Jay has held my hand against his face the entire ride home, alternating between kissing the top of my hand and my palm. It really shouldn't feel as erotic as it does right now, but whatever it's doing to my body makes it incredibly hard to sit still.

He grins against my fingers as we near his street. I swear I'm within arm's reach of jumping his bones right in front of his damn parents' house.

Pulling into his driveway, he zaps around to my side of the car, opening the door before I've even had time to take my seatbelt off. He lifts me into his arms, sealing his mouth over mine in a burning hot kiss while he somehow transports us to the front porch of his guest house prior to even breaking apart.

Something carnal snaps inside me. Jay helps me maneuver to wrap my legs around his waist without ever letting me touch the ground, all while twisting the doorknob to get us inside.

There is something about him being completely vulnerable—showing the superhero den, revealing his new self, and introducing me to people like him—that has me feeling even more special than ever before.

Once the door clicks shut, he pushes my back against the wood, moaning against my mouth. "I don't think we're going to make it to the bed," he mumbles upon my lips, driving me wild.

"Here," I mutter, pulling at his hair before running my hands down his chest to the hem of his shirt.

No sooner do I get his shirt off, I hear his belt clink against the floor as a wrapper crinkles at the same time, and milliseconds later, he's inside me.

We move in tandem with each other, a dance exclusive to only us.

"You're ethereal, Tatum." Jay kisses up one side of my neck and down the other. I sigh, looking up at the ceiling in ecstasy, my eyes almost rolling back inside my head.

"Please," I whimper.

Suddenly, he moves faster. My vision goes black the higher I climb. Our speed picks up, sweat sliding down my back.

Then, I feel him jerk against me and empty somewhere deep inside as he grunts into my ear. I quickly follow after him.

After our breaths slow down a bit, Jay leans back and grips the side of my face, staring deep into my eyes. The blue bolts scattering across his irises almost seem to reach out and flick across my skin. "I super love you," I mouth.

He kisses my forehead, "I super love you most."

CHAPTER FIFTEEN

Spring is turning out to be one of the best parts of our first year of college. There's been no sign of my dad, this semester has been going great, only a few more weeks of school before we are off for summer, and we have some really exciting things planned during our spring break.

After a weekend of lying around, we are starting off our Monday with the first actual plan we've made: a picnic date down by the riverfront a few cities over. Pulling in, the bridge towers over us, its sheer size taking my breath away the way it usually does. I watch as a huge burgundy freighter pushes through the water, a powerful wake following its course.

"You ready?" Jay asks, unbuckling both of us from the car before squeezing out his door.

I'm out before he even has a chance to open mine. "No speedy service today, stud?"

He shrugs. "Gotta keep you guessing."

I chuckle back at him as we walk a little ways down the boardwalk, the fresh breeze sweeping off the water and flowing over our skin.

Today is thankfully a somewhat warmer day in the good old thumb of the Mitten State. Jay and I are both in a pair of jeans and superhero t-shirts. The only difference is his backwards hat. I swear we didn't coordinate. He chose The Hulk and I chose Wonder Woman, and I can't help but appreciate the cloudless, sunny day because it makes the colors of our shirts seem so much brighter than they usually are.

Jay has wandered a few feet ahead of me, and is already laying down the picnic blanket on a patch of grass next to the walkway when I feel a boop against my leg. Looking down, I find an adorable, black, wiry-haired dog. "Hey, little fella." I pat him a few times on the head as he pants, staring up at me with dark brown eyes.

"He's friendly, I swear." A man with hair as black as his dog's runs up, huffing and puffing when he reaches us. "His name is Darth."

"Darth? Like, Darth Vader?" My eyebrows rise in question.

He swipes his hand horizontally down Darth's coat, telling him what a good boy he is. The guy looks to be about our age, maybe a little older. He's tall and has a friendly face. "Sorry he ran up to you like that. We jog together, but sometimes he gets a bit too excited."

"No problem. He seems very sweet." I reach out my hand, "I'm Tatum."

He shakes it gently. "Luke." Luke's eyes widen the moment I feel Jay's arm slip around my waist.

"Correct me if I'm wrong, because I don't know as much about Star Wars as I do superheroes, but Luke as in—"

"Skywalker, yes. My mom had a thing for Star Wars." He glances back down at his dog. "I guess it sorta rubbed off."

"Sounds like you all have great taste," Jay says, pulling me closer and reaching his hand out next. "I'm Jay."

"Nice to meet you." He quirks his brow when his and Jay's hands meet. "Well, I gotta get going. Darth here needs to get home. Great meeting you guys. Enjoy the day!"

"You too!" I yell, watching them pound the pavement away from the bridge.

Jay and I meander back over to the red plaid blanket. The picnic basket lays open in the grass, containers of sandwiches, chips, strawberries, and chocolate chip cookies spread out before us. "This looks great, Jay." I lick my lips, ready to dive in.

"I really hope you're licking your lips because you're envisioning me lying amongst all this delicious food, and not because you just met Luke Skywalker."

I laugh right out loud, smacking his chest. "I mean, space people with glowing swords compared to a superhero? Nah, they're not even in the same bracket." I nudge him with my shoulder. "The fact that he's a dog dad, though? That's something I could get behind." I waggle my brows.

"Siri, remind me to look up new puppy ads," he says out loud.

"Adding look up new puppy ads to your to-do list. Is that correct?"

"Yep!"

We both laugh our way down to the blanket, picking food from all of the containers. I move to sit in between Jay's legs, leaning against his torso as I look out at the water, smiling to myself as I enjoy the beautiful view and the rock-hard body behind me.

Ding, dong! The doorbell to Jay's guest house rings throughout the space around us— alerting me that Friday has already arrived—followed by a slew of snorts and laughter outside the door. I get up from the couch, excited to greet my girls, when Jay gently pushes me back down.

"You have no idea how jealous I am of the fact that those girls are about to come in here and share a bed with you tonight." He towers above me, looking me over with a hunger in his eyes.

I walk my feet up his thighs, stopping on his abdomen. "Think you can last one night without me?"

He continues to stare for a quick second before grabbing both feet and pulling my legs apart, which makes me gasp out loud. His eyes start to glow before he wraps my legs around him and leans down.

"Hello? Tatum? Jay? Are you guys shabanging?" Lex yells.

My laugh is cut short when Jay reaches behind me, lifting and holding me close. He skims his nose along the outside of my ear, walking over to the door. "Will you be able to last for one while snuggled up in my sheets that reek of me?"

Rolling my eyes when we make it to the door, I reach down to grab the handle and pull it open. All three of the girls stop mid-sentence when they see us in the doorway.

Jana snickers, patting Jay's shoulder a few times before moving inside. "That didn't last very long, did it now?"

"Jana!" Toree scolds, her ponytail bobbing as she runs to catch up to her.

Jay leans in to give Lex a hug. They've both always had a very sibling-like friendship. I wrap my arm around her, too, since he's still holding me to him. "Hey, Lex. Are you sure you can handle it here with this chaos?" Jay slowly lets me slide down his body, and even though he is waiting for Lex's answer, I'm preoccupied with thinking about every muscle I can currently feel through his clothing.

I clear my throat and focus on her, a smirk creeping across her face. "Come on in, Lex. Let's get these girls wrangled so Jay can leave us be." I pat his chest, signaling for him to let me go before moving to help Lex grab all the bags, since the girls left her behind.

Jay pins me with a stern look. "I will get the bags. You guys can go find the girls."

I shoot Lex a look, tilting my head toward Jay. We both dive in, kissing one of his cheeks as he goes to grab all three *huge* bags in one fell swoop. "Thanks, babe."

"This place is huuuuuuge!" Toree screeches, jumping up and down in the kitchen.

Once we walk around the island that serves as the divider between the actual kitchen section and the dining room/living room combo, I find Toree and Jana gazing at everything.

I appreciate their taste. Jay's parents did a great job with helping him design the place upon moving in. The dark wood floors and white cabinetry are a stark contrast to one another, the silver appliances completing the sleek look.

I lean against the counter. "I'm so excited for tonight."

Lex sits down onto one of the barstools while Toree and Jana lift themselves up onto parts of the free counter space. Jay walks past us, plopping all the bags down on the couch.

"I'd stay and sort things for you, but I know you want to get to whatever girly things you have planned." He shifts back and forth, looking lost about how girls' nights must work.

"You carried all of those bags with one hand?" Jana gapes her mouth at me. "I bet he can really toss ya around, eh?"

She has definitely always been the most outspoken of the group.

"Oh my gosh!" I cackle. "You guys are killing me."

Jay places his elbows on the counter, resting his chin on

his piled-up hands. "Like a ragdoll." He shoots a wink at all of us, and the girls squeal in unison as they pretend to melt. He laughs as he smacks the granite surface. "Well, girls. This has been fun, but I must be going. Take care of my girl, and don't get into too much trouble. I'll be right next door."

He walks into the kitchen, giving each girl a quick peck on the cheek before making his way over to me. Wrapping his hands around the sides of my face, he firmly presses his mouth to mine, and I swear it makes me liquefy like a stick of melted butter.

I rest my hand against his stomach gently, trying my best to push him away as the girls hoot and holler behind us.

"Love ya, T." He pinches my cheek and starts to walk away.

"Love you too!" I shout, watching him leave, trying not to feel too sad that he didn't say *super love you.*

The girls all hop down, running around the counter, yelling out, "But we love ya more!"

We bust out in a fit of laughter, watching as Jay's head shakes back and forth, closing the door behind him. I'll bet he's grateful he won't have to deal with us all night. We're a lot to handle, to say the least.

"It's girls night, bitches!" Jana screams, pulling us all to her the moment she realizes we are alone.

This is going to be an interesting night. *Fun,* but interesting.

It's getting dark by the time we wrap up dinner: pizza from the best place in town. We all chipped in to get a quarter of the pizza with our favorite toppings on them. I got pepperoni and mushroom, Jana chose pepperoni and jalapenos, and Toree and Lex continued their weird obsession by getting their ham and pineapple. I mean, pineapple doesn't even belong on pizza! *Bleck!*

Moving into the living room, we flip on Magic Mike, a movie my grandma took us to see when it came out. We were a bit young to see it, seeing as it premiered our junior year, but my grandma talked all of our parents into letting her take us to the theater. Needless to say, we love Grandma; she's spunky, and she claims taking us to see a movie like that in high school was "educational" and showed us real-life experiences. I think she just wanted an excuse to go watch Channing strip on screen. Can't say I blame her.

Nearly two hours later, I turn the screen off as we all shift to face each other. There comes a time during every girls night that calls for what we call the Talk-and-Turn; we take turns asking random questions and giving everyone the time to talk. It's the only way to keep things fair.

"Well? Let's hear it, T. Any updates on dating Mr. Captain America himself?" Lex snuggles farther down into the couch cushion, looking over at me with hopeful eyes. I perk up at this, hoping like hell I don't manage to let Jay's secret slip at some point; the ease of discussing superheroes has always been effortless.

The footrest of the recliner bangs up as I pull the lever, and I smile at all of them since the new angle gives me the perfect view of them squeezed together on the couch. "I mean, what do you want to know?"

Jana throws her hands up in the air. "I've been asking you

to rate the spice on our pepper sheet scale for months! Where does he rank?"

"Hm. Let me see…" I hold up all five fingers on my right hand, ticking them off as I list them. "I need to remember them all first." I start with my thumb, "Green for one, yellow for a two, orange for a three, red-orange for four, and red is a five." I tap my finger against my chin as I ponder before throwing up all ten fingers, having nothing else to compare it to like some of them.

"I knew it!" Jana screams. "That man could blow the sheets off any bed! The highest I've ever rated a man was a four. I'm saving my five." We all fall into a laughing fit, and I dry my eyes from the tears flowing down my cheeks.

When we finally calm down a bit, I find myself wishing I *could* tell the girls Jay's secret. The thought has my mind wandering. Am I okay with a life full of so many secrets? Secrets I can't even tell my best friends?

"T?" Toree questions, handing me a glass of water.

I grab it, taking a sip before placing it in the cup holder on the chair. "Hm?"

"You okay?"

My middle finger traces the mouth of the glass. "I'm fine." I smile up at her. "Can we please change the subject? I need to know all about what's going on with you guys."

Toree gives me a small grin before squeezing back between Lex and Jana on the couch. "Well, I met this guy in my weights class," Toree starts. "His name is Dean, and he's a total dream. He asked me to go on a date tomorrow!"

Even though Toree recently tried out for the Pistons dance team, she is going to school to be a personal trainer, so meeting someone who likes working out as much as she does will be perfect.

"That's great, Tor!" Lex cheers, resting her head on her shoulder. Lex is always supportive, getting excited over things that don't always feel that big and celebratory. That's why Lex will make a great teacher. She'll be the best at cheering on her students.

"Jana? You're next." Toree pokes her arm.

Jana leans her head back against the couch with a huff, "I think I'm switching my major again. Criminal Justice was not for me. I think I was only in it for the hot cops." We all chuckle. "Up next is Dental Hygiene!"

Toree rolls her eyes. "Those aren't even remotely related, Jan."

Jana is a certifiable free spirit. She has infinite potential, seeing as she's good at basically everything she does, and has hobbies up the wazoo. But there is one thing I've always noticed she enjoys the most: doing her own thing. I've often thought about it, wondering what might grant her the freedom to go wherever and do whatever.

I guess now is the best time to mention my idea. "Have you ever thought about being a blogger?"

"A blogger? Why the hell would I do that?"

"Just hear me out," I beg. "We all know you are incredibly indecisive, overly independent, and extremely adventurous. What if you traveled, finding random jobs here-and-there, and blogged about it? You could teach people how to do the same thing."

Jana stares off for a second before bobbing her head in a thoughtful *yes* motion. "Actually, that might not be a bad idea. I'll think about it."

Lex shoots me an appreciative wink, dangling a thumbs-up over the side of the couch that only I can see, prompting me to remind her that it's now her turn.

"Lex? What's going on in your life?" I ask.

She moves to sit up more before she starts. "Remember how I did that special college program during high school? And how I earned that associate's degree from it?"

"Yeah, I wish I would've done that…maybe I could've at least tried out a career path for free before jumping from major to major, racking up the loans as I go," Jana throws in.

"I have a feeling you'd still be switching anyway," Lex points out. "But like I was saying, since I did that, I've been able to start some of my actual core classes at Oakland while also finishing up things here, which means I've started some field placements. I'm in one right now, and oh my gosh, these little kindergartners are the cutest! I just want to read to them all day. They run around after every story, pretending to be the main character." She throws her hand over her heart, and if I didn't know better, I'd swear her eyes have taken on a misty sheen.

Toree playfully smacks down on one of both Lex's and Jana's knees, pushing herself up, letting one of Jay's comic-themed blankets fall to the floor. "Ladies, I don't know about you, but after all that, I think we need to finish with our favorite game."

"*Mario Kart*?" Jana screams, rushing over to Jay's refurbished Nintendo 64 to blow in the cartridge and get it set up. Not to be that person, but I demolish at Mario Kart, so I'm more than ready.

"Game on, bitches!" I yell, grabbing a controller to get started.

Five rounds in, I glance over at the clock, noting how it's already 3:00 AM. "Holy shit! How did that happen?"

"Girl time can't be measured. You know that." Lex grabs all the blankets, rolling them up and placing them inside the basket near the TV—a recent addition I talked Jay into adding to his house since we've started dating.

Jana and Toree have already made it to the bedroom by the time we've tidied up and are snuggled in the center of the bed, their eyes getting heavy. Jana's head pops up the moment she hears us enter the room.

"Hold the hell up. These aren't your dirty sex sheets, are they?" She looks around her like a fish stuck in the middle of a group of sharks.

I laugh, slipping out of my outfit and pulling on one of Jay's t-shirts over my head. "Shut up, Jan. Jay changed the sheets this morning."

"Well, they smell like him." Toree mutters, her eyes still closed.

My skin crawls at that admission, suddenly aware of what Jay meant exactly when he talked about his aroma being on the sheets. *Little shit.*

I type out a quick text to Jay on my phone.

> Me: The girls like your smell. Too bad I like it on your skin more ;)

I don't wait for a response as I'm the last one to puzzle-piece my way into the bed. "I love you guys," I whisper.

Not a single one of them answers as I close my eyes right behind them.

I wake up to a half-whispered, half-shouted "*Fuck*" coming from somewhere in the house. Peeling myself from the tangled arms and legs of our girl pack, I stealthily slip out of the bed and into the hallway, softly pulling the door closed behind me.

"My damn toe," Jay mutters. I'd recognize that silky-smooth voice anywhere.

I lean against the counter, watching him as he limps his way around the kitchen, cleaning up our mess. He has yet to notice me, and I love watching him be completely unaware. I find it hard to suppress my laughter as I take in his Avengers pajama pants and black t-shirt. His hair is disheveled, bits and pieces poking up every which way.

I glance at the clock on the stove. It reads 11:00 AM. I'm sad the girls will all be leaving today, because after our last plan Jay and I have tonight, that means spring break will officially be coming to a close. How we've already worked our way through a picnic, a reading day at my house, a Marvel movie premiere, and a girls' night, I'll never know. Breaks always go by way too fast; that's one of their biggest downfalls.

"I was going to get that," I say softly, hoping not to startle him.

He turns around, a sleepy smile forming, earning a smile from me too. "I didn't want you guys to have to worry about this. I figured you could sleep in some more."

I walk over to him, standing up on my tiptoes to kiss his cheek. "I *was* sleeping until *someone* massacred their toe, apparently."

"That cupboard is tougher than it looks," he remarks, pointing at the wood that has a surprisingly deep dent in it now. I guess the cupboard could say the same for him.

I push his shoulder playfully, "Don't tell me that counter is your kryptonite, Mr. Super—"

He shushes me by placing his hand over my mouth. His lips cup over my ear: "Don't finish that." A shiver runs down my spine as I feel his hot breath brush over my skin.

Jay picks me up and places me on the counter, walking between my thighs, his hand grasping the fabric of his shirt I'm still wearing and yanking me closer until our bodies connect. His touch is addicting. I bite my lip and rub my hands up and down his rigid torso.

"I missed you," I murmur, looking up at him through my eyelashes.

"I missed you more," he mumbles right against my lips, drawing a gasp from me.

"Don't you mean *super* miss you?" Sliding my hand around the back of his head, I pull him in until his mouth reaches mine. Our lips dance and sway with each other, heavy breaths escaping through each tiny crevice as we come up for air.

I notice our hands frantically reaching for random sections of our clothes, trying their best not to take anything off, as our chests heave against each other.

"Oh great!" I jump back at the sound of Jana's voice. I whip around with wide eyes to find her in the entrance of the hallway. "I dropped a slice of my pizza on the counter yesterday and still ate it…"

Lex guffaws next to her, "Nothing like a piece of pizza with a side of canoodling."

Jay laughs huskily against my shoulder, "Morning, ladies. I swear my counters are clean. Or, they were."

The girls walk in, Toree trailing behind them with a smile on her face. They each have a bag in their hands, messy buns on top of their heads, still rocking their pajamas.

"Hate to bust up this spice-fest, but we should probably get going," Toree admits, her eyes downcast.

I hop down from the counter. "Are you sure you don't want to stay for breakfast?" I look up at Jay, double-checking that it's okay.

"You're more than welcome to," he urges.

The girls cast glances at each other, smirking. "Looks like you guys already have breakfast plans," Jana winks, dropping her bag down and opening her arms up wide.

I rush over, pulling all three of them to me. "Please say we will do this again."

"Absolutely." They pull away, grabbing their things and heading toward the door.

Jay somehow already slipped around us to hold the door open for them. "Bye, ladies. You're welcome to come back anytime."

"Better watch it, Jay-Man. We'll make this a girl pad in no time with that offer," Lex teases. "Have fun, you two!"

"Bye!" I yell, hugging myself as I watch Jay close the door and lock it behind them.

When he turns back to me, his stare is wild, the glow growing increasingly brighter with each step he takes toward me. "Now…where were we?"

CHAPTER SIXTEEN

It's starting to get dark out by the time Jay swings by to pick me up for the bonfire tonight. April is a bit of an odd time for a bonfire in Michigan, but Jay claims Maleko has a firepit at his house, and that it will do a decent job keeping us warm on the beach.

Thankfully, we've been pretty lucky weather-wise for spring break. So, for a Friday night, I'd say it's looking good for our last big hurrah before going back to wrap up our first year of college.

"Bye, Mom!" I kiss her on the cheek, running toward the door.

Jay opens the door, and I leap into his arms before he even makes it inside.

"Bye, sweetie! Love you," Mom yells behind me.

I breathe in his musky scent as he spins me around in a circle, kissing my neck as his laughter sends vibrations across my skin.

Sliding down the length of his body, I come nose-to-nose with him. His smile is breathtaking. "Hey, gorgeous."

"Hey, hot stuff." I lick the tip of his nose before grabbing his hand and yanking him back through the door. "Love you, Mom! See you tomorrow!"

Like a flash of lightning, Jay appears on my side of his

car. He opens the door, softly grabbing my hand to help me in. I slide in, and before I even have a chance to look over at his seat, he's already there. "Ready?"

"Ready," I reply, shooting him a wink. "I'm so excited!"

"You act like you're getting ready to meet the Avengers or something."

I smack my hands onto my thighs. "I sorta am, though!"

As the GPS signals we are getting closer to our destination, anxiety starts to pool in my stomach. Nothing like the anxiety my dad so easily causes though; this kind is different. It's due to all the excitement because I finally get to meet more of the REDs Jay works with.

"How old is Maleko?" I ask, looking up at his impressive lakefront home.

Jay grabs our bag of clothes from the back, just in case it gets chilly since we'll be sitting right along the water. "Twenty-three. Why?"

"I guess I thought he was our age. But judging by this house, I knew I must've been wrong."

The beep of the car door being locked has us heading toward the house, but Jay stops me as he gently pinches my elbow to get my attention. "Hey."

"Hm?"

"We're obviously going to be here for a while, which means there's going to be lots of talking and questions, but please do me a favor. Don't ask any of them how they became REDs. Not all of them will want to tell you that just yet. Okay?" His furrowed brows relax after the question is finished.

I loop my pointer finger with his, tugging lightly. "No problem. I don't want to make anyone uncomfortable. I want your friends to like me."

Just as he nods, the front door swings open as we close in on the porch, a very smiley Maleko hanging his body outside. "*Aloha*! Welcome to my humble abode!"

I smile, waving up at him. "Hey, Maleko! It's so good to see you again."

Jay shakes Maleko's hand, letting me slip through the door before he follows behind me. I look all around us, taking in the beachy, nautical theme Maleko has decorated his house with. I wonder if he misses home. By the frequent instances of using the Hawaiian language, I'm assuming he lived there for a decent portion of his life.

"Are you ready to meet some REDs?" Maleko asks, leading us through toward the back of the house, where there's a sliding glass door leading out to his own private beach.

I nod, a gasp escaping my mouth as I take in the beautiful section of sand. The water has taken on a deep navy color close up, while a bit farther out is a little lighter due to the sunset. Maleko has logs he must've cut himself spaced out around his firepit for seating, and strings of lights hang from the trees overhead.

Once I've surveyed the space, I notice that I'm being stared at by quite a few new people. Jay grabs my hand, kissing the back of it, drawing my attention to him. "Guys, I'd like you to meet my girlfriend, Tatum."

"Hey, everyone!" I say, inwardly cringing at my sudden awkwardness.

Maleko pipes in, "Tatum, these are the McCoy twins: Maze and his sister Dola." Maze and Dola flash their gorgeous smiles at me, the pearlescent gleam extremely bright against their rich black skin. Maze lifts a hand to wave.

I wave back. "Great to meet you both."

"That's Nate and Koral," Maleko continues. Nate holds two fingers against his reddish-brown hairline before giving me a sort of salute. Beside him, Koral's blonde hair takes on a fiery glow from the flames. She pulls her hair all to one side, giving me a soft grin.

"Nice to meet you guys."

Koral gets up from the log, walking toward us. I can't help but notice the rippling muscles along her forearms. Maleko wasn't kidding when he said Koral could kick some ass.

"What's up, newb? I see you wrangled yourself a RED, eh?" My eyebrows raise in confusion. I can't tell if she's being a bitch, or if she's just a lot to handle.

"Koral," Jay quips.

That just might be my answer…

"Actually," I take over, "Jay and I have known each other almost our whole lives. I guess we should've seen this coming." I shoot her an innocent smile. Her face goes rigid, her eyes squinting as she assesses me from head to toe. This is going to be a hard one to crack.

Koral extends her hand, and it takes everything in me to shake it. "Ouch," she says, yanking her hand away. "You shocked me." She shakes it out as she passes by, tripping for a split second before heading into the house.

"Sorry!" I call after her.

"Don't mind her," Nate speaks. "She's a sour puss." Everyone erupts in laughter.

"Yeah, she'll come around. Now, I'm a hugger, Tatum. Is that okay with you?" Dola gets up and holds her arms wide open.

"Absolutely," I reply before she wraps me in a welcoming hug. Her arms are gentle, her scent like flowers.

Maze gets up and hands me a water. "Come sit down. We're excited to finally get to talk with you. Jay over here never shuts up about his sweet T."

Jay punches him in the shoulder. "Shut up, ya prick." Maze sticks his tongue out at him. We all break into roars of laughter, and then we're welcomed to the fire.

I glance at Jay's watch and notice that it's been about fifteen minutes since Koral went into the house. I'm starting to wonder if I should go check on her…until the questions get turned to me.

"So, Tatum," Nate starts, holding a fist up in front of his mouth as he clears his throat. He has nice arms. The sort of arms a woman would want to reach out and touch just to see how hard they are. "Jay claims the both of you have been obsessed with comics and superhero movies since forever. I gotta know… Marvel? Or DC?"

I stroke my chin, pretending to really contemplate his question. He chuckles, giving me his full attention. "Well, can I be honest?"

"I'd expect nothing less," he answers. He perches his elbows on his knees, leaning over the ground.

"In my opinion, DC's characters are a bit more in depth in the comics, but Marvel has done a better job with their cinematic universe. I really am a fan of both, but they each have their own successes."

Nate's eyebrows rise as he tilts his head to the side in a sort of "good point" gesture. I glance over at Jay, who is giving me a proud smile as he reaches out to rub his hand across my lower back.

"What about you?" I ask Nate in return.

He shifts in his seat, yanking the fabric of his pants that rests on his quads to get more comfortable. "I'm actually pretty partial to DC, myself. One of my mom's ex-boyfriends got me on the Michael Keaton *Batman* movies when they were dating. I guess it's stuck with me ever since."

Okay…that's just about the sweetest thing I've ever heard, and I can't say I'm shocked. Nate seems like one of those authentically nice guys. I bet he was the high school jock that not only joined the quiz bowl team too, but also volunteered. He seems really well-rounded and down to earth.

"Are you serious?"

He smirks. "Deadly."

"Favorite villain from those?" I ask.

"The Penguin. Danny DeVito played him so well."

"Right on, bro," Maze chimes in, offering up a closed hand that Nate fistbumps. In the excitement of it all, I must've missed how deep Maze's voice was earlier; it is actually so baritone that it intimidates me.

"I've always been partial to The Riddler, myself," Dola adds. "It was fun trying to guess the riddle, and besides, who doesn't love Jim Carrey?"

I'm just about to join in and say the Joker, but Jay distracts me as he squeezes my knee before giving his input. "You know The Riddler was from *Batman Forever* with Val Kilmer, right? Michael Keaton was only in two of them."

I roll my eyes, unable to stop the groan moving up my throat. "We were just talking about villains from the *Batman* movies, Jay. Doesn't matter who played Bruce."

Moving to scan the rest of the group, I pause at the spot

where Dola just was. Jay's head jerks to the left, and I can't help but stare at him.

"Damn it, Dol." Jay rubs the right side of his head, surveying his surroundings.

I join in too, until Dola pops up right in front of us and meanders back over to her seat. "Thank you, Tatum. As for you, it serves you right, trying to sass me like that. Watch your mouth, boy."

My hand covers my mouth, and I try to hide my laughter, but Jay's stare holds my own.

Now really seems like a good time to go check on Koral. "I'm going to use the bathroom," I say to the group, rising from my place.

He pulls me in for a kiss before moving his mouth to my ear. "Need me to come?"

I shake my head, standing up to face Maleko. "Where's your bathroom?"

"Once you reach the edge of the kitchen, turn right down the hallway. It's the first door on the left." I watch as his finger points in each direction that he lists.

Stepping over everyone's legs, I slide the glass door open before slipping inside, making sure to shut it directly behind me. There's nothing worse than a bonfire smell seeping into your house.

"Koral?" I softly call, hoping she's okay. I guess I need to talk with Jay more about REDs. Do they get sick? Is it normal to worry about them on a day-to-day basis?

The toilet flushes and when Koral comes out of the bathroom, she looks fine... I almost miss the line of sweat above her top lip, but not quite. "Can I help you?" Her tone is short and void of emotion.

"I...uh, was just checking on you." I shrug my shoulders,

not wanting to make anything weird. "Plus, I gotta use the bathroom."

She quickly wipes her lip. "Go on, then. It's free." Her arms signal behind her before she slips past me and heads back down the hallway.

Nice talk.

Once Koral joined the group again, it seemed to ignite something in the REDs. Suddenly, I am catching all sorts of small details that clue me in to what they can do.

Maze and Dola have been playing a game for the last five minutes where Dola has been turned toward the house, her eyes staring straight ahead, while Maze stands behind her, his hands and legs switching from weapon-to-weapon, as she calls out each one without looking back at him.

Roots of nearby trees have been periodically reaching out like arms with fresh pieces of cut wood from Maleko's pile and adding them into the fire.

Apparently, mosquitoes have been kept out by Maleko's force field that still somehow lets in a soft breeze, or so I'm told by Jay. I can't see it, but I can tell he's feeding me the truth.

Nate, whose power I find the most interesting at the moment, has spent the last few minutes shapeshifting his right hand into those of various creatures, having us guess them like it's some sort of trivia. Jay and I haven't done too bad, mainly because besides superhero shows, we grew up on *Animal Planet*.

A couple hours of talking, eating, and laughing later, Jay pulls me up by the hand. "We should get going. Our spring break is coming to an end, and we need to get back at a decent hour so I can take her home in the morning."

I grin at all of them as Jay holds me close. "I really appreciate you inviting me, Maleko. It was so good to finally meet all of you."

Maleko stands, coming around the fire to pull me in for a giant bear hug. His enormous stature seems to cover every inch of me. "*'A'ole palikir*, Tatum. Thanks for coming."

"I have no idea what you just said, but I hope it's good?" I question, looking up at the towering man in question.

"*'A'ole palikir!* It means you're welcome. Looks like I'm going to have to teach you some of my Hawaiian language, my friend."

I pull away, smiling up at him. "Please do! I can't wait!"

Everyone else waves and says their goodbyes before I jump onto Jay's back. He piggybacks me through the house and to the car, plopping me onto the hood. His lips softly kiss my forehead, his hands smoothing back my hair. "Well?" he asks.

"I had a great time. I'm so glad we came."

"And what did you think of everyone?"

I hug him to me. "They were amazing. Well, except for Koral. I don't think she likes me."

Jay laughs, his chest shaking against my cheek. "Koral is a whole other breed of woman, I'm pretty sure. Let's get going." He helps me down, getting me in the car, before putting it in drive and heading home.

The whole ride, I stare up at the moon, resting my head against the window, listening as Jay hums the *Avenger's* theme tune.

It's after midnight by the time we get back to Jay's house. I close the door behind me, watching as Jay walks through the living room. He lays his hoodie along the top of the couch and slips his shoes off and places them on the shoe rack, flipping the lights on as he goes.

He must sense I haven't followed, because he quickly turns around, cocking his head as he gazes at me. "You okay?"

I nod my head. Biting my lip, I head toward him. I don't know if there's something in the air, or if it's the combination of meeting the REDs and the smell of bonfire on Jay's skin, but I'm suddenly not ready to go to sleep.

"I know that look." Jay meets me halfway, picking me up. I wrap my legs around him, kissing along his jaw as he carries us to the bedroom.

I'm just waving Jay off as he leaves when a crash in the distance has me jumping back from the door like it's on fire. *What the hell was that?* I rush through the entrance, stopping dead in my tracks at what I hear next.

"Where the fuck is Tatum, Anne? If you don't open your mouth, I swear I'll—" Without thinking, I slam the door shut behind me, the walls shaking with the force, hopefully hard enough that the hinges fall off.

"Tatum? Honey? Is that you?" My mom comes running through the doorway and pulls me in for a protective hug like debris from an explosion is about to head our way. I squeeze her back hard.

"Are you okay, Mom?" I whisper, hoping Adam can't hear us. If he touched her, I will kill him.

"I'm fine, baby. Why don't you head up—"

My heart drops as my mother is yanked away from me. She screams as my dad drags her back by the ponytail and throws her toward the staircase, her head crashing into the banister before she slams against the last couple of stairs like a bag of garbage, her body thudding onto the wood floor as it lays still.

"*Mom!*" I scream, running toward her. *No, no, no no no, please don't be dead...*

Adam grabs me by both arms, using his strength to rip me away from her and slam me against the wall, pain reverberating through me. I instantly see red, something foreign coming over me, but I find myself unable to use that to help me. The fear fights to keep it at bay.

"Where the fuck have you been?" His voice booms, shaking my eardrums. His face has completely morphed since I last looked at him. He resembles a horrifying monster with his bloodshot eyes, blotchy face, and grayish-black bags. And even though I was feeling brave a moment ago, every ounce of fight I had is washed away by the look in his gaze alone. The panic settles at the base of my throat, ready to emerge at any moment. *God, no. Not right now.*

"D-don't hurt her," I beg quietly. His hands cover his stomach as he throws his head back in laughter. It's a manic noise.

I move to help Mom again, but Adam charges me, cornering me by the door. I close my eyes and try to blend in with the wall. If only I had just enough space to slip out...

But I'd never leave my mom behind. I could never.

"*D-don't hurt her,*" he mocks in a baby voice. If I could knock his lights out, I would. Where the hell did my mom *find* this piece of work? "W-What's wrong, T-Tatum? Cat got your fucking tongue?"

The panic is still there, swimming beneath my skin, but it's stuck. I don't know why it's not consuming me like usual, but…

"Leave me the hell alone," I snap in the most confident voice that I can muster. I just keep telling myself to appear brave. If he senses even an ounce of fear, he will strike.

I scream when his fist flies at me, but I dodge, and it crashes into the wall next to my head. Some of the plaster splinters onto my shirt. My resolve is chipping away the same way.

"You listen here, you little brat. You think you can run off while I'm gone and not tell me where you are? Bribe your mother into silence? You are a stupid, naive, bitchy, sorry excuse for a daughter. You think you have a life of your own?" He ferociously laughs, and for the first time in my life, I see that there's no saving this man in front of me. He is ruined for life. He has never been, nor will he ever be a father to me. He is nothing. "Think again! You will never be free of me because you owe me."

"I don't owe you anything! Please, just leave!" The minute the words leave my mouth, I feel a little better. I am so tired of his bullshit that I couldn't care less what he does to me anymore. I just want him gone.

Without another word, a murderous sneer takes over Adam's face, a terribly insane smoky darkness rushing over his eyes, blocking out the color.

Holy shit. We need to get out of here. Something is wrong with him.

All of a sudden, tendrils of dark shadows erupt from him,

swirling all around us. I hurry backwards, tumbling into the wall.

"Well, well, well. Looky here. Someone has grown some balls now that they have a superhero boyfriend, huh?" My eyes fling wide open. "Yes, I know all about your precious Jay's secrets."

"What the hell are you?" I chance a glance at my mother, who seems to still be unconscious. The panic starts to rise up my throat.

The black shadows swim over to me, wrapping me up like a cocoon, bringing me dangerously close to Adam's face. I fight to get out, almost reduced to tears because of the terror eating away at my insides.

"I'm glad you asked." He tilts his head up as his skin ripples in front of my eyes. When he looks back at me, the cloudiness in his gaze has left, and now his irises have taken on the blackish-purple I saw in my nightmare not too long ago. "Let me introduce you to Daddy Dearest, Dark Doom."

"Are you saying you're a—"

He laughs again, "A villain?" He lets me go, and I fall to the floor, pain radiating through my legs. "That's right. And do you know what that makes you?"

I look up at him, confusion stirring my thoughts. "A psychopath's daughter?"

His sinister cackle chills me to the bone. "Oh no, sweetheart. That just means you're part villain, too. What do you think your super boyfriend will have to say about that?"

My heart drops. "No. No, that's not true." I push up, frightened urgency coursing through my veins.

My dad's shadows swivel together between us, obscuring my view of him. "You mean to say you haven't noticed anything weird about yourself? No weird sensations sweeping through you? No odd happenings when you've touched someone?"

I rack my brain, trying to see if there's anything I can possibly link to this asinine thought. I blanch when I remember the indescribable feeling that came over me when I got home…almost like if I would've let it take over, I would've actually been brave and tried to fight back, but it wasn't strong enough to help me.

My breathing goes ragged when I recall the way Koral felt a shock that I didn't before tripping into Maleko's house.

And then it really hits me. That day Jay could feel the shock…it wasn't because *he* was glitching and shocked us. It was me.

No wonder he'd looked so shaken up.

No, no. This can't be real. "It can't be. You're lying." This all must be some crazy coincidence.

"I wish I was. But you see, I knew something was off about you whenever I was finally able to get my hands on you. I could feel the power beneath your flesh." The smoke clears from between us, moving to surround me in a dark, whirling cloud.

I smack my hands at it, yanking them away just as fast when the shadows inflict searing pain against my skin like burning hot lashings. "Stop it! Stop it! *Please!*"

Adam's hands push through the black smoke, wrapping around my wrist. "Not before I figure out your power. I must know what I have in my arsenal to wipe out every existence of those heinous REDs before *he* comes. He'll already be shocked someone like you even survived to this point."

He? And what does my survival have to do with this 'he?' But those thoughts vanish almost as quickly as they formed, because at the idea of even the slight possibility of Jay's extinction, a foreign power engulfs me from the inside out that I've never felt before. My hand rises of its own accord and takes hold of my dad's hand.

He bellows in pain as I close my eyes, an addicting darkness being absorbed through every pore. *What is happening?*

I come to when a *thud* moves the floor beneath me. Looking down, I find him struggling to get up, his piercing eyes losing a bit of their glow as he glowers up at me. "Why, you little—"

I hold up my hand, and his mouth closes in surprise, but I see he's ready to try and attack again.

"Get the hell out." My trembling finger points at the door —I'm unsure of whether I should be trembling out of fear, or because I just did something to stop Adam—but my eyes never leave his.

I will not show weakness.

I will not back down.

I bow to no man.

"You can't make me leave," he snarls. "I will strip you of whatever power you have, bit by bit."

My mom stirs across from me. I have to get rid of him before she comes to. I can't have her seeing this, not before I know what's wrong with me and what story I'm going to have to create for all of this. I just need time.

"Would you like to try? Or shall I repeat what I just did?" I question. Maybe I should still be scared. I'm not exactly sure what I did to Adam, or if I'll ever be able to do it again, but something inside is willing me forward, pushing me to change, challenging me to be brave.

He barely pushes up from the floor, staggering to the wall. His gaze drifts between my mom, me, and the door, weighing his options carefully.

"This isn't over," he says over his shoulder, ripping the door open and slamming it behind him. I leap to turn the lock and lean my back against the wood. My breathing quickens, but not because I'm on the verge of a panic attack; the complete opposite, honestly. I've never felt more alive, and that thought is enough to scare the shit out of me.

"Honey?" My mom's voice is soft and barely audible. Her arms shake as she lifts her torso off the ground, wincing from the pain.

I rush over to her. "Mom? Are you okay?"

"Where's A-Adam?" She leans into me, wheezing against my chest. "What happened?"

My mind tries to conjure up any possible reason it can for how I was able to get rid of my dad. "I started recording him, threatening to show the evidence to our local authorities if he didn't leave."

She stares at me, her eyebrows pulling together. "But he *is* part of the local authorities?"

"How could he deny actual proof, though? He had no choice."

She seems to accept the truth. I'm sure only because of how tired she is from this hellish encounter. "Well, thank you." Her hand reaches up to cup my cheek. "You saved me."

A sudden sadness creeps through me. How could I possibly save her, when in reality, I was the product of a villain? I mean, what does that make me? Half of a villain? A full villain? Something else entirely?

Surely nothing even remotely close to being a hero.

"We should get you to the hospital. You hit your head really hard."

Her voice cracks, "Honey, I'm fine. I just need rest. But do you think he'll come back?"

I pull her up, letting her rest her weight against me. "He won't. I promise. I'll lock everything up and set the alarm. I'll even call Jay to let him know what's going on."

"This is bigger than Jay, honey."

I smile sadly at her words. If only she knew the truth.

I always knew Jay was too good for me. Hell, too good for this planet. And now that I know exactly what I am…what does that mean for us?

Getting mom settled into bed, locking the doors, arming the alarm system, and making my way up the stairs seems to last a lifetime. I was never able to talk her into going to the hospital, which pisses me off. If she sleeps her way into a coma, I'm going to lose it.

My thumb reaches for my ring finger in comfort, but comes up empty. *Where's my ring?* I slam my bag onto the carpet so I can check my pockets. Coming up empty, I take the room key out of my bag and insert it into the lock, happy to hear it click, ensuring me that the coast is clear inside. I pick up the strap of my bag and drag it with both hands into my dark room, exhaustion slowly taking over.

At last, I make it inside, close the door, and lean against it, shutting my eyes for just a brief period of reprieve.

When they open, they zero in on a hooded figure on my bed.

I scream wildly, clumsily reaching for the doorknob behind me, not wanting to take my gaze off the man in my room. The man's face lifts and his eyes connect with mine—intoxicatingly blue. They still me.

"Jay?" I whisper, praying to God that I'm right.

"Tatum? Are you all right? Did you hear that?" my mom yells from downstairs. She's always been a light sleeper, and with her head, I'm relieved it took her no time at all to answer my distress call.

I flick the light on and come face-to-face with Jay freaking Tenlin himself as I holler back, "I'm fine, Mom! Just got frightened. Sorry!"

"Okay!" Her voice has already grown more depleted. I'm grateful she didn't try to make her way up here.

My hand flies to my chest as I gulp big breaths of relief. My heart tries to beat itself directly out of my chest. "Holy shit, you scared me half to death."

"I'm so sorry. I didn't mean to scare you. I just had to make sure everything was okay." His voice is so sweet and reassuring, but guilt laces his tone like poison. Or maybe it's my own deathly toxin seeping through, trying to reveal itself.

"Would you like to tell me how you got in here?" I ask.

He pauses before answering, "Flew in?"

"Okay? Why did you even come back?" I slowly turn to face him, pinning him with stern eyes.

"I had to make sure you were okay."

"Well, thank you. I'm fine now, but…" I stop dead in my tracks. How did Jay even know something was wrong? "How did you know you needed to check on me?"

"You, uh…forgot this." He draws a hand from his pocket, my ring held between two of his fingers.

"You found it! I didn't even realize it fell off." His eyes flick back and forth for a few moments. What is that look? Shit, did he hear everything? How long has he been here?

"I found it on the bedspread when I got home, so I came back as soon as I could" His face remains stoic as he slides the jewelry back on my finger.

"I appreciate it, but you should get going.."

He walks up to me and pulls his hood down before running both of his hands up and down my arms. Goosebumps travel behind his touch, fear following in their path. He shouldn't touch me. It's dangerous. "Go? What happened?"

I nod, carefully moving out of his reach. I make myself busy, trying to avoid suspicion. "Adam was here when I got home. He… I…" I sigh, running a hand through my hair. "It could've been bad, but I was able to outsmart him and get him out." *Outsmart.* I mentally roll my eyes. That's a good word for learning I'm actually part villain and using my "powers" for the first time tonight.

Jay's mouth is on mine before I even know what's happening.

"What the hell was that for?" I breathe.

"By the time I got inside, you had Adam scrambling from the house. Since when did you become such a warrior? It suits you."

It takes everything in me to pull the corners of my mouth into what I hope is a grin. I want to smile so badly, because I should be so proud to take on that title, but all I feel is shame.

When he discovers the truth about me, it'll change everything.

I fight back tears as I answer. "I have this badass superhero guy I'm trying to impress. Do you think it's working?"

He tries to pull me to him, but I move away, putting more distance between us. "It's not going to if you don't *come here*," he answers.

Swaying from right to left, I force a small laugh. "Jay…" My breath comes out in short gasps.

"What's wrong?" He stills when I hold my hands up, silently urging him to stay back.

I shake my hands out, letting them fall to my sides. "I just…need some space. Do you mind sleeping downstairs tonight?" I wait a beat. "Please?"

The light in his eyes flickers in and out as he peers between both of mine. I can feel him desperately searching for reasons to explain what's happening.

"Uh, sure. Yeah. That's fine."

I kiss his cheek as he passes by, a spark tickling my lips. *Oh no. This can't be happening. Not again.*

Jay grabs his cheek. "Sorry. I must be short-circuiting from all of this."

Putting my hand to my mouth, I watch him stumble into the doorframe as he leaves. I so badly want to reach out and touch him, but resist. "Love you," I whisper.

He looks back at me, the color of his eyes slowly drifting away. "Super love you…JT forever?"

I pause almost a beat too long, "And always."

I close the door behind him, my hands cupping my face as I slump to the floor. The emotion rips through my chest and tries to tear me apart from the inside out as tears glide down my face.

Trying to keep quiet, I bite down on the skin of my forearm, mouthing into it, "There's nothing super about me." My body starts to rock back and forth as I silently scream toward the ceiling, feeling that same power try to consume me once more. "There's nothing super about me."

CHAPTER SEVENTEEN

After a week of isolating and hoping to wake up from this freakish nightmare, I finally let Jay talk me into going out to dinner in honor of getting rid of my dad again.

For now, anyway.

I just finish up getting ready when I hear the honking of Jay's car from the driveway. "Mom! Jay is here. Will you please tell him I'll be right down?" I shout from upstairs.

"Sure! She can let me know!" Jay shouts back. I smile to myself. That man and his super speed.

"Shut up, ya jerk!" I holler, packing my things up quickly, anxious to see how I'll feel once I see him. I know I can't keep something like this a secret for much longer.

I can just picture him placing both of his hands around his big mouth as he yells back to me, "Sorry, can't hear you!"

I roll my eyes. He is something else entirely.

Slipping on my boots, I look in the full-length mirror that hangs on the inside of my closet door. My black leggings are a stark contrast against the white, long-sleeved sweater that falls to my knees. It's the perfect somewhat chilly spring ensemble for me.

I huff a breath, steadying myself enough to make it down the stairs and attempt to pull off some normalcy. *Deep breath, T.*

When I make it to the bottom of the stairs, it's like all the breath has been sucked right out of my lungs. Jay is leaning his left shoulder against the wooden front door, peering down at his phone, his right leg crossed over his left ankle. He looks so damn fine, and I'm thankful he didn't hear me come down so that I can take the time to study just how good he looks.

He oozes liquid heat. The jeans covering his legs are not too tight, not too loose, and hug in all the right places. His muscular quads stretch the upper leg of the material, showing off just how much he works out…or maybe it's just the super-hero hormones that keep him buff. The bottom of his pants cover just enough of his dark leather brown Timberlands, a small detail of Jay's style that I very much admire.

Letting my eyes wander upward, I find a baby-blue polo that clings to every single part of his deep chest and thick arms that I love. My mouth goes dry at the sight.

Reaching his face, I take note of the very sexy five o'clock shadow that coats his skin, but before I make it to the hat covering his hair, I'm mesmerized by his brilliant blue eyes that are even brighter because of his shirt color. My eyes don't dare flinch; they stay locked on his, tantalizing heat scorching me from afar.

Jay finally breaks the silence by cracking his heart-stopping smile my way. "Don't you look gorgeous, as always." He pushes off the door, removing his hat to comb a hand through his hair before walking over to the stairs. "You going to come down here, or do I have to come get you?"

The question startles me. I'm still five stairs away from him, but it suddenly seems to be too close, the secret I'm keeping crowding the distance between us.

I make my way down to the landing, where he's holding out his hand to help me step down. "Ever the gentleman," I say, my gaze remaining on him when we touch, looking for any signs of whatever evil powers lurk beneath my skin.

"For you? Always." His warm mouth gently kisses mine. I resist pulling him in deeper, but man, do I want to. "Spin around. Let's see just how good you look in this new outfit."

I hold onto the finger he dangles above me and spin around like a ballerina in a music box, cackling as I go. When I stop, I fall into his rigid chest and look up at him through my lashes. "Well? What do you think?"

His strong grip squeezes my butt, sending shivers up my spine. "What do *you* think?" He pulls me closer, and I gasp when I feel the hardness pressing into my stomach. He shoots me a cheesy wink and lets me go.

I spin around and grab the doorknob, "Bye, Mom! We're heading out!" I've got to get out of here before he makes me do something I shouldn't do with my mother in the house, or before I just go back to pretending nothing has changed.

"Have fun, you two. I love you!"

Jay leans down to kiss me behind the ear. What I was just about to say suddenly leaves my mind, but I quickly regain my composure and respond, "Love you more!"

Closing the door behind me, I check that it's locked and am swiftly lifted by Jay's arms. "What the hell are you doing?" I yelp between fits of laughter.

"Oh, just sweeping you off your feet," he smirks, carrying me to his car.

I kiss his cheek, secretly taking in a breath of his cologne. "You are so punny, Jay Tenlin."

"I know," he whispers in my ear. "Now, let's get this over with so I can show you how serious I can be, too."

The way he says that last part has me swallowing loudly. There's something about hearing him declare how badly he wants me right now that has me wishing this date was already over.

After he sets me down next to the car, he kisses my forehead before opening my door to usher me inside. I slip in and buckle the seatbelt, watching Jay strut to his side in the rearview mirror.

This is going to be interesting.

Taking our seats, I look around at the very fancy restaurant Jay's chosen for dinner tonight. "This place is gorgeous," I mutter. "How can you afford this?"

The glass water cups, linen napkins, and shimmery chandeliers are all the tells I need to know that this place isn't going to be cheap. We really have no business being here. What kind of date is this, anyway?

"Tonight is special. I wanted to make it one to remember."

Hm. Interesting.

I raise my glass and wait for him to do the same. "I guess time will tell." We clink them and take a sip before setting them down.

Idle chit-chat keeps us busy as we eat our delicious dinner. Waiting for dessert now has my stomach grumbling, making me wonder if my meal consisted of air. I place my hand over it, wondering if my nerves are getting to me.

Staring over at Jay as he scans the room, I wonder if he could ever find it in himself to love someone—or some*thing* —like me. I mean, does it ever work out between the hero and the enemy?

All of a sudden, our love seems to hold some sort of catastrophic risk. And I know how risks work—I can either see what happens, or run from it. And even then, there's a chance everything will go wrong. In the case of heroes and villains, someone always has to be the bad guy; someone has to lose; someone has to make a sacrifice.

Would I be willing to sacrifice everything I have with Jay just to protect him from me? Absolutely. Could I live without him? Yes. But would I want to? Never.

Jay clears his throat, ripping me away from my dark inner dialogue. "Baby," he says in a voice that sends me shifting in my seat.

"Hm?"

"I have something to tell you." I search his eyes for any signs as to what this might be about, but all I find in them is love and excitement. What could he possibly be so excited about when I feel as if everything is over?

"I want to start by telling you that you are the strongest, most courageous woman I've yet to find. I'm so proud of you for standing up to your dad, even though I know it hurt you."

Bullshit. How could someone you hate hurt you? If only he knew how much bigger than my dad this was.

"You may not think it hurt you, but it did. I know this might not make much sense, but ever since I got home, you've been different, even when you were with me. Now that Adam is gone, things will start to get better for you." He reaches for my hand. I almost fight to yank it away, but I talk myself down from whatever I might do to unintentionally hurt him. "I've missed you. I just wish I could've saved you from the pain that locked you away in the first place, and for that, I'll never be able to apologize enough.

"With that being said, these last couple months have been nothing short of amazing. If I knew my life could've been this great all this time, I would've made you mine sooner." He stops suddenly, and I give him a questioning glance.

"What?" I ask. He shakes his head like I just woke him from a dream. What the hell is going on with him?

"I'm sorry. Your eyes are just so beautiful when you have tears lining them…happy tears, to be precise."

"What has you so sappy, Jay? You are killing me over here." I lift my glass to my lips and take a sip of water, washing down the heightened emotions this conversation has coursing through me.

"I'm sorry." Jay arches his back and huffs out a deep breath. "Enough waiting. Okay. So, I received a new mission." A wide smile spreads across his face. His enthusiasm is contagious, but I can't help the worry spreading throughout my stomach.

How could he possibly leave when there is so much going on? Even though my dad left, it doesn't mean he'll stay away. Apparently, Jay's mind control couldn't even keep him at bay. It obviously has an expiration date of some sort. And don't even get me started on what needs to be done to figure out what the hell is going on inside of me.

"So you're leaving me?" It slips out without a second thought. The smile on his face instantaneously drops, a frown quickly taking its place.

"T, it's not like that."

But it *is* like that. He's going to leave, and who knows what will happen to me in the meantime.

"When do you leave? How long will you be gone? Where are you going?" I gasp for air before trying to continue my slew of questions.

"Tatum," his calming voice has my eyes snapping to his,

"breathe." I take a deep breath, closing my eyes and imagining I'm anywhere but here.

"Jay, I just—"

"Just let me finish, all right?" I try my best to nod. Probably best if I don't say anything right now anyway. "My dad asked me to go on a mission throughout South America. There are some promising leads on new REDs there. This will be my first time traveling to try and get more heroes trained throughout the world!"

"Wait a second…let's go back to my first question. So you're leaving me? At the very moment that I need you the most?"

"What? Are you listening to yourself? Did you hear a single word I said about you just a few minutes ago?" His hands are waving in the air now. "I'll never leave you. The only way this will ever end is if you leave me. I'm in this 110%." *Until you hear the truth about me…* "And what do you mean about leaving when you need me most? Are you…okay?"

I stare down at the table, pinching my nose and trying my best to ignore that last question. "Please tell me then, Jay. Please tell me when you're leaving, how long you'll be gone, and when I'll be seeing you again. Lord knows I'm holding onto my seat, waiting to know when I'll be alone again."

The sad look in his eyes tells me that this conversation is not going how he planned. He's fully regretting it. "I need to be in Brazil by the end of the month."

"End of the *month*? We won't even be done with classes! What about final exams?" The fight in his eyes is gone. I'm coming at him from all sides, draining the excitement out of every aspect of his big news. Maybe that's another power of mine: devastation.

He ignores my extra questions and starts finishing what he started. "I'll be there for a full month, returning the last week of May. All of my professors agreed to let me take my exams early."

I want to cry. Not just because he will be leaving me soon, but because the light that covered his face when he started telling me about this trip has now dissipated, and I'm fully aware that it's all my fault. This darkness is already starting to seep into everything good in my life.

"How can you possibly leave at a time like this?" I slam my hand down on the table, the glasses and silverware clinking against each other and the table. Fellow customers look over at me, giving me questioning glares. "Do you know how much is at stake?"

"Tatum…" he's staring at me when I move my gaze over to him. "*What* is wrong?"

He takes my hand in his, and we both blanch when the now-familiar ricocheting, painful shock flows between our hands. "Damn it! Not again!"

"I'm sorry, I didn't mean to shock you." He pulls away, looking at his own hands as if *he's* the one who's damaged. How he could ever even consider that *he* might be the problem is baffling. The sight makes me sick to my stomach. "I don't know why I keep doing that."

"It's fine. I-I have to go. I need air." I stand and blindly round the table, confusion and anger swirling its way through me.

"Tatum," Jay says, standing up too. I hold my hand up, urging him to stay put, and I continue on, leaving him behind me.

I abandon him in that stuffy, fancy restaurant and walk out

the front door. I have no idea where to go from here. What do I tell him? How do I tell him? Who do I ask?

While I know I shouldn't be walking in the dark alone, I just can't stand to be anywhere near Jay at the moment. Slipping through a nearby street, I sneak my way toward home, praying that paying the bill will stall him long enough.

The walk home is quiet and dark, giving me loads of time to think about what to do from here. Not that I've got anything yet. It's obvious that there is never going to be the perfect moment to tell Jay what is wrong with me.

After all he's done for me, he deserves to know. He deserves the chance to get away from me.

I forgot how much being outside has always had a way of calming me down. While Jay was gone, I was too afraid to even walk past Adam half the time, so staying holed up in my room felt easier.

Trudging along the edge of my fence, I wind my way down the ditch behind our yard. This has been my favorite outdoor place ever since I was a kid. I love the way the branches and leaves cover the walkway with moonlit shadows, giving it a magical fairy garden vibe.

Making it to my favorite tree, I cast a glance up at the full moon.

I run my hand along the cracks and sinews of bark that cover the tree's trunk and pat the area that's been perfectly carved by nature to resemble a seat. The stepping hole still remains in the trunk, so I push my foot into it and hoist myself up.

Once I settle in, I breathe a sigh of relief. This tree has

been my faithful companion for most of my life. Leaning against one of the thick branches, I whisper, "It's been a long time, my friend."

After wrestling my phone out of my tiny clutch, the lit up screen makes me cringe. It's way too bright for being out here at night. I have no missed calls or texts, but I'm surprised to see that it's 9:00 PM and Jay still hasn't found me. It took longer to get here than I thought.

"I knew I'd find you out here, Pink Moon." Right on cue, Jay's angelic voice breaks through the silence of the night.

I chuckle, but even that feels forced. "Pink Moon?" Now that is a nickname I've never heard him use on me before.

"Yeah. It's April."

"And?" I urge on.

"You have loved the night sky your entire life…particularly the moon. Ever since, I've studied tiny tidbits about that giant ball of cheese and all the balls of gas that surround it to try to understand you better."

Is he being serious right now? He has studied the night sky just for me?

"Prove it."

I watch as he wanders over to me, careful not to trip over any of the roots jutting out of the ground. "Do you think this old guy will still hold the both of us up?" he asks, patting the patch of branch next to me.

I shrug, watching as his strong arms reach the limb above us that he then uses to lift himself into the air before plopping down next to me. The bough sways a little, but stands firm. "Atta boy, Old Man Hickory."

I laugh, lifting an eyebrow at him, "You remember that?"

"I remember everything."

I smile sadly at his truth. Jay has always had such an easy

time reminiscing about all the years of our friendship, some-times remembering things about me that I have since forgot-ten. There was even one time he reminded me about the day I kicked Landon Starnick's shin on the playground in first grade for pushing Jay off the monkey bars.

I'll deny it until the day I die, but Jay swears by the memory. He said that was the moment he knew that I'd always have his back. I never let him down, and I've had his back ever since. Can I handle disappointing him like I'm about to?

"Yeah, yeah. We know. Now, get to proving." I just want a few more minutes of being the same old JT we've always been before I break his heart and ruin everything we've built.

"Every month of the year, the full moon goes by a different name. Remember in *Pocahontas* when she sings about being under the 'blue corn moon?'" I nod. "That moon phase occurs in September and is also known as the Full Harvest Moon. It's close to the time when crops are harvested."

"What did you call the moon tonight?" I question, growing far more curious about this topic than I was expect-ing. If nothing else, it serves as a great distraction.

"The Pink Moon, because it's April. The Native Ameri-cans call it that because of a certain wildflower that grows at this time."

I stare at the moon. How can something remain so beau-tiful when it is surrounded by darkness?

"Can you tell me more about the moon names?" His laugh rings out in the night. "What?"

"I told you. You're such a Uranophile."

"A what?" The term sounds dirty in some way.

"A person who loves the moon, stars, and everything

found in the sky." I hesitantly lean into his shoulder as he speaks, and feel his arm wrap around me to pull me closer. I guess he knows me better than I actually know myself.

"You really have always loved me, haven't you?"

"Always. And I plan to keep loving you, T."

"Time will tell, won't it?"

"Mmhm," he agrees, kissing my hair. "I'm sorry, T."

"For what?"

"I should've told you about the mission thing in a different way." There he is, feeling bad again when he shouldn't.

I pull back and look at his face. "Don't be sorry, Jay. It's me who should be apologizing to you."

"For what?" I lean forward and kiss his mouth, trying desperately to memorize the feel of his lips against mine.

"There's something wrong with me."

He jumps down from the tree, startling me, before turning to face me. His hand cups my cheek, bringing tears to my eyes.

"T, what do you mean?"

"I-I-I just found out something, and I'm not sure how you're going to take it."

"Are you sick?" His other hand comes up to cup my other cheek.

I shake my head. "No. No, nothing like that. It's worse. So much worse."

"What could be worse than you being sick?"

I place my hand over his, accidentally shocking him again. But this one is bigger. Jay's hand falls from my face and he staggers backwards, leaning against a tree.

"Fuck! I'm sorry, T. I don't know what is happening to me."

I jump down from the tree next, going to reach for him, but just as quickly let my arm fall back down. "It's not you."

"Don't be silly. My powers are messing up and—"

"Stop!" I yell, unable to take it anymore. "It's not you, damn it! It's *me*! Can't you see? I'm not good for you!"

Recovering, he starts to walk toward me. I throw my hand out, urging him to stop. "Stay away from me!" I scream, squeezing my head between my hands. Pain courses through my brain, my eyes feeling like they're being warmed up in a microwave.

Suddenly, blue lightning flickers between us, but it's different. There's a dark purplish tinge to it, and it seems to be staring directly into my eyes.

The lightning. It's not coming from Jay. It's coming from me, and it's trying with all its might to make it to him. I slam my eyes shut, trying to fight back.

"Make it *stop*!" I shriek, falling to the ground and curling up against the tree trunk.

"Tatum! Tatum! What is happening?" His hand touches my shoulder, but I push him away, looking up to find him soaring through the air and into a nearby oak before slamming to the ground. I so badly want to run over and help him, but I resist, afraid I'll inflict more damage.

"You can't save me, Jay! You can't."

Jay looks at me, a slight shift in his eyes. If I'm seeing correctly, I swear he is almost afraid of me. "T, l-let's call my dad. He can help."

"No! You don't understand." I sit up, propelling myself back into the bark of the tree, letting the wood scratch my skin through my clothes.

"Then help me to understand. It's obvious I did something to you—"

"It wasn't you! It was my piece of shit dad!"

Jay's eyebrows furrow. "What did he do to you?"

"He made me, Jay. He made me what I am."

"What do you mean?"

I heave a deep breath. "He's a villain, Jay."

He snorts as he shifts against the opposing tree. "I mean, we all knew that."

"No." I shake my head again. "No. He's an *actual* villain. Your enemy, Jay!"

"Wait…you mean…a VOE?"

"If that's what you call the bad guys all of you at RED are trying so hard to defeat."

Jay starts to pace. "Shit. Holy shit! I'm going to kill him." He presses something on his watch before making his way over to me.

"Don't touch me. There's more."

"Tatum, I need to get to RED. We have to get rid of your dad and figure out who he's working for."

I completely ignore what he's just said. "It's me who's been shocking you. You're not the one malfunctioning, Jay. It's me."

"You're being ridiculous. There's no way. Your dad's just getting in your head."

I press against the ground, forcing myself up to stand before him, staring deep within those breathtaking blue eyes. "There is when you are the product of a villain."

"You can't be serious, T."

"Did you not see what I just did? I am a villain, Jay, and my dad will stop at nothing to figure out what powers I have."

If I didn't know better, I'd think Jay just became a statue. "You can't be. No."

"But I am. You aren't the first person I've done this to. Koral. I—"

He rakes his hand through his hair. "She stumbled after you touched her! And when she came back out, she looked like she'd just gotten over having the flu for a week."

"I know. I—"

"We've gotta go," he says, reaching out to take my hand.

I wrench it away. "Jay, wait!"

He whips around, looking at me, his shoulders sagging. "We'll fix this. I'll find a way to fix you."

My knees almost give out, because just as I feared, there's something inside me that needs to be fixed.

I'm broken.

"I need you to come with me, baby. Please." His voice comes out in spurts as he begs.

I shake my head, my face crumbling. "I can't risk it. I can't." And before I know what I'm truly asking him to do, it's out of my mouth. "Just go."

"I will not leave you here. No way!" His chest is heaving, his face pinching tight in pain.

"You have to."

"Why?"

"Because I'm asking you to."

A sort of frustration comes over him, and without another word, he catapults into the sky. The leaves of the trees and the plants along the ground bend and bow beneath his power.

I stare up after him, tears streaming down my face, knowing that the danger of hurting him mid-flight could be disastrous. There's no way I could chance it.

Observing the sky once more, I silently talk to Jay, hoping with all that I have that if there was ever a time I would want him to be reading my thoughts, it would be right now…

You can't fix the darkness, Jay. Not even the stars and moon can get rid of it. They shine what they can through the murk and gloom, but everything still hides away.

Even the daylight holds consequences. Shadows follow everything, permanently tying us to the ruin.

I am no different.

There's devastation, and destruction, and even catastrophe.

I just so happen to be desolation.

CHAPTER EIGHTEEN

Three days pass before Jay finally comes to me again. While I know he didn't want to leave me behind, I needed him to. And even though I probably shouldn't have been alone the last couple days, I needed that too; to come to terms that things are going to change, and I hate that.

In the meantime, I've done what I could to distract my mom. Lies about staying with Jay, seeing my friends, and studying for exams while sneaking around without being seen have kept her at bay so I could keep her safe from me until her busy weekend of work.

Now that I know what I am, I don't want to risk a single thing where my mother is concerned.

I break my stare from the glow-in-the-dark stars dotted along my ceiling when I hear my phone chime next to me.

Jay: Meet me outside?

Me: On my way...

Moving through the house and out the front door, I stop on the porch, focusing on Jay, who is standing on the sidewalk three steps down from me.

"Hey," I whisper, rubbing my hands up and down my arms.

He gives me a somber smile. "Hey. You okay?"

I lift a shoulder. "How am I supposed to know?"

"That's why I'm here. I'm going to take you to RED. Let's see what we can figure out on our own."

"It's not safe, Jay."

He comes up a step, freezing when I hold my hand up for him to stay put. "Baby, if you want to talk technicalities, it's probably not safe for you to be around me either."

I laugh. "How the hell could you possibly think that?"

"Well? Why do you think so many superheroes in the movies don't end up with someone in the end?"

"Not true! Iron Man ended up with Pepper." I choke back a sob, so desperately wanting him to be wrong.

"And look how that ended up for them!"

"Take it back!" I yell, moving closer. "Take it back right now!"

He conquers another step, reaching out to me, his fingers brushing my arm. "I can't. Not if you don't give this a try. We can do this, T."

I grab my head. "You don't know that! The good guys don't end up with the bad. That's not how it works." I move closer this time, my skin vibrating. "I am your sworn enemy, Jay! There's no way you can love me."

"But I do, damn it!" His voice booms, but he just as quickly quiets it back down. "I do love you. More than anything. I know your heart, T. Your heart is not evil. Far from it, actually."

I close my eyes, trying my best to believe that what he's saying is true. "I'm scared, Jay." My voice is just barely a whisper, but he catches it, flashing next to me and pulling me tight to him. I don't have the energy to resist him this time.

"Tatum, just think about it for a minute. Think about who

you are, who your mom is, what we've built." His large hand cups over the right side of my head as he hugs me to his chest. His heart lub-dubs against my ear, and the sound works like magic. "Listen to my heart. You might not always believe what I say, but I hope you can believe that. It only beats for you."

"But what if I hurt you?" I whisper.

He must sense I'm about to pull away, because he pulls me even closer before saying, "Your touch could cause me physical pain for the rest of my life, and I'd still love you through it."

I force myself to breathe deeply, fighting off any worry that could potentially hurt him when he's this close to me, trying my best to absorb his words at the same time.

After a few minutes, Jay gently pulls my arms from around him, pushing me back a smidgen to stare into my eyes. "I need you to come to RED with me, okay?"

I reluctantly nod, knowing this is something that must be done. "I'm ready."

He takes my hand in his and pulls me to his car.

Pulling into TI Industries has my stomach in knots. "Have you told anyone?"

"Only Maleko and my dad."

"They must hate me, huh?" I look out my window, noting the mostly empty parking lot as Jay puts the car in park. Pa is probably beside himself with this news.

"Pa could never hate you. If nothing else, he's sorry you're going through this. He wants you to know that he'll do anything he can to help." Jay pauses. "As for Maleko, he has a hard time hating anyone. He agrees with me that this is just an unfortunate situation, T. But that doesn't mean people should hate you. You can't help what you're born of. All you can do is make a difference with what you've got. Maleko believes in you, and so does Pa."

I smile at my lap. Getting out the door, I reply, "I hope they're right."

"They're both pretty wise, I'd say." Jay takes my hand in his, gripping tightly when I try to pull away. "If you keep thinking about it, you're going to hurt me."

"I'd never mean to."

"There's the T I know. That T could never be the enemy in my story."

There's good and evil in all of us. I'm just a firm believer you don't always have a choice in what life tries to mold you to be. I know I'd never want to be a villain, but what if Adam never meant to be either?

What if it wasn't always a choice? What if it sometimes came down to fate?

Maleko is peering through the eye of the microscope as I sway my legs back and forth on the medical bed in a replica of a doctor's office of sorts. "What's this room for?" I ask him, trying to fill the silence without Jay in here.

"This is the room we sometimes administer injections in." A shiver ripples over my skin as I glance at the restraints near the top and bottom of the bed, a jar of bite splints sitting on the counter.

My eyes scan the only picture in the room, a painting of red splotches that don't seem to have any rhyme or reason for their placement. "Does everyone get the same injection?"

"Yes. It conforms to everyone's DNA differently, which is why each hero gets a unique power."

"Right." I kick my legs now, growing more antsy. "Jay's unique power was mind control."

"Was?" Maleko looks over his shoulder at me before moving to write on a piece of paper.

"I've noticed him doing some other things that don't seem to be the regular RED powers that you all get. What's that about?"

His pen twitches. Most would probably miss it, but when your brain is working as fast as mine is, you can't pass over it. "I'm not sure what you're talking about, I guess. Might be something you need to ask him about."

The tone of his words holds so much power. He just confirmed what I thought. Jay is different from the rest of them. How, I'm not sure. But maybe it's best if I don't know. If my dad comes back, I don't want to have information that could put Jay at risk, that he could potentially try to torture out of me.

"Did Jay's dad teach you how to do all of this stuff?"

Maleko nods as he continues writing, "Oh yeah. And he's since hired some really great experts. I'm no professional, myself, but I know enough. Plus, the more you come around, the more you'll see him down here. My education with him never stops."

I silently nod my head—not that he is looking at me to see it—and enjoy the sound of his pen on the paper while I wait for him to finish.

"What ya scribbling over there, Doc? How's our patient?" Jay's voice breaks through the silence.

Maleko turns around, leaning against the counter as he faces us. "She definitely has some of the bad stuff in her."

"So, what does this mean? What do I do now?" I ask.

"Since your only problem right now seems to be accidentally *shocking* people, I'd say you're pretty stable." Maleko scratches at his temple before crossing his arms over his chest. "Unfortunately, we don't know much about this. Other than keeping this a secret as we find out more, I think you should just watch for any changes. We should document this entire process."

I leap down off the table. "Let me get this straight. I'm supposed to just go about my merry way without knowing if I could seriously hurt someone? Are you *nuts*?" Jay laughs next to me. I glare at him, feeling as if heat waves are cascading off of me. "What the hell are you laughing at?"

"T. You act like this is only you. What do you think we do after we receive our injections? We gotta wait around to see what our powers even are, constantly unsure of when they'll show, how they'll make their presence known, and what exactly will trigger them. We're not so different."

"For being your enemy, you sure have a lot of faith in me."

"Never doubted you for a second," he says before placing a kiss on my cheek. "Let's go home."

I stay back as Jay makes his way to the door. "Wait." I spin around to face Maleko. "Thank you, Maleko. I really appreciate your help."

"*Ko 'u hau'oli.*"

"What does that mean exactly?"

"No problem, sweetheart," he answers, moving over to Jay.

Grabbing my bag, I make it to the doorway, smiling for

the first time in what feels like a lifetime. These men have no idea how much they've calmed the storm brewing inside of me. They make me feel like everything could actually turn out okay.

"See ya, Mal." Jay and Maleko fistbump before Jay moves back over to me, sliding his hand around my waist.

"Maleko?" I start once more. "Could I have your number, please?"

Before I even have a chance to explain, Jay's arm drops from around me, and he and Maleko look at me with wide eyes and even wider mouths.

"Well, fuck. Tell her she's a safe-for-now villain and she's looking for a new man," Jay groans.

"I'm confused," Maleko adds.

I can't help but burst out in laughter. "You guys are so dense. I just mean for emergencies."

"What kind of emergencies are we talking, babe?" Jay's hands collide, and my eyes can't resist watching them wrap around each other. Seeing him wringing his hands sends my mind reeling, remembering how that was a tic of mine not too long ago when things were really bad with my anxiety. I've come a long way, and my problems have only grown bigger.

"Forgive me if I'm wrong, but is a certain someone in this room not going on a mission on the opposite side of the world soon? Who am I supposed to call when I blow a fuse in the house getting mad at my blow dryer?"

Maleko wipes at the sweat along his forehead, casting a glance at Jay.

"Oh. Damn it." He moves over to me, fishing my phone out of my pocket before walking it to Maleko. "Will you please put your phone number in here? And not under some stupid name like Mal the Hunk or Hawaiian Horn Dog.

You're the only one I trust to look over my girl, but I know how she is with superheroes. I don't need her looking for an extra man."

"Extra?" I ask, giggling to myself.

"I have high hopes you wouldn't up and leave me, but I'm not exactly sure you'd shut down a throuple."

"Jayson Tenlin!" I yell. "You are terrible."

He winks at me, and that distant, familiar spark inside my belly seems to erupt throughout my body. "You have no idea how terrible I can be, baby."

The tone of his voice sounds much more seductive than it should within the confines of this office and a foot away from one of his closest friends.

Maleko finishes up with my phone and tosses it to me. I catch it and slide it back into my pocket. "Don't ask me to be your stand-in boyfriend while this dweeb is away, okay? Get out of here before he tries to *oof* you in this room."

That is one Hawaiian term I don't have to ask for interpretation of. "I think that's our cue, Jay."

Jay zips through the door, pulling me behind him. "Say no more, T."

I laugh as he zooms along with me in tow, not entirely sure how I'm somewhat keeping up with him. "You are too—"

Jay cuts me off: "Too sexy for my shirt. I know. I know…"

We make it back to his car and to his house before I know it. All the while, I think about how at ease Jay and Maleko have made me feel. Maybe Jay was right; maybe being born evil doesn't have to be my ending. Maybe it's my origin.

CHAPTER NINETEEN

I'm swaying back and forth to Justin Bieber while cooking eggs in Jay's kitchen. Being sure to keep the music low, I watch as the eggs get more firm each second they cook, the steam wafting up to blow across my face.

I was so unsure about staying here last night, let alone letting Jay touch me, but just like when I was battling my debilitating anxiety and panic attacks over my dad, Jay has found a way to help ground me once more, assuring me he can handle whatever might happen.

I know that Jay is obviously a superhero—in so many words—but they have their own kryptonite; that I'm sure of. Now that I think about it, Jay has never mentioned what his weakness is. And at this moment, I really don't want to know. I'm adding it to my list of TBTs (to-be-tolds) for once we are officially safe from Adam.

"I'm starting to think all my shirts were specifically made just for you," Jay says with a croaky voice.

I smile to myself before looking over my shoulder, my eyes moving over every inch of him. I lick my lips once I turn back around, "I assure you, they were made for you. They just so happen to look good on me too. Luck of the trade, I guess." I grab the salt and pepper on the counter next to me and shake both of them over the eggs, one after the other, before stirring it a final time.

Jay's arm brushes my side as he turns off the burner, his mouth kissing my ear at the same time. I close my eyes and sigh heavily. "Smells good in here," he whispers.

"After all our exercise last night, I thought we needed a protein-filled breakfast, ya know?" I turn around, grateful he spins out of my way to let me by. I don't want to take too many chances where he's concerned. Last night was more than enough trial for a twenty-four hour period for me.

He pretty much poofs into existence on the opposite side of the island, facing me. Our eyes latch onto each other's as I scoop the eggs onto two plates that already have some turkey sausage on them. Jay glances down at his watch. "Post-breakfast workout in fifteen?" He winks at me, a devastatingly handsome grin putting his perfect teeth on display.

I shake my head, laughing. "I don't know…maybe."

"We'll see about that." Jay leans across the counter and pulls his plate toward one of the chairs on his side of the island. I toss him a fork that he catches with his eyes closed.

Staying on my side so I can see his face, I plop some eggs into my mouth, wondering how nonchalant I can make this conversation. "Can I ask you something?"

"Sure."

"You have more powers than the other REDs, don't you?" I question, noticing his fork freeze in mid-air.

He chews slowly, his eyes locked on mine as he nods. "Yes. I was waiting to tell you since you've had so much information to take in these past few months. Would you like to know how?"

I hold up my fork, shaking my head. "Nope. Don't say a word."

"What? Why?"

"I don't want to know anything that Adam might use against me. I just wanted to know if I was right."

A moment of silence passes before I glance up from my plate again. "What's wrong?" I ask Jay, who is concentrating way too hard in my direction.

"I can't get into your head."

"And you want to?" My mind races, wondering how often he tries to. I wouldn't want him to know half of what's going on up there these days.

"I just wanted to see if it's changed since your powers started developing. Don't worry, I never did it often. I would never infringe on your privacy like that, T."

My fork tumbles onto the plate as I straighten and place my hands on my hips. "Why did you ever do it, Jay? What were you looking for?"

"I only did it once or twice, just to see what was going through your head." He runs a hand through his hair and pushes back from the counter, starting to pace back and forth. "Do you know how hard it was to resist when you were so plagued with darkness? I wanted so badly to know what was happening to you, but wanted you to be the one to tell me. I would never take your truth from you, not without your permission."

I let out a hefty breath, leaning over the counter while pushing up on my toes and then back down. "But you could have."

"I could have, but I'd never. Your thoughts are your own. I would never want you to think I manipulated anything about you or us. The only thing I ever did was help calm you down after the fight between Adam and I."

My mind goes back to that day as I swallow down the emotion building in my throat. "Thank you."

Before I realize he's rounded the corner, Jay is softly lifting my chin so that our gazes meet. "You don't have to thank me for the bare minimum, Tatum. My job is to protect you, not own you."

I nod in his touch. "I have one more question. I don't want you to get specific, but I'd like a yes or a no so that I know what I'm dealing with. Okay?"

"Mhm. Go for it."

My eyes move between his. "Do REDs have weaknesses?"

He drops my chin and moves back an inch. "Yes."

"Okay."

So many thoughts are dashing through my mind. Ever since my villainous side started to show up, Jay now has a hard time reading my mind. It's also somewhat dangerous for us to touch. And now I know that REDs do have weaknesses.

How in the world am I not only supposed to protect this man from me, but also my dad *and* any other villains who might be after him?

I now understand the pressure Jay is constantly under. There are too many variables when it comes to keeping those you love safe.

There's a certain standard to be expected pertaining to keeping loved ones safe from harm, but what about when it comes to protecting them from yourself? How do you know when the darkness is starting to take over?

"Where are you going?" Jay asks, combing through his hair with his hands as he walks out with just a towel wrapped around his waist.

I try my best to look elsewhere because I cannot be late for what I have planned. "I have some things I need to do."

"Are you sure that's a good idea? Adam could be out there."

I glare at him, keeping my eyes trained on his face. "Let's call it like it is, Jay. Adam *is* out there. He's coming for me whether we like it or not. I can't hide in the shadows from the darkness."

Jay saunters over to me, lifting my seemingly light bag from the floor and setting it on the bed. His gaze is hooded as he stares down at me. "Damn."

I half-grin. "What?"

"Normally, darkness eats away at people, making them crumble from the inside out. You seem to be having the opposite effect. Instead of incinerating you, it seems to be catching, growing stronger and stronger within you. I don't know whether to be scared or impressed."

I try not to flinch. "Well, I hope you don't *have* to be afraid."

Jay presses his lips to mine, and electricity shoots off everywhere throughout my body. I pull away, frightened I'm hurting him again, but he holds me still against him.

My hands move from his waist, over his chiseled abs, and up to his powerful chest as I moan into his mouth. The sparks dancing across our lips are addicting.

When he pulls his mouth from mine, there's a carnal hunger in his eyes. Our breaths come out haggard and loud. "If you have somewhere to be, I suggest you get out of here before I do everything in my power to lock you in this room."

I grab my bag and lift it onto my shoulder, dancing up on my tiptoes to kiss Jay's cheek. "Love you. I'll call you later."

He smacks my butt as I walk by, making me squeal. "Text me when you get where you're going, or the hero in me will have to come searching for his damsel in distress."

I blow him a kiss and rush through the house toward the door, screaming when I grab the door handle as Jay appears out of thin air next to it to kiss my forehead. "Love you more, T."

My phone beeps with a new message as I hear the door click behind me. It's Maleko.

> Maleko: I'll be at RED in fifteen minutes. See you guys there.

I round the corner of the house, glancing behind me as I slip into the back of the UBER I ordered half an hour ago. I sort of fibbed to Maleko and told him Jay was coming with me, so I obviously had to beat him with a text first, or he probably would've started a group chat. I can't have that. This is something I need to do on my own. I'm choosing to operate on a "do first, tell later" agenda for right now.

"Where to, ma'am?" the older gentleman from the front seat prods.

"TI Industries, please."

Repeating the process I watched Jay do not so long ago, though I enter a code Maleko gave me instead of the whole fingerprint ordeal, I find my way into RED headquarters below the main floors of TI Industries.

When the elevator doors ping open, I scan the floor, looking for signs of inhabitance.

"Be right there, guys!" Maleko calls from somewhere nearby. I wring my hands together, nervous he is going to be unhappy with what I'm doing.

He rounds the corner, almost backtracking like he hit a wall, when he notices me alone. "*Aloha*, Tatum. Where is Jay?"

I clear my throat, twirling my hair around my pointer finger. "He didn't come."

"No? Is everything okay?"

I set my bag on the ground, looking up at him as if I find it hard to lift my head. "Actually, I was hoping to ask for your help."

Watching Maleko lift his bulky arm to scratch at his cheek is like watching a thick tree lift a limb all the way to the top to touch the leaves. I continue to be impressed by this tall, burly man. I'm not sure if it has anything to do with his injection, but he is beyond intimidating.

"Okay?"

Putting my hair behind my ears, I huff out a breath before continuing. "Just hear me out…I know I should've told Jay I was coming here, but I don't want to worry him before he goes off on his mission. He's really excited about it, and I have to know that I'm safe for him to be around until he leaves." I carry on before pausing too long, feeling the worry start to stir within me. "Well, I mean, I want him to be safe with me when he returns too. But he's leaving so soon, and I guess I just need some peace of mind."

Maleko sighs like a parent about to say no to their child when they so badly want to say yes. "I will help you, but you're going to have to tell Jay, Tatum. This isn't right."

"I know. I know. Can I just wait to tell him, though?"

He runs a hand through his wavy hair. "Where does he think you are now?"

I shrug. "I wasn't exactly specific. I just told him I had somewhere to be."

A long pause passes between us before Maleko speaks again. "Follow me."

***

"And you're sure this is all for safety precautions?" Maleko questions, his eyes squinting at me every so often.

"What do you mean?"

"You're sure you haven't seen your dad or anything?"

It takes me a second before what he is really asking me registers. "Wait…do you think I'm trying to help my dad? He's a villain! Are you crazy?"

Maleko's hands pulse up and down. "All right, all right. Calm down. I had to make sure. I can't have any VOEs getting secrets through you."

I shake my head, "I'm sorry. VOE?" Jay said that word once, but I never asked what it stood for.

"Yes. Villains of Earth. That's what we call them here at RED."

I blink my eyes quickly. "Does that mean RED stands for something too?"

His smirk is sincere. "Jay never told you?" I shake my head. "It stands for Rare Earth Defenders."

"Wow. I had no idea there were acronyms to study."

"There's a lot to learn about our world, but in the meantime, I think we need to focus on what's going on with you. What do you need me to do?"

I rub my hands along my thighs. "I really just need to know how to control the short-circuiting thingy that keeps happening to me."

Maleko gets up from the couches we've been perched on in the main office to grab a pen and pad of paper from his desk. "Let's break down what we know. When does this short-circuiting happen?"

"As of right now, it's whenever I'm panicking or thinking about it too much."

I think back to when I accidentally shocked Koral, when my mind was reeling about meeting all of the REDs for the first time, worried about what they'd think of me. I also reminisce about the time when I shocked Jay by accident, how he flew into the tree and fell to the ground, and the weird thing it did to my eyes.

How on earth was this really happening to me? It all felt a hell of a lot like when Bella woke up to find herself a vampire, almost crushing Edward to death, and knocking the piss out of Jacob…

I grin to myself. The simple days of reading *Twilight* in my bedroom while Jay read his comics seems like centuries ago.

"Let's try it out, then." Maleko's voice pulls me out of the memories, spiking a new fear inside of me.

"Are you batshit crazy? I could seriously hurt you. Jay got knocked on his ass the last time I shocked him."

He laughs. He actually laughs! "I assure you, I'll be fine."

"Suit yourself," I warn, getting up to throw my hair in a ponytail. "Do we need to go to a training room or something?"

"Nope," he answers. "This is going to be quick. I don't plan on keeping you here all night, *Lolo*."

"That a new nickname for me?"

"Nah. It means crazy." Maleko smacks a giant hand to his abdomen, laughing heartily.

"Very funny, jerk face."

He shakes my shoulder. "I'm just messing with you."

I purse my lips, giving him a glare. "Yeah, yeah. Let's get going."

"Close your eyes," Maleko starts. "Good. Now, I want you to picture your dad."

I wince, betrayal washing through me. I conjure up a recent image of him, his teeth bared at me, black shadows unfurling from all angles of him. "Okay," I whisper shakily.

"I'm going to take your hand now." I'm glad he warned me. "I want you to picture him hurting Jay. He has him backed into a corner, Jay's powers aren't working, and he's quickly losing consciousness."

I shake my head, my eyes suddenly feeling hot. "I don't like this, Mal. Do we—"

"You wanted my help. Do it."

I nod my head, imagining what it would be like to watch Jay be hurt by Adam. Seriously hurt by him.

Before, it wasn't a worry, because once I knew Jay was a RED, I knew he was basically invincible. Now that I know what my dad is, I know that there is some real risk and danger here.

The feeling starts to course through me again. A foreign darkness. It cascades through my body, reminding me of what it feels like to have someone snap a sheet over you so that it can almost pepper over your skin before resting against you. It's not as comforting as that. This feels more like an invader that could be either friend or foe.

"I'm scared, Maleko. Something's happening!" My voice

rises in pitch as the power begins to consume me. "I think we need to stop!"

"Fuck!" Maleko half-yells, his grasp falling away. I stumble back, staring at my hand in bewilderment.

"I'm sorry! I didn't feel the shock. I usually do!" I look over at him, slightly paled, assessing his palm. "Why aren't you on the floor?"

He keeps prodding at his hand before answering, "Did you forget that I'm a RED? I have powers too. Obviously better powers than Jay."

My head tilts in question. "I don't understand."

"My power is a force field. I was able to contain feeling to just my hand, but trust me, I felt it. If I wouldn't have used my power, I think you could've done some real damage. I'm going to be honest, this is all new to me. We are experimenting as we go."

I sink to the floor. "Just what I thought…I'm damaged. I'm no good for Jay. He shouldn't even be near me." I look up at Maleko through blurred vision. "I shouldn't be here."

Maleko moves to sit in front of me, crossing his legs, staring right into my soul. "Tatum, don't throw the towel in just yet. You being here shows me just how badly you want to be good. Focusing too much on the darkness only welcomes it."

"But I'm unpredictable. How come each time I touch someone, the result is different?"

His mouth moves into a straight line as he shakes his head. "I'm not sure. There's a lot we don't know. My guess is that maybe since you haven't fully harnessed your power, you don't inflict the same amount of damage on everyone you come in contact with."

I wipe my eyes. "So, what do I do? What's wrong with me?"

"You go home."

"What?" Is he out of his mind?

"There's a little bit of darkness in everyone. We see our own shadows every single day, even in the daylight. But just because they follow us, doesn't mean that is who we are. You have the power to manipulate that murk and gloom housed inside you. Even heroes have to do things that are questionable sometimes. But you're different. If I didn't know any better, I'd say you were a phoenix, rising from the ashes…"

He pauses, and I use the time to interject. "What if I can't shake off the ashes? What if some of them get stuck on my wings?"

"Then you try to find that in between; that morally gray part. You try to find the good in the bad. Think you can do that?" Maleko pushes up from the ground, offering me his hand once more. I hesitantly take it, wondering if his force field is activated at this very moment, or if he's trying to trust me.

I grab on and pull myself up, "I don't know…"

"Think on it. It's time you go."

I head toward the door, listening to Maleko's stealthy steps following me. I grab my bag and make my way to the elevator, pressing the button. "Thank you, Maleko. Really."

His smile is small, not quite reaching his eyes. "You're welcome."

The elevator dings, and I slip inside, holding down the doors open button. "Will you let me know what you find? About my… condition?"

His nod is short and curt. "I'll research as much as I can. But listen…tell Jay, please?"

"But I—"

"You should tell him, T. He'll kick my ass if you don't."

I let go of the button, just bobbing my head up and down. "Fine," I whisper.

The see-through doors close, and my eyebrows come together as I stare at Maleko. His face concerns me, because if I didn't know better, he was studying me like he's unsure whose side I'm on.

The thing is, I'm starting to wonder that too… Even though I so badly want to be good, I worry that's not enough.

Jay thinks I'm his saving grace, but what if I happen to be his undoing?

Getting into another UBER, I jump when my phone rings, my mind busy thinking too quickly about what to tell Jay. "Hello?" I breathe into the phone, my heart thumping wildly, anxiously awaiting what he'll say.

I jump in my seat when shaky breathing greets me on the other line.

"Hello? Is someone there?" My eyes flinging wide, I glance down at the screen. It reads 'restricted.' I hang up quickly, concern wafting through my too-awake mind. Scanning the parking lot of TI Industries, I can't help feeling like someone is watching me.

The driver's eyes meet mine in the rearview mirror. "I'm sure it's nothing," I quietly say aloud. "Stupid sales call."

CHAPTER TWENTY

Over the course of the last week, I've done everything in my power to keep things under wraps. Between school, trying to figure out my powers, and keeping Jay and my mom safe from me, time has been flying by.

Now, here we are, the morning of Jay's departure, and I'm just not sure how I'm supposed to finish this semester without him.

So much has me uneasy, but just thinking about asking him to stay seems entirely too selfish.

Not wanting to waste a minute, I slip into my closet to change. By the time I make it out, he's already sitting on my bed with a mischievous grin on his face.

"What?" I ask, blushing under his gaze. How does he always make me feel so shy?

"Changing without me, eh?" He wiggles his eyebrows. "I would've loved to help." Hearing the desire in his voice makes my legs shake.

Later, Tatum. Later.

I give him a scrutinizing look. "Not with my mother home, mister." That's the last thing I need.

"She's not home."

Oh no. Dear God, no.

This revelation only heightens my desire, which is at a dangerously high level as it is. I wanted us to do all sorts of stuff today, but with that look he's giving me, I'm starting to think we might not be leaving my bedroom. I look up in deep thought. It wouldn't be the worst thing…no, not at all.

When Jay pushes off my bed and stalks toward me like a lion hunting its prey, a chill runs through me. I've never felt so desired in my entire life. I gulp loudly. "What are you doing?"

"Walking toward you," he murmurs. The blue color of his eyes starts to brighten, making it seem like they are the only light source in the room. They call to me with the voice of a siren, but I have yet to move.

"Y-yes, but why?" I swallow what little spit is in my mouth. My throat runs completely dry. Where is some damn water when you need it? But when Jay stops short, a few steps in front of me, I suddenly realize that I've been looking at my own tall glass of water the entire time.

He chuckles. "Oh, I think we both know why. I'm not going to be able to lay my hands on you for almost a month. I plan on collecting early." The depth of his voice sends a wave of warmth through me. Has he always wielded this much power over me?

When his lips crash into mine, I'm lost in a sea of blue. The lightning that strikes between us is absolutely incendiary; every part of my body feels like it's on fire. I feel Jay's hot touch on the back of my legs as he bends down to effortlessly swoop me into his arms.

I squeal when he tosses me onto the bed, both of us busting out into a fit of laughter. "Every time," he laughs deeply.

"What's every time?" I question, biting my lip. His gaze turns greedy as he moves over me.

"You squeal every time I toss you onto a bed, like you're going to get hurt. You should already know by now that whenever you're with me, you're—"

"Safe," I finish for him, shushing him with a finger on his lips. "Every part of me is always safe with you. I know."

Grinning like a fool, he sucks my finger into his mouth. I groan in response. The color of his eyes burns even brighter than before, and I latch onto that, trying my best to ignore the warning beeping in my head to be careful of touching him too much.

Pulling his mouth off of my finger, he knees open both of my legs, settling in between them, his weight resting softly on top of me. I close my eyes, willing my emotions and concern to stay locked away.

"Look at me, baby," Jay urges.

I open my eyes, staring deep into his. "I don't want you to go."

There it is…exactly what I didn't want to happen. I knew getting tangled up in his web would get me all emotional.

He presses two hard kisses to my mouth. "I don't want to go either, but I have to. I'll be back before you know it."

I swallow down my emotions. "What if I need you?"

"Then you call me. I'll get a hold of Maleko, just in case, and I'll be there before you can even say my name."

"Speaking of Maleko, I have to tell you something." Now is probably not the best time to admit to going behind Jay's back and meeting up with Maleko, but hearing his name reawakens my guilt.

Jay's fingers caress the side of my face, "I already know."

I blanch, "Know what?"

His tone has a smile to it. "That you went to Mal for help."

"And you didn't say anything? How did you know?"

Jay's eyes sway between mine. "I have my ways… besides, I trust Mal. You have been working through a lot, and if you needed someone else to help confirm what I've already been saying, then so be it."

"So, you're not mad?" I question, staring at his face, searching for any signs of frustration.

Instead, Jay shakes his head and grabs one of my hands in his, pulling it up over my head before running his fingers down along the underside. "T, there's nothing to be mad about. I trust you. You obviously need to get through all of this in your own way. I'm more than happy to let you do that. You don't need my permission."

I shiver beneath his touch. "Can I ask you about something he mentioned while I was there?"

"Sureee," he draws out.

"Mal mentioned the word VOE, and how it basically means villains. Have you fought one before?"

"Besides your dad? One. But to be honest, there aren't many out there."

My mind swirls around what he just said. "What do you mean?"

"Just that," he sighs. "Very few have been encountered by a RED. We're not sure why, but their population is very small. We run into more fakes than actual VOEs."

"Fakes?"

"Yeah. There are these creeps who *claim* to be VOEs. To be honest, they look rough; every single one we've met. Sometimes, I think they're sent out to gather information for the very few actual VOEs that *do* exist. They obviously don't have many to chance losing."

"And who's they?" I ask.

Jay doesn't answer. Instead, the conversation dies as he softly drags his lips across mine.

Unable to resist any longer, I pull him down to me, my mouth finding his once more.

My tongue breaches the line of his lips, forcing its way in. His quickly meets mine, and I hum out a moan in reply.

When he breaks away, his mouth moves to my ear, whispering sweet nothings to me. I smile, listening to them until his tongue runs along the outline of my ear, making my heart stop.

I squirm under him, my skin tingling with anticipation.

"Stay still," he whispers in my ear as his hands dance around me, magically breaking my body free of its clothing.

"Jay..." I beg, finding it harder to stay put with each passing second.

"Shh," he orders, positioning himself just right. "You ready?"

I nod, grabbing onto both sides of his face with my hands. "Whenever you are."

When I open my eyes, I find Jay staring out my window. The sunlight dancing around him makes him look like an angel.

Jay has always enjoyed sunrises and the way the earth looks in the morning, while I prefer the moon and starry night sky. I guess opposites really do attract. Just like the moon and sun taking turns, he is always willing to set in order to let me shine.

Quietly digging through the covers, I find my phone and press the power button to check the time. 7:30 AM. *Shit.* Jay's flight is somewhat early today; combine that with him having to be there two hours before, plus the hour drive, and we'll have hardly any time together. Guess I'd better get the day started.

"Morning, baby," I say softly, not wanting to startle him. Instead, his entire body goes rigid at the sound of my voice.

Jay turns around and pins me with his electric blue gaze. It's enough to siphon the air directly out of my lungs. "Hey, baby." His voice sounds dull.

"What's wrong?" I ask. He plops down next to me on the bed and reaches for my hand. I let him take it. I'd let him take anything; he wouldn't even have to ask.

"I'm just going to miss you," he whispers.

Tears prick at the back of my eyelids, but I beg them to stay back. *Make this easier on him, Tatum.*

I pull myself up using the hand he's holding mine with and hug his waist. "I'm going to miss you too, but just like you said, time's gonna fly by."

"You don't have to be strong for me, T." *Damn it*, this man really knows everything. I'll never be able to hide from him, I swear. "I'm just afraid to leave you…" I remain quiet, giving him time to finish. "I can't protect you when I'm not here."

"Jay." I lean back and hold both sides of his head, using my thumb to softly rub against his cheek. The color of his irises seems more stunning than usual. "Don't worry about me. I'm going to be just fine. Maleko is here, and Adam is probably too afraid to come find me after what happened last time."

"You've always been strong, T. You just didn't see it

before because you were smothered in darkness. *You* are my hero."

"No, Jay. It's *you* who's my hero." I slowly lean closer to him, the word 'villain' running through my head. I can't be his hero with what I am, but I'll let him call me that for now. I'll let myself pretend it's the truth.

The ride over to the airport has been stressful, to say the least. I can see the sadness in my mom's eyes as she glances back at us in the rearview mirror. Jay has an iron-tight grip on my hand that somehow feels soft as he rubs his thumb back and forth over my skin.

"Do you have everything, sweetie?" my mom asks from the front seat.

Jay squeezes my hand. "Almost."

"What did you forget?" I prod. "We can stop by a store on the way."

"It's not something I can buy at the store."

"Then what is it?" My eyes search his.

"You." Every single emotion is wrapped up inside that one word. My heart throbs.

"Jay," I whisper, "I—"

Jay doesn't let me finish. He just plants a chaste kiss to my lips and squeezes my hand a little tighter. I squeeze his back in understanding.

I notice my mom's hand flash by in the mirror and find her face donning a bittersweet smile. I wish Adam would've loved her the way Jay loves me. It's so unfair that she lost so much, just to have it come back even worse.

The rest of the ride goes by in silence. When the airport

pops up in the distance, Jay lets go of my hand and holds tight to my thigh. I place my hand on top of his, feeling the warmth travel through my palm.

My mom clicks the car into park, and that's when I feel the fear take hold of my body. There's no way I'm going to be able to say goodbye to him *and* be okay without him here. We haven't had enough time to figure things out.

Making our way out and around the car, we seem to have all of Jay's things. My mom has a small bag dangling from her arm, while her other is locked around Jay's waist. I'm holding another small bag in one hand while my other holds onto Jay's hand, and Jay is smack dab in the middle of both of us, somehow dragging his suitcase with the arm that's wrapped around my mom's back.

After Jay drops off his bags and finds where he needs to check in, I watch my mother dive into his chest. I can't help but feel a twinge of guilt at the fact that Jay's parents aren't here. *Did he already say goodbye to them?*

My mom's arms slip out from around Jay as their embrace ends. Jay's emotional blue eyes snap to mine, and they narrow at me.

"I'll be waiting for you just outside those doors," my mom says, patting my shoulder. I shake my head, my stare never leaving Jay's.

"I can't do this."

"You can and you will," she whispers. "Don't let him down." And when I watch Jay's arms drop to his sides and open slightly, I know just how bad he needs me.

Just like the day he came home, I fling myself on him again, crashing into his unmovable body.

He holds me up, pulling my legs so they wrap around his

waist. "I'm going to miss you so much," Jay murmurs in my ear.

I kiss his cheek. "I'm going to miss you more."

He pauses. "I'm sorry."

"For what?" I ask.

"For having to leave."

"I know. Now, listen to me." Jay lifts his head, scanning my face in question. "You go and do what you need to do. I only ask one thing."

He pushes his forehead to mine and closes his eyes. "Anything."

"Come back to me." I don't know why, but I feel the need to say that to him. Ever since everything with Adam happened, there's been a different kind of worry housed in my stomach, waiting for the perfect moment to reveal itself.

His eyes whip back open and stare into mine with a blue fire I've never seen before. It pulls me in.

"Always." Our mouths come together on their own as we pass every unspoken word we intended on saying to each other. Jay's arms loosen and I slowly slide down his body until my feet reach the floor. "I love you more than anything on this earth, Tatum."

"And I love you more than that," I reply.

Jay pushes a strand of hair behind my ear before rubbing his thumb along my jaw. I extend my arm up and grab onto his wrist, feeling his veins tighten beneath my fingertips. "Bye, baby," he mutters.

"Bye." His touch falls away from me as he turns around toward the gate. I watch him go as my heart shatters into a million pieces and escapes my body, going to follow him where I cannot.

When I can't see him anymore, I run toward the entrance

and smash my way out of the doors, into my mom's arms, my sobs racking my body against hers. She holds strong, squeezing me close to her, trying as she might to absorb some of the pain, having no idea what is really going on.

What would she say if she knew what I was? What Adam was? What I was really involved in?

Could she ever grow to love something so dark?

"I'm sorry, my darling."

I only nod, unsure what to say back.

Getting back into the car, I choose the back seat to ride back to the house, wanting nothing more than to lay my head where Jay last was. I buckle in and close my eyes, my nose yearning for any remnants of his scent.

"Check the seat." I peer at my mom through the mirror of her visor, a sweet smile crossing her face.

"What did you do?" I ask, scanning the seat next to me. *Nothing*.

"It wasn't me."

I lift up in the seat, scared that I might've squashed whatever the surprise was—but that fear evaporates when I find a Pegasus constellation necklace with two envelopes taped to it. I rub the constellation between two of my fingers, admiring its beauty.

Taking the first note out of the smaller envelope, I unfold it, my breath hitching when I find Jay's handwriting inside. My eyes sting with unshed tears.

"Go on," my mom urges. I wipe away the wetness and begin reading what isn't covered by my blurred vision.

Dear Tatum,

I had no idea how little I was living until

my heart collided with yours. Years of your friendship gave me more than I could've ever dreamed, but it was the day you decided to love me in ways we never had before that I reclaimed my life and dedicated my heart to you. Thank you for being mine. I truly don't deserve you. And please don't ever change, not even for me.

While I know there is so much going on for you right now, I hope you know that I'll always do everything in my power to protect you. I need you to survive. Not just literally, but metaphorically. Don't give up while I'm gone. You can't thrive in the darkness.

I love you more than all the stars in the sky. I hope when you wear this necklace of your favorite constellation—you thought I forgot, didn't you?—you look into the sky and find Pegasus; he will always remind me that your love is being sent over on his wings.

All my love,
Jay

I fold his note and push it as far down in my pocket as it will go and fasten his necklace around my neck before pulling out the next paper in the bigger envelope.

The reveal takes my breath away. It's a comic Jay drew himself. There are no boxes with different scenes; it is just a postcard-sized drawing of him in all black—a cape billowing out behind him—holding me while he flies us through the night sky.

I've never felt love as powerful as the love this man has for me, and I'll be happy to spend the rest of my days trying to be deserving of that sort of love, no matter what becomes of me.

CHAPTER TWENTY-ONE

One week. I've made it one whole week without Jay. I sort of feel like there's a missing piece to my puzzle, but I've done my best to make do. Between helping my mom around the house and wrapping up the semester, things have been super busy.

Jay has kept his promise and has been in contact with me every day. It's been really hard not to express how much I miss him, but hearing how happy he is while completing RED tasks on his mission makes it all worth it.

Jay's duties sound like something out of a movie…and I guess they sort of are. Between training at secret facilities, meeting other possible REDs—though I have no idea what it means to be a possible RED—to have join the force, and searching for any VOE activity, he's living up to the reputation of all of the heroes he's always hoped to grow up to be.

At the sound of my phone ringing, I rush over to grab it off my desk, red marker in hand. "Hello?"

"Hey, baby," Jay's voice coos in my ear.

"Hey! You okay?" I mark off another day on my calendar while I wait for his reply.

After a rushed sigh, he starts off, "Yeah. Everything's okay. I just miss you and needed to hear your voice." I smile to myself; I'm honored he found a way to sneak off and call me just because he misses me.

"Well, how's my voice treating you?" The bed creaks as I flop back onto it, reminding me of the many years we would sit and chat on the house phone into the wee hours of the night.

His chuckle is music to my ears. "It's exactly what the doctor ordered. But hey, will you do me a favor?"

"Anything."

"Go out and look at the stars tonight. I'm going to fly as high as I can and try to take a trip around the moon. Let me know if you see me."

I roll my eyes, smiling to myself. It's not every day your superhero boyfriend is willing to breach the ozone layer just so you can spot him thousands of miles away.

"You can do that? Wow. I've gotta try to find my binoculars. I'll text you?"

"Still can't stand people talking while you stargaze, can you?" He crows. "Yes, that's fine. I wouldn't want my annoying voice to disturb your view while I literally circle the moon to impress you."

Jerk. But he's right—I've always hated idle chit-chat when looking at the stars. They seem brighter when surrounded by silence.

"Thank you," I reply sarcastically.

"Oh, yeah. You're welcome. No problem."

"Shut up. You'll survive, you ass!"

"Me?" He feigns innocence. "You're the one who said you don't want to hear my loud mouth while you look at some big balls of gas up in the sky, trying to catch a glimpse of me."

We both break out into a fit of laughter that lasts for a few minutes. I clutch my stomach, doubling over in pain.

"Ow, okay. My abs hurt. Listen, I have to go so I can have dinner with Mom and finish everything before Jaygazing. I mean, stargazing." He snorts out a big laugh at that. "I'll talk to you later, okay?"

"Okay. I love you, T."

"Super love you, Jay." I hang up before he convinces me to stay on the line. That gives him the chance to get sappy, and nobody needs to be getting all emotional. Emotions are sometimes a breeding ground for guilt, and Jay has no reason to feel guilty for what he's doing.

Running down the stairs, I'm greeted with a warm, garlicky scent. I breathe in deeply, my mouth salivating.

"Tatum?" Mom calls.

"Yes?"

"Dinner is ready. Your favorite!"

I burst into the dining room. "Chicken alfredo? *Yes*!"

She chuckles at my excitement and gestures with her head for me to sit. We both chat our way through dinner and cleaning the dishes. The daylight fades quickly, and excitement buzzes in my chest as the stars start to make themselves known in the sky.

I make my way toward the stairs to head up and grab a jacket and a blanket when the house phone attached to the wall rings.

I answer quickly. "Hello?"

No sound.

"Hello?" I prompt. "Is anyone there?"

I jerk the phone away when labored breathing on the other end sends a cold chill down my spine. I slam it back into place, grasping at my throat. I thought these stupid phone calls were done, but apparently, I was wrong.

My hands rub up and down my arms, trying to wipe away

the goosebumps covering my skin. I want to tell my mom, but don't want to worry her. I mean, it could've been a misdial for all I know. I just can't shake the feeling of impending doom…

No. I'm okay. I'm safe. Everything is fine.

I dash up the stairs, grab my things, and race back down to find Mom once more. The television is playing in the living room as she starts a movie. Taking a deep breath, I try to compose myself. Moms can sense that shit.

"Mom?"

"Yes, honey?"

I clear my throat and peek at her through the doorway. "Jay wants me to stargaze at the same time as him, so I'm going to be outside for a little while. Do you mind waiting up for me?" I don't know why, but knowing that someone is inside waiting for me to return helps put me at ease. It just seems a bit irrational now that I know I'm growing villainous powers inside of me. Shouldn't anything possibly waiting for me out here be more afraid of me than I am of them?

"Of course." She turns around to smile at me. "It sounds romantic. I'll wait. Why don't you head out the back door so I can hear you come in? I'll turn the volume down."

I mentally wipe the worried sweat from my forehead. "Thanks." I wrap the blanket I grabbed around me and turn to leave the room, snagging a pillow off of the couch as I go.

"Have fun."

Stepping out onto the small wooden deck—with no railings, and only two steps leading down to the grass—that I helped my mom build by hand as a kid, I spread out my blanket, dropping the pillow on top of it.

Once I'm settled outside, I admire the way the moonlight shines down on the fenced-in backyard. It's a rather large yard, with only a few trees and a small blue shed that sits next to my old, rusty playset. I begged my mom not to get rid of it in eighth grade, and I still swing on it from time to time.

I scan the space, looking for anything that might be even slightly amiss. *Damn it.* Why am I worrying so much? What is it about that phone call that has me so nervous?

I lay back on the blanket I brought out and stare up at the sky. The crescent moon seems to shine extra bright this evening, taking my breath away. My eyes bounce between the hundreds upon hundreds of stars twinkling above me as all the stress and worry from the phone call seems to wash away with the gorgeous view.

Me: This view is amazing.

My phone buzzes a second later.

Jay: I have to be honest. This view doesn't even come close to comparing to you. :(

His thought is ridiculous, but I still blush at his admission.

Me: You're sweet <3 Where are you?

Jay: Um, in the sky? Are you ready?

Me: As I'll ever be.

Jay: Don't blink ;)

Suddenly, a figure flashes across the face of the moon. I gasp, sitting up quickly, typing away on my phone.

Me: I saw you! Oh my gosh!

Jay: Does this make me your favorite constellation now?

A lightbulb blinks on in my mind. Opening my camera, I face it toward me. I hold up my hand, making sure my Pegasus pendant is visible in the photo, and send it to Jay.

Me: I don't know if you count as one, but this really cute guy bought me this Pegasus necklace, so I'd have to say that I'm really fond of that constellation in particular ;)

Jay: Have I ever told you how absolutely gorgeous you truly are?

Me: Not nearly enough as you should. Please, go on :p

A rustling next to me sends me nearly soaring off my blanket. I squint my eyes hard at the bushes, trying my best to peer at what's hiding within them. As much as I'd love to stay out and watch the stars some more, something in my gut feels like it's sending me a warning. Ripping my things up off of the ground, I rush inside, slamming the door behind me and locking it quickly.

"You okay, sweetie?"

"Ah!" I scream, clutching my chest. "Sorry. You spooked me. Yeah, uh—I'm fine." I shake the doorknob one last time before going to meet her in the living room.

"Why did you scream?" she asks, giving me a look of concern. "Are you sure you're okay?"

I am far from okay. Between hiding the fact that I'm actually part VOE from my own mother, choosing to leave out the creepy phone calls bit, *and* my superhero boyfriend who's currently thousands of miles away while I try to figure out what will become of me, I'm anything but okay.

I rub my arms again, sneaking glances out the windows. "Yes, I'm fine. I'm going to head to bed. Is it okay with you if I set the alarm before I go?"

I punch our code into the alarm system Mom had installed a few days after Jay changed our locks.

"Sure. I'll be heading to bed in a few minutes too. Night, Tatum. I love you."

"Love you too." I spin on my heel and head upstairs, racking my brain the entire time to try and figure out what has me feeling so jumpy. Adam has been gone for a while now. It couldn't be him…right?

After changing into my pajamas and settling into bed, I pull out my phone to check if Jay texted me back during all the commotion. There are multiple messages to scan through.

> Jay: Well, here it is again…you are the most beautiful being I've ever laid eyes on.

> Jay: You still there, or did you fall asleep on the blanket again?

> Jay: T???

> Jay: Tatum? You're worrying me. You can't just sleep outside. If I don't hear from you in five minutes, I'm flying back home. I can do that now, you know.

The screen of my phone lights up with Jay's face, and all my worry dissipates just from looking into his gorgeous blue eyes and at his snow-white teeth. I click *Accept* and raise it up to my ear.

"I want to know why you think I'd fall asleep on a blanket outside in the middle of the night…"

Jay cackles. "Like it's never happened before."

"Not with my VOE of a father existing somewhere out there! By the way, thank you for the kind compliment."

"You're welcome. Is everything okay?"

That uneasy feeling returns to my stomach. Do I tell him what happened, or not?

I don't think so…for all I know, it could've been an animal. Why would I tell him something like that, knowing he would rush home and risk everything to keep me safe? No, he doesn't need to know unless something significant happens. I can handle this. I mean, I have some sort of dark power growing inside me. I'm sure it will reveal itself when I need it most. That's what usually happens…I think.

"My mom needed me inside. Sorry, I was totally going to call you when I got into bed, but you beat me to it."

"That's okay." He pauses. "You know you can tell me anything, right?"

Such an odd thing to say at this moment. Did he find a way back into my head while being in a completely different country than me? *Play it off, T.*

"Of course. Here's something I need to tell you: I'm tired as hell, but I love you more than all the stars in the sky."

"I love you more than that. Night, T."

"Night," I reply.

***

Now that I've made it to the end of the second week since Jay left, I notice that a phone call hasn't come tonight, giving me a very small window of reprieve. They seem to be getting more frequent. Mom thinks they're spam calls, and while they very well could be, I just can't shake the feeling they're not. I decide to take advantage of the brief moment of respite and pull my phone out to text Jay again.

Me: Guess what?

Jay: Chicken butt?

I smirk at his reply.

Me: No. Even better—I'm in bed. ;)

Jay: Thank God. Please say you're in MY bed...wait. Are you trying to prep me for phone sex?

I think about all the things I could do with a simple text to really get Jay going, but decide against it. Keeping it simple, I snap a quick picture of my kissy face and send it through.

Jay: How many more days until I get to kiss those lips of yours? I already know you've got some sort of countdown going on over there.

He knows me too well. I don't even have to look at the calendar to know how many days until he's set to come back.

Me: 14 days. :) I can't wait.

I start to drift off before hearing back from Jay and plunge into dreams of a dark sky and flashes of blackish-purple and blue.

No sooner do I close my eyes than a scream breaks through my dream, jolting me awake. I scramble my way out of the covers, deep breaths quaking through my chest. The anxiety rebuilding itself within me feels so foreign inside my body.

"Shit," I say aloud, my heart pounding through my chest. I shake my head, finding it difficult to recall anything from my dream; all I know is that the scream I heard sounded like it was somewhere else; almost like it was here.

After taking a few deep breaths, I check my phone before trying to fall back asleep and am happy to find Jay texted me back.

> Jay: Remind me to never be away from you again after this. I can't take the separation. I think you'll just have to come with me next time. :(

> Jay: Did you fall asleep on me? I'm trying not to worry here.

> Jay: Goodnight, my love <3

After sending a goodnight text in return, I set my phone down on the bed, wide awake and listening to the house, wondering if I should check to see if the scream came from downstairs, or if it was all in my dream.

CHAPTER TWENTY-TWO

Seconds later, I bolt upright when a second scream shakes me to my core. There's no way in hell that was in my dream.

"*Mom?*" I yell, clambering out of bed and running to the door. I look around my room for some sort of weapon, only finding a pocket knife I shoved in my junk drawer one time. I pick it up and flick the blade out, unsure if I'll be able to conjure up any of my powers should I need them. I don't even know what mine are yet, let alone how many I actually have.

Winding my way down the stairs, I crane my ear, listening intently, but the house remains silent. Could my mom just have been having a bad dream? I tiptoe my way to her room, trying my best not to disturb her, and quietly open the door.

"Mom?" I whisper. "Are you awake?" The door creaks as I push it open a little wider and step inside. The room is dark, only a tiny slit of moonlight peeking through a crack in her curtains. "Mom?"

I reach for the corner of her comforter and pull it back, shocked when I find it empty. She must be in the bathroom.

This isn't adding up. *No…something doesn't feel right.*

My blood runs cold, reminding me of the beginning layers of ice that form on top of the lake in the first freeze of winter.

Before moving much farther, I halt, frozen in fear. The

floor behind me groans under the weight of someone's heavy steps, and I have a sinking feeling they don't belong to my mother.

"Thought I had disappeared for good, huh?"

That voice is the very voice that fuels my nightmares and wakes my anxiety like a bear coming out of hibernation. *It can't be.*

"You and your mother are so stupid." I sense him inch closer, desperately praying he can't see me well enough in the slithering darkness. It's hard to tell if it's this dark because it's the middle of the night, because his shadows are blocking out any light, or a combination of both.

I turn toward him, my mind spinning.

"I've been watching you the entire time. Being a cop *and* a VOE has its advantages. I just had to wait for your precious *Jay* to leave." His mocking laughter sounds in my ear. This cannot be happening.

"Where is my mother?" I grit through my teeth. I'm done living in fear of this man. He needs to go—for good.

"Oh, let me take you to her, Daughter."

It's the last thing I hear before something hard hits the side of my head, taking my consciousness away. My last thought is of Jay and how I wish he was here to save me. *Will I ever get to see him again?*

When I come to, I find myself blindfolded and tied to the base of a tree in the freezing cold. I struggle against my binds, giving everything I have to try and free myself, but the ties are so tight that I just end up inflicting more pain on myself.

I rub both my middle and pinky fingers against the ring

finger on my right hand, searching for some sort of comfort. There's a possibility I'll never see Jay again after this.

"Mom? Jay? *Help!*"

"It's no use," Adam's evil voice starts. "No one is going to hear you. We are in the middle of nowhere, and your little Jay is thousands of miles away."

Hands grip my blindfold hard, pulling some of my hair with it as it's being undone. Blinking a few times, I come face-to-face with my dad. The disgusting police uniform he's wearing looks as if it hasn't been washed in months, and his unshaven face and terrifying gaze rattle my bones.

"What the hell do you think you're doing?" I scream at him through the tears that threaten to break through the dam. Why couldn't he just leave and never return? We don't want him. He doesn't want us. Why does he keep coming back?

His hand flies out, making me flinch, and he grabs onto my chin aggressively, forcing me to look at him. His eyes flash with hatred. "You listen here, you little bitch! If you and your mother would've just listened to me, we wouldn't be here right now. But no, you had to go and fight back, which only pissed me off more."

I yank my chin away from him, opening and closing my mouth a few times to make sure my jaw still works properly. "We aren't your property. Women weren't created to simply obey."

"That's honestly what you think?" He laughs madly. "You're sadly mistaken."

"Can you just tell me why?" I beg. I think I deserve answers after all this time.

My right arm twitches as a shock travels through my body, starting at the finger I wear Jay's ring on. *Oh, great. My powers are starting up again, and I have no idea how to use them yet. Really useful…*

"Your mother and I were so in love until *you* came along. The minute you arrived, I saw how she would neglect me to be with you, to soothe your cries, to take care of you." He starts to pace back and forth in front of me. "I was being pushed aside for some stupid kid, and I was not okay with that."

My heart starts to beat erratically, not out of fear, but of sadness. How could my own father say this about me?

"Why did you *have* me then, you piece of shit?" I screech.

His gaze turns away from me and focuses on the blade of a knife in his hands—a knife that I somehow missed before. What would he need a weapon for when he has powers of his own?

I swallow loudly, staring at the glimmer of silver as small tendrils of dark shadow start to wrap themselves around the handle. I guess that answers my prior question.

I have got to get out of here.

"Well…you see, your mother begged me for a child. I wanted to give her everything she wanted, so I did it, but the minute I felt her love for me diminish a fraction to make room for you was the exact moment your existence became nothing to me. Truth is, I didn't like it; I still don't. You weren't meant to survive infancy anyway."

I still. "What does that mean?"

His booming laugh washes over me. "So many questions."

"*Tell me!*" I scream.

"Long story short, sweetie, I was injected years ago. Went through a fucked-up change, got some kickass powers, and used your mother as a cover-up. Well, all of that got me into a little…predicament, so when you came along, I could feel the presence of my potential beneath your skin. The transformation is so grueling; I figured either you wouldn't live more than a few years possibly, or nothing would happen at all, so after giving it some time, I left. Wasn't worth it to stick around.

"After my trouble started catching up to me, I hatched a different plan to come back after I heard a rumor of RED being housed here. And lo and behold, when I caught a glimpse of you at the grocery story with your mom, I knew I had to weasel my way back in. Surely, you had powers that I could turn over to earn my freedom. What a shame that turned out to be..."

"What are you going to do to me?"

"The only thing that makes sense." His eyes bore into mine with an intensity that would normally have me shrinking back in fear, but I've now accepted my fate. If I can't wiggle my way out of this, I'll be damned if I slink away in fright; especially not with what I know about myself now.

"Which is?"

He leans so his face is within inches of mine. "Kill you."

My eyes widen, my body trembling with terror at the two words that fall from his mouth. He wouldn't kill his own daughter, would he?

"You're a monster. Mom? Mom, *where are you*?"

He rolls his eyes with a low chuckle. "No worries; your mother will be joining you. She'd never agree to be mine without you. Don't you see? You're a package deal, one I never ordered."

"No! You cannot kill her! Please don't. Just take me instead!" I lean around him, searching for my mom in every stretch of land I can see.

We truly are in the middle of nowhere. Woods surround us

on each side, not a lick of grass to be found beneath us…just soil and rocks.

That's when I spot a giant hole in the ground; one big enough for a couple of bodies to fit inside. *No, this cannot be happening.*

Adam crouches down and begins digging through a bag nearby. As I rack my brain, trying to think of anything that could get us out of here alive, I hear a groan not too far away. My eyes peruse the area once more, but evening light makes it difficult to see. Thankfully, the moon that has captured my heart my entire life gives me just enough light to see.

That's when I spot her: my mom, tied to the base of a tree across the clearing.

"Mom!" I scream at the top of my lungs. "Mom, wake up!"

I notice the strain on her face as she fights to lift her head. Her eyes dart around in a haze until they latch onto mine. When our gazes lock, her eyes swing open wide and she starts to fight against the ropes.

"Tatum! Honey, hold on!" She rocks back and forth against the tree, desperately working to break free. I wish I could tell her to stop, that the fight isn't worth it, and that we are going to die out here. I was worried she'd be disappointed in what I am the entire time. Instead, I let her down by doing nothing. I couldn't even learn to harness my powers to save her.

Just as I thought... I'm no hero, only a failure. A true villain.

"Mom, I love you."

She stills at my words, her face contorting in rage. "Oh no, you don't! You are not giving up! We are getting out of here! Adam, what the *fuck* do you think you're doing here?"

Adam pulls something different from his waistband as he tosses the knife to the ground and stalks toward her, pushing what seems to be a rectangular-shaped cartridge into the bottom of the new object.

My breath catches in my throat. *A gun.* Moonlight shimmers along the shining silver object, sending me writhing and pulling against the cords binding me. I can't sit here and watch him kill her.

"If I can't have you, then I must rid my life of both of you. Why wasn't it enough to just have a husband, Anne?" He pokes at her temple with the barrel of the gun, making her eyes go wide with fear. Why he hasn't chosen to reveal himself and use his dark powers, I'm not entirely sure.

"You're making no sense! Stop this!"

He hits the side of her face with the gun. She goes limp.

"Leave her the *fuck* alone, you monster! You don't deserve her. Get away from her!" I cry out.

"What did you just say?" he seethes.

Good, that got his attention. *Keep up the good work, T.*

"You heard me! You don't deserve her. You never have." He gets closer, but I hold steady. His leech-like instincts will use my fear to suck the soul right out of me. Maybe that's another power of his. "You only lost my mother because you turned into a psychopath. There is nothing even remotely lovable about you. Do us a favor and get the hell away from us!" All the words I've so badly wanted to say to him my entire life start to spill out of my mouth until he is standing directly in front of me.

"Can't you see that's what I'm trying to do? The sooner I get rid of both of you, the sooner I can move on."

"I wish you never came back!" I gasp for breath. "And just like I thought, you never needed or wanted us. You said so yourself that all of this—of me—ended up being a shame. So, what was with all that 'need to take your powers' bullshit? Too scared to touch me now?"

"The original plan ceased to exist when I wanted to find a way to take your powers and make myself stronger. Although, I knew my best shot was to turn you over to a doctor I know. However, I think your abilities will only cause more trouble. They could be used against me. I'm better off disposing of you and leaving before he comes to collect."

I rack my brain, trying to think of what exactly he means. Original plan? He wanted to make sure I had a power that would help him. But now that he knows what I can do, I'm better off dead? What?

"I hate you. You're that afraid of what I can do? My, my, my…how the tables have turned." I spit in his face, the corners of my mouth curling upward. "Fuck you."

"Good," he starts with a snigger, "you're angry. At least we can agree on one thing." My eyebrows twitch up in question. "I hate you too." The back of his clothed arms wipes over his face, a low snicker escaping his mouth. "Oh, and I wish you were never born."

My heart shatters as I watch the gun slowly rise until I'm eye-to-eye with the barrel. Only a villain would suffer a powerless death such as this.

"I love you, Mom. I'm sorry," I whisper, quietly enough so he can't hear me. I beg God to deliver my whispered words of love to her and close my eyes to accept my demise, the last picture in my mind being one of her and Jay hugging each other…the two loves of my life.

My scream rings out in the night as a gunshot goes off, and I scrunch my eyes tightly closed, knowing I'm already gone.

CHAPTER TWENTY-THREE

Dying doesn't feel all that bad. Being shot is actually a hell of a lot better than being torn apart by those dark shadows.

I pop my eyes open one after the other, ready to see where I've ended up, when something catches my eye. Mom is still tied to a tree, but it's the manly grunts that throw me off.

Where the hell am I?

My stare scans the night for a sign of what the sounds could be when I find Adam wrestling with someone on the ground. I squint my eyes, imploring them to see better. Is that a man fighting him? Where did he come from? How did he find us?

"Help us!" my mom screams at the stranger. The sound of the gunshot must've stirred her awake.

She shouldn't be screaming for him to save me, though. I'm beyond saving. Maybe she can't tell I'm gone, but her occasional looks say otherwise. Is she hoping this man can revive me?

THUD.

My eyes snap up in the direction of the noise. Adam's body lays still on the ground, the stranger hovering over it, heaving breaths big enough to see from afar. Did he kill him?

I watch as the stranger's gaze dances around the ground until it lands on Adam's bag. He rushes over, digging through it before pulling what he wants out of it. It must be rope, judging by the way it's dangling from his hands; that must mean Adam is definitely *not* dead.

I wish I could tell the man that ropes will not bind someone like Adam. What he cannot maneuver out of physically, he'll command his shadows to take care of for him. Those bindings won't last long.

The figure lifts Adam from the ground like he's a doll, walks him over to a nearby tree, and tethers him to the trunk in a standing position. Once he's restrained, the newcomer puts their hands on Adam's head, going ramrod still for what feels like a lifetime.

He stands like that for a few short moments. Pulling away, he makes his way over to my mom, and I wonder if he could be just as dangerous as Adam. Then again, he just knocked out my horror of a father, so he must be helping…right?

The stranger helps her up, and she collapses into his arms, crying inconsolably. "Sweetie, thank you. Oh my gosh, thank you."

Sweetie? Who the fuck is she talking to? Who is that?

When he turns around to face me, his eyes take the breath right out of my lungs. I'd know that penetrating blue gaze anywhere.

"Jay?" I whisper in disbelief. The figure remains silent, coming my way. My eyes stay locked on his, utterly baffled. Will he be able to bring me back?

I try as hard as I can to focus on his eyes when he makes it over to me, but the mask on his face covers all of the skin surrounding them. He reaches behind me, quickly releasing my bound arms. I'm surprised I'm still able to move my hands.

My eyes run over every inch of my body I can see as I quickly inspect my injuries. No sign of a gunshot wound. Adam must've missed. But how?

"I'm okay?" I ask. The man nods his head, a smile growing on his face. It's just enough to confirm my assumptions. "Jay?"

His arms slowly rise. He presses a button right above his ear, the mask collapsing itself into a small singular piece. He takes it and pushes it into a hidden pocket on his hip.

I reach out to him and lift his head to look at me again. My fingers graze his cheek, and he leans into my hand, gripping it tight to keep it there.

My breath hitches as he slowly lifts his eyes to meet mine, and I nearly choke on my spit when our gazes lock onto one another. It really is him. How?

"Is it really you?"

"It's me, T. I'm here. You're okay."

My vision goes blurry with tears. "How did you find us?"

Jay pulls my hand off of his face and pokes my ring.

"My ring?"

"I can see your heart rate, where you're at, and can tell how you're feeling through an app I created on my phone. I started checking it more after your ring fell off the last time, and when you were acting strange earlier, I had a bad feeling." I stare down at the jewelry in awe, suddenly grateful I've kept my word in keeping it on. It saved my life today. Well, Jay saved my life, but it sure helped.

I grab both sides of his face. "So you knew something was wrong and came to help me?"

"I came to save you," he replies, sealing his mouth over mine in a worried kiss.

After he backs away, I finally get a chance to look at him. Jay is wearing a black, one-piece, scaly suit that covers every inch of his body except for his neck up, a reddish-black cape billowing behind him to the ground. The slick boots on his feet are covered with almost-iridescent blue lightning bolts that catch random bits of moonlight.

Altogether, his look is extremely sleek and intimidating. I study the way the suit molds to his body, putting his muscles on full display.

"What are you?" I prod, desperately searching his eyes for more of an explanation than I've received before. I've never seen him in action, and I've had yet to see him in his superhero form.

But when a groan sounds a few feet from us, he slinks away from me and runs toward Adam's body, diving straight for him. Jay's fist collides with his head, knocking him out cold.

A second later, my mom slams into me. "Tatum, are you all right?" She leans back to scan my body. "Let me take a look at you."

"I'm fine, Mom. I'm okay."

She peers at me with tears in her eyes. "I was so scared."

"I know…me too. I'm so sorry."

Her gaze turns toward Adam. "For *what*?"

My heart sinks.

For being me, I want to say.

"What do you want to do with him?" Jay's voice shocks me back to attention, hurriedly waving his hand in front of my face.

"I'm sorry, what?"

"What do you want to do about your dad?" His eyes flick back and forth between mine.

I struggle to come up with words. I mean, what should we do? How am I supposed to know?

"Tatum, are you listening to me?"

How could I possibly be listening? There's no way this is real.

My mom's hand squeezes my shoulder. "Sweetie, are you okay?"

"Okay?" My face snaps between the both of them. "First, Adam tries to kill us, then Jay swoops in to save the day, and we don't even know what Adam wanted me for? How am I supposed to be okay?"

"Tatum, what would Adam want you for?"

I swallow hard, suddenly realizing I've said too much.

What on earth are we actually going to do? I mean, we can't just kill him. Can we?

Jay freezes, his stare bouncing between my eyes. Did he just tune in to my thoughts?

"Mom," Jay starts, "can Tatum and I have a moment alone?"

Her wide eyes reflect the worry building inside of her, but she nods and walks a few feet away.

As she turns, I watch as two, thin streaks of blue lightning erupt from Jay's eyes and waft after her. My body stills, watching him do his work.

The bolts dance around her head, and her body goes stock-still. When they retreat back to him and disappear, he zooms over, catching her just in time and laying her gently on the ground.

"What are you doing?" I ask, surprisingly calm.

"Figured you wouldn't want her to know too much." He assesses me from head to toe, walking closer to take both of my hands in his. "Tatum, there's something I have to tell you."

"All of this has been a dream?"

"No. Um, you know how you said you wish your dad would forget you?" I bob my head up and down. "What would you say if I told you I could help with that?" I try to pull away, baffled, but Jay holds steady. "Hear me out."

I stare at his face, unblinkingly.

"T, I am able to erase people's memories and replace them with new, fake ones. If you really wanted to, I could make your dad completely forget you and your mom ever existed and reconstruct his brain with new memories that aren't true. Would you be interested in that?"

"Wouldn't he still be a villain?"

His head signals a *yes*, his eyes sad.

"Jay, no." I push him back a fraction. "I can't risk that."

Moving to glance at Adam, I notice a black tendril playing with his bindings.

"Jay! Watch out!"

But I'm too late. Adam breaks free, and my screams drift into the night as a wave of dark shadows lifts him above us. He peers down at me with a sickening grin, the dark purple hues in his eyes chilling me to the bone.

Jay pulls the mask from his pocket, slams it to his face, and I watch as panel after panel of the foreign material puzzle-pieces its way across his face and around his head.

Adam spits down at him and shouts, "You think you can save them from me? Even without me, my darkness will follow them. He's already coming. This is ten times bigger than you, boy. There's not a thing you can do to keep them safe! You are nothing against the Doctor!"

"They're both better off without you, and they will *always* be safe with me." Jay's voice booms into the sky, and I notice the tension in his shoulders as he flies up to meet Adam.

"Oh, really? And what are you going to do about me, then? Kill me? Someone will find out. Especially with that getup. You don't seem like someone who could possibly withstand blood on your hands."

I squint my eyes as a bright light permeates through the night, bright enough to resemble the sun. I slap my hands to my face.

Peeking through my fingers, I watch a stream of glowing blue flow from Jay's eyes straight for Adam's head.

As soon as his lines of energy reach Adam, they are slapped away by strips of shadow. Adam's hand directs one to wrap around Jay's throat, and I cry out as I watch him pull and scratch at it, choking.

"Let him go! Stop it!" I break into a run, chasing down Jay as he falls from the sky, slamming to the ground.

The shadows engulfing my dad start to swallow him whole as they bring him to the ground. I try my best to pull Jay away as Adam exits the dark cloud and stalks toward us, thick lines of smoke billowing up his arms.

"All you REDs are the same. Thinking you can save the day and defeat us VOEs when we are the least of your worries. I am nothing but a grain of sand in the grand scheme of evil."

I hold my hand up to him as he closes in, Adam pausing in his tracks.

"Are you afraid of her?" Jay chokes out, trying his best to look between us with tired eyes.

Adam shakes with evil laughter. "Afraid? Of a wimpy-ass girl? Please."

"I touched him at my house before he left and it did something to him, just like what happened with you and Koral," I whisper into Jay's ear, my lips barely moving.

His arms slowly move over mine. "Let's try it again, then."

Before I can even comprehend what is happening, I am screaming at the top of my lungs as Jay catapults us at Adam, full-force. He attempts to build a screen of black smoke at the last second, but for some reason, I'm able to breach its doors.

My hands slap against his face, and I fight to hold on as he screams and thrashes. Flashes of black and purple spark around us, but I refuse to let go.

Adam's knee comes up and bashes into my stomach, knocking the wind out of me. I gasp for air as I fall backwards to the ground.

Jay grabs me under my arms, shuffling us backwards. "Did it work?"

I nod, air finally sweeping into my lungs before Jay is wrapped up in a shadowy arm, his eyes bulging as it squeezes him tight.

Doing what Maleko taught me, I use the nightmare in front of me to draw a rage from somewhere deep inside that I never knew existed. Within seconds, a black force explodes out of me, knocking Adam over.

He was already weaker from my touch, but now Jay is completely free of his reach. Adam seems stronger this time, because he gets up quicker than he did at the house.

"It all makes sense now," he sneers with a manic voice. "You're a fucking siphon."

Jay is up and moving for me, but stops in his tracks at the word.

"I'm sorry, a siphon? Like, I can suck out your powers?"

His hideous laughter gets louder. "Yes, just like that." He stumbles, but quickly rights himself. "The Doctor will be so pleased once he knows you can suck every single one of those REDs dry that he won't even think about using them on me. The world will be ours!"

I stare up at him when Jay mouths something to me: "Cover your head."

I slam my eyes shut and wrap my hands around my head as bolts of lightning erupt from his eyes. It takes a second for my eyelids to open, but when they do, I find Adam kneeling on the ground, seemingly dazed.

Spinning around, I come face-to-face with Jay. Only able to see his eyes, I finally get the chance to see the symbol on his suit. It is a blue 'J', the long arm jagged like the shape of a lightning bolt. I hope I get the chance to ask him about it later.

"Tatum." Jay takes my face in his hands. "Look at me."

I feel strange. I swear I'm looking at him, but I find it hard to move.

"You need to breathe, baby. Breathe for me."

Putting his hand to my chest, I feel a slight jolt to my chest. I gasp for air, my lungs expanding and deflating with each rapid breath. "What happened?"

"I think you were in shock for a second, but I need you to listen to me." I nod for him to continue. "We need to kill Adam."

"What?" While I always wanted Adam out of my life, I never thought it'd be quite like this. Looking over at him, I watch as his eyes begin to twitch, the once-bright glow now slowly transitioning back to the blackish-purple they were a few minutes ago.

"We don't have much time. He's going to come to shortly, and he's not going to stop."

"I want to do it." Jay freezes at my words, his eyes growing wider. "I want you to help me take his powers and tell me what I need to do to end this. We'll never be safe until we do."

He grasps onto my shoulders. "Come with me."

Following Jay over to Adam, he places my hands on either side of my dad's head.

Dad. That word suddenly feels disturbing in my head. Adam has never been a dad to me.

I think I always knew he was destined for darkness. And while I always hoped for better for myself, I'm not sure something like this exactly breaks me free from the bleak side of my DNA.

Without instruction, my hands start sparking, painful jolts of electricity slowly moving up my arm. "Ouch, fuck!"

Jay pulls my arms away. "I don't think you should do this."

"What? Why?" I stare up at him, baffled. "I need to learn how to harness my power. He's going to come to and kill us! Are you crazy?"

"T. You're already part VOE. Should you really take on more darkness?"

I study my hands, noticing black tendrils snaking their way through my veins. Maybe this isn't such a good idea. Maybe something like this will wake the evil lurking beneath my skin.

Or maybe it will just save us—save Jay—from Adam forever.

"Just tell me what I need to do."

Jay doesn't seem sure, but he says, "From what I've heard before, it's more thought than anything else. Once you touch someone with powers, you're going to want to picture the power swimming within them. After you find it, you need to do whatever it takes for you to activate that energy of yours. It draws it in. But there's a catch…do it quickly, for a short amount of time, and you can take on their powers for a brief period. Do it until they go unconscious, and not only do you kill them, but you permanently take their powers. Siphoning is risky business, T. Very risky."

Abruptly, Jay and I are catapulted back, Adam's shadows back with a vengeance.

"How dare you think you can kill me! And my own daughter at that. What, Tatum? Scared of the dark side? Scared to actually become powerful?"

Pushing myself up from the ground, I gasp as I spot Jay dangling from a shadow eerily shaped like an arm. He is grasping at his throat again, the blue in his eyes fading fast.

I run straight for Adam, but his silhouettes knock me back down.

"Let him go! Let him go, right now!" I fight to get back up, instantly remembering that I still have some of Adam's powers housed within me.

Turning around, I close my eyes and breathe through my nose, readying myself for battle. *You can do this, Tatum. Darkness doesn't make you bad.*

"Awe…poor thing has to turn around and hide her tears from Daddy. What say you, Jay? Who's supposed to be saving Tatum no—"

He doesn't get to finish. The shadows billowing out of my fingers seize every single one of his limbs, and I stare up at him, his body dangling like a starfish in the sky. "Let. Him. Go." My voice has taken on a very cryptic, echoey tone. Whatever is wrong with it does the trick. Jay falls to the ground, unmoving, which only fuels my rage.

I pull him closer, using his own power against him. "You see, *Daddy*, you thought you helped create the villain of your dreams. Instead, you only helped form the monster of your nightmares. And as for the saving bit, I can do that myself, thanks."

His evil cackle ricochets off each part of my eardrum, sending boiling hot fury coursing through my veins.

I slam him to the ground, waves of power flowing beneath the surface of the earth. Standing over him, I command the shadows to pin him to the ground. He twitches this way and that, fighting against what will soon be *my* power.

"What's wrong?" I sneer. "Afraid of the dark?"

And with that, I run around his body toward his head. I sneak a glance back where my mom remains unconscious, hoping and praying this doesn't change me like Jay thinks it might.

I grasp onto both sides of his head again, and I do what Jay told me. It only takes me milliseconds to find the beast housed within him, and I latch onto it with my bare hands. It thrashes, trying to fight off my grip, but I hold steady.

I'm getting closer to pulling it out from its hiding place when I feel something calling to me.

"Tatum, no! Stop!"

Jay...

Unsure how my brain is able to do two things at once, I send a shadow out to hold Jay back, ordering it like it's my own pet.

It feels wrong for a second, but quickly passes. *I have to do this.*

Adam is my problem. He is my fight.

I find the beast once more, yelling to it. "Dark Doom!" It rears its ugly head. Long, yellow teeth hang from its mouth, dark purple eyes staring straight through me. "You're mine!"

I take on all that darkness and consume it, falling backwards. It doesn't seem so scary when it's stealing you away…

CHAPTER TWENTY-FOUR

 loudly.

"Try to catch me, Daddy!" I yell behind me, turning back to see him chasing me, so much loving light emanating from his eyes.

"I'm gonna getcha, Tater Tot!" he says in a silly, booming voice.

I yell out as he grabs me, throwing me over his shoulder with a swift grace. "Let me go!"

"Never! Now that I've caught the princess, I need to take her to the grand ball. Princesses can't miss their own balls. Don't you want a fancy introduction before you bound down the stairs in your big fancy dress?"

I giggle as I bounce against his back, watching the driveway filled with chalk drawings pass us as we go. "But I don't have a prince to escort me!"

He spins us around, and I scream again before he carefully places me on the ground. He bends down and takes my hand like the princes do in all those fancy princess movies, looking into my eyes with a warm gaze. "Never fear, sweetheart. I will always be there to escort you, should any undeserving prince let you down. Shall we go for tea?" He lightly kisses the top of my hand and arches his eyebrow.

"We shall," I say, leaping into his arms. "I love you, Daddy."

"I love you more."

Sucked away from the dream is like being sucked up by a cyclone. I cough and sputter for a few seconds as I fight to get my bearings about me.

"What the hell was that, Jay?" I gaze up into his wonderfully blue eyes.

"That was me showing you what it could be like if you wanted me to give you new memories of Adam. He could be the dad you should've always had." I push away from him and scooch back until my body slams into a tree. The pain doesn't faze me; it only briefly distracts me from the ache spreading through my body. *What have I done? Where is my mom? Where's Adam?*

My eyes scan the treeline until I find Mom quite a ways away. She's still lying soundly a few yards over, safe and undisturbed.

"Tatum?" Jay calls, inching closer.

"No."

His brows lift in surprise. "No, what?"

"I don't want new memories."

"Are you sure?"

I bring my knees to my chest. "I am who I am because of what I went through with him, Jay. I was strong enough to make it through my entire life without him, and even when he did come back, I grew far stronger and braver than I've ever been. I don't want to forget where I came from, or how I made it to this. I don't want to forget how bad things can get, or how good it can make you."

My eyes wander to him, my tears blurring his face. "A part of me died when he left as a kid, but I rebuilt myself.

Then, another part of me died when he came back and turned out to be an utter failure, but I fought my way out, hoping for change. The same part died again tonight as I watched someone who helped create me become my worst nightmare right in front of me." I stop, closing my eyes with a difficult swallow. "But you saved us."

"No, I didn't."

I stare directly into his face, confusion seeping through each of my pores. "What do you mean?"

"You did it, T. You saved yourself. You saved all of us." He smiles warmly at me. "You're the hero in this story."

My gaze drifts between the sky, the trees, and my hands for a few minutes. Bewilderment creeps across my mind, the gears spinning round and round as I try to recall what happened before everything went black.

"Are you okay?" Jay asks, his voice quiet and almost muffled.

I look up at him. "What happened?"

"You don't remember?" His brow quirks, and I swear if I didn't know better, he was looking at me like he didn't recognize me at all. "He's gone."

"How did he get away?"

Sadness washes over Jay's face briefly. I so badly want to reach out, but something inside stops me from doing it.

"He didn't. He's…dead, Tatum. You killed him."

I blanch. "But I—but where's his body?"

Jay's Adam's apple bulges with a large swallow, the blue of his eyes so dismal, it's almost nonexistent. "T, you siphoned his powers. You did what I told you to, and it took the life right out of him. His body disintegrated the moment you fainted, and the dark particles he was made of blew away. I watched it with my own eyes."

Time stops. My eyes stare, unblinking. Jay stills. My chest locks.

I killed him…

I actually killed him.

I took my dad's life, and I'm not sure how to feel.

"I-I murdered him. I'm a murderer, Jay!" I move my eyes down to my hands, watching them tremble and shake. "I'm just like him! I'm bad!"

Jay takes my hands in his, a dangerous move in and of itself. "Tatum, look at me." I do. "You are nothing like him. You did what you had to do. He was never going to stop. Do you hear me? If you didn't kill him, he was going to kill all of us."

I nod, my mind trying its best to go somewhere else. "I know. I know. You're right. But why do I feel like I didn't do enough? Why does it feel like there's more left?"

Jay gets up, lifting me and drawing my body to him. He then grabs both of my shoulders and leans back, holding me an arm's length away. "I need to tell you something."

"Okay?"

"Adam was not the only VOE after you…there's another."

"Worse than Adam?" I glance over at Mom again, wondering why she's still out.

"Much worse." Jay takes hold of my chin, bringing my attention back to him. "I'll wake your mom once I get her back home. You don't need to worry. She's fine. But listen…" He steps back from me, shifting from one foot to another. "The VOE who is after you is bad news."

"Like…Thanos-level bad news? Are we talking 'world-ending' bad?"

Jay scans the perimeter before looking back at me. "Not that bad. Think more *Spider-Man's* Green Goblin…he goes by the name Dr. Desolation. He is a scientist who ends lives with almost a snap of his fingers, and twists science in ways no one should…"

"What would he want with me?"

"Revenge. Adam was made, Tatum. He wasn't meant to be a VOE. He stole serum from Dr. Desolation before you even existed, somehow hearing about what it could do to him. He thought he could hide here, using your mom as protection, but when you came along, he knew he had to leave. You were born from someone injected with the serum, which has never happened before. Adam knew he had to wait until you developed your powers because you'd be worth way more than sacrificing his life. He meant to give you to the Doctor to avoid retribution."

"He was planning to sacrifice me? Fucking hell! As if we haven't been through enough—"

He takes my face between his hands, staring straight at me, the blue hues of his irises roaring back to life. "It's no longer a plan, Tatum. This is going to happen."

"How do you know?"

"I went into Adam's mind while you were in there and asked him myself."

I grab onto Jay's wrists, pulling them away from my skin. "What did he say exactly?"

Jay's eyes flutter as he sighs. "Darkness is coming."

"Are you sure about this?" I question, suddenly very worried about Jay having us on full display up in the sky.

He lifts me into his arms. "Absolutely," he answers, kissing me square on the mouth and rising into the night, carrying me close to the moon and stars that are suddenly so beautiful, they take my breath away.

Neither of us utters a word as Jay soars through the air. The cold breeze drifts over my skin as I try my hardest not to close my eyes. I don't want to miss a second of this.

I'm pretty sure there is not a single movie out there that could prepare you for something like this. Magic seems to be the only thing I can compare it to. This literally feels magical. The way the lights are glistening down below resemble the twinkling of Christmas lights. The peaceful dark of night seems unreal this close to it. Even the air seems clearer.

For a moment, I can almost forget what has transpired tonight.

Once Jay drops me off at home, I shakily make my way up the staircase.

Arriving at my room, I weasel my way through the door and station myself in front of my window, wanting nothing more than the chance to stare up at the moon, taking any amount of time I'm given to pretend my evening didn't turn out the way it had.

Even though I managed to rid this earth of my evil father, I can't help but feel like I'm taking too big of a chance walking around with a power like his swerving its way through my body, taking up space in what was a decently *good* body.

After about thirty minutes of waiting for Jay to show back up, I maneuver toward the bed, lean against the headboard, and try to let my eyes rest.

"What are you doing?" I nearly jump out of my skin at the sound of Jay's voice.

Whipping my eyes open at the speed of light, my hand thumps over my chest. "Holy shit. You scared me. What the hell are *you* doing?"

"Uh, coming back?" he questions, his eyebrows lifting in wonder. He holds up his hand to silence me. "I know. You're confused. Is it okay if we sit down and talk about what just happened?"

Jay's knee pops when he takes his first step toward the bed. His delicious scent wafts through the air and fills my nose the moment he plops down next to me. "He's gone, T. You're safe now."

Safe…such a loaded word. A part of me should be over-the-moon excited about the fact that we *should* be able to rest easy with Adam being gone. But that was taken away from us just as quickly as it was given.

Adam fucked us over from the beginning, setting us up for destruction…destruction that *should* be destroying *him* instead of us.

Life can be so unfair.

"Thank you," I softly whisper.

"Tatum…" he starts, pulling my attention to him. "I'm sorry."

"For what?"

"This isn't fair." He couldn't be more accurate. When I don't respond, he picks up where he left off. "You deserved a dad who loved you, a dad who wanted to keep you safe. You didn't do anything wrong, and whether you believe it or not, you have grown so much stronger over the course of this past year; far stronger than anyone I've ever met."

"I haven't been strong, Jay. I've been terrified, hoping and praying you would always be there to protect me from what I couldn't."

He stiffens. "No. Don't say that. Tatum, you may feel that way, but it's not true. Despite everything that went down, you didn't give up—you pressed on and eventually took a stand against him. Heroes aren't created overnight. You are amazing, and I'm in awe of you." His arm wraps around my back as he pulls me close. "Please promise that you believe me."

His words bounce around in my mind. Maybe there is some truth to what he's saying. Even though I have been terrified for months, I tried not to give up. I did what I could and ended up taking matters into my own hands, ending the raging battle that swept through our house for so long.

"But I'm not a hero, Jay."

Silence stretches between us for what feels like eons.

"Don't say that."

"It's true. You know as well as I do. I'm born from evil, and now I made the decision to take more on. I'm nothing but a ticking time bomb." *And a murderer…*

"You're different from them, Tatum. I don't care how long it takes to convince you of that fact, but I'll spend the rest of eternity doing it. You will *not* go bad. I won't let you. There's too much light in you to go dark."

Jay has an awful knack for always seeing the good in everyone. I am no different. What he fails to realize is that it doesn't matter how long you know someone—or how well you know them—people can change.

Just like the sunset being swallowed up by night, it's only a matter of time before the bleak shadows try to devour me from the inside out.

I obviously would never want this for myself, but there's a

part of me that thinks you don't always get a choice in what cards you've been dealt.

I just have to hope and pray I can overcome this, that I can keep hold of the flame inside me, even when the gloom tries to snuff it out. Or most of all, at least hold it back long enough to get everyone else as far away from me as they can go.

CHAPTER TWENTY-FIVE

I wake up the next morning to an empty bed. Jay must've left sometime after I fell asleep. After such an eventful night, I barely had any energy to discuss what happened much further.

Turning over, I find a note on the pillow Jay should be resting his head on. I blink a few times before zoning in on his scrawled handwriting:

> Morning, T. You should really discuss things with your mom when you get up, but be warned, I wiped away the entire night. Let her tell you what she remembers. Fill in the blanks with what you deem necessary. Then, come to my house. We need to talk.
>
> XO - Jay

"We need to talk" are words no one ever wants to read from their significant other. But when one of you is an actual superhero, and the other was born part villain, I guess there can be lots to talk about.

I groan loudly as I stretch my limbs like a stiff rubber band before tossing the comforter off of me.

Spring is in full motion now, and I'm excited to slip on some leggings and a long-sleeved shirt. The action feels *normal*…as normal as it can feel on a day like today.

Coming down the stairs, I throw my hair up in a ponytail as I listen to the clatter of Mom doing dishes. I almost want to stop and head back upstairs, but after everything she's been through, the least I can do is provide her with an explanation.

I peek at her through the doorway to the kitchen and knock on the doorframe. "Mom?"

"Morning, sweetie." She remains stationary as she says it, her stillness drawing me closer.

"You okay?" I ask, slowly walking toward her.

She turns around, my eyes latching on to her blackish-blue bags and ashen skin. "I'm not sure, Tatum. What happened last night?"

My eyebrows quirk in question, hopefully not giving too much away. "Do you remember anything, Mom?"

She nods solemnly before bringing her hand to her forehead, her fingers stretching and bending as she rubs the skin with force. "I…I remember waking up in the middle of the night. Someone was knocking on the door."

"Then, what?"

"Adam. He was the one knocking. He was going on about how he needed you, but when you came down the stairs and told him to leave, he swore he'd never come back. It got really dark and smoky after that. Next thing I know, I'm back in my bed." She pauses, staring at me in a way that makes me feel like if she could read my thoughts, she'd be doing it right now. "Did that really happen?"

Internally, I sigh with relief. She doesn't remember anything about Jay, and so far, she doesn't seem to remember anything about what I did either; other than something entirely made up. Although, I'm worried about her being under the impression Adam is out there somewhere.

Why did Jay leave me to do this on my own? I don't know what to say. Let alone what I'm *allowed* to say.

"It did, Mom. All you need to know is that Adam is gone, for *good*. We're safe."

Tears begin to roll down her cheeks, her whole body sagging with astounding relief. "Oh, Tatum. Thank God. My girl, come here." She holds her arms wide open, and I slink in, pulling her tightly to me.

"It's okay, Mom. We're okay." The relief only lasts mere moments before the guilt sets in. We're anything but safe. If anything, we are in even more danger.

Adam was terrifying enough, but of course he had to be a total fucking prick and screw us completely; putting our lives at actual risk all to save his own ass.

At least it didn't work out in his favor. Now I just have to find a way to fix all of this with the least amount of collateral damage.

"Why don't you go lay down, Mom? You need some rest. I'm going to see Jay. He's probably worried about us."

She leans back, staring at me as if she's memorizing everything about my face. "I am utterly exhausted, honey. Are you sure you're okay?"

I nod, my lips in a tight-lipped grin. "I'm fine, Mom. Lay down. I'll see you later." I kiss her cheek before turning around to grab my purse off the table by the front door.

Wiping a stray tear from my cheek, I push through the door, softly pulling it shut behind me and double-checking it's locked. Could my mom love me as I am? Knowing what Adam has made me become, would she still recognize me?

Staring up at Jay's house, I find my throat suddenly way too dry, my feet glued to the sidewalk.

My body jerks at the sound of the door creaking open. Jay meanders onto the porch, looking as delicious and rested as ever, besides the dark hue to his eye color. "What's wrong?" he questions.

"Nothing." I shake my head, looking down at my feet. "You wiped everything from my mom's memory?"

The silence stretches on for too long. I lift my head and find Jay observing me, his hands shoved into the pockets of his sweatpants. For a brief moment, I wonder if it's because he wants to avoid touching me, or if he's trying to come off as *untouchable*.

"I did." My eyebrows raise before he continues. "It's more dangerous for her if she knows. Don't you think?"

"Yeah. I totally get that, but what happens now? The Do—"

He holds up a hand to stop me. "Come inside, okay?"

Jay walks back to the door and swings it wide open, his right hand sweeping toward the inside. I walk past him with my arms folded, unsure of where we stand. We were cuddling last night in my room, but today suddenly feels different.

I move to sit on the couch and smile when Jay appears next to me before my behind has even hit the cushion. "As I was saying, the Doctor is coming. We know that. Should we really keep my mom in the dark?"

Jay sighs, "Tatum…can we talk first?"

I swallow hard, nervous about what he could possibly want to discuss. I give him a curt nod before my hands begin to wring of their own accord. It's been a bit since they've done that. "About what?"

"I think we need to lay it all out there before we take on this Doctor. I want to know everything you never told me, but I also feel you should know how I became what I am." Jay sits on the opposite couch, a haunted look in his expression. Could the way he became a RED be that daunting?

"Do you want me to go first?" I ask, my voice small and higher-pitched than normal.

He adjusts himself on the couch to face me, giving me the utmost attention. "If you'd like to."

"I guess mine is shorter? I don't know." I shake my head, trying my best to gather my thoughts before explaining. "You know the original story behind Adam. Mom always told me he started out so great, but the minute I came along—as Adam mentioned in the forest—something changed. Mom said he became dangerous; doing things that frightened her. So, she asked him to leave. And at the time, he was more than willing to go…to leave us behind." I sniffle, wiping a stray tear from my cheek.

"I spent so many years of my life wondering about him. What he would look like, or how his voice would sound, should I ever run into him. But I never did…sometimes I'd almost search his name online, wondering if he was even alive." I sigh, my mind winding its way through years of memories where I often wondered what I could've ever done to lose the love of my own father. "When he came back, I really thought I'd finally have the chance to know what it was like to have a dad, but as you know, that never happened. I have been wishing all this time that he really was dead. He did something to me. And I know that you might say it's because there's a villainous part inside of me, but just being near him affected me…it was almost like he changed something about me, and even when he wasn't doing anything, there was this fear that would take hold of my insides and twist them until I could barely breathe."

Jay gets up, and my eyes follow him like those flashlights at the optometrist's office, trying to keep track of where he's going next.

He sidles up next to me, spreading his arms wide to pack me into his lap. "You didn't do anything wrong, Tatum."

"I was born, Jay. Just being made was what went wrong."

Jay shakes his head above me, his chin grinding against the top of my head. I close my eyes and snuggle in further, doing everything I can to keep my mind from focusing on what's buried within me.

"Adam was never supposed to be created. He messed with something he never should've. Truth be told, he did a damn good job covering it up, but he reaped the consequences of that. He created someone so unique that not even what he chose to become could earn the love of you or your mother. You were his kryptonite. Don't you see? You were his Achilles' heel."

He pauses to swallow before continuing, "And I have a theory about why you felt like you were changing. I've been talking to my dad. Not only do we think that being so close to Adam could've started your metamorphosis, but we think his shadowy powers could've had something to do with your emotional state."

"How do you mean?" I prod, looking up into his face. I want to reach out and touch his cheek in hopes that it will bring some sort of light back into those gorgeous eyes. Seeing them so dark feels almost hopeless.

"All of us, in some way, shape, or form, fear some sort of

darkness, right?" I nod against his chest, and he adds, "We think his shadows held some kind of power to manipulate emotions, making you constantly feel on edge and afraid."

"So, he made me develop my anxiety and depression?"

Jay looks down at me, studying my features with grace. "I think so."

"Fucking bastard." I push off from Jay's lap and begin pacing his living room. "I did not have to live like that all this time…I hate him! I hate him. Jay, why me? Why couldn't he *love me*?" I fall to the floor, heartbreak seeping through my body, weighing me down.

Abruptly, all of my senses are so in tune, I can't breathe. I can feel the change in temperature in the air surrounding us, can hear the creak of the boards under the rug as Jay moves off of the couch, can feel every carpet fiber against the palms of my hands.

"Get back!" I scream, terrified of what might happen, should he come closer. "*Get away from me!*"

His footsteps freeze before I sense him moving back behind the couch; not exactly a promising barrier to the power welling within.

"Tatum…come back to me," he whispers soothingly. My breaths sputter out of me as he starts to break down my walls. "It's okay. You're safe with me, every single part of you, even the parts you might not like right now."

And just like that, my walls crumble under his words. I look up at him, tears in my eyes. "Jay, I'm sorry. So sorry…"

"For what?" He leaps over the couch with ease, closing in on me. Not even holding my shaky hand up can stop him. "You don't scare me, T."

When he crouches beside me, I leap onto him, throwing my arms around his neck. "Thank you for loving me."

"It's a privilege to love you, Tatum. Your shitty father should've known that. He missed out on you, perished because of it, and not an ounce of pity will ever be found inside of me for him. He chose his path, and it destroyed him. I'm just sorry you had to have any part of it."

I close my eyes as his soft lips kiss my cheek. "I don't want to talk about me anymore."

"I'll go next, then," Jay begins, holding onto me as he stealthily slides his legs out from under him and almost floats down to the floor. "My dad had another sister once, other than my Aunt Heidi. Aunt Jayda was younger than my dad, and he loved to look out for her. When he started TI Industries, which obviously specializes in scientific engineering, she wanted to work there too.

"At the time, he had a potential business partner who approached him, wanting to branch into some sort of human enhancement, hoping to cure the sick. That man's name was Desmond. He fell in love with my aunt, and all seemed to be going well with a potential collaboration."

Jay hugs me tighter, and I feel a chill run through him. "What happened to her, Jay?"

"Desmond started acting funny during the meetings at TI, always finding a way to beat around the answers to my dad's questions, all the while wanting to focus on Jayda. So, my dad started to look into him, even did a scan on his hard drive. And let's just say, what he found was some dark shit.

"He forbade Jayda from seeing Desmond, telling her what a danger he was to society, and that pissed Desmond off. You see, he had plans to create an army of enhanced humans, using some of the darkest elements known to mankind. It had nothing to do with his original proposal, and the fact that he had been within TI Industries, working so closely with my dad, was petrifying."

Jay lets go of me, spinning me gently to face him before resting his forehead against mine.

"You don't have to finish, Jay. It's okay."

"No. No, I have to. For *her*…"

"Okay," I whisper, taking his hand in mine.

"Desmond took the information he had gathered from TI Industries, and when my aunt tried to stop him, tried to protect her brother…"

"No…" I murmur when Jay's hand begins to tremble. "Don't say it."

"He killed her."

Moments later, I've managed to pull Jay to the bedroom. Pulling the blankets aside, I crawl in, silently convincing him to join me.

Once he pulls me to him, our bodies molding into one, he heaves a deep sigh. "He had to watch it, Tatum."

"What?"

"He had to watch her die. There was nothing he could do. He had to watch his own sister die at the hands of a man who was supposed to love her just as much as he did."

"What happened to him?" I question, finally realizing why I've never heard of his Aunt Jayda before. How could anyone chance discussing this in a world so ignorant to power-possessing beings?

"He became Dr. Desolation."

I blanch, turning out of his arms to face him. *"What?"*

How could our stories be so closely intertwined without either of us knowing from the beginning?

His nod is slow and laggy. "He took the information from TI, created an injection in secret, and succeeded in turning himself into the ultimate villain, creating the term VOE. Desmond left after that, not a hint of regret on his face."

I bring my hands up to my mouth. "Your poor dad. It wasn't his fault."

"He feels like it was. That's why he started RED. He wanted to build an army of good to save those who couldn't be protected from the dark forces that work to destroy those we hold most dear." Jay rubs a hand down his face, looking at me once more. "He wanted me to be able to be safe and secure, and he wanted to ensure that I could protect those I loved too."

"Like your family."

His head shakes back and forth. "No... Like you."

"I don't need protection...not now."

"But you did. You just needed someone to watch out for you while you figured out how to save yourself."

My right hand swings around to the back of his head as I pull him close, molding my mouth to his.

Jay was right. For so long, I thought I needed a hero to save me.

Turns out, I did.

It just had to be me...

My only concern is...if I was able to save myself, but had to kill someone in the process, what did that truly make me?

CHAPTER TWENTY-SIX

I JOLT AWAKE TO THE FEELING OF MY BODY VIBRATING. Casting a glance around the room with tired eyes, I rub my hands along my skin, feeling for anything that could be causing this strange feeling.

"Jay?" I call, my mind tingling with confusion.

The door swings open, making me jump. Jay walks through it, his hair sticking up every which way, like his hand has been running through it all night.

"What's wrong?" I question, moving to get off the bed.

"He's coming."

Just as I'm about to ask who, it hits me.

Dr. Desolation…

He is coming for me. Already.

I knew this day would come, but I didn't realize it would happen so soon. I've only just learned how to siphon, and now that I've taken on Adam's powers, I don't even know how to control them.

Being a superhero is all about control; being able to use your powers at will, knowing when to stop an attack, and having the power to decide what to do next.

I don't know how to do any of these things without Jay, and now that the Doctor is coming, there's no way he can be by my side throughout the entire showdown.

As Jay moves over to his dresser, I'm plagued with questions...are our families safe here? Do we need to get them out? Is there a light to signal the rest of the REDs for help? Will the Doctor be bringing more VOEs with him?

Before I realize what's happening, Jay has my face between his hands. "Tatum, look at me."

I blink a few times before latching onto his gaze, the blue color masked behind a smoky sheen. "Huh?"

"I have to go." My eyes widen at his admission. "I need to figure out what's going on. Can you please get our families out of here? I'll meet you at RED in an hour."

"Don't go. Please."

He pushes my hair back and peppers my forehead with kisses. "This is it, T. You're a RED now. Sometimes, we have to do things we don't want to. Now, get up. You have a job to do."

Everything inside of me wants to smile because I might finally have a chance to prove to myself that I have everything inside of me to be a RED, but the fear of what's to come is quickly taking over. "I'm scared." *What if I kill someone again? Someone important...*

Jay yanks me up to him, his hug slowly pushing the air out of my lungs. "Just because you are strong, doesn't mean you can't be scared."

I squeeze him as hard as I can, the weight of what we're up against crushing us closer. "Just promise me something."

He leans back, holding me at arm's length. "What's that?"

"Find me again. You have to."

"As long as you promise me something in return." The hint of a smirk rests around his mouth.

I quirk a brow. "Okay?"

Jay huffs before a sinister whisper floats toward my ear: "Kick the Doctor's ass. Make him pay."

A triumphant feeling washes over me, a mixture of who I've been and who I'm becoming, turning and twisting together to create an even better version of who I once was.

I puff out my chest, a devilish grin sweeping over my face. "Oh, I plan on it."

***

"We've gotta go, guys." I usher Jay's parents out to the driveway, where my mom is already waiting.

"Tatum…" Jay's dad beckons, gently pulling me to walk with him behind his wife. "I need you to listen to me. The REDs are already at TI. We have a couple of premade RED injections in the lab office there for the possible recruits we've been meeting with. You need to go there. Tell Maleko they need to be hidden. We can't risk the VOEs taking them."

"Okay. I'll do it." I kiss his cheek and go to pull away, but he hugs me tightly. "It's going to be okay." I have no idea why I even said that. I can't guarantee anything, and if there's anyone who knows how dire this situation is, it's this man.

"You have no idea what you're capable of, my dear. Please look out for my son. I'm going to take your mom away from here. Take care of yourself. We love you."

"I love you too. Mom is going to seem a bit out of it. Jay had to mess with her mind a bit to keep her calm."

His sad smile is grim. "We'll take good care of her. Get going. You should be with the others so they can protect you."

I wait on the porch, watching them load into the Tenlin's Cadillac before pulling away. Neither Jay nor his parents told me where they were going with Mom. They figured the less I knew, the safer they'd be. There's no telling what Dr. Desolation will try to do to me, and we can't risk him taking information, hence why I didn't ask Jay more about what he is.

After they turn the corner, I sprint to my mom's car, checking my phone for any messages. Still nothing from Jay...

The drive over to TI Industries, as well as the elevator ride down to the RED floor, pass by in a flash. Either I'm barely paying attention, or I'm suddenly able to move at the speed of light.

Dashing through the entryway, I find the REDs scattered around the main room, all at what I assume are their own desks.

"Tatum?" Maleko calls, confusion blanketing everyone else's faces.

"What the hell is she doing here?" Koral's menacing tone floats over to me.

I clear my throat, avoiding everyone's questioning glances as I pin Maleko with a stare. "I need you to take me to the lab office. We need to talk."

Once we get in there, I start ripping open drawers and cabinets, rifling through their contents.

"Whoa, whoa, whoa. What is going on?" Maleko walks closer, grasping both of my wrists with his ginormous hands. "Tatum, what are you looking for?"

"Mr. Tenlin. Injections. He needs us to hide them."

Maleko turns around and presses a button I never noticed before along the side of the hospital-like bed I sat on not too long ago. A hidden drawer pops out, containing three small syringes filled with red, almost-shiny liquid. The sight is mesmerizing. How can a shot be so beautiful?

"Here, take them. I need to let everyone know what's going on, and then I'll help you hide them before we figure out where we need to be."

I take the injections in my hand, staring at them a beat too long. I find myself wanting to run my fingers along them, wondering what they'd look like in the daylight. I wonder if they have the power to change bad powers into good. Could I be injected with one?

Maleko clears his throat, waking me from my stupor. "S-sorry. I'm ready," I reply shakily.

He glares at me a beat too long before leaving the room. I shove the small syringes into my pocket, patting them for safety, making sure to move nimbly so as not to break them.

Exiting the hallway, I come face-to-face with my own set of Avengers. My jaw goes slack as my eyes move across the league of heroes standing before me.

Koral stands as still as a statue, her serious look terrifying enough to turn someone to stone. The only part of her skin I'm actually able to see is her face; everything else is covered in her suit. It's a deep brown, with some lines of varying cocoa-colored and tan hues cast throughout it. It resembles the bark of a tree.

Nate stands next to her, pulling on a pair of sleek, flat-soled shoes. His suit is interesting and unique. Each limb is a different muted color—one of his legs is a silvery shade, the other a dark black, one of his arms a golden yellow, and the other a deep red. Smack-dab in the middle is a rigid, muscle-accentuating white mixed with a blue hue. Nothing dons his head, leaving his red hair on full display.

Maze and Dola sit on their desk chairs, their attire

capturing all of my attention. Maze is sporting a metallic black suit—one that doesn't look very comfortable or flexible —with bits of gold found along each jointed area, a mix of a pair of sunglasses and a classic cloth mask covering the area around his eyes, giving off major *Robocop* vibes.

Dola is the most breathtaking of all. Her suit is almost non-existent, barely visible to the naked eye. If I didn't know better, I'd say she was wearing a suit made of the same material as an invisibility cloak. It puts her ebony skin and navy leotard on full display. The almost-invisible suit casts a sparkly, iridescent-blue sheen over her skin.

Tied around her waist is a sky-blue belt, and flowing toward the back from that belt is a lightly evident, glittery, blue tulle-like material. It just barely brushes the floor. On her feet are a pair of stark black, ankle-high boots. And finally, a helmet similar to a globe protects her braid-covered head. If I didn't know better, I'd say she resembled a queen.

On the other hand, Maleko is still wearing his civilian clothes, suddenly making me feel more comfortable in mine too. In all the rushed time since finding out what I am and taking on my father's VOE powers, I don't even know what I should be wearing, let alone what I can consider calling myself.

"We will head out and confer outside, Mal. I have a feeling Dr. Desolation will be bringing the fight here. I'm sure he knows where Tatum would be, and he has things he wants here. We need to scout the area." Dola's voice is assertive and intimidating. She tilts her head toward the elevator and all of the REDs—minus Maleko—walk briskly in the direction of the doors.

"Wow," I whisper to myself, in awe of the group moving out to battle for me, someone they barely know. In my chest, there's a deep pounding that tells me I'm not beyond saving, but something in my heart tells me not to jump to conclusions too quickly.

"Are you ready?" Maleko asks, checking his watch as he awaits my reply.

I cough into my arm. "I have no idea what I'm doing, Maleko."

"None of us do."

I shake my head, "Not true. You guys know you are REDs. You all know what you're doing. You've done this before. I—I don't even know what I am."

He saunters over to me, putting his hand on my elbow. "But you know who you want to be. Remember that when we're out there. I can't tell you what we're up against." His eyes flick between mine. "None of us can. All we can do is fight for the greater good."

"Do you think Jay will make it in time?"

Maleko looks at his watch again. "I just pinged him. I'll check it once we get outside. Can I have the syringes now?"

I pause, suddenly feeling protective of them. I want nothing more than to be able to say I've been injected with one of those rather than admitting I have remnants of VOE powers coursing through my veins.

"Tatum." Maleko's tone is urgent and forceful. I stare up at him, wondering what would happen to me if I were to administer the serum on myself. Would it kill me? Would it make me strong? Would it wipe out the darkness inside of me? Or could it possibly make me both RED and VOE?

Not wanting to panic Maleko, I quickly slip the injections into his hand and curl his fingers in, asking a question to avoid speculation. "Where's your suit?"

His grin is soft and lopsided as he presses a button on his

watch before shoving his other arm with the injections into his pocket.

Before my very eyes, a bright red material sweeps over his skin. I jump back with a gasp as I watch it slither over every inch of his body, skipping his head.

When it finishes its route, a shiny yellow material stitches its way along the outline of his body. The finishing touch is a single, deep green leaf that covers the tops of each foot. I wonder if it's native to Hawaii, where he is from.

"Wow, Mal. You look fantastic."

He bows his head toward me. "*Mahalo*, Tatum. Shall we?"

I swallow loudly, glancing down at my feet before casting my gaze back up at him. "Sure."

CHAPTER TWENTY-SEVEN

Emerging from TI, we are greeted by darkness; the sky is so dismal, I suddenly feel like days have passed since walking inside the building.

The property surrounding us is wide and expansive; flat land circles us for miles, sparse trees and foliage throughout it, and then massive groups of trees bordering the perimeter, along with a tall, iron fence.

TI Industries probably resembles the large areas some factories are housed on, but their spacious land and extensive buildings are more for security and privacy than anything else.

Something beneath my skin starts to tingle, and I twitch.

"Tatum? Are you okay?" Maleko asks.

I hug my arms around myself. "I'm not sure. Something feels off."

"I'd say you're spot on with that." His eyes inspect the sky before he turns to me once more. "Stay with the others. I need to go hide these. I'll be back before you know it."

"But what about J—"

Maleko's gone before I can finish my question, leaving me reeling. I turn my attention back to the other REDs. They have scattered throughout the property—Koral floating up in the sky, her head sweeping right and left, while the McCoy twins and Nate alternate between walking the perimeter and playing with their watches.

I wonder what all they can do on those devices. They must be important for all of them to be this focused on them so frequently. It makes me wish I had one.

A flicker of movement near Dola catches my eye, and adrenaline nearly stops my heart.

"Dola! He—"

The words are knocked right out of my mouth as something crashes into me, sending me flying backwards, my back skidding across the cement parking lot. "Fuck!" I yell out, the pain slowly working its way up, seeming to never end.

When I'm finally able to lift my head and open my eyes, I scream as I come face-to-face with a hideous beast. Its dog-like body is halfway between hunched over and being on all fours.

Before I can gather my thoughts, it lunges at me. My hands fly up as if they'll be able to do something, but with me barely knowing how to conjure up my new shadow powers, I don't stand much of a chance.

Nothing happens, and as I squint my eyes back open one at a time, tilting my head in question, I find the heinous beast gnawing on an invisible barrier between us.

"What the—?" I swivel my head and find not only the REDs battling tons of terrifying creatures, but Maleko about a mile off, hidden beneath a tree, his attention completely focused on me.

I reach my hand out and attempt to touch what protects me, coming to the realization that Maleko must have thrown up a force field. *Thank God for him!*

Just as I'm about to nod in thanks to him, a scream erupts from my mouth as he gets knocked over by what appears to be nothing. My hands feel around for an escape to go help, quickly breaking through the area that was protected mere moments ago.

The beast's growl is louder than it was when I was sheltered inside that bubble, and I back away slowly, trying with all my might to get my body to conjure up something from the plethora of power living within me.

"Come on now, little doggie. Shoo shoo…" I wave my hands in his direction, hoping like hell there's some sort of natural instinct that will drive this thing away.

Instead of running away, the creature continues closer, stalking me like the prey I am. As I turn to run, a searing pain shoots through my left calf, knocking me back to the ground. I crawl away, the beast's growl growing louder and louder.

I close my eyes before flinging myself onto my back, the dog leaping onto me at the same time. My hands grasp around its leathery neck, attempting to fight it off as it nips at every bit of space between us.

"Get off of her!" Maleko runs full-throttle at the beast, slamming his body into it, sending it flying. He moves to help me up, but his arm gets snatched up into the jagged jaws of the beast. He cries out in agony.

"Maleko! *No!*" And with my screech, black tendrils of shadow erupt from my fingers, riveting through the air before snatching up the beast by the neck and snapping it. It falls to the ground, lifeless.

I tremble. *Not again.*

I take a few steps back, heaving breaths too quick to take in enough air, my eyes wide with the realization of what I've done. The shadows recede back into my body, leaving me feeling weak and vulnerable once more.

The pain serves as a reminder of my injuries, and as I

sneak a peek at the back of my leg, my gut wrenches at the sight of mauled flesh. There's no way that was just a single bite.

"Tatum! Holy shit! Are you all right?" Maleko's panicked face checks me over from head to toe, his stare latching on to my leg. "I'm sorry. I tried to get to you faster."

I stare up at him, speechless as I watch the rest of the REDs attempting to fend off the rest of the creatures behind me. "This isn't working."

"What do you mean?"

"You can't do this on your own, Maleko. You can't fight *and* protect me. We need Jay."

His chin tilts up toward the sky as he closes his eyes and takes a cleansing breath. "I have an idea."

"Okay, what is it?"

"You're not going to like it…" He grabs onto my forearm. "Can you walk?"

"Um…"

Before I can get out another word, he scoops me into his arms, pulling a yelp from my throat. "Forget it. There's no time. Hold on."

He catapults into the air, and I watch as the force field slides into place, almost invisible, but casting just enough of a sheen that I can see it. "The others!"

"They'll be fine for now."

Seconds later, we land on the roof of TI Industries, hidden behind rows of solar panels. I'm just barely able to see Maleko's face because the panels block out almost the rest of whatever light was left down there under the darkened sky.

"Tatum, I need you to listen carefully, okay? I'm going to speak fast."

I nod at him, not giving myself time or room to interrupt.

"I think Jay is in trouble." He pauses when my eyes widen. "We are losing out there, and I have a bad feeling that the Doctor is close. If we're having this much trouble, we're really in for it when he arrives. You're our only hope. You're the only one who can find Jay, because like you said, I can't fight *and* protect you."

"What does this have to do with me?"

He leans in close, his mouth skimming the edge of my ear. "You need to siphon my powers."

I jolt backwards, "What? No! I'll kill you."

His hand slams over my mouth. "Shh. No, you won't. You're going to siphon just enough that you take my powers. Yes, I'm going to pass out, but I'll live. I'll just be normal again. There's something I need to do. In the meantime, you need to find Jay and rain hellfire on Dr. Desolation's ass."

"I can't."

He stares straight into my eyes with a power that over-throws my thoughts. "I'm not asking about your ability. I'm giving you an order. As a hero, we need you."

My breath squeezes out through my scarcely open mouth before I answer, "Okay…tell me what I need to do."

"I assume Jay explained how the process works, yes?" Maleko suddenly seems nervous, and I can't say I blame him. The strong hero he has become is about to be stripped away, all because I can't fucking figure out how to control my own power to save us from something that is my own fault. I'm the reason Dr. Desolation is coming here. I'm the reason we're in this war.

I nod. "Yes." My swallow echoes through my head. "I think I can do it again."

"Okay. Before we begin, I need to give you my watch. You'll need it to find Jay. But Tatum…" He freezes. "When I pass out, you will have no time to waste. You need to take the powers you've acquired and find Jay. Don't wait for me. I know what I'm giving up."

"I'm so—"

His finger presses against my mouth. "Don't be. You can't help your circumstances, Tatum. Whether we be hero or villain, all of our stories begin somewhere. That's why there's an origin story for each of us. You need to finish writing yours. I'm just grateful to be part of it."

My vision goes blurry as he moves to sit on the roof. "Maleko…thank you for believing in me."

"Every hero needs someone to believe in them; someone who reminds them what they're fighting for. You can do this, *hoaloha*."

I sniff back an almost-sob. "What does that mean?"

"Friend." His smile is small and tired. "You have been my friend. We don't get many of those outside of what we are. Now, let's begin."

Maleko lies down on the ground. I take a cleansing breath before squatting down to follow him and allow my hands to latch onto his head. All of a sudden, the pain in my leg dissipates, swiftly becoming the least of our problems.

Just like Jay told me, I close my eyes, pushing my thoughts deep into Maleko's. I'm instantaneously sucked in through a kaleidoscope of greens and blues as bright as the plants and waters of Hawaii itself; at least, that's what it feels like.

Where I found the dark varmint growing within Adam, I'm relieved to find a giant sea turtle within Mal. The animal sits along the sands inside of Maleko's mind, almost as if he is enjoying the sunset. I want nothing more than to push him out to sea and free him, but immediately realize the end of his journey has come.

"*Aloha, hoaloha.*" I clumsily repeat the words Maleko has slowly taught me over the course of our short friendship.

At the sound of my voice, the turtle's head swivels to the side, his friendly eyes latching onto mine.

I walk closer, the sand squeezing between all of my toes.

When I make it beside the creature, I sit down next to him and rest my hand on his shell, closing my eyes. "Thank you," I whisper, softly and gently siphoning his power from him; it's warm and comforting, like a cascade of warm bath water covering my skin.

"Stop, Tatum. It's enough." Maleko's small voice murmurs through my mind.

It takes everything in me to rip my hand from the shell, and before I realize what's happening, I'm sucked out of the scene, almost like waking from a fever dream.

Sweat drips down my face as I look down at Maleko. A tear squeezes out of the corner of my eye and slips down my cheek to join the droplets of sweat. He appears so peaceful and serene, but I know better. He just had everything ripped from him, his whole life changing in an instant.

While part of me wants nothing more than to take him in my arms and beg him to wake, his power quivers beneath my skin as if it's having a hard time coexisting with the shadows lurking within.

I gasp and sputter for breath, urging and begging them to coincide. "You will bend to my will. I am in charge here. I make the rules." I say the words aloud, ordering the newness inside of me to bow down to its new master.

Pushing myself up off of the ground, I feel the change. A new world order has begun. It's time to find Jay and end this.

It's time for me to be unleashed.

And no one knows what is coming…

CHAPTER TWENTY-EIGHT

It seems to take forever, but I finally figure out how to decipher my way around with this stupid watch. Two dots popped up on the GPS feature when I first opened it, and clicking upon both, I found that they were both labeled.

The first one I clicked was Jay's location, but the second one was tagged with a simple car emoji. I decide to follow the second one first, because with how far off Jay seems to be, I'm going to need some transportation to get there quickly.

As stealthily as I can with my injured leg, I climb down the ladder from the roof, maneuvering all the way down the left side of the building. It's quiet over here, and seemingly deserted. Once my feet touch the ground, I practically tiptoe toward the tree line, winding my way to the gate.

Looking up at the massive height of the fencing, I sift through ideas of how to get out of here, not wanting to waste time that might lead to me being caught by one of those beasts again, or worse, the Doctor himself . . .

Supposedly, I should have all of Mal's powers, including the ability to fly. While I'm much too nervous to fly myself to Jay and don't have time to practice, maybe I can at least gain enough height to make it over this partition.

Closing my eyes, I concentrate on the task at hand. I focus on what it felt like to fly with Jay, squatting down in an attempt to direct the energy I need to push myself into the air. Propelling upward, I set my mind up for trying to keep myself in the air, even if only for a short period. I hover for maybe two seconds, but fall back down, almost toppling over in the process as I cry out in pain.

This is taking too long, Tatum. Fucking jump! I internally holler at myself. Anger starts to sweep its way through me as I squint up at the top of the stupid barrier, instantaneously aggravated at how hard this is. If only one of these powers could heal my injury.

After jumping two more times to no avail, something behind me catches my attention. I whip around, and instead of coming face-to-face with one of those hideous creatures, I find a smoky shadow hovering before me.

Of course. Now they decide to come out.

I almost dismiss it and turn around to try again, but instead, a smirk grows on my face as I command the dark silhouette to help me climb my way over.

It works. The figure multiplies to resemble tentacles, and as they grab on to different parts of the bars and rails, I shriek as I'm lifted into the air, rapidly slapping my hand to my mouth so I'm not heard.

Landing on the other side, I take off limping at what feels like lightning speed, not giving myself time to think. And after wandering around a few random roads outside of TI's property limits, I've come to an abandoned street, save for a single gray car.

Dashing over to it, I try the door, which swings open easily. I slip inside, searching for a set of keys.

Feeling around, I discover a single key deep down in the cup holder. I push it into the ignition, start it up, and take off, following the GPS as best I can.

It takes almost fifteen minutes of driving before I finally pull onto the street Jay's location has brought me to. I click off the headlights, slowly and quietly making my way down the road.

After passing by numerous dilapidated houses, it's obvious the one on the very end is where Jay is at. Hoping to remain as conspicuous as possible, I park the car in the driveway before it.

Unsure of who or what I'll find in there, I almost silently shut the door behind me, looking for a place to hide the key should anyone try to steal it from the car or take it off of me.

A random rock catches my attention nearby. I lift it, placing the key underneath before letting it rest back in place.

I dust off my hands and make my way toward the building, dread filling every part of my body.

My feet begin to feel like I'm wading through quicksand as I peruse the shabby houses along the street, and I can't help but wonder if it could be because I'm so terrified of what might be happening to Jay, or if I'm suddenly having a reaction to the RED powers acclimating inside of me.

Briskly walking through the neighborhood until the watch buzzes against my skin, I come to a halt in front of a run-down, piss-yellow house; the windows are broken, and only half of a front door dangles from a single hinge.

My chest tightens because there's no way Jay would be wasting time here by choice. I can't help but feel like something happened here. Something tells me he needs my help.

My eyelids droop, suddenly heavy, which is only adding to my level of anxiety. Could my body reject the RED powers? And if so, who would know how to fix me? Can I even find and help Jay at this point?

I'm not so sure, but I have to try. He would do the same for me. It's time for me to be *his* hero.

Stumbling up the oddly quiet steps, I wrench my body through the incomplete door and crane my ear, trying to listen for any sign of life.

Roughly a minute passes in silence; I have to assume no one's here, but it's hard to see, so I force myself to move fast. I have no idea what's happening to the REDs I left behind, or if Maleko made it out okay.

"Psst. Jay?" I whisper out, my volume seeming loud enough to shatter glass.

I wince in both anticipation and pain because there's now a stabbing ache in my side, almost begging me to turn back. That thought is appalling enough.

Before I waste more time, I push myself to start making my way through the house.

Coming to the only closed door in the empty hallway, I grasp the tarnished doorknob and slowly give it a turn. The simple motion is enough to take the rest of the energy right out of my body.

Once the door is open, it's almost impossible to see. At least in the rest of the house, the broken openings to the home had some light from the streetlamps out front shining through. In here, it's almost like someone purposefully blocked off the windows.

Just as I'm about to call out Jay's name again, a quick intake of breath has the hair on the back of my neck standing on end. I slam on the watch with my hand, hoping with all that I have that the screen will provide enough light to see inside the room.

Somehow, with all the buttons I've pressed on the screen,

I notice a little lightbulb on the display. I click it, squinting my eyes in anticipation of blinding brightness.

Thankfully, a light starts to stream from the screen. I tilt my wrist and all but scream at the sight before me.

My poor, sweet Jay is bound so tight, he could pass for a chrysalis. His face is beet-red from the pressure being put on his upper body from being hung upside down. But it's the way his eyes are squeezed shut in pain that has me staggering away to throw up anything I've eaten today in the corner of the carpeted room.

The light dances around the space, bouncing off of walls covered with torn, striped wallpaper.

I can't do this. I seriously can't do this. I am no hero.

I close my eyes, begging whatever new, parasitic-like DNA is being created internally to help provide me with the steps of what I need to do to not only save the love of my life, but to help me become some sort of half-hero, at least.

My chest huffs out one last big breath before I force myself to turn around and move.

I rush over to Jay, using the light available to me the best I can, and take Jay's face in my hands. "Jay. Baby, I need you to wake up. Please wake up."

His eyelids flutter a bit but remain closed, and he groans low and deep.

"Damn it, Jay. I need you to wake up!"

My emotions start to get the best of me, and before I know it, a small, glitchy coil of blackness slowly crawls its way out of my hand and starts wrapping its way around him.

"Hey! No! You better not hurt him!" I yell at this thing, as if it's not sprouting from my very own flesh—but it's strange. It doesn't look like my normal shadows. It almost looks like a sickened version of one; hairy and jagged in appearance rather than the normal smooth smoke.

Abruptly, a thought bursts into the front of my somewhat-foggy mind: what if I'm able to tell this shadow to cut through ropes and set Jay free?

As soon as the thought appears in my mind, the shadow disappears without a trace, and my knees give out.

I fall to the floor, my flattened palms trying their best to keep me upright. "No! Fuck no! Come on!"

This cannot be happening. You cannot tell me that someone who thought she was just a regular old human, but then discovered she's actually part villain and took over powers from both a VOE and a RED, is destined to die in this piece of shit hellhole when she's literally standing next to the love of her life she's meant to save, on a day when the world could fucking implode because of her, all because the powers she siphoned like she was *meant* to might not adapt to wherever they are inside of her.

"This is just my luck," I say to no one.

Well, I suppose it could be Jay, but it's not like he's going to answer me.

"Well, well, well…look who we have here," a sleazy voice almost chants behind me. "If it's not Dark Doom's dopey daughter, come to…what? Save the day? Some hero you are, mere inches away from the person you're supposed to rescue." His heavy footsteps move closer. "Looks like you're meant to follow in your father's footsteps of being nothing but a damn fraud!"

I snarl at the sound of his phlegmy cackles…until I feel another presence enter the room.

"I suggest you both get the fuck away from me before I kill you both without even laying a hand on you." I try to keep up the volume, but whatever is happening to me is getting worse, and I'm wanting and wishing for whatever they know about me to be enough to scare them away, or at least keep them at bay; but at bay from what, I'm not entirely sure.

The rest of my energy is wiped out as something hard and metal bashes against my head, making everything go darker than it already was. I thought the bite on my leg was bad, but that's long since been forgotten compared to what's happening now.

Jay...

I blink rapidly, my head feeling swollen and heavy with the pressure being exuded on it. Something about the room is different, though. If I could just open my eyes enough, I'd be able to figure it out.

As a sliver of light catches my attention, my eyes fling wide. The men who walked in are now sitting in folding chairs along the opposite wall, albeit upside down. Their sneers fuel a rage in me I didn't know I possessed.

"'Bout time you wake up. Things are just about done. Looks like you let your precious REDs down."

I spit toward them. "What the fuck is that supposed to mean?"

The confidence I'm exuding is nothing compared to the fear building inside of me. What is happening out there? How long have I been out? Is there no one coming for us?

My gaze slips over to Jay, my heart sinking further seeing him still hanging there, unconscious. What did they do to him? He's supposed to be invincible...

Anger stacks on top of the rage, and I swear I see red. I

close my eyes, begging at least some remnant of my power to come forth. I have no idea how to do this, but if no one else is going to come for us, I guess it has to be me.

The blonde-haired, greasy man to the right of me starts to laugh, and I pin him with my gaze, which only makes him laugh harder. I force a swallow, because something about his appearance has me wanting to throw up all over again…not that there could be much left inside of me.

His pale, blotchy skin and dark, saggy eyes resemble that of a sickly man. Could this be a VOE gone wrong? Did he try for an injection and his body gave out?

Moving over to the second man, I shiver at his putrid stare, his eye color a haunting gray that appears to almost disappear. The high arch of his eyebrows and greasy slicked back, collar-bone length hair has me wondering if his injection went wrong, too.

Whatever is wrong with these guys, they definitely don't look—or act—right. We have *got* to get out of here before they kill us. And they will. I can feel it.

"Just wait until the Doctor gets a hold of you. That's what he needs to fix us. Ain't that right, Hex?" the blonde asks his accomplice.

Gray-Eyes punches him in the shoulder, "Shut up, Trace."

"Good to know you can't even keep your lips shut. I bet the Doctor would love that." For some odd reason, being upside down is not as tiring as it was when I first woke up. It's just annoying.

"Listen here, you little bitch!" Trace screeches, rushing over and slapping me across the face. Something starts to boil within me, sudden aggression coming over me.

Hex gets up to drag him back. "Stop it! Just stop! The Doctor will be here soon. We just need to sit tight." His eyes latch onto mine. "And you! Your shithole dad should've taught you a lesson or two on how to talk to men. Watch your mouth, or next time, I won't be so kind as to hold this asshat back."

ZING.

Here is the moment I've been waiting for; that cosmic shift that starts to create every hero and villain's origin story. The time when our minds race through every piece of darkness that got us to where we are now.

I stare down at the floor, gathering all of my worst memories: my dad treating me like shit and laying his hands on me, the moment he put his hands on my mother, his admission in the forest to the plans he had for us, how dark his mind was, finding out what he made me, and the words I just heard.

My neck starts to sway back and forth as I mentally click together the pieces of my life's puzzle, and when it's finished, I am met with the visual of a cracked orb—similar to the force field I'm supposed to be able to conjure up now, but the fractures are filled in with dark, sinews of shadows.

There's no one here to teach me how to use my powers. So instead, I need to trust myself; I need to trust that even though I possess so much corruption, the power of the person I truly am will be enough to make it something it wasn't inherently made to be.

That cosmic shift cracks within me, and I look back up at the men, my stare boring holes in their souls. "And what gave you the impression I'd be afraid of you?" My voice leaks death, its tone chilling me to the bone.

"What did you just say?" Hex shoots back. He gets up, his eyes squinting at me, while his fists squeeze tight.

"Why would I be afraid of you when it was so easy to kill my own father?"

Both of their faces go slack. "He's not dead," Trace fires off. "We're going after him next."

I command a shadowed hand forth, opening and clenching it in front of me. "You need not go far. I have his power right here. I took it after I killed him."

Trace gets up to join Hex, and they both begin to fumble backwards. "Get it out. The thing! Get it out!" Hex tries to dig in his pockets, and I almost cackle in disgust.

"I would ask you what you're getting, but there's no point. I have a more important question for the two of you."

I swear their gulps are loud enough to be heard down the whole street.

"Are you afraid of the dark?" And before I await their reply, I send a second hand out to join the first. They shoot out as fast as bullets and grasp their throats in a tight grip.

SNAP.

They go limp before I let them fall to the ground, and I sneer at my victory before sweeping my stare to Jay.

A second later, I'm shaking myself from a daze. This isn't me, but even I know we wouldn't be safe if they were to live. I can't have them knowing what I can do.

Murderer chants in my head again.

Please don't hate me, Jay. I'm going to get us out of here.

Murderer...

Monster...

Villain.

CHAPTER TWENTY-NINE

Bringing forth my shadows once more, I use them to not only cut me free from my bindings, but also to catch me before crashing to the ground.

They slowly bring me to the floor and gently lay me down. I scramble up, running over to Jay. Almost sensing my urgency, the shadows spiral up the outline of his body. They cradle his upper half while simultaneously cutting the large rope attaching him to the ceiling, repeating what they did for me as he slowly descends to the floor.

I push off the ropes after they cut through all of them, uncovering him. My hand flies to my mouth as I look at his amazing suit covered in cuts that go all the way to the skin. How could they have done this?

"Jay! You have got to wake up, damn it! Wake up!" I yell. We really need to get back to the fight.

Running through my new powers, I try to come up with a plan. There's nothing I can do with the force field, but maybe there's something the darkness can help me with.

They must have injected Jay with something for him to be out this long while still being able to breathe, but maybe I can siphon whatever it is out of him if I focus hard enough.

This couldn't be a better time to test my powers. All of them will have to work together to force Jay to wake up.

I push out a force field to cover the both of us, filling it with smoky shadows in hopes it will block our view as well.

As soon as I know we are safe, I focus all of my attention on him, kissing his forehead. "I'm going to save you, Jay. Just hold on."

Placing my hands on his chest instead of the head, where I've done all of my siphoning thus far, I close my eyes to begin.

Pushing my mind into his body, I search for something that might be out of place. His warmth and pure energy wafts over me, making me feel safer than I have since the day began. I smile with bliss.

My body twitches as I come across something unfamiliar. It's a dark energy, seemingly red in color, which I'm guessing isn't coincidental. His injection would've been red too, but whatever this entity is, it isn't friendly.

Latching onto it, it begins to fight back, almost cutting my presence with razor-sharp claws. I duck and sway, trying my best to stay out of its way.

Begging for back-up, I bring in the shadows to hold it steady, darting my hands out to where it can't hurt me.

The siphoning begins, but as it tries to attack my body, I remind it that I don't want any part of it either by sending it to the dark, murky shadows. They gobble it up like it's fuel and recede back inside me.

I start to drift out, sensing an ease from within Jay, and when I come out of the haze, I discover that Jay is starting to come to.

His eyelids quiver before opening. He stares up at the ceiling while I stare at those beautiful blue eyes, having missed them more than I thought.

"Jay?" I whisper, catching his attention.

With lightning speed, Jay whips around to face me, somehow still sitting on his bottom. Even with my own shit going on, his powers never cease to amaze me. I wonder if I'll ever get used to them.

After my mind is done trying to distract me from the scene behind me, I'm able to utter the words plaguing me.

"I killed them," I mutter. "I swear I didn't mean to." I wrap my hands around my head and start to rock back and forth.

"Shhh. Hey, hey. I know you didn't. You saved me. It's okay." Jay's arms wrap around me, his hands rubbing up and down my back.

I push his arms off and stand up, moving away from him. "But I didn't need to kill them, Jay! Damn it! What is happening to me?"

Jay follows suit, rushing toward me, but staggers as he slams into something I can't see. He rubs his forehead, and I quirk a brow, confusion setting in until I realize I must've put up a second force field by accident.

"How did you…?" Jay questions, his eyes growing wide.

I fall to the ground, utterly exhausted from everything. Between the battle raging outside, having to strip Maleko of his powers, killing the two VOEs behind me, and now the fear of what Jay is going to think of me, I cannot handle much more. "Mal gave me his powers. Fuck! This isn't fair. I mean, he's still alive, but now he's just a human. Jay, I'm scared! I don't know what is going on inside of me, and I'm fucking scared!"

My eyes slowly open as a warmth crawls over me. I find Jay's hands on the barrier, slowly stroking the orb like he would if he were smoothing my hair back.

"Tatum, why are you so afraid to be different? Being a RED is not sunshine and rainbows; saving everyone and killing no one. It's much more complicated than that. It's making the hardest fucking decisions you can possibly fathom to protect the ones you love and those you don't know. Just because you've had to take on things that feel more like burdens than blessings, doesn't mean they have to ruin who you are. I think you're more afraid of finding out what you might become, rather than staying where you've been. Change doesn't always have to be bad."

"But I can't control this." I gesture at myself. "I have no clue what to do with these powers, and I'm scared I'm going to hurt the people I love…specifically you."

He shakes his head. "Fear only harbors nightmares, but those dark dreams weren't prepared for me, nor were they prepared for what you truly are. Don't hide from your purpose. In time, it can help you. So can I."

I stare deep into his eyes, those opulent blue hues returning to his irises. "But what if you can't?"

"Well, we won't find out unless you let me try." He pauses a beat. "Trust me."

The shield breaks, disappearing into thin air, leaving me a confused heap on the floor. "I'll try."

"Super swear?" he adds. I nod. "Good, because we have a Doctor's ass to kick. Let's go."

***

Arriving back to the chaos on TI Industries' property, I can't help but throw up in a bush on the outskirts where we're standing. I was able to manipulate the shadows to somewhat stitch together the laceration on my leg during the car ride over here, but apparently, that was too much work on top of the RED and VOE concoction brewing inside.

"You okay?" Jay asks, patting my back as he assesses the situation.

I wipe my mouth, nodding as I stand back up. "Yeah…" My eyes move over the nearby crowd, and they stop at each RED, all of whom are still fighting against the VOEs' creatures. My heart pangs with regret as I feel Maleko's absence. He should be here, not me.

Koral and Nate are double-teaming what seems to be a pack of rabid wolfish creatures. Koral's hands swish and flow through the air, tree branches and clouds of dirt winding their way around the legs of the beasts. Nate, I realize, is not himself. He has since shapeshifted into a terrifying rhino and is spearing all the animals around him with his horn, scooping them off and stomping on them when he's finished.

Meanwhile, the McCoy twins are fending off a league of devilish dragons and bat-like beasts, Maze shooting bullets from one arm shaped like a rifle and slicing from his other shaped like a machete. Dola, on the other hand, keeps appearing and disappearing before my very eyes, somehow spotting the brutes behind her before they even realize it themselves.

Bodies of beasts and pools of blood and flesh litter their wake. I shiver as I watch them move and fight with ease, not thinking twice about the powers they possess and how to use them. I'm not sure I'll be able to do that, not even on a day as big as this one.

"What if I can't figure out how to fight today, Jay?" Unease settles in my gut, and I feel like puking again.

He grabs my hand, pulling my gaze to his. "The RED

becomes you. Instinct takes over. You'll see how much you're meant for this."

"I'm read—" My words are stolen from my lips when a wild whoosh of energy slams into my back, sending me soaring across the pavement and knocking the wind right out of me.

I cough and sputter, gasping for breath as I turn over onto my back. My hands glide up to my throat, trying their best to fight for air.

Jay's yells seem lightyears away as a frightening face hovers over mine. The man's skin is such a translucent gray, you can almost see through it. His piercing, purple eyes seem to grab right onto my soul, almost scaring it out of my body.

Finally, his mouth pulls up into a sickening grin. Each one of his teeth are slanted down into a spike, a disgusting yellow in color.

I try to scream, but nothing comes out.

"Don't fret, pretty. The Doctor is in." His voice slithers over my skin and settles in my stomach.

I have never felt fear like this before now.

CHAPTER THIRTY

Pushing myself up takes tremendous effort, especially with the scream I belt as I turn around to find the Doctor heading straight for Jay.

It takes everything in me, but I quickly push my force field out to encase him. Dr. Desolation's fist bounces off the barrier, the ricochet ringing out through the air as Jay stills inside, as if wagering with what his next move should be.

The Doctor's stare slowly turns to me, and he resembles someone out of a horror movie with that eerily slow pace. "Ah. Force field, eh? Your father made it sound like you had much better powers than that, but it will do. It's something neither me nor my few VOEs possess, so it will be perfect in helping me to hold off the REDs."

I scrunch my brows in question. He doesn't actually know what I can do? My insides smile at the prospect of actually being able to take this guy by surprise.

The thought quickly passes, because Dr. Desolation holds his hands behind him, his fists clenching and glowing brighter and brighter with each passing second like they're charging up.

Before I know it, two huge boulders whizz past my head, my body swaying this way and that with the force of the wind.

I brace my force field for impact to protect Jay, closing my eyes in the process—but they come flying back in my direction. I yell out, temporarily dropping the shield as I try to run out of the way, but one of them lands on my foot, trapping me in place.

"Fight back!" Jay yells. "Fight back, damn it!"

Jay whizzes through the air, landing a few punches to the Doctor's head. They stun him briefly, but he continues his attacks, landing just as many on Jay.

At one point, Jay is catapulted to the ground as I grit my teeth in pain, giving it all I have to try and pull my foot out from under the boulder. Agony shatters through my leg, and I collapse to the ground on my back. Meanwhile, he basically floats back up to his feet, neon-colored lightning bolts flickering through the air zapping the Doctor all over his body. His hands try to swipe them away as his body jerks in pain.

I slam my head back to the ground, the fear almost sucking all the energy from my body. I just need to rest a second before I try again.

Jay's hollering travels through the space between us. "Tatum, get up! *Now!*"

I lift my head, staring him down, excruciating pain rippling through my body. I can just barely shake my head at him. If I'm going to defeat the Doctor for good, I have to keep up the facade that I'm not only as strong as he thought, but as unique as he was hoping I'd be.

Dr. Desolation stalks toward me, and I swear he is unusually tall. I glance at his legs, wondering if something about his power has made them longer than average.

Behind him, Jay presses a hand to his ear. I start to wonder if he has an earpiece I missed earlier as huge flames sprout from his palms. Wha—how?

Jay throws two balls of fire toward the Doctor. They strike him, making him yell out in pain, but he quickly shakes it off.

Scooping up something that looks a lot like a winged bat, he flings it in Jay's direction, and I watch as the two collide, attacking one another.

The Doctor's quipped cackle sends a chill to my core, and I find myself having to request that the shadows stay trapped within. *Not yet,* I beg them.

Just as he gets too close for comfort to me, absolute chaos ensues.

My eyelids blink rapidly at the flashes of Jay's lightning, the beasts coming to the Doctor's aid, the McCoy twins shooting and disappearing, tree limbs flinging around us like lassos, and a dragon-form I'm positive is Nate—because of the flashes of orange color along his scales—flying straight for the Doctor.

While everyone fights to distract him from me, I get to work with my foot. The sinews of darkness are begging me to let them help, but I can't chance it. Not yet.

I startle at the silhouette that appears behind the giant boulder on the opposite side of the fight.

My eyes widen when they latch onto Maleko's face, and I almost cry in relief. "You're here."

"Of course I am." His eyes shift to the battle raging behind us as he pulls out a giant branch that he wedges beneath the rock. I grin at the fact that he's strong enough to not only lift a limb as large as this one, but that he has the strength to attempt to get this thing off of me.

"But why? I'm part enemy, and I took your powers."

He dusts off his hands in preparation to try hoisting this thing up before locking his eyes with mine. "You didn't take anything, Tatum. I gave them to you. Sometimes, friendship means sacrifice. I couldn't risk your life." He swallows before assessing my situation. "Ready?"

I grimace, realizing that this rock could crash right back down on the top of my foot if I don't move it out in time, and then I nod.

Maleko crouches down low before catapulting as high as he can and slamming his body down onto the limb. I feel it rise a smidgen and attempt to move my foot out from under it, but am not fast enough. It slams back down, this time crushing my foot from the side.

My body convulses and thrashes in pain. "Fucking hell!" I scream out, having to release the agony in some way.

But then something strange happens…the pain starts to lessen, and as I close my eyes to try and understand what's happening, I begin to feel the shadows working their way through me. They have contained some of their power to my buried foot, helping the skin expand and acting almost like the force field I wasn't able to use in time.

It's weird, because I am appreciative of what they're doing. I'm not sure if that means they're starting to like me more, or if I'm starting to like them…even so, I'm worried that isn't a good sign, but I'll take the reprieve for the time being.

Maleko grabs my hand, holding it against his chest. "I'm going to get you out of here, T—"

His words are cut off as a bat-like creature swoops in, flying him through the air until he crashes against a tree.

"Maleko! *No!*" I shriek. "Let him go!"

Thankfully, Nate plummets down from the sky, using his powerful jaws to eat the beast whole. His nostrils puff out a tendril of smoke in what I assume is satisfaction.

Maleko doesn't move, and Nate doesn't stick around.

Instead, he turns toward me, quickly stomping his way toward the giant rock. His claws wrap around the limb and push gently, moving the rock off of me long enough to get my foot out.

I grab onto my ankle, looking over it for injuries, but find none. The pain actually feels as if it never existed, and I'm guessing I have the darkness to thank for that. Without their protection, I wouldn't be able to move and help the others.

"Thank you," I say to Nate before glancing at Maleko once more. "Please. Get him out of here."

Nate's slanted yellow eyes glance toward Jay before turning back to me. I can tell he is internally struggling with what to do. Jay would want him to keep fighting, but I also know how much they care for Maleko. They want him safe too.

Before weighing his options much longer, I break him from his thoughts. "Please."

He nods curtly before flinging himself into the sky. My head tilts up, watching as his wings wrap around himself, resembling a missile. His body swoops through the air, one scaly arm reaching down to scoop up Maleko.

Mal dangles from the dragon's claw, his arms stretched backwards as his neck overextends. I close my eyes, desperately hoping he will be okay before preparing myself to join the fight.

Sneaking a peek around the boulder, I dart toward Dr. Desolation as he holds Jay up with an invisible grip around his throat, high in the air. Jay's face is red, his eyes bulging as he fights for breath.

Just as I prepare to release my shadows, utterly fed up with hiding them, my body's ability to move is stripped from me. My mind whirls as my limbs move of their own accord, and I'm hauled into the air, directly in front of the Doctor's face.

"Looks like your sweet old pops left out the fact that you have nothing of real value for me." His eyes scan me from head to toe in disgust. "But your man, on the other hand, might just have something useful."

Confusion settles in my gut, wondering what he could possibly want with Jay. Not that I'm some big prize to be won, but Adam made it very clear that the Doctor's whole intention was to come for me. Unless…

Unless he was waiting to tell him in person.

Unable to physically move, my mind is still on high alert, the paralysis unable to completely take over.

Dr. Desolation's actual hand reaches toward Jay's head, and it takes everything in me to stretch a shield of protection around him. The invisible grip on him slips away, and he free falls toward the ground.

Again, I rely on the shield, urging it to break Jay's descent. It lays him down on the ground, and my heart clenches when he doesn't move.

"Think you're slick, don't you?" the Doctor croaks, his covert grip on my body pulling me closer to him.

It's then that I feel it; the peculiar feeling a foreign presence has taken up residence in my body as it renders it useless.

I close my eyes, focusing on the strange feeling. "How do you feel about darkness, Doctor?"

He sneers, a deep cackle escaping him. "Darkness? I created it, my dear."

My left brow lifts. "Then your last name is very fitting, because now, the darkness will destroy you."

"What do you—"

I cut off his words as my shadows plunge out from within me, encasing us in a sheen of blackness.

Another set of tendrils finds the internal foreign occupant and holds it steady. The Doctor's eyes actually widen with surprise, and the sight makes me smirk with delight.

"What are you doing to me?"

I command the shadows to form a sort of platform beneath my feet, holding me still in front of his face. "It seems you were wrong about me." I twist my wrist as a shadowy snake slithers up my arm. "The greatest powers can't always be seen."

The serpent darts toward the Doctor's neck, and he cries out, his arms flying to get it off. The others go to work inside, moving to still the stranger.

Just as it feels like I'm about to succeed, that out-of-body feeling returns, and I plunge to the ground, unable to move.

Screams and yells from the REDs swirl around me during my descent, and as my head sways this way and that, I watch as each of them are sent down, one after the other, unmoving. He got them too…

What do we do now? Who can stop him?

When my head collides with the grass, my consciousness slips away…

Coming to, I find myself feeling even weaker than before. Still unable to move most of my body, my head actually starts to swivel with maximum effort. I turn it slowly, desperately searching for the others. Nate and Koral are completely unconscious, but Jay is sitting up against a nearby cement pillar, bound to the rock, forced to face me and watch whatever the Doctor is doing to me.

"Ahhh, glad you could join us, Tatum. I was actually just taking your blood. I finally figured out why your shitshow father ended up fucking me over when it comes to you…" He halts, sending a debilitating pain through my body. If I could scream, it would be deafening. "He truly thought your siphoning powers would be enough for me to forgive his transgressions. And while they somewhat interest me, he hid the most important details."

He stares into my eyes, acting as if he thinks he'll get a response from me, when he very well knows he is the one putting me in this immobile state.

"You're probably wondering what I'm doing, and the truth is, I need your blood. You see…all your little RED friends have spent years thinking there were very few of us out there, but I've been building an army. A faulty one in many ways, but a following nonetheless."

Searing agony shreds its way through my body, and it feels like it's completely tearing apart each of my muscles, piece by piece.

"There, there. I'm almost done." The pain remains steady as he leans further over my head. "When I left dirtbag Tenlin and his science, I was screwed over with the injection I stole and worked on for my precious VOEs. I thought it was just going to be a few of us who actually acquired powers, and then a few sick shits who would eventually die off, until this thought popped into my head."

The muscles in my neck loosen up, and I raise my head to

try and look around. My voice almost doesn't make it out. "And what thought is that?"

"I'm sure you've heard the pathetic story of your father, am I right?" I nod in answer. "Well, he was so busy seeking retribution that he didn't realize he was one of the very few VOEs who actually succeeded in his transformation. I never planned on killing him." His evil guffaw floats up toward the sky. "But I'm thrilled that the fear he had sent him looking for you, because your blood is the key I've been searching for."

My eyebrows scrunch in curiosity. "Huh?" seems to be the only word I can muster.

"You were born of someone injected with the VOE serum. It is lethal, and not many survive it. So, for you to overcome the mortality rate of it as merely an infant, your blood could help others do the same."

The Doctor looks over his shoulder at Jay, who is only able to move his eyes back and forth. "You hear that, lover-boy? Your girlfriend is giving me the nectar of the gods, and it will solve all my problems. Just wait until you see how many villains I have in my arsenal, eager to take all of you REDs right out of the picture."

Jay's voice breaks through the void. "Let her go, you piece of shit! Stop! You're going to kill her!"

Dr. Desolation has given him just enough mobility to talk; probably to make me suffer more.

"Oh, but that's the plan. Her death was imminent. I can't have her running around, stealing my VOEs' powers, or anyone else using her blood to come up with some new way to defeat me." He grabs the last vial from the ground and attaches it to whatever he is using to drain me of my blood. I wonder if he planned on doing this to all of us. Why else would he have doctor supplies on him?

My consciousness starts to slip away, almost too easily; how much blood has he taken already? How much can I lose before I follow it?

"You—beast," the Doctor calls as a stomping sound ricochets off the surface I'm lying on. "Take this to headquarters. You know who to give it to." My heart sinks as I realize he now has a new accomplice, someone who will get my blood and start working straight away. If the creature makes it there…

"Jay…" I barely whisper. "I…love…you."

"No! Fuck no!" Jay screams at the top of his lungs. "Don't you give up, Tatum! Not now!"

But I'm too weak. My consciousness starts to slip away.

That is, until I feel a slight twitch deep down inside.

I close my eyes, Jay's voice sounding too far off, listening to the shadowy whispers I somehow understand.

We can fight, they whisper. *Let us start*, they beg.

Please…help them… I command, my body's functions diminishing.

"Tatum? Baby? Answer me, damn it! *Stay with me!*" Jay's yells rush through me as my eyes slide shut and my head falls to the side.

"One down," Dr. Desolation sings. "One to go, loverboy." He walks away from me—why I'm still conscious, I have no idea. Maybe it's the shadows' consciousness I'm observing, or maybe it's an out-of-body experience, but Jay needs help. The REDs have to survive.

Do something, I implore. *Don't let them die too.*

Jay's howling turns to gurgles and then to silence, which awakens something left deep inside of me.

That's when I feel it. Some part of the Doctor is still present.

Find it, I order.

The darkness begins the hunt.

Using my siphon within my own body, they search desperately to find the stranger, grasping onto it with all the strength left in whatever alertness they are keeping alive.

The Doctor cries out as we grab onto his invisible form, and it begins. I pull as much out of him as I can, my eyes snapping open and my mind waking up. Whatever the internal corruption did, it managed to bring me back.

Reeling with the realization that I am truly awake, I watch as the Doctor all but floats toward the ground. The beasts rush beneath him, but he starts to break apart and float away before our very eyes.

The REDs—who have since been released from their paralysis—attempt to ambush the pack, but I hold my hand up to stop them, the Doctor's body-control power already rippling through my skin and being put to use. I roll my neck as it adapts to its new environment. "His power has been depleted. There will be nothing left of him to take back." I sweep my gaze across the monstrous beings. "Let this be a reminder to the other VOEs of what awaits them, should they decide to reveal themselves after being cured by my blood."

The coils of darkness start to recede as they usher me back to solid ground. I'm surprised when my body doesn't react the way it did to Maleko's powers.

Instead of feeling woozy and unsteady, I feel powerful and daunting. I guess what I thought was true…darkness works well with company.

"Go," I instruct the brutes, and they scatter, almost vanishing into thin air.

Rushing through the other REDs, I sink to my knees beside Jay, taking his head in my hands. "Wake up, Jay. Wake up! I'm not doing this again, damn it!"

I can feel the pulse beneath his flesh, the life inside him unsure if it's safe to come out, so I do the only thing that makes sense. I press my mouth to his, silently begging for him to come back to me.

I can tell he's come to when his mouth moves against mine, his hands wrapping around the back of my head, holding my face against his.

Breaking away, I stare deep into those beautiful blue eyes, grateful to have the chance to see them again.

"Did you do it?" he asks, his voice tired and dreamy.

"Save the day?" I question, an odd swarm of misplaced absurdity settling within me. "I mean, duh."

Jay laughs, pushing himself off the ground, yanking me up into the air. I swing my legs around his waist, and pull him close, hugging him as if my life depends on it.

"I told you so."

I shrink back, pinning him with a questioning glare. "Told me what?"

"Heroes aren't always born. They're made."

Only problem is, whatever new being that has joined the league swimming within my body doesn't feel like it'll help me be a hero. If anything, it feels like something I have to hope I can bend to my order. Because if not, I have a sneaking suspicion that it could not only be *my* undoing, but the downfall of all of us.

CHAPTER THIRTY-ONE

It took three days for us to clean up the mess from our battle with Dr. Desolation and his league of mutated beasts. Three days to get my mom and Jay's parents home. Three days to try to formulate how I'm going to voice my worries to Jay.

Looking in the mirror in his bathroom, I take one last deep breath before venturing back to his bedroom. He's leaning against the headboard, shirtless, his hair a tousled mess, and the blanket covering only his bottom half. The muscles of his arms twitch and bulge as he reads through one of his favorite comics. All in all, he drips liquid heat.

His eyes move slowly from the comic to where I'm leaning against his door frame, wearing nothing but one of his baggy t-shirts. A quiet groan moves up his throat.

"After everything we just went through, this is the best wake-up call I could've asked for."

I smirk before pushing off the doorway, sauntering toward the bed. I crawl across the comforter, noting how fluffy it feels against my skin, and take the book out of his hands to place on the nightstand, straddling his lap.

Jay peruses my body with hooded eyes, lifting me with one hand so that he can pull the comforter off of his lap, before pulling me back to him. He's in nothing but a pair of boxer briefs, granting me the feel of all of him. I smile as he moves in to kiss me.

Our mouths come together in a soft, warm kiss as Jay's hands rub up the length of my back and along my arms as he pulls them above my head. He bends them back at the elbow, holding me still as his mouth moves to my ear. "There's something different about you, and whatever it is, I like it."

Goosebumps erupt along every inch of my flesh, and I close my eyes, letting his breath flow over my skin.

He's right. There is something different about me. I don't know if it's the new powers, or the mixture of all of them within me: the realization that I defeated the Doctor, the pride of feeling like I'm finally becoming a hero despite what I was born as, or maybe a combination of all of those things, but whatever it is makes me feel like I'm finally discovering who I'm meant to be.

Turning my head, I nip Jay's earlobe. He releases my arms and uses both of his hands to now grasp my face.

His tongue plunges into my mouth, coercing a moan out of me. I thread my arms through the space he's created with his and lock them around the back of his neck.

Before I realize what's happening, he's removed most of our clothing and is pushing inside of me. Our position has me completely full of him, and I rock up and down with the help of his strong arms.

When we both reach that blissful finish together, the flashing streaks of blue in his irises catch my attention, while he mouths my favorite phrase to me: "Super love you."

A smile stretches across my face. "And I super love you, too."

Once Jay and I finally make our way out of the bedroom and into the kitchen, I lift myself onto the counter to watch him cook some breakfast.

Jay flips our pancakes, using just the pan, with ease. "Spit it out, T."

I roll my eyes, annoyed with how easy it is for him to read me. "Ugh, you're the worst." I stick my tongue out at the back of his head. "I'm just scared."

"Of?"

I look down at my toes, wiggling them in the air. "How am I supposed to figure out what I'm truly becoming? Or how to use my powers? What if something goes wrong, and I go bad? Are the REDs going to hate me now that I took Maleko's powers? Do you think taking the Doctor's powers could hurt me? Will the VOEs come looking for me? Are we going to get my blood back? Wh—"

Jay's finger goes to my lips, his body wedged between my legs where I'm perched. "Take a breath, babe."

I breathe through my nose, blowing out and around his finger, watching as his eyes darken at the action. "Sorry," I whisper.

Putting his arms on either side of my hips, he stares straight into my eyes. "I have no idea what will come of this —or who—but I assure you, I'm on your side. I'm going to help you through this. RED will help us figure out what to do about your blood, and we will try to formulate a plan when it comes to the VOEs, because honestly, we have no idea what to expect from them. In the meantime, I'll make damn sure you don't go to the dark side, because the only *bad* you should be is in the bedroom."

My eyes widen at his words, my jaw going slack.

"Jayson!" I yell, smacking him playfully on the chest. "You're awful."

"Only for you, babe." He winks before kissing me on the cheek and turning back around to take care of our food. "But I'm being serious…we're going to figure everything out—your powers, our future. I'm in this for the long run with you, T."

I melt at his words. "Ever the hero."

"For you, I'll always be there to save the day."

My skin prickles as I lift my hand to ring the doorbell of Maleko's beach house. I'm not sure what condition he's in, or how he will feel about seeing me after everything that's happened, but I just had to come. There's so much that needs to be said.

Dola comes to the door, her beautiful smile helping to ease some of the tension inside. "Tatum, it's good to see you. You look well!"

I nod my head at her, "You too!" My eyes drift past her, into the house. "How's he doing?"

She glances over her shoulder. "Better. He'll be happy to see you."

"Thanks for helping to take care of him." My hands grab onto each other of their own accord. Old habits die hard, I suppose.

Dola steps aside, pulling the door open wider. "Us REDs look out for one another."

Her words sink deep as I recall all of them helping to fight the Doctor both for me *and* with me. "I know I'm not really one, but I'm still grateful for all of your help with defeating Dr. Desolation."

"No two REDs are the same, Tatum. Neither are our origins. Just because yours might contain a little more darkness than the rest of us, it doesn't mean you're any less deserving of this title. You're a RED to me."

Wrapping my arms around her, I breathe in her fresh scent. "Thank you."

She lets up, patting me on the head. "Thanks isn't necessary. Follow me."

Leading me down the hallway, past the bathroom where I found Koral after I accidentally siphoned her and two more rooms, Dola finally opens the last door on the right. Maleko is sitting up in his bed, a bowl of popcorn resting on his stomach. I smile at him as I watch a kernel miss his mouth and tumble down his chin.

"Why is this one of the messiest snacks to ever exist?" he questions, his face muscles pulling tight as he searches for the missing piece.

I scrunch my eyebrows in deep thought. "Actually? I have no clue." We both burst into laughter, and I make my way to his bed. "Mind if I sit here?"

He pats the space next to him. "Not at all."

I crawl onto the tall bed, sitting atop the blankets next to him, our shoulders barely touching.

"Maleko," I start, pulling his attention to me. "I'm sorry."

He blinks a few times before replying. "What for?"

"This." I motion toward his body, noticing the cast around his leg and bruises along his tanned skin. "Your injuries, your powers…it's all my fault."

Mal pushes himself up a little more, wincing as he turns his body to face me better. "Tatum, being a hero means sacrifice. This was always meant to be a part of my journey."

"I know…but I'm not just some civilian. You know what I'm made of."

He sighs, rubbing a hand down his face. "I've told you so many times before. You cannot help the path you were sent down. All you can do is figure out where to go next, and who it will help you become. I don't know why you feel undeserving of being rescued."

I close my eyes, suddenly feeling emotional. "I don't know either."

"Look at me, Tatum." I cast my gaze up once more. "It was an honor to give you my powers. You have become a friend, and friends are always worth saving."

Leaning over, I give him a peck on the cheek. It's amazing how much I love talking with Maleko. I talk to him differently than I even talk to Jay. Who knew a friendship like this could come from such unfortunate circumstances?

Just goes to show you that no matter where you come from, you can always find someone who doesn't give a shit about your background and is willing to help you through it.

Hearing his voice grow quieter, his actions becoming less animated, I know I should leave him to rest. "Thank you, Mal. You saved me."

"It was an honor," he answers, his eyes drifting closed. "But from what I understand, it's you who is the real hero in this story."

With a big smile on my face, I move carefully off the bed, placing the bowl of popcorn on the nightstand, and pulling the blankets back over him, the rogue popcorn kernel flinging into the air. A quiet laugh shakes my chest as I pluck it from the comforter, rubbing it in between my thumb and forefinger.

The floor is thankfully quiet under my feet. I pull the door closed behind me and move back toward the front of the house, finding Dola in the kitchen humming while making some food.

"He's asleep. I'm going to go."

She looks up at me, stirring something that smells delicious. "Sure you don't want to stay for some food?"

I shake my head, "No, thank you. I've got somewhere to be."

"Good to see you, Tatum. Don't be a stranger."

I tip my head at her and head for the front door.

Time to go home.

Pulling into my driveway, I wonder what my mom will say once I see her. Jay never told me what she thinks happened over the course of the last few days. And until I have everything under control, I'm still not chancing exposing the truth of what I am, what Adam was, or about the clashing worlds of REDs and VOEs. It's still not safe.

The front door creaks when I open it, and once I shut it behind me, I lock it, listening for sound. It feels weird being back in here after all that's transpired, attempting to adjust back to a new normal.

"Honey? Is that you?"

"Hey, Mom!" I yell. "I'm home!"

Emerging from the kitchen with a dish towel in her hands, she opens her arms to me, urging me closer for a hug. I walk over and squeeze her tightly, so grateful she's here and safe.

Ending our embrace, she keeps holding my shoulders.

"Why do I feel like you've changed so much? It feels like I haven't seen you in months."

My mind runs back through the moment I thought the same thing about Jay. "Not sure, Mom. Maybe it's because Adam's gone."

A flash of pain comes over her. "Could be." She gently pats my cheek. "I'm so happy you're okay."

"Me too."

The kitchen timer beeps in the background, and Mom starts to head in the direction of the noise. "Would you like to get washed up? Dinner is ready. Is Jay joining us?"

Hearing his name makes my heart flutter. "Sure thing. And no, not tonight."

"Oh. Okay, sweetie. See you in a few."

Once she disappears into the kitchen, I carefully make my way up the stairs and into my bedroom.

My eyes peruse the space, the area somehow feeling different. I shut and lock the door behind me, beelining for the closet.

I reach up and pull on the corded light. It clinks on with ease, casting a yellowish-haze over the contents inside.

Glancing back at the door, I push the clothes aside, in search of my old keepsake box from when I was a kid. It still sits inside a hole Jay carved out years ago; he's long since forgotten about it, I hope.

I flinch at the chiming of my phone, clutching a hand to my chest before delicately pulling it out of my stuffed pocket. It's a text from Jay.

Jay: You okay?

> Me: Yes. Went to see Mal, and now I'm home to have dinner with my mom. What did you end up telling her?

> Jay: I'm glad you got to visit him :)

A second ping comes right after.

> Jay: Kept it simple. Told her my parents were renting out an Airbnb in the city and wanted to treat her to a trip after everything that's happened. She deserved it.

I smile to myself. Here we were, fighting for our lives, and Jay was kind enough to make sure Mom was completely oblivious to the situation.

> Me: Thank you <3

> Jay: Anything for you. Want me to come over for dinner? I can be there in a minute flat.

Chills wash over me.

> Me: Not tonight. I think I should just be with my mom right now.

Jay takes a second to respond, and I press my ear to the closet door as I wait for it, sliding the lock in place.

> Jay: No worries, babe. XO

> Me: XOXO

Placing my phone on the shelf under the window, I pull

the blind down, fishing in my pocket for the remaining contents I stashed away after the battle ended.

Removing my fist from the section of my jeans, I open my palm and stare down at the item, my head swimming with so many thoughts.

There was a recent time when I thought I was destined for destruction; a feeling that was so dark and gloomy, I didn't think I'd survive it.

But after everything I've learned from being born a villain, falling in love with a hero, and watching people sacrifice so much just to save a version of me I didn't feel was worthy…I've come to accept the fact that I'm a power and force to be reckoned with.

There is no one like me. I'm an anomaly, unique and strong.

I have realized that no one knows what I'm capable of doing or becoming. This is something I have to discover on my own.

As I stare down at the red vial in my hands, I know there's a strong possibility I've made the wrong decision, but I needed to have some sort of back-up plan…

With all the darkness and murk swirling inside of me, we have no idea what to expect of any transformation I go through. I have to ensure I won't go bad…which is why I secretly took one of the injections.

When I gave them back to Mal, I purposefully closed his fingers around them quickly, hoping the dire situation we were in would be enough distraction for him not to investigate too much before hiding them away. I then wiped away the thoughts that only two of the syringes made it back into his grasp—basically creating a scenario in my mind that all three were returned and nothing was amiss—that way, if someone was going to search my mind for information, they'd come up empty. I doubt anyone at RED would approve of what I've done, but I had to assemble something.

Jay would be most disappointed of all, only because he'd never take a chance where my life is concerned. Not like this. But he said it himself; he trusts my decisions. Should I need to use it someday, I hope he can understand; I never intended to do something like this, and choosing to keep it from him will be difficult, but I refuse to risk anything where he's concerned, especially when it comes to me. There's a huge possibility that I'm a ticking time bomb, and just thinking about the fact that my darkness could someday consume me and hurt—or even kill—someone I love is repulsing enough to convince myself that what I'm doing is right.

So, I place the syringe carefully inside the keepsake box, lock it up, and slide it back into hiding—my own little insurance policy.

Taking a step back and closing my eyes, I prompt the shadows to take these memories and hide them away. Opening them again feels like the start of a new era; a new beginning.

When it's needed—and I'm ready—I'll inject myself with the RED serum. And while the world might never be prepared, they'll someday meet an antihero like they've never seen before.

I'm both the calm *and* the storm.

And I will change everything.

THE END

ACKNOWLEDGMENTS

Let me just start by saying that I've dreamed of this very moment my entire life… *cue tears*

First and foremost, I'd like to thank God for my love of reading, passion for books, and the gift of writing, which He so kindly bestowed on me. Honestly, I would not be here without Him.

My WHOLE family: I truly have the most supportive bunch out there, and I don't know how else to put my thanks into words. I love you all.

My sister, Kaitlin (aka my NaNoWriMo drill sergeant): I never would've finished that first draft without you yelling at me. Thanks for loving Jay as much as I do. You are my biggest supporter, and I'm so blessed to call you my sister.

Grandma and Papa: Gram, you've been screaming my name and cheering me on since I brought up the idea of writing. Thanks for loving my passion right along with me. Papa, thank you for being so supportive of my dreams and teaching me the importance of reading. You're the best grandparents in the universe. I'd be lost without you, and I'm so lucky to call you mine.

Mom: Thank you for fostering a love of reading in me for my ENTIRE life, for always offering to help me out with anything I need, and for supporting my multi-fandom obsessions, no matter how old I get.

Purdy People: You have helped me through SO many stressful waves of panic, and I'm grateful. You've sat at your table, listening to me anxiously ramble on about everything I have to do. You've helped me create timelines, put dates in your phones, checked in with me, and everything in between. Thank you. You've helped make this journey possible.

Bex: One of my first beta readers, a fellow bookish lover, and my amazing cousin. Thank you for freaking out over my book and for being you. You're the BEST!

ALL my friends: I don't know how I got so lucky to call you mine, but I'll claim all of you time and time again. Thank you for sticking by my side, no matter what life brings.

Lindsay: Twenty-seven years of friendship this year. Can you believe it? And you've loved and supported me through all of them. Thank you for not only supporting my dreams, but also for loving me, even when I might not always be so lovable. Having a chosen sister like you is the best feeling in the world.

Amanda: Seventeen years of friendship. Holy cow. Thank you for the work days so I could meet deadlines, for checking in when you know I'm struggling, and for letting me cry when I'm stressed. You always know how to calm the storm within, and I'm so grateful each time you share your umbrella to keep me dry.

Abbey: Eight years of friendship. For real? Your excitement for all things Saving Tatum saves me more than you know. Anytime I'm feeling insecure about my work or myself, you know just what to say. Thank you for all you do. You're the sparkliest human I know, and you bring light to the darkest days.

To Melissa Frey and Carly Martinez (aka the best CPs I could've asked for): You helped me bring this story to life. It started small, but you watered it, and it grew to be so much more than a little seed. I'll never be able to thank you enough.

To Cassidy Clarke: To be honest, this book would've NEVER ended up where it did. You changed so many things for me. I'm incredibly thankful to have found you. You deserve an award for BEST EDITOR.

To Murphy Rae: Thank you for the best cover EVER. Despite my indecisiveness, my numerous idea changes, and everything in between, YOU are the one who got this cover to where it is today. Your mind is magical; I know it.

To my proofreader, Allyssa Painter: Thank you for working my book into your hectic schedule. I know it wasn't easy, but I'm very grateful you were willing to work with me. You're a super mom!

To my formatter, Victoria Ellis: Thank you for making the interior of my book beautiful! You're AMAZING at what you do, and I'm so freaking happy I found you!

To my beta readers: Rebekah Stout, Lindsay Johnson, Amanda Fair, Abbey Berger, Kris Sweet, Julie Leister, Jennifer Lashbrook, Stephanie, Amanda Creek, Kate, Michelle, Marisa Fink, Lindsay Scharff, Averyn Vanhouteghen, and Erin Wolak. Thank you for your honest feedback, constructive criticism, and continuous support. I appreciate your dedication more than you know.

To Kear Simmons and Marisa Baratta: Thank you for helping to keep me accountable. I know I stink at answering messages, and it's been a while since we last talked, but I still appreciate both of you SO much.

A huge shoutout to ALL of the writing groups I'm in on Facebook, Discord, and Patreon. Even if you don't see this, I'm beyond grateful for your support and help throughout this entire journey.

And to the writing community in general: Authors are some of the most supportive, creative, helpful, and hard-working people I know. Thank you for existing and for being amazing human beings to look up to. Your stories change the world!

To JJ Otis and Amanda Creek: Thank you for answering my countless questions. You've helped me with SO many things while I've been juggling this author thing and teaching full-time. Thank you for being such EPIC humans.

To Brittany Wang: I was at a standstill with my writing journey until you came along. Joining your Patreon and getting to know you AND so many writers in your Discord has been a huge blessing. Thank you for teaching me so much and for being an inspiration.

To Sarra Cannon and Tomi Adeyemi: Thank you for the infinite knowledge and guidance you offer through your courses. I admire you more than you'll ever know.

To Twice the Jennifers (you know who you are): Meeting both of you so early on in my journey truly helped shape me into the writer I am today. Thank you for ALL of your help.

My ARC Team: You took the time to read my very first book baby and tell other people about it. I am speechless and touched. There are no words to thank you enough for that.

My readers: Wow. I never thought I'd get to say those words out loud. You're real, so very real, and I'm in awe of you. Thank you for reading my book. Thank you for supporting my dream. Thank you for existing. You add so much color to my world.

To all comic creators, Marvel, and DC: This story started because of you, and I'm grateful for the superbeings you created. The power of your stories helped bring mine to life.

And last, but most certainly NEVER least... My dog,

Finnick: Named after one of the best fictional characters ever created, YOU are my real-life hero—a little furrier than most, but a hero nonetheless. There was a time I thought I'd never see the light again, but you truly taught me that there's power in silence, and that even when there are dozens of shattered pieces on the floor, it's still possible to work to put yourself back together. That's a superpower I'll never be able to repay you for. Thank you for saving me, sweet boy. I love you.

P.S. To anyone I might've missed typing in here, I promise you haven't been forgotten, my mind is just jumbled from the stress and excitement of this journey. I could never forget you. Thank you.

I SUPER LOVE YOU ALL. XO

Meghan Monarch loves athleisure wear, Disney, movie theaters, dancing in grocery store aisles, loud music, and even louder laughter.
She writes from her Michigan home, where she lives with her dog, Finnick—a super cool standard poodle with a colored mohawk. When she's not writing, she's reading, relaxing, or going out on solo dates.
Find her and other bookish goodies at
www.meghanmonarch.com :)